The
Age
of
Blessing

A NOVEL

MASCOT® BOOKS

Dedicated to

David, my wonderful husband,
From the moment you read my first short story, you believed in me. You are
a never-ending source of strength, encouragement, and optimism. It was
pouring rain the day you walked to my check-out counter at Sears. You were
a ray of sunshine. The sun has been shining for 35 years.

Davie and Joanna,
My tough and tender son, and my adorable and lovable daughter;
as children your easy laughter at my stories encouraged me. You pooled your
funds to purchase a laptop so that I could finish writing this book. Children
want to be like their parents. When I grow up, I want to be like you.

My Dad and Mom,
My first memories are belonging to a loving devoted family. Watching you
deal with the challenges of raising a large family, persevere during tragedy
and death, continue to write editorials while ailing, volunteer from a wheelchair, and refuse to let the twilight years hinder you from serving, have
inspired me beyond words. You are the blessing.

"Praise God from whom all blessings flow!"

www.mascotbooks.com

The Age of Blessing

For more information, please contact:
Mascot Books
620 Herndon Parkway #320
Herndon, VA 20170
info@mascotbooks.com

Library of Congress Control Number: 2017916228

CPSIA Code: PBANG0718A
ISBN: 978-1-68401-631-0

Printed in the United States

The Age of Blessing

A NOVEL

CHATTANOOGA (WRCB) — Twenty-five years ago, Eunice Rooks decided it was time to retire. At the age of 65, she had put in more than forty years teaching in elementary schools throughout Chattanooga and Georgia. But when her 80th birthday rolled around, Mrs. Rooks decided to put her considerable energy to good use, returning to the classroom. Ten years later, she's still going strong as an interventionist at Chattanooga's Bess T. Shepherd Elementary School.

Vickie Morrow

Chapter One

Swing Low, Sweet Chariot, Please Come and Take Me Home

I didn't die, doggone it. I see you saw fit to let me live to see another sorry day. Cori was not dead. She knew it as soon the chill reached her aged-spotted wrinkled face. All Corinthia Pearl Jacobs wanted in life was to die. Was that too much to ask? Why was death so difficult for her, when it was so easy for others? She turned 92 this year and she believed she had seen it all, heard it all, and frankly she just didn't want to see or hear anything else.

She never dreamed she would live this long. Robert Edward had been dead nearly fifty years and she would never understand why God saw fit to let her live such a long life without the man she still loved so dearly. Every night she hoped to sleep away to death and wake up between her precious Robert Edward and sweet Jesus.

"Miss Cori, you're still spry. You still have a lot of living left in you. People your age are doing amazing things, walking in marathons, still teaching school, still making contributions to the world."

If someone tells me one more time all the things folks my age are doing, I'm liable to scream right in their face. I don't care about none of that mess. I just want to go on to glory!

What was it that jolted her awake? Something caused her to want to stay motionless, to avoid the stillness that summoned her to endure another day. She struggled to go back to sleep as the reality of life awakened her.

It must have gotten close to zero last night. She lay still, fearful that movement would invite the frigid temperature into her multi-blanket cocoon.

I'm alive again, Cori stated without feeling. Lying perfectly still, she began her ritual of talking to her Lord, something she had done each morning for what seemed like an eternity.

Well, Lord, I didn't die peacefully in my sleep like I asked. I guess I should say thank you. I know I have a lot to be thankful for, but it sure is hard to say thank you these days. Whew! It's colder than it was yesterday. I feel the chill straight to my bones. I just don't know how much longer I can stand this. I sure can't cut that thermostat up any more, with them charging that extra every month. I've never been in debt to anyone in my entire life. The Bible says it as plain as bread, 'Owe no man nothing but the debt of love.' I wouldn't be in debt now if that little hussy at the gas place hadn't looked down her nose and told me the biggest lie straight to my face.

"We're gonna let you pay your bill a little at a time, Mrs. Jacobs."

Little did I know, they charged a little extra for letting me pay just a little a month. Cori shook her head in disgust. *Ump, ump, ump! I guess I better get on up. Why I keep getting up, only you know, Lord. You know I've long since stopped praying, "if I should die before I wake."* Cori closed her eyes tight and continued, *"Let me die before I wake. I pray dear Lord, my soul to take." That's my prayer now.*

She opened her eyes and stared around her cold, lonely bedroom. *I surely didn't think I'd be this old and find myself in this situation.*

Cori's husband, Robert Edward Lee Jacobs II had been dead for nearly fifty years, and after years of being the grieving widow, the caring mother, the town matriarch, she just wanted to join her dearly beloved Robert.

Lord knows I didn't think I'd be over 90 years old and facing what I have to face every day, pray tell. I sho' didn't. Now on top of everything else, that buck-toothed Billy Joe Croftin keeps hounding me to sell my house. I know he's in cahoots with his ole Uncle Barnett.

"Now, Mrs. Jacobs," Billy Joe said, "You know you can't afford to keep this big old house anymore. Let me take it off your hands and you go on out to that nice Blessing Rest with the rest of the folks your age."

I went on to tell him how he ought to be ashamed of himself for hounding the elderly about selling their homes. Plus, he didn't give Sally Mae Perkins pert near nothing! Advertised it right here in the Blessing News as a historical home. Got nearly five times what he paid poor Sally Mae for it. Was right nasty with me after I told him that.

"Before you know it, they gonna find you frozen to death, or you'll lose it to taxes. Either way, you gonna lose it," snarled Billy Joe.

Well Lord, as bad as my knees hurt me, I knew I had to get down on them that night and pray for forgiveness for the awful things I called that scarecrow. Shucks, I knew his great-grandpappy when he lived in that old run-down mill home, where you could see the chickens running under the house through the boards in the floor. Didn't have a pot to pee in and stole the pot they had. But I still couldn't risk having things on my list, with me having one foot through the Pearly Gates. And I told him so!

What in the world could he have been thinking? He's just as foolish about money as his crazy uncle who bought up just about every inch of dirt in this town. Then his no-account money hungry children didn't want to use even six feet of the dirt to bury his sorry old self in. Went and cremated him! Lord, I never! I guess they figured he was gonna burn anyway.

But, I'll never sell this house! I was born in it, married in it, had my babies in it, dear sweet Robert Edward died in it, and I plan to die in it too!

Ump, ump, ump! Now those little hoodlums have moved in next door and stole my plums the entire summer. When I asked them not to steal them, they started throwing them at me! Worst of all, when I called the police, old Snoot Snead came out here and threatened to put ME in jail.

Just 'cause I got me a switch and told them I'd cut their legs from under them.

"Now Mrs. Jacobs, the children are just playing," Snoot said. "You can't go around here threatening little children. We'll have to lock you up for child abuse."

Well, I never! Plus, that teenaged girl don't have the sense God gave a bumblebee. Walking around talking on that funny looking phone and all kinds of things just a beeping. And those kooks they have for parents. They say they are professors at the university. But ev'ry time you look, they're loading up that van to go save some animal. Looks to me they need to try to save those two they leave here to drive me nuts.

And Lord, one more thing. I never thought I'd see the day when I'd live right next door to Coloreds. Now I know they don't like to be called Colored any more. Wants to be called African-Americans. Shucks, I know most of them never set foot in Africa. Now one of them wants to be President! And he ain't even a real Colored… one of those Black Muslims or something. Lord Jesus, oh my soul! And that big boy just gives me the heebie jeebies. He's headed straight to the chain gang. I just know it. Looks at me like I've done something to him and I don't even know his name.

Lord, I know you said you don't put more on us than we can bear. I just don't know how much more I can bear. Robert Edward left me almost 50 years ago, and each day I still miss him so much. Now I can't pay my bills, when teenagers who never lifted a finger to do a thing, get checks every month, just 'cause they laid up with some boy and got themselves knocked up. I'll tell you what. That big rascal on the radio is right. I listen to him every day! We need to thank God, we finally got some God-fearing people out there telling the truth. But anytime you see fit, you can just take me on to glory!

The room felt deathly cold. The sheets pricked her skin like icy needles as she moved under the layers of heavy handmade quilts that were nearly as old as she. As much as her 92-year-old body cried and as much as she wished to lie there and wake up at heaven's door, Cori began the slow laborious task of facing another day.

Even with the wool socks on her feet, her toes ached to the cold. She stuck her feet into her worn, tattered slippers, reached for her heavy robe that she tied securely around her thick flannel gown, and slowly made her way to the small bathroom next to her bedroom. Just entering it was painful. It was a luxury they could not afford, but her Robert was determined that she should not have to go downstairs.

It seemed that it was taking forever for the water to warm. Fortunately, she let it drip throughout the night to keep it from freezing. Bobby Lee had called her and insisted that she let it drip. He didn't want the trouble he had the last time they had a freeze. He fussed for days when the pipes burst. Of course, he could let his water run through the night; he could afford to pay his water bill.

As the water slowly warmed, she quickly washed her face, stuck her toothbrush in her box of Arm & Hammer baking soda, and brushed her teeth. Bobby Lee fussed about her brushing her teeth with baking soda, too.

Well, I still have my own teeth. He can't say that.

Slowly she made her way down the twenty stairs that creaked in rhythm with her body. How many times had she counted those stairs? Each year the count became as painful as the steps. Bobby Lee fussed that she should move to the downstairs rooms, but she felt so close to her beloved Robert in the bedroom they had shared. She could not bear the thought of sleeping somewhere else.

Breakfast was the simple meal of hot coffee, oatmeal, and toast. She ate it without tasting it and waited for Bobby Lee to come in for his morning cup of coffee. Though she looked forward to the company, she didn't look forward to his whining and complaining about the new S-Mart taking his business.

How many times did she have to hear about his General Store being the oldest business in the county, how his great-grandfather had opened it after the Civil War, how they kept it open to Blacks even when others wouldn't let them shop in their stores, and now Barnett Sampson opens his S-Mart with its low prices and Bobby Lee's business may soon have to close. If it weren't for the old folks who like to shop in a familiar place, his business would have closed long ago.

I've listened to that story every day now for five years. I would feel sorry for him if he wasn't so hardheaded. That store had never been in debt a day until Bobby Lee took over and caught hold to every wind of doctrine that passed his way.

He invested in records. That boomed until people stopped buying records. Then he started selling food, and McDonald's came to town. He started renting movies, and that ole Blockbuster came to town. He started selling toys, and Toys "R" Us came to town. As much as I dislike change, this place is changing and Bobby Lee should be able to see it.

She could hear Bobby Lee murmuring to himself before he got into the house.

They say that folks who talk to themselves are crazy. I guess they never lived by themselves. Course now, Bobby Lee doesn't live by himself, but everybody knows that he and Grace simply live in the same house when she is at home. So, I guess that's just like living by yourself.

Bobby Lee threw the door open, as he had done on every morning for more years than she cared to count.

For some reason, he thinks he needs to come by and have coffee with me. I think he just wants to check and see if I'm dead before he goes off to the store.

He sat down, hurriedly drank his coffee, fussed about the S-Mart, griped about how cold the house was, and fussed about the items on the grocery list. They both laughed at the joke about Hillary Clinton's pantsuits. After the show ended, he left proudly, as if he had done a good deed for the Lord.

He acts like I don't know this house is cold. Just went on and on about how cold the house is, as if it's news to me. I wish it weren't so cold so I could do my own grocery shopping. Bobby Lee always gets more than I ask for. He says I need the stuff. For some reason, people think that when a person gets old they don't know what they need. All that instant mess Bobby Lee brings home sets right there in the cabinet.

Folks didn't start getting cancer 'til they started getting lazy and started cooking all that instant stuff. But I had to give in and let him do the shopping this week on account of it being so cold. If it weren't for my daily walk to the post office and to the store, I probably would never leave the house.

All my friends in my ladies' club have died or moved to an old folk's home. All my church friends and neighbors are pushing up daisies too. I don't know those folks who moved into the houses on either side, and I don't want to know them. Came here from God only knows with those unruly, disrespectful heathens they call children. I can barely recognize the houses with all that "renovating."

Twasn't nothing wrong with the houses, but they had to have a room for the sun. If you want sun, why don't you go on out in it? Had to add a hot tub. What's wrong with cutting the hot water on in the tub that they have? Had to add closets, and bathrooms, and decks, and gazebos, and bonus rooms, and I don't know why they just didn't build a new house. Oh, I forgot. They want to live in a historical home. Well I 'spect they got rid of all the history when they added all those other things.

I guess I should be thankful that they finished all that pounding. I know my dear neighbors Janie and Lessie turned over in their graves at what those scalawags did to their homes. But still, they are definitely better off rotting in their graves than to be on this pitiful Earth with all these fools running around.

I guess there's not much for me to do but pity-pat around here until "The Price is Right" comes on.

Tidying the kitchen did not take much time. Cori pulled the new word search magazine Eddie had purchased for her. He always dropped a word search or crossword puzzle magazine off for her to keep her mind occupied during the day. Today she would search for "Animals of the Rainforest."

What in the world is a Rainforest anyway? I'll have to ask Eddie when he comes by Wednesday evening.

Cori sat engrossed in her puzzle, when she suddenly heard a knock at the door.

Chapter Two

The Arrival of the Cold Day in Hell

The evenings were the hardest for Ada Passmore. She and Mr. Passmore, Frederick, didn't sit in front of the television until they dropped off to sleep like so many of their friends. They had talked about everything and before you knew it, the evening was gone. Ada loved their conversations, which began when they had first met.

Most couples spent their time googly-eyed, staring at each other, but not she and Frederick. Hours of sharing their deepest thoughts and dreams dissolved entire evenings. And now there was silence...still...cold...silence. Ada went to bed earlier and earlier to absorb the loneliness of the evenings, but even her bedroom was no refuge. Emptiness waited for her in the room she had shared so long with her Mr. Passmore. After tossing and turning until sleep overpowered her, the torturous dreams returned.

They took her husband. They took her children. They took her home, and now they are back! Why do they keep taking everything? Oh, my God! They're coming! They've taken everything! I have nothing left! They are coming back! What do they want! Oh, my God! It's me! They're coming for me! They're tearing the door down! They're coming for me!

She awoke with sweat running down her face.

It was just another bad dream. Thank God, it was just a dream. She lay in her warm, comfortable bed with a grateful heart that it was a dream. As she glanced around the bedroom at the dark cherry Queen Ann furniture, she was reminded of what had precipitated the dream. The boxes were stacked from the hardwood floors to the tiled panels on the ceilings. Slowly, it all came back to her.

Dear God, this is the day, she cried to herself.

This was the day she had dreaded for the past six months. This was the day she was to leave her home of over forty years. This was the last day she would spend in the home that she had shared so many years with Mr. Passmore.

He had stolen her heart when she was a young schoolteacher and he was the Principal of the Rocky River Elementary School. She liked to call him Mr. Passmore, after all no one deserved more respect than her dear Mr. Passmore.

Her son, Frederick Jr., would be arriving from North Carolina soon to move her down South with him. It had been so long since she had left the South and Detroit had become her home. She could barely remember living anywhere else. It was inevitable. She could hardly walk. The doctors confirmed that her arthritis was not getting better, and the harsh Detroit winters made it even worse.

"You ought to move on down South with your children," Dr. Lacy said in a matter-of-fact tone.

"I swore I would never live in that evil place again as long as I lived. Just mentioning the word 'South' sends chills straight to my spine."

"Well, move on out to California where you can get lots of sunshine," the dear old doctor and family friend continued.

"Now why would I want to move out there, where it seems half of it is going to fall into the ocean and the other half is sinking right to hell?"

"You need to be near some family who can take care of you."

Family, Ada thought to herself. Her eyes wandered to a familiar but distant place. *It was so precious to me after growing up so alone without anybody. I promised the Lord that if He ever gave me a family, someone to love, to take care of, and have them love me back, I'd serve Him all my days.* As joyful as her wedding day was, she never felt so alone.

Of course, Miss Steepleton was there, as she had been for her since Mother Damaris died. Her future mother-in-law and Frederick's sister instantly made her feel as if she was part of their family, but she still felt a sense of loneliness. They were shocked to silence when she told them that outside of the teachers that she and Frederick planned to invite, she only needed one invitation.

But the Lord answered my prayers. After all those years of not having anyone, He blessed me with Frederick and soon I had my precious little family.

Just the thought of family caused her hazel eyes to glimmer with tears.

My family—how it has changed. Frederick Jr. is so caught up in achieving success. And Lord, when he told me he was registering with the Republican Party and was against Affirmative Action, it was as if someone twisted a knife right in my heart. All those marches, voter registration drives, and now he is going to turn his back on the very party that opened doors for him. Lord Jesus, oh my soul!

Then there's Damaris, or "Naana Yaa."

"I'm changing my name to Naana Yaa. I no longer want to be known by the name of some old White woman," Damaris stated defiantly to her mother after another exhausting argument.

"But Damaris, I owe my life to that White woman. If it wasn't for her, I wouldn't be where I am. You wouldn't be where you are. And it is taken right out of the Bible."

"I don't care about some book that the White man read to keep us oppressed."

I didn't intend to slap her. It just happened before I knew it. And the worst part was her threatening to press assault charges against me. Precious Lord Jesus, I just don't know anymore.

Then there's Martin. After six years, he drops out of college, gets kicked out of the Air Force, and now he goes from pillar to post looking for a six-figure job.

"I'm not settling for less than $100,000 a year," he said.

My Lord, did I fall off the Earth and the world went on without me? Or have half the folks on this planet just gone completely crazy? When did it all happen? Frederick and I taught them and raised them by your word. We tried to guide them in your way. But Lord, it's as if I don't even know my own children anymore.

Now I'm moving back. I vowed it would be a cold day in hell before I returned to the South. Ada's body shook as memories of dark, cold nights raced through her mind. Many nights she woke trembling with fear.

Frederick had always been here to hold me when I awoke sweating and trembling from nightmares. I was so young, and most children would have forgotten it by now. But the dreams always remind me. Now Frederick's gone. I can hardly bear to get up out of this bed.

Lord, how I miss my precious, sweet Frederick. I know when you took him last fall, the angels shouted on high for his precious soul coming to join them. I just wish you had taken me right on with him. For nearly 50 years I lay in bed waking up to face each day with him. They say time heals. I must need some more time, because my heart hurts as bad today as it did when he closed those big brown eyes that last time.

She made the painful steps to get ready. Frederick Jr. was so impatient and hated to be kept waiting. She bypassed the wheelchair that she didn't need even though Frederick insisted on buying it. However, she did grab the cane because her legs gave out at times. She quickly took a bird dip in the sink.

That's what Mr. Passmore called it when you washed yourself off in the sink. It was too difficult for her to climb in and out of the tub. *At least they have a shower that I can sit in and wash myself good.* She dressed in the jogging suit that Denise said would be comfortable for travel.

I guess they think since my bones are in bad shape that my mind is in bad shape also. They really mean well and I guess I should be grateful for children who care enough to want me to live with them. Some folks' children don't care anything about them.

At the noise outside the window, she crept over to peek. There was Frederick Jr., Denise, and a moving truck right behind them.

I guess it's really going to happen. Another phase of my life is ending. Another change I will have to go through.

She sat down by the window and tears slowly slid down her caramel face.

Chapter Three

Somebody Knows the Trouble I've Seen

"Now, who in the world could that be?" Cori asked. "Nobody comes to visit me during the day anymore. Probably a Jehovah's Witness. One thing you have to give them, they are persistent!" She walked to the door and peeked out the window at Grace, Bobby Lee's wife.

"Well my word! When did she get back in town?" Cori said to herself. "Just a minute!" she yelled through the cracked windowpane. "I see you're back. Didn't think you were coming back," Cori stated, opening the rickety front door.

"I almost didn't," Grace stated with equal emotion.

"Well, don't just stand there letting the heat out, come on in."

Grace stepped through the wooden door, quickly surveying the familiar room that had not changed in all the years she had been a part of the family. Every piece of furniture, picture, and ceramic what-me-not were in the same places they were in the very first time she crossed the threshold. Her mind quickly wandered back to that joyous day, but something snapped her back to the present.

"Lord, Mother Jacobs! It's as cold in here as it is outside. Why don't you have your heat on?" She reached to hug Cori's thin, fragile body. She could feel Mother Jacobs' body tense and pull away from her.

"I just use the oven in the morning for heat," Cori answered abruptly.

"But you need more heat than the oven today," Grace continued.

"You just need to wear more clothes. You gonna have arthritis for sure if you don't start wearing more clothes," replied Cori.

Grace followed Mother Jacobs through the icy house into the kitchen and took a seat at the table. As she glanced around the kitchen, her mouth formed a slight smile as she looked at the old Formica table, which was nearly identical to the one she had seen in an antique shop while visiting her sister.

Most of this stuff should be in a museum. Why this entire house could be a museum.

The thought of Mother Jacobs' reaction to visitors walking through her home nearly brought her to laughter, but she contained herself. Mother Jacobs set two half cups of hot coffee on the table.

"Here, have a cup of coffee." Grace reached for the sugar dish and saw that it was empty.

"Too much sugar is not good for you. You'll get sugar diabetes for sure," Mother Jacobs stated with a tone that let Grace know that she would be taking hers without sugar also.

Grace slowly sipped her weak but piping hot coffee. She glanced around the kitchen and just as the living room, everything was exactly the same. She thought back to when the dark wood panels with the matching cabinets were built. They seemed extremely dark to Grace, who preferred a bright cheery kitchen. It was especially dreary today.

"Mother Jacobs, it is so dark in here. Let me turn the lights on," Grace asked.

"I just pull the curtains back and I get all the light I need," responded Cori.

"But Mother Jacobs, it's so dark in here. It is bound to affect your eyes."

"You the one with the glasses," Cori stated.

"Where are your glasses?" asked Grace.

"I don't need them anymore. Probably never did."

Grace gripped the side of the cup tightly to warm her fingers.

"I just don't see how you stand it in here as cold as it is."

"Well, if it's that cold, why don't you leave?"

At one time that comment would have offended Grace, but she had long since gotten used to Mother Jacobs' acid tongue. She simply walked over to the oven, longing for some of the heat that was escaping from the oven door. As she walked to the stove, she caught a quick glimpse at the gas thermostat and noticed that it was off.

"Mother Jacobs, you don't even have your heat on! No wonder it is so cold in here."

"Now you know I never did like that gas heat. I should never have listened to Bobby Lee and kept my wood stoves. I changed my heat to gas, put in all that new stuff, and it took nearly my entire nest egg. Now gas is sky high and I can't pay those high prices."

Grace nodded to that truth. They were having a hard time with the requests for assistance at Social Services and Mother Jacobs would never qualify, considering she still owned her home. Bobby Lee had lost that battle too. He tried to convince Mother Jacobs to put the house in his name or even Eddie's name. But she was resolute that she needed to have something of her own. Plus, deep down she believed Bobby Lee would sell it and put her in a nursing home.

"Mama," Bobby Lee said, "you could get all sorts of assistance if you would put this house in my name. You could qualify for meals, gas assistance, someone to come in to help you or you could move into Blessed Rest and have everything on one floor."

But Mother Jacobs had looked at him as if he was insane.

"Bobby Lee should help you with your gas bill," stated Grace.

"Bobby Lee is a fine son and he takes good care of me."

"I see how well he takes care of you. Just about as well as he takes care of me."

No sooner than the words left her lips, Grace regretted it. Mother Jacobs was not only Bobby Lee's mother, but also his number one defender.

"I think he's done well by you. Bought you that fine house. Bought you all that fancy furniture. Sent you back to school. Let you have your career when most women were home taking care of their families. Sent your young'uns to college. Seems to me, he took really good care of you."

Grace knew it was no use arguing with Mother Jacobs when it came to Bobby Lee.

Mother Jacobs' selective memory conveniently deleted the facts that Grace and her children went to college on scholarships, Grace was a stay-at-home mom until her children began middle school, worked at the Social Services office as a receptionist, took night classes, and moved up the ladder to her present position. Sure, Bobby Lee bought the house, but they would have lost it many years ago, if it had not been for her income. And that fancy furniture, she purchased with her own money.

It was like talking to a brick wall when it came to Bobby Lee. Mother Jacobs could fuss about him until the cows came home, but if anyone criticized him you would think he walked on water after she finished with them. She was the only person on Earth who was allowed to say anything bad about him. Grace learned that lesson many years ago.

"Besides," Mother Jacobs continued, "What's he gonna help me with? That ole S-Mart is running him right into the ground."

Grace knew that the S-Mart was having an effect on Bobby Lee's business, but in her travels, she had seen how many general stores in the South capitalized on their history and made quite a bit of profit. Bobby Lee was just so stubborn and would not listen to anyone, especially her.

"Mother Jacobs, you can't keep living like this. Why, at the rate you're going, you will surely freeze to death or starve. You just have to move in with Bobby Lee and me."

Mother Jacobs' eyes quickly turned to daggers. "I was born in this house and I'm dying in this house. I would rather be dead than have to live off anyone. I've been taking care of myself all these years and I will take care of myself until I die."

"Well, if you won't move in with us, how about someone moving in with you?" Grace studied the house carefully. "This is such a huge home. It's big enough for you to have a boarder and still have your space. You could share the kitchen, keep your privacy on the second floor, and the rooms that Grandma used could be for the boarder."

Grace was getting excited just thinking about it. "One room could be the bedroom and the other could be a sitting room. Plus, the bathroom is right by the bedroom. You would only need to share the kitchen. People are doing it all over the country. They're turning their homes into bed and breakfasts, but in this case, you would keep the boarder permanently."

Grace saw the sharpness in Mother Jacobs' eyes soften a little, but an edge was still in her voice as she said, "Do you think I want some stranger rambling through my things? Why, I'd be worried to death about being murdered in my sleep!"

"I would screen them very carefully. I could run a background check at the agency and I could get Eddie to help me. He's such a good judge of people."

With the mention of Eddie's name, Grace saw Mother Jacobs' eyes soften even more.

She truly adored her grandson, even if he did marry what Mother Jacobs considered a crying, sentimental simpleton.

"I would run an ad, and Eddie and I would interview them. I interview people all the time, and I could evaluate them just as I do on my job. I have a really good feeling about this."

Yes, that is true, Mother Jacobs thought. *Grace has many friends who confide in her and she has a genuine understanding of people. I guess that was why she was elected homecoming queen.*

"What do you think about this?" Grace continued. "I will pick up a newspaper and see how much people are charging for rooms. With us being so close to Chapel Hill and Durham, I wouldn't be surprised if you could get about $600-$800 a month for the three rooms."

It was then that Grace saw a bit of excitement flash across the stern face.

"I am off the rest of the day; I will just run on over to the store, let Bobby Lee know I'm back, and pick up a paper. I should be back in about an hour."

Mother Jacobs sat there with no expression. Her mind was a whirlwind of thoughts as she began to debate herself.

What will people think? Me taking on a boarder?

Who's alive that would care anyway?

What about my privacy?

What, pray tell, do I have that is private?

What if they aren't clean?

Grace said she would screen them carefully.

Who would have thought I would have come to this? Having to take on boarders to survive. I thank God all my dear friends are not alive to see me in such a state.

She looked around the kitchen with the dark paneled walls Robert Edward put up as a distraction from the Watergate hearings. She glanced at the cabinets that matched the paneling. She glimpsed the downstairs bathroom that had been their only bathroom for many years.

She caressed her chipped china coffee cup that had belonged to her own mother and now she may need to rent out her mother's bedroom. She gazed at the door that led to the basement where Robert Edward died. Cori Jacobs did something she had not done in a very long time. She put her head down into her frail arms and sobbed.

Chapter Four

Home Is Where the Broken Heart Is

The cold was absolutely unbearable. Grace almost regretted taking the short walk to the store. She walked a little faster examining the surroundings for any change, but everything looked the same. Although her life was changed forever, everything looked exactly as it did when Grace left three months earlier.

The service station, which no longer sold gas due to the new environmental laws, was still open. The fading sign of the blonde lady drinking the Coca-Cola was in the same place it had been for as long as she could remember.

A few of the remaining World War II veterans hung out at the nearly deserted spot discussing the Battle of the Bulge, Iwo Jima, or whatever battle they had been a part of. The owner was retired, and although he only sold a few loaves of Sunbeam bread, he opened the store every day for the daily debates and heated discussions.

These men, though having never finished high school, were probably the most brilliant minds in the town. They had lived in the county all of their lives, except for their brief stints serving their country, but they were more knowledgeable about the world and politics than the most educated Harvard professor. Even before she came into their view, Grace could hear their animated conversation.

"That young whippersnapper can't take on those Republicans," said Mr. Jim. "He's still wet behind the ears."

"He's a smart'un though," added Mr. Raymond. "Graduated from Harvard. They don't come much smarter than that."

"It don't take smartness these days. Look what we had the past eight years," Mr. Pate added as all three men joined in laughter.

"It ain't no way folks gone vote for a Muslim," said Mr. Jim.

"I done told you, he ain't no Muslim," stated Mr. Raymond. "His daddy was from Africa and his mama was a White woman from Kansas."

"Well, you know what ole George Jefferson used to say. He's a zebra!" said Mr. Jim.

Once again, the three men erupted in laughter.

"I still say Hillary can take on ole man McCain, Huckabee, or any of them. That's one tough woman," said Mr. Pate. "Shucks, McCain is about as old as I am and I know I am too old to run the country. I can't even remember where I put my teeth most mornings!"

They were still laughing at that line when Grace approached.

"Good morning, Mr. Jim, Mr. Raymond, Mr. Pate."

"Good morning, Miss Grace," said the three men.

"I was so sorry to hear about yo' sister," added Mr. Raymond, with the other two joining in expressing their condolences.

Grace thanked them for their concern and continued her walk. Just as she passed, she heard Mr. Raymond remark in a soft voice, "That's the nicest white woman in town, the salt of the earth."

Grace's cold walk felt warmer. She was still basking in the warmth of the dear old men as she passed Mrs. Emmaline's house, which was still standing, although it should have been donated to the fire department many moons ago. It was one of the most beautiful homes in town, but after she died her greedy children couldn't agree who would live in it, so it sat lonely and haunting.

Grace continued her stroll down the street and was about to pass Herman's Barber Shop when she saw Taliaferro Johnson, Jr. heading in her direction. His dad was proud of being named after the first African American to be drafted into the NFL, but Taliaferro, Jr. was nicknamed Kung Fu by his friends.

He was probably making one of his many trips to the store for his Grandma Polly, who refused to make a shopping list, even though her memory was quickly becoming a thing of the past. Tal Jr. was a classmate of Eddie's and lived with his grandmother and dad in Pearl Harbor, the Black neighborhood.

Grace never could figure out how it got the name *Pearl Harbor*. Apparently, when Pearl Harbor was attacked during World War II, the name somehow became attached to the neighborhood. It was no more than a row of small three-room shanties. A few years ago, the owner of the properties was ordered by law to bring them all up to city code by adding indoor plumbing and aluminum siding to the outside.

Tal Sr. had gone to Korea around the time Bobby Lee went to Vietnam.

After the troops returned, Tal came home with a tiny Korean wife named Yaki, which was short for something Tal's family and everyone else in Blessing had trouble pronouncing. She lived in Pearl Harbor with Tal's family for a while but left suddenly.

The story was told that they had a big Fourth of July celebration and all the neighbors joined together under the large oaks at the end of the road. There was a makeshift table covered with numerous large bowls of fried chicken, fresh fish was frying in iron cookers, one table had a variety of cobblers, pies and cakes, and another table had platters and pots of every possible part of the pig, from the pig ears to the pig feet.

Apparently, there were several pots of chitterlings, which Tal's little Korean wife refused to eat. Tal's family was insulted and began a verbal assault about how Yaki's people ate rats and cats and anything else that had four legs. She tried to leave with Tal Jr. but Tal Sr. stood firm that his son was not leaving Blessing. Yaki disappeared shortly after the celebration, but every birthday and Christmas, little Tal received gifts from her. The last folks heard, she owned a chain of nail salons down in Charlotte.

Anyway, Yaki and Tal's little boy had to have a nickname because just about every little child in Pearl Harbor had a nickname. Since he was part Korean, it was Kung Fu for little Tal Jr. after the television show, which was popular at the time. It was cute when he was little, but as he grew older he insisted that he be called by his name.

Tal Jr. was a very bright child and an excellent student. He could have succeeded in college, but worked as a maintenance man with his dad at Sampson Industries until it closed. He and his dad were responsible for all the HVAC repairs at the mill. Tal Sr., although trained in the army, was never licensed and because of new regulations, had to cease repairing the industry's HVAC systems. He continued to make repairs in his community until one of his neighbors reported him for charging $20 for a job that normally cost $200.

The three generations lived on his grandmother's Social Security, which wasn't much. Even though she worked for the Sampson's for over 30 years, they never paid her Social Security. Her small check, plus the odd jobs Tal Jr. was able to acquire, and Tal Sr.'s disability check, provided a decent living.

"Hello Tal Jr., how is Miss Polly?"

"Good Morning, Miss Grace. Grandma is doing just fine. I just left your store picking up some things for her. She's getting more forgetful, but her body's holding up fine. I know she's going to be sending me back to the store when I tell her you're home. She'll probably want to make some kind of cake or pie on account of your sister dying. We were sorry to hear about her. I remember her from school. She was a little older but was always real nice."

"I appreciate that, Tal Jr., and tell your Grandma don't go to any trouble trying to make me a cake. I am really trying to lose some weight."

Grace hoped her true thoughts didn't show. Even though Miss Polly once had the reputation of being the best cook in town, she was just about as blind as a bat now, and there was no telling what might wind up in that cake.

"Tell Eddie I said hey when you see him. He's still on me about going to college," Tal Jr. said smiling.

"Well, I agree with Eddie. You are so smart! You know it's never too late. Remember, I didn't finish college until my children were nearly grown. Why, I was older than you are now. I know there are several programs out there that could help you get started. If you get a few minutes, stop by my office and we can discuss it some more."

"You know what Miss Grace? I just might do that. I just might."

Grace smiled at Tal Jr. and continued her walk toward the store when she saw Opaque Albright heading in her direction.

"I wonder whose husband's she's after now." Grace immediately reprimanded herself, *"After all God loves Opaque too."* Only God knew why. How she wanted to cross the street to the other side to avoid Opaque, when she was reminded of the promise she made while taking care of her dying sister.

There is nothing like watching life slowly ebbing away to realize how precious life is…each life. She promised herself that she would try to treat everyone just a little bit better. And that included Opaque Albright.

Although Opaque had gained weight in the wrong places, as had everyone else in her age group, she refused to update her wardrobe to her age. The fact that she believed she could wear a mini-skirt in this cold weather alone caused Grace to question her stability.

Although the top waistband was completely covered by an extra layer of belly, and the tightness caused the black leather skirt to rise and form horizontal wrinkles that resembled an elephant's legs, Opaque thought she was still God's gift to all men.

Grace thought her eyes were playing tricks on her, but they weren't. She truly questioned Opaque's sanity. Opaque wore a matching leather jacket that was obviously two sizes too small, but that was not what was most bizarre. The jacket was unbuttoned due to the fact that two torpedoes refused to let the sides of the jacket meet.

Grace's eyes bucked as they zoomed in on the bright red wool turtleneck and focused on the tip of the torpedoes. Opaque did not even have on a bra! And how she could still walk in those high heel boots was a complete mystery to Grace, who had not been able to wear high heels ever since she had children.

She hated to admit it, but she envied Opaque's confidence. Oh, she was still good looking in her own way. Blonde highlights carefully camouflaged uninvited, unruly residents who had staked their claim throughout her thick auburn tresses.

She slyly caught glimmering gazes of men in her peripheral vision, but even she was aware that parallel lines had usurped the curves which once framed her body. She was starting to understand her mother's appreciation for elastic waist pants.

Opaque spotted Grace with a smile that resembled a buzzard after discovering road kill.

"Well Grace Jacobs," Opaque said, "Why…I mean…when did you get back in town?"

"Hello Opaque, how are you?" Grace responded casually.

"I am just fine. I am so surprised to see you."

"I don't know why, after all this is my home."

"But Bob, I mean Bobby Lee, said he didn't know when you would be returning. I don't mean any harm, but I got the slight impression he didn't think you were coming back at all."

"Well, I don't know what gave him that idea. He knew I would be returning as soon I took care of my sister's affairs."

"Oh my, please forgive my rudeness. I did hear that you lost your sister. You do have my sympathy, but for the life of me, I cannot place her."

"She was a few years behind us, and she left Blessing as soon as she graduated. She went away to college and never came back."

"So sad and such a young age. Had she been sick long?"

"No, not too long. She found out she was sick last summer and by the time the doctors diagnosed her, it was too late to do anything. Since she was single and didn't have any family but me, I stayed with her until she died. And now I am back."

"So, I see." A strange look went over Opaque's face, one Grace could not or did not want to even try to discern.

"Well, Opaque, it's been good seeing you again. But I need to head on over to the store to let Bobby Lee know I'm back."

Opaque stared at Grace as if she was seeing a ghost. Grace's comment seemed to startle Opaque back to the present.

"It was good seeing you too, Grace," she added somewhat forcibly.

Did Grace detect anger in Opaque's voice?

"What's eating her? Maybe she has an icicle up her butt. Who can tell with her?"

Grace continued walking down the main street, and after having to relay the details of her sister's death to just about everyone she passed, she almost regretted walking to the store.

Finally, she arrived at the Jacobs' General Store. Bobby Lee was in the back talking to PM, another gifted man who seemed to be stuck in a rut. He, Bobby Lee, and Johnny were the same age, although PM went to what was then the "Colored" school across town. When they were sent to Vietnam, the three stuck together since they were from the same hometown.

It was during the Battle of Hamburger Hill that PM saved Bobby Lee's life. He jumped in front of Bobby Lee and was shot multiple times. He was sent home in a wheelchair but slowly regained his strength and began walking, but with a terrible limp.

Bobby Lee and Johnny returned home from the war, too. Bobby Lee took over his parents' store, Johnny became Pastor of Blessing First Church and PM became the town drunk. Bobby Lee always felt like he owed PM something, so he let him hang out at the store, and kept him and his friends supplied with cheap wine. It was the least he could do.

"Now PM, I know it's cold, but I can't have y'all hanging out in here. It ain't good for business."

"Naw, Bobby Lee. I was just thinking we could hang out in your cellar where Mr. Robert's old pool table is. We'll be quiet as a mouse. It's just that the fire in the old barrel just ain't standing up to the cold today. I told Tadpole and Leroy, Bobby Lee won't mind us hanging out in the cellar, if we don't make too much noise."

"Well, I guess it'll be all right. But I don't want no smoking down there. Mess around and set yourselves on fire and burn my whole place down."

"No siree, we couldn't smoke even if we wanted to. Can't find a decent butt anywhere. Cigarettes so high I guess we all just quit at the same time." PM burst out laughing at his attempt at humor. "We just gone play some cards. I promise you, we won't set nothing on fire." PM looked up and saw Grace.

"Well I know spring's coming now! How ya doing Miss Grace?"

Grace began, "Now PM, didn't I tell you not to call me Miss Grace? We are the same age."

"I know that. But I also know you are a fine lady, and you deserve to be called Miss Grace."

"I appreciate the compliment, PM but I think of you as a dear friend, and I would appreciate it if you would call me Grace."

PM broke out in a smile. "I'll try Miss, I mean Grace. It's gonna be hard, but I'll try." He turned and winked at Bobby Lee and headed out back to tell his friends the good news.

"So, you're back," said Bobby Lee.

"Yes, I am back," Grace replied.

"Sorry I couldn't make it to the funeral. Couldn't close down the business with things as bad as they are."

"I didn't expect you to come."

"You all right?"

Did Grace detect some concern?

"Yes, I am fine."

"Good."

"I saw Opaque Albright this morning." Grace noticed Bobby Lee's face contort strangely. "She seemed surprised to see me. Seemed to think I wasn't coming back."

Bobby Lee returned to his work as if he had just finished with a customer. Grace stared at his back.

After a depressing period of silence, Grace said, "Bobby Lee, I saw your mother this morning."

"Yeah?"

"She doesn't look well to me."

"I saw her this morning. She looked the same to me."

"Bobby Lee, she looks thin and her house feels like an icebox."

Bobby Lee nodded when she mentioned the temperature of the house.

"I don't think she can afford to live there anymore."

"What do you want me to do? I've offered to take the house. I offered to help her find her assisted living. She won't listen. She is as stubborn as a mule."

"Well, I was thinking about maybe finding her a boarder. Maybe she can rent a room out or something."

"She won't want anyone staying with her. You know that."

The crash startled them both. Bobby Lee let out a few words that Grace hadn't heard in quite a while. "I wish those drunken winos would find somewhere else to hang out. Why do they keep hanging out here?"

Grace wanted to reply, "Because you keep giving them that cheap wine."

"Bobby Lee, what do you think about a boarder?" Grace yelled as Bobby Lee headed to the back of the store.

"Do what you want to do. You always do anyway."

He stomped as he headed down the stairs and left Grace standing there. Grace stared at his now empty space. So much had changed in her life. All of her immediate family was gone. Bobby Lee despised her for reasons only he knew. The man who abruptly turned from her showed no resemblance to the one who not only turned her head, but stole her heart.

He hadn't changed much physically. His piercing blue eyes still had a spell-casting effect, and he knew exactly what lonely, needy soul needed the captivation of his charm. His gray edges only made him more magnetic to women. She smiled as she was reminded of something she heard in the office.

"At a certain age, 'abs' is short for absent." Yes, with all his good looks, he couldn't hide the fact that his sturdy, firm, athletic frame had acquired a kangaroo pouch.

Slowly she turned and walked out. She stopped by the entrance and dropped coins in the paper machine and headed back home. The temperature seemed to have dropped a few more degrees.

***

Cori was still at the table when she heard Grace returning with copies of the Durham Herald and the Chapel Hill Gazette. Her spry steps were gone and the familiar dejected look on her face spoke volumes.

"Mother Jacobs, I picked up these papers," she stated in a monotone. "Opaque Albright said hello. She also said she was surprised to see me. Apparently, Bobby Lee had told her he didn't think I was coming back."

"Well, you didn't let anyone know your plans." If Cori felt any concern about Opaque, it didn't show on her face.

"Anyway, let's look at the ads."

"I don't think I want to do this," Cori began. "It just ain't natural letting strangers live with you for money."

Already feeling somewhat defeated, Grace's first response was to tell her she could sit there and freeze for all she cared. But that wasn't her nature, and as much as Bobby Lee's uncaring attitude at the store affected her, she was resolved to try to help his mother.

"Mother Jacobs, it's totally natural to seek help and it's totally natural to give help. You could look at this as you helping someone else instead of them helping you out. Johnny is forever preaching about us helping the less fortunate, even if he does have trouble practicing what he preaches. Besides, it won't hurt to look at the ads."

Grace began sifting through the pages until she came to the classified page. She skimmed quickly and found the *Rooms for Rent* section.

"It says right here that a single room goes for around $400. You would be offering two rooms plus a bathroom, and kitchen privileges. Let's see if I can find something close to what you are offering. Here we are. Two-room apartment for $750. Now that means that they have total privacy, so you probably would not be able to get that much. I wouldn't be surprised if you got at least $500."

Mother Jacobs' eyes lit up. *Five hundred dollars*, she thought. *What I could do with five hundred extry dollars a month! Why my Social Security check doesn't even amount to $500!*

Grace continued, "I say we run an ad for $600 a month to allow for some wiggle room. Now let's see how we want to word it. Elderly Lady…no…we better not advertise that you're elderly or you may become a target. As a matter of fact, I will put my phone number down, and I will only bring clients here who pass Eddie's and my inspection."

Grace began scribbling on her notepad.

"How about this? *Share a beautiful turn of the century home in the historical part of town. Two rooms, a private bath, and kitchen privileges. Lots of privacy. Perfect for studying or simple solitude. Only $600 a month.* Now we probably won't get that much, but we can negotiate down to $500."

"Whatever. Suit yourself. You probably won't get any phone calls at all. It seems like if a person had $600 extry a month, they should buy a home. I imagine $600 would make a house payment."

"Do you know how much Eddie and Lindsay pay for their two-bedroom townhouse out near the interstate? Fifteen hundred dollars a month."

"Fifteen hundred dollars a month for that cracker box?"

Totally ignoring Mother Jacobs, Grace continued, "Real estate has gone crazy around here."

"I guess that's why that old bumpy-faced Croftin boy is so anxious to get his hands on my property."

"You got that right. You have some of the most prime property in the county and everyone knows it. That's why I don't think it will be a problem getting a boarder. I'll type this up for you and drop it off this afternoon."

"Like I said, suit yourself," said Cori. She sat there as Grace let herself out. It was still hard to believe her long life had come to this.

Chapter Five

There's Nothing Like Southern Hospitality

The days were getting warmer. Redbuds peeked on Mrs. Emmaline's trees as a reminder that life goes on. Crocus boldly poked through the soil, signaling their victory over another winter. Several weeks had gone by and Grace had not brought anyone by to see the house. Cori was relieved. The relief was brief however, because Grace had called earlier to inform her that she was bringing a client by to look at the two rooms. After fretting the entire morning, Cori made up her mind that she was not going through with it.

The knock startled her. *Why did I let her talk me into this nonsense? I don't want some stranger living in my house. She'll probably cut my throat and throw me in the Country Line Creek! That Grace is always sticking her nose in my business. I should have left well enough alone.*

There was another knock at the door, then she heard the door unlock.

"Mother Jacobs, are you at home? Miss Petronella is here. She's on time. You like that."

I never should have given Grace a key, nosey heifer.

"I'll be there in a minute!" She started toward the parlor, but stopped dead in her tracks. She could hear Grace attempting to make the young lady feel at home.

"So, you're from the university. I wanted to attend the university, but I got married instead."

The rest of the conversation went silent as Cori took in the stranger who had invaded her home.

Well I never! Did she forget her clothes? Why, those are no more than drawers! Who in their right mind would go out in public with that short skirt on? And I swanney! If she makes a wrong turn, her bosoms will fall right out of that little rag that's barely covering her up. Don't she know it's still wintertime?

"Mother Jacobs, come meet Miss Petronella," Grace stated joyfully.

Grace's call snapped her to reality, and she began the dreaded steps toward her parlor, which now felt alien. She sat down without addressing either woman.

"Mother Jacobs, this is Miss Allison Petronella," Grace began. "She's studying Astronomy at the university. She wants to move away from the campus and spend more time studying the stars. Isn't that fascinating?"

"I get so distracted at college," added Miss Petronella, "and with the construction of the new high rises, I really don't have a good view of Sirius, Capella, and Vega."

Miss Petronella continued talking as Cori wondered who Sirius, Capella, and Vega were.

"I volunteer at the planetarium where we run a program that names stars. For $50 you can have your own star too. You would get a certificate certifying that a star is officially yours and your star would be registered in the Worldwide Catalog of Stars. You would even be able to locate your star," Allison said, quoting the information from the Catalog of Stars brochure. "Isn't that awesome! To have a star in the heavens named after you? Would you like a star named after you?"

Mother Jacobs finally found her voice.

"You mean to tell me if I pay $50 I will get a star in my own name and I'll get a letter stating that it is mine?"

Miss Petronella nodded, her eyes beaming with pride.

"That is about the dumbest thing I've ever heard! How do I know that someone else doesn't have my star? Is somebody gonna fly up there and put my name on it or something? Can I bring it home to make sure it is mine? What scatter brained dimwit would actually fall for such stupidity?"

Miss Petronella moved so far into the corner of the sofa that it nearly swallowed her. Finally, a fragile and nearly inaudible sound came from her mouth.

"Actually, we have sold over a million."

"Well, I hope John shoot the bull! You mean to tell me that a million people have purchased stars for $50 a pop? Well, I thought I had heard it all."

Grace decided she needed to change the subject, and quickly.

"Mother Jacobs, Miss Petronella would like to see the house."

"Petronella? You ain't from round here, are ya? You a Yankee ain't ya?"

"I'm from Brooklyn, New York," she said, her voice cracking.

"Y'all dress like that up north? Down here the only people that dress like that are floozies looking for trouble. You looking for trouble?"

"Mother Jacobs!" exclaimed Grace.

With every bit of courage she could muster, Miss Petronella began to speak. "Thank you so much, but I probably should try to find a place a little bit closer to the campus. I'm sorry I wasted your time."

"No, I'm sorry," said Grace. She walked Miss Petronella to the door, wanting to exit right along with the traumatized young woman. Yet, she knew she had to return to face her mother-in-law.

"Mother Jacobs, you were simply rude to that young lady," Grace began.

"What's rude about telling the truth? Would you pay $50 to have your name put on a star? And don't tell me that you saw nothing wrong with her looking like a slut."

"That is the way young people dress today."

"I don't care if they do. It still looks slutty and I will not have anyone dressing like that in my home. This here is a Christian home."

"Mother Jacobs," Grace began firmly, "I don't know how to say this, but times have changed, and if you want to find someone to help you with your situation, you have to be more accepting."

"Well, if I have to starve to death I won't have a trashy Yankee dirtying up my God-fearing home. I opened my home to trash one time and look where that got my sweet Bobby Lee."

"Why do I even try?" Grace shook her head with disgust and left in silence.

Chapter Six

The Unwelcome Mat

"Scat you ole Tom Cat! I can barely feed myself. Go find yourself another home!" Cori continued to beat the old, frayed rug against the rotting wooden steps. She beat it with all the fervor she could muster. With each swing, more fabric than dirt floated through the air, when she heard a knock at the door.

"Now who could that be?" Cori pondered. "Grace is at work, thank God, and Bobby Lee has already had his morning coffee."

She dropped the rug on the porch and made her way through the kitchen, down the hall to the door. She pushed the curtains back for a peep, and gasped at the sight that stared back at her through the windowpane.

"What in the world?" Cori pushed the worn curtains to the side again and peeped at the oddly clad stranger on the porch. Standing on Cori's front porch was what appeared to be a young lady covered from head to toe. Only her eyes were visible to Cori.

"Lord Jesus! It's one of those folks who flew those planes into those buildings in New York!"

"What do you want?" Cori shouted through the window.

"I come to rent room!" stated the young lady in an accent Mother Jacobs had only heard on the news.

"Room not for rent! Go way!" stated Mother Jacobs, mimicking the accent. "That's it. I am telling Grace to pull that ad today. I am tired of all these strange folks showing up on my porch. First, I had that hussy from New York, then that kook from out west somewhere. Now it's a steady stream of folks. It was just like that little wench at the newspaper to give my address to everyone who asked about the ad. I got a good mind to march myself over there and give her a good piece of my mind!"

She practically threw the curtains back into place and stomped through her house, ranting to herself, "When you live this long, you ought to be able to have some peace! I don't have peace of mind, peace in my home and…" The noise in her backyard caused the white in her eyes to turn blood red. "And I definitely don't have peace in my yard."

With traumatic urgency, she headed toward her back door. The door nearly fell off its hinges with the force.

"How many times do I have to tell you brats to stay out of my yard? Leave my plum trees alone, you little heathens!" Her body jerked as the loud startling noise drowned her shouts.

"Cut that noise down! I can't even hear myself think!" Cori shouted.

"Shut up, you ole hag," shouted Tay from the upstairs window. He proceeded to turn the music volume up louder.

"Just keep it up, you little pissants!" yelled Cori. "I hope a hornet nest falls splat on your heads!"

"You crazy ole lady. There are no hornets out this time of year!" yelled Tay.

Cori glanced at Tay with disgust and threw her old rag rug out in the yard, as if to scare Lizzie and Summer. This only brought the girls to further rowdy laughter as pieces of the rug floated through the air. They not only doubled over in laughter, but picked up the rug pieces and proceeded to run around Cori's yard, screaming.

This was all Cori could take. She turned around and marched back to her kitchen, slamming the already dilapidated door so hard it rattled the entire house. She sat at her table, totally exhausted.

Dear God, what did I do to deserve this? Why, I ought to go on and kill myself since you don't seem to want to take me. Lord, animals are treated better than I am. I see on the television about all kinds of laws protecting animals. Just last week I heard a news report about some military people out in California who can't even go to the beach because of a little bird that lives on the base. Lord, it said that they actually pay people to watch the beach to make sure the bird is safe, and I don't even feel safe in my own home. Please, Jesus, take me. I don't want to live on this earth anymore. If you're not going to take me, then please help me. God knows I need your help.

Cori didn't know how long she sat at the table. The noise finally died down and she was as drained as if she had worked a day in a hot, scorching tobacco field. She was sitting at the table with an empty stare when Grace entered the kitchen.

"Mother Jacobs, I knocked. I thought you might be sick, so I let myself in." Grace looked around the kitchen and everything appeared to be normal. "Mother Jacobs are you sick?"

"Yeah, I'm sick. I'm sick and tired. I'm sick of living and I just want some peace and quiet." She knew it was no use telling Grace about the trouble she had just experienced. Of course, those little demons were always on their best behavior whenever Bobby Lee or Grace was around.

Grace began quietly, nearly whispering, "Well, I hate to bother you right now, but I met the most delightful woman today and I brought her right over. Her name is Mrs. Ada Passmore and she just moved here from Detroit. Her husband died last year, and she had to move to warmer weather because she has crippling arthritis."

"Her kinfolk can't help her?"

"Well, she's been living with them for a few weeks, but wants a little more independence. She's a retired schoolteacher and she didn't as much as flinch at $600 a month. Just come in and at least meet her."

Cori's body began to move even though her mind was still fragmented over her most recent assaults. With the vitality of a wounded kitten, she followed Grace through the kitchen.

As she entered her parlor, she abruptly staggered and whispered somewhat loudly, "You didn't tell me she was Colored."

Grace saw Ada's body stiffen. "Mother Jacobs, please."

Grace began the introductions, "Mother Jacobs, this is Mrs. Ada Passmore. Mrs. Passmore, Mrs. Corinthia Pearl Jacobs." Neither woman said a word, but stared at each other as if they had been lifelong enemies.

Grace continued repeating some of the information she had shared with Cori in the kitchen.

"Mrs. Passmore's son lives out in the Cypress Springs Country Club."

"I didn't know they allowed the Colored out there," stated Mother Jacobs. Ada's body contracted even more.

"My son was the first African American family to move into Cypress Springs. He is now president of the Homeowners' Association."

"Well, I heard you people were trying to take over. I guess it's true."

"Yes, my people have worked as hard or harder than any other group in this country, and they can live anywhere they can afford."

Grace jumped in, "Mrs. Passmore is very interested in renting the two rooms."

"Why don't you move on out to Cypress Springs like your young'un?"

Trying to remain calm, Ada began, "I prefer to live in town. Even though I drive, I don't like to drive on country roads." Mrs. Passmore looked directly at Grace and continued, "I really appreciate you taking time out of your busy schedule, but I believe I will examine some other options. You have been most kind."

Mrs. Passmore flashed a smile at Grace, quickly smirked at Cori, grabbed her cane, and began her painful walk to the door. The grimace on Mrs. Passmore's face was not lost on Cori as she absorbed Mrs. Passmore's pain with each step. The anguished sadness in her eyes was too familiar.

Before her mind could seize her mouth, Cori heard words escaping, "You didn't even look at the rooms." The sound of her voice penetrated the tense silence and Grace saw the opening she prayed for.

"Mother Jacobs' home was built after the Civil War and is one of the oldest homes in the county. Bobby Lee, my husband, had gas heat, central air, and new electrical wiring put in a few years ago."

"I paid for it," interjected Cori.

"Indeed, she did," Grace continued. "Mother Jacobs is a proud woman and is known throughout this entire town."

"I'm sure she is," stated Ada somewhat sarcastically.

Grace continued, "She is a pillar in the community, and during the Civil Rights movement, her store was the only one that continued to allow Blacks…I mean, African Americans, the opportunity to shop."

Ada paused briefly, taking in the last statement.

"My Robert and I were always good to you people."

Grace's eyes rolled as she continued, "You see, the two rooms are right off the parlor and are not far from the kitchen. It has a private bath, also."

Ada looked in the rooms and was impressed at the space. She despised small, closed-in spaces. She appreciated history, and could see that this truly was a beautiful home.

Grace led Ada through the living room to the kitchen. Ada glanced around the kitchen and was drawn to the old, red Formica table with the silver chrome sides. She rubbed her hands over the table and fought back tears.

She and Frederick had one just like it when they first started their lives together. It was one of the first pieces of furniture they bought. Her eyes continued to scan the room, glancing at the outdated cabinets and matching panels. She gasped as her eyes focused on the object in the corner.

There, sitting off in the corner of the kitchen as if it had been discarded, was an old cast iron cooking stove. Ada didn't move, and was quickly transported to another time. She stared at the iron legs that held it firmly. Years had not weakened it in any way as it stood solidly defying time. Her eyes were transfixed on the white shiny porcelain doors at the top.

"The lady who raised me had an old stove just like that. She would bake bread in it during the day and keep it in the little cabinets at the top."

"I used that stove every day until Bobby Lee talked me into buying that electric one. Food never did taste as good to me with the new one," stated Cori. Ada's nod in agreement with Cori was a glimpse of hope to Grace.

"Where are my manners?" Cori asked. "Would you like something to drink? Do you have your own teeth? Cause if you got your own teeth, then I'll offer you some Mary Janes. Now most folks don't buy Mary Janes anymore. They're still a penny at the store. I think the only reason that Bobby Lee won't raise the price is because he knows I'll have his head on a platter. They're about the only thing extry I buy. So, I grab a handful every time I go to the store.

"I offered Tator Jones some, he's the fellow who helps out round here. He helps out 'bout everyone in town. He's as good as an ole shoe, even if he is a little sissified. Bobby Lee and his ole friends even call him 'Sweet Tator.' Now, I don't know nothing 'bout that heathen stuff and don't care to learn nothing 'bout it. Seems like every time I turn that TV on, you see men kissing men and women kissing women.

"I been around here over 90 years and he's as good a soul as they come. I offered Tator a Mary Jane, and course he took it and started chewing. Well, he had just gotten him some new false teeth. Answered some ad in the paper about 'false teeth for $100'. Well, he sho' nuff got them teeth. He had 'em in his mouth the day he came to get the garbage. I burned garbage in my barrel out in the back for nearly 60 years and all of a sudden, it was against the law. Now, it didn't happen to get against the law until the Sampson's bought the Heckton's land and turned it into the city dump.

"Then Barnett Sampson, being the Chairman of the City Council, had the City Council make it a law that all trash had to be taken to the city dump.

Now I have to pay a little dumping fee to have my own trash taken to the trash yard. So Tator figured he'd load his truck up with as much trash as he could since they charged by the vehicle, not the amount of trash on the vehicle.

"Anyway, Tator sat there chewing and chewing and the next thing you know, he started making these ugly faces and strange noises and before you could slap a tick, those teeth flew across my table and nearly landed in my sugar bowl.

"Well, they were just a mess. I couldn't tell if it was the Mary Jane that made them look so bad or if it was the fact that Tator probably hadn't brushed them since he bought them. Now, you don't brush false teeth, do you? I saw it right on the TV. You set them in some bubbly stuff. Well, they hadn't seen no bubbly stuff either. Anyways if you got yo' own teeth, you're welcome to some Mary Janes."

"No thank you," replied Ada. "I do have my own teeth though."

Grace thought she detected a slight smile from Ada.

There was an invasion of silence once again. Grace, feeling that too much silence would give Mother Jacobs the opportunity to end the tranquility with another ignorant statement, broke the stillness.

"You have a beautiful car. Did you drive it from Detroit?" asked Grace.

"Oh, no. Frederick Jr. drove me down here. I still drive, but I don't like to drive long distances, especially on unfamiliar roads. I am a nervous wreck on those narrow roads out where Frederick lives. But I still like my independence, and I don't like the thought of having to ask someone to take me everywhere that I want to go."

Cori nodded in agreement.

"Speaking of driving," Ada continued, "I need to head on back to Frederick's. I am still learning my way around, and he is already angry with me for coming to look at the rooms. My daughter even called me senile. What makes young people think that just because you start to age that you don't have any sense?"

"Or feelings," Cori added softly.

The look of mutual understanding on both faces was not lost on Grace.

Ada grimaced again, shaking her head from side to side as she struggled with her cane and with her new reality.

"I have lived right here all of my life. I walk to the store, to the post office, and to my church. That has been a blessing. Lord knows, I don't know what I would do if I had to ask someone to take me everywhere that I needed to go."

"Mother Jacobs' house is very convenient and is close to just about everything. I imagine she is in better shape than most folks in town because she walks so much," added Grace.

What was it the doctor had told her? Ada thought. That she needed to walk more. Of course, she couldn't walk the streets of Detroit, and even though Frederick Jr. had bought her a treadmill, it wasn't the same as walking down a street and waving to neighbors.

"Well, do you want the rooms or not?" asked Cori with her usual tact.

Cori's tone caused Ada to turn abruptly to face the woman. Even though her mind wanted to tell this woman that hell would freeze over before she lived with her, her heart softened as she looked at the gray eyes that penetrated from the aged wrinkled face.

There was something so familiar in her eyes; something she had seen before. It vanquished the words in her head and instead she answered, "I do like the rooms and they are very spacious. I also like the idea of being able to walk down safe streets. But I don't like to make hasty decisions and I probably should discuss it with Frederick Jr."

"Suit yourself," Cori said, getting up from the table and heading to the porch. Cori pulled the door open and peered through the rusting screen door as if searching for something, something that connected her with anything kind.

"It just don't seem natural to not be putting something in the ground in the spring. Robert Edward and I planted a garden every spring, come hell or high water."

As Ada started towards the parlor, she stopped and turned to Cori who had briefly drifted to another time.

"Do you have a garden spot?" asked Ada.

"I guess you can call it that. It once was a beautiful garden. Last summer I put a few tomato plants out, but they didn't amount to much."

Ada turned and joined Cori at the back door. "I have always wanted a small garden. The woman who raised me planted one every year. The three of us would put the seeds in the ground and would wait and watch until the first sprouts showed.

"We took care of the garden like it was a member of the family. We planted enough for the whole town it seems, and when it was time to pick the plants, it was just like Christmas.

"After I moved to the city, every spring I would think about those times. I even put a flowerpot in the window and tried to grow some tomatoes too. They didn't grow to any size; probably not enough sun."

"I imagine so," said Cori.

Ada stood beside Cori and looked at the garden spot now overgrown with weeds. Both women solemnly gazed at the mound of dirt.

"I bet it was a beautiful garden."

"That it was. It kept us fed and healthy for many years." Cori let out a deep sigh. "I've been on Bobby Lee to plow it up for me, but he can never seem to find the time. Maybe this spring."

"Hopefully," Ada said in agreement.

Ada once again struggled with her cane and began her painful walk to her car.

"I really need to head on back before Damaris sends the State Patrol out for me. They said they are going to get me a cell phone. Can you see me with a cell phone?"

All three women laughed.

"I do like your house, but as I said I need to talk to my son," said Ada.

"And like I said, suit yourself," replied Cori.

Grace knew this was as much as she would get out of either woman today.

"Let me walk you to your car, Mrs. Passmore."

"Thank you, Mrs. Jacobs, for showing me your home. Have a good day."

Cori stayed in her position, fixated on the garden spot. It didn't resemble the fertile, fruitful spot it had been so long ago. But nothing was the same anymore.

Grace walked Ada to her car, moving slowly to match Ada's pace.

"Mrs. Passmore," Grace began. "I do hope you will consider moving in with Mother Jacobs. Deep down she really is a good soul. She can be crusty, ornery, and sometimes just downright mean. Over the years, she has rubbed me the wrong way and aggravated me so much. I just think of her as my sandpaper. Even though she rubs me the wrong way, as I get older I think I am a better person because of her.

"She was born and raised during a different time. The world changed, but she didn't. Life has been extremely hard for her, but she keeps plucking right along, and what I said earlier is true. During the Civil Rights Movement, they had a cross burned in their yard because they continued to let Black patrons shop at their store. When Papa Jacobs died, I imagine there were just as many Black people at the funeral as Whites. And you know what else?"

Ada's face searched Grace's face for a possible answer.

"She likes you. She only rambles with her old stories like that with people she likes."

"Mrs. Jacobs."

"Call me Grace. All my friends do."

Ada smiled, "Grace. I've lived long enough to know the difference between good and evil. And one thing that I've learned is that evil has no color. Actually, I can relate more to Mrs. Jacobs than she knows. She reminds me a lot of the lady who raised me. You see, I was adopted by an elderly white woman."

Chapter Seven

Caswell County, North Carolina, circa 1930

Vivian had seen the moon three times now. Each night before she and her little sister collapsed in slumber, Vivian counted how many times they had seen the moon. She was so tired that the hay was a comfortable soft mattress.

They had walked for forever in their little minds, mainly walking in the woods because games of hide and seek had taught them that the woods were a good hiding place. As her baby sister's legs buckled in weakness, Vivian, who had always been an attentive older sister picked her up and let her ride piggyback.

"It must have been a bad dream," Vivian thought, retracing the horrible events of the past days. She was asleep in a warm bed when she heard her papa talking real fast. As her mama quickly grabbed them out of the bed, she heard horses and saw fire through the windows. Her mama told her to take Georgia with her and run out back.

"Run as fast as you can and don't stop!" her mama cried.

Vivian grabbed Georgia's hand and ran just like her mama said. Vivian tried not to look back but the gunshot caused her to stop and look back at their home. It was then that she heard her mama's screams and saw her home in flames. She heard more gunshots, which caused her to grab Georgia's hands and run with all her might. She tried not to stop like her mama said, but her legs gave way to the pain.

Georgia had not ceased from crying as Vivian tried to quiet her. She didn't know how far she had run, but she and Georgia were deep in the woods when they stopped to rest. Georgia's sobs turned to sniffles as Vivian sang the song that her mama sang to them, "Swing low, Sweet Chariot. Coming for to carry me home." Vivian secretly hoped that if she sang it long enough, a chariot would indeed come and carry them home. Georgia eventually went to sleep and although she tried to fight it, Vivian's weary body soon joined her little sister's peaceful rhythm.

It was a distance away, but it was the clear sound of a rooster that awakened Vivian.

Although her mind was somewhat fuzzy, the memory of the previous events cleared the haze. Her first thought was to go back, but as soon as her thoughts were lucid, she knew they must do what her mama had told her; they had to keep running. She woke Georgia who immediately started crying. Vivian picked her up, cuddled her, and began walking through the woods.

They found a blackberry patch and sat down, and ate until their hands were completely blue. They continued walking, stopping for water from springs and to eat more berries. Occasionally, they came across a desolate farmhouse where they hid in the woods until night and fed on tomatoes, potatoes, and other vegetables from the farmer's garden.

As the warm sunrays beamed down, awakening them, they returned to the woods that had become their refuge from the heat and strangers.

The third day brought the rain showers. They found an opening under a cabin porch and hid until the rain subsided. Vivian held Georgia, who had always been afraid of the dark, tightly, whispering for her to keep quiet.

And now they had seen three moons. It was the day after the third moon when they found another farmhouse sitting out in a field with an old barn out back. It was already getting dark, and Vivian decided this would be as good a place as any to sleep. It would probably be warmer than the old porch they had slept under the previous night.

As they slowly moved toward the barn, they could hear a dog barking some distance away; Vivian hoped the dog was tied. She quickly picked her little sister up and headed to the barn.

They found the creaky door in the dusk and slipped quietly through it into the dark, musky barn. Vivian surveyed her new dwelling for animals and found none. Weary from another long day's journey, she found a mound of hay and an old dirty blanket and made a little bed.

As Georgia began to cry, Vivian began singing to her again, and Georgia's cry soon faded to light breathing. Vivian got on her little knees as she had done with her mama, and prayed to God to help them. After her tearful plea to God, she lay beside her little sister and fell asleep too.

***

Mrs. Damaris Jane Gilliam had lived alone for five years now. Her husband, Bill, tried to help the horse that had broken its leg, when the horse kicked wildly, hitting Bill directly in the temple, causing his instant death. Their farm was a prosperous farm, which enabled them to have a very comfortable living. They worked side by side, managed their money well, and Bill left her in very good shape financially.

Damaris was one of the wealthiest women in the county. She and Bill had achieved every goal they set when they married, except they never had their much-desired children. Sharecroppers ran the farm now and Damaris spent her days working right along with the sharecroppers and running the lucrative tobacco farm.

Many of the other landowners clung to the old ways and abused or took advantage of the people who worked their land, but not Damaris. Some evenings she sat on her porch listening to their *Come to Jesus* meetings. Their gut-wrenching spirituals and heart-warming prayers often caused her own soul to quiver.

It was in one of those moments that she made up her mind that even though she could not change the times they lived in, she would do all that she could to ensure that the people who worked for her had a decent quality of life. She doctored, clothed, and protected them fiercely. In return, they worked hard and were very loyal to this woman, who some had named their daughters.

Of course, there were those who thought Damaris Gilliam was a little bit strange or just downright crazy. She dressed in Bill's overalls, would be seen in the field working right beside the sharecroppers, and hunted and fished right along with the men in town.

Something was in the air, Damaris could feel it. She had seen her people whispering on several occasions and stop abruptly when she approached. As loyal as she felt they were to her, she knew that they had a code of loyalty to each other that even she could not break. She was glad it was her day to go get supplies. If anything was going on, she would definitely find out in town.

Folks still looked at her strangely when she drove her truck to town, dressed in men's clothes. She was so glad that Bill taught her how to drive the old truck, and she could not care less what the town folks thought about her clothes. Just as she headed toward the square, she noticed a congregation of people huddled under the Civil War Soldier statue.

Damaris parked the truck and started into Smith's Mercantile. She saw

Lucinda Mutts and Caroline Beach talking with such excitement she thought they would burst. She headed towards the ladies who were so engrossed in deep conversation that they barely noticed her arrival.

"I never thought such shenanigans went on around here," Lucinda said.

"It's just a shame, just a shame," interjected Lucinda. "Oh Damaris, I didn't see you walk up."

"What in the world is going on?" asked Damaris.

"Haven't you heard, child?" replied Lucinda.

"Heard what?" asked Damaris.

"There was a killing over in Caswell," said Lucinda.

Caswell County was the next county over from Alamance, near the Virginia line. Many folks in their community had relatives over in Caswell, so Damaris figured that's why there was so much commotion.

"Yes, yes. An awful killing," Lucinda continued. "A few days ago, a farmer found his po' wife murdered somewhere near Wilmington and they arrested a Colored man for it."

"Lord Jesus, you don't say!" a shocked Damaris said.

"Sho' nuff. Well, folks are riled up and some Ku Kluxers showed up at this Colored fellow's house in Caswell and killed his whole family. Young'uns and all."

"Lord, have mercy!" shouted Damaris.

"Yes indeedy," Lucinda continued.

"Shot some and burned the rest in the house," added Caroline.

"Who was the family?" asked Damaris.

"Some new folks. Came down here to open a Colored school," stated Caroline.

"So, that's it," Damaris thought to herself. "That's what all the whispering is about."

Damaris stood with her mind transfixed on the terrible information she had just received.

"This is just awful," she thought. There had been stories of things like this happening across the state, but not in their own backyard. "Yes indeed, this is awful."

Lucinda continued, "Now, there are some who said the Colored are getting ready for an uprising. If I were you, I would call that nephew of yours on over to keep an eye on things for you."

Damaris tried to dismiss the thought, but remembered the whispering and huddling she had witnessed before leaving the farm. *Surely her people wouldn't turn on her. This was a mess. Just a mess.*

"Johnny Beau is over at the store now, buying more bullets," Lucinda went on. "You know he never trusted the Colored anyway. I need to get on over there before he buys enough stuff to blow up the whole state."

"This is the last thing we need," Damaris thought. There were several old Civil War veterans who lived in the area who never got over the South losing the war, and even though they were old as dirt, this was just the ammunition they needed to start another one. She grew up hearing about the dark deadly days when other killings took place in her county and over in Caswell.

Damaris no longer felt like shopping, but being a practical person, she didn't want to waste a trip either. So, she quickly dismissed her uneasiness and headed on to the Mercantile. The store was more crowded than usual and just as Caroline had said, the men were stocking up on supplies.

When Rev. Abe Jones, the Negro preacher, walked into the store, there was sudden silence. Not a soul spoke to him. Damaris couldn't believe her eyes. This community had gotten along with each other fairly well, as long as everyone remembered their places.

"How do, Mr. Beach?" said Reverend Jones.

Silence.

"How do, Mr. Mutts?" Reverend Jones continued.

Silence.

"How do, Miss Damaris?"

"I'm just fine, Rev. Jones," Damaris said.

"Can I help you find something, Abe?" shouted Mr. Smith from behind the counter.

"I just came in to see if the Bible I ordered had come in."

"Naw. It ain't in. I'll let you know when it comes in. Anything else?" he said in a dismissing tone.

If Damaris hadn't witnessed it with her own eyes, she wouldn't have believed it. Rev. Jones was the most respected Colored man in town. He was respected by both Colored and Whites, and he definitely didn't deserve the treatment he received from the people in the store.

This man had the voice of an angel, and had sung at just as many White funerals as Colored. Yes, this was bad. Damaris quickly made her purchases and headed towards her old truck. Rare tears appeared as she struggled with the clutch. "Lord, have mercy. These are praying times."

Damaris pleaded all the way home for God's help and intervention as the details of the killings raced through her mind. As she approached her yard she continued to search for some answers.

Realizing she wouldn't need the truck anymore until her next shopping day, she headed toward the old shed where she kept her truck when she didn't need it. She parked it and went to open the two doors so she could put it in the shed. Just as she pulled the door open and the sunlight provided light to the shelter, she thought she heard a sound from the corner.

Grabbing a stick to fight off a stray animal, Damaris cautiously entered the shed. She walked softly over to the area where she heard the sound, and was startled by what she saw. Sleeping soundly on a mound of hay were two little girls. Why, one was no more than a baby, and the other one was just a small child. As Damaris stepped closer, her next step broke the silence and caused the bigger one to jump. She immediately lay down over the little one.

The smaller one woke at the movement of the older one and began to cry. Damaris started to take a step towards them, but something told her to sit down on the ground and talk to them from a distance.

In a soft voice, Damaris told them her name and that she wouldn't hurt them. She asked them their names, but they didn't answer. She asked them about their Ma and Pa, and the smaller one continued crying with the older one joining in. Damaris walked slowly over to the little girls and sat down beside them. She didn't say anything for a while, but then she started caressing them in a soothing way that reminded them of their Mama. She didn't know what else to do, so she began talking to God as she had done so many times.

"Dear God, I know I just finished talking to you, but here I am again. Lord, I don't know who these little girls are or where they came from. Lord, they are just babies. Please show me what to do. Show me how to help them. Be with their family wherever they are. I thank you and I will trust you Lord. Amen."

The girls seemed to calm down some. Damaris took the bigger girl's hand and helped her up. The bigger girl continued to hold the little one as Damaris took them to her home.

Chapter Eight

"The biggest disease today is not leprosy or tuberculosis, but rather the feeling of being unwanted."

– Mother Teresa

Ada's family's response to moving in with Cori was just as she had expected. Ada didn't rush into the decision and really tried to adjust to life with Frederick Jr. and his family.

She attempted to help with the cleaning, but was reminded that they paid a housekeeper to do the housework. She cooked what she thought were delicious meals, but was informed of the carbohydrates, fats, and calories that were in her cooking. She was available when the grandchildren arrived home for school, but they rushed in, dropped their belongings, and headed back to their after-school activities.

When they returned home, technology was their companion and Ada was no competition for the interactive, vigorous challenger. She spent much of her time just as she had in Detroit…alone. So, she made her decision; she was moving out. Just as she figured, there were questions about her stability and her senility. The only person who offered no opposition was Denise. She guessed the old saying was true, "You can't have two queens in one castle."

Frederick and Denise scheduled an appointment to meet with Grace and were won over by the caring, kind lady. So, they decided to support this little venture of Ada's. Ada Passmore and Corinthia Pearl Jacobs would become housemates.

The day finally arrived for Ada to move in with Cori, who was apprehensive but strangely excited. Grace spent her free time tidying the rooms. The bedroom was emptied because it was agreed that Ada would use her own bedroom furniture. Cori could relate to Ada wanting to keep the bed that she had shared with her husband.

It was also agreed that she could use the basement to store her extra items, which were in a storage facility near the interstate. After wearing a path to the front window, Cori headed to the back and gazed at the lonely little garden spot.

Perhaps with the extry money, I can hire someone to plow my garden, she thought.

The sound of the truck caused her to jump. She returned to the window and saw Frederick Jr. backing the U-Haul into her driveway. She recognized Ada's daughter-in-law driving the car Ada had driven to her house for her first visit. The two teenagers who sat in the backseat were probably the grandchildren.

Grace had tried to get Bobby Lee to help with the move, but of course he couldn't close the store. So Eddie, who had taken the teacher's workday off, hired PM, Tator, and Tal Jr. to help move the items. In very little time, the house was in order. Cori was amazed at the quality of the furniture Ada had.

Most of it looked just like the items she saw on *The Price is Right*. When they brought the refrigerator with the ice and water on the door, Cori couldn't contain herself. The new side-by-side refrigerator found a spot in Cori's kitchen, and her little round-topped refrigerator was placed on the screened-in porch for cold drinks on hot nights. Because of the many years Tal Jr. had worked in maintenance at the factory with his dad, he connected the icemaker in no time. Cori giggled like a schoolgirl when he handed her the glass of crushed iced water.

Tator secured the handicapped rails in the bathroom that Grandma had used, and just about the time the furniture was in place, the cable man arrived and appeared to take over each room in the house. Soon Cori's historical home was connected to cable.

Denise was arranging photos on the dresser as Ada searched for the A&E channel where she watched *Murder, She Wrote* and the The Hallmark Channel where she watched *Little House on the Prairie*. Kenya, Ada's teenaged granddaughter, was busy inserting everyone's number in the cell phone they had purchased for Ada. Carr had struck up a conversation with Eddie, one of the teachers from his school.

Finally, everything was in order and Denise and Frederick had to admit the rooms looked warm, cozy, and very much at home. Cori stayed in the kitchen much of the time Ada's family was there. Grace, who had formed a quick bond with Denise, left to show Denise the new slicer she had just purchased from a Queen's Kitchen party.

Finally, she heard them exchanging their goodbyes, so Cori joined them on the front porch. They visited a little while longer and after another lesson on the cell phone by Kenya, the family left their matriarch in her new home.

And now it was Cori and Ada.

"I thought they would never leave," Ada said breaking the ice.

Cori laughed.

"That nearly wore me out, even though I didn't lift a finger," Ada added.

Cori was somewhat tired too.

"I hope you don't mind, but I need to rest for a minute. You want to watch *Murder, She Wrote*?"

"I didn't know it still came on," Cori responded.

"It doesn't come on the local stations, but it still comes on cable."

"Hush yo mouth and get away! I just love Jessica Fletcher."

Now it was Ada's time to laugh.

They both went in to what was now Ada's sitting room and Ada relaxed on a beautiful chaise.

Cori took a seat in the lazy boy recliner and thought it must have been the most comfortable chair she had ever sat in. And sure enough, there was *Murder, She Wrote* on the 32-inch color TV. It was just like going to the movies. The ladies enjoyed Jessica like she was an old friend. Cori couldn't believe she had spent so many years afraid of the rays in colored televisions.

After the show ended, Ada jumped as if she had seen a ghost.

"Lord, have mercy! I haven't even paid you for the rooms. You must think I am an awful moocher."

"Honestly, I hadn't even thought about it. I figured Grace had taken care of it."

Ada grabbed her purse and began counting the money to Cori, since she had specified that she wanted it in cash.

"Just like we agreed, $600 a month and $600 deposit."

Cori felt her heart skip a beat. She didn't know if she had ever seen that much money at one time in her entire life.

"Maybe I better go on over and put some of this in the bank."

"I think that would be good idea. It is not good to keep too much cash around these days. How about I drive you? I need to open an account myself, and then we can go out to dinner and celebrate our first night together."

They both laughed at how that sounded.

Cori couldn't remember the last time she had eaten in a restaurant. When Robert Edward was alive, they always went to the Pig Out Palace to celebrate their anniversary, but that closed when the new restaurants came to town. Dinner at a restaurant sounded like a great idea to her.

It was agreed, and they headed towards Ada's Lincoln. Cori ran her hand across the smooth leather seat, curiously eyeing all the gadgets on the dashboard. Ada instructed her as to how to adjust the seat, and she giggled once again as the seat moved to the front or reclined.

She hesitantly put her seat belt over her and held it in her hand instead of fastening it as she had done so many times with her family. She just could not stand the thought of being strapped in the car and not being able to get the seatbelt unhooked if she needed to. But after the incessant beeping, she finally agreed to hook her seatbelt.

Ada drove to the bank, which was only a couple of blocks away. The people in Blessing appeared to be friendly, as just about all the townspeople spoke or threw up their hands. Everyone in town knew Cori, just as Grace had said, and they were already aware that Ada was living with her.

Cori wanted Ada to see the General Store, so they left the bank and walked the block to the General Store. Ada thought it reminded her of a tourist trap she had seen one time down in Alabama. The items were somewhat pricey to her, and the group of young men huddled behind the store by the barrel reminded her of the gangs who had taken over her neighborhood in Detroit. Bobby Lee was engaged in an intense conversation with a man in the front, whom Ada soon learned was Barnett Sampson, the patriarch of the Sampson family.

The conversation was the same one that dominated nearly every living room or dining room table.

"It's going to be hard for me not to support a fellow Vet," said Bobby Lee.

"I'm telling you. Huckabee is the man. All the good Christian folks are throwing their support behind him. They can't stand McCain, and it will hard for them to support him," stated Barnett.

"Well, all I can say is the man was a POW. Anybody who survived those hell holes in 'Nam can stand up to anything and anybody, and I'm supporting him."

"If he gets the nomination, of course I'll support him. I'd vote for a rattlesnake before I'd vote for anybody on that Democratic ticket."

Bobby Lee looked up at that moment and saw his mama entering with her new housemate. He introduced Ada to Barnett, who was cordial, but had a distinct air of confidence and superiority that was all too common to Ada.

"I believe I met your son at our monthly Republican League meeting. Now that's a fine boy...ah, young man. I know you are proud of him living out there in the Country Club and being the first Black member of the Club."

Ada thought back to the argument she and Frederick Jr. had over his joining the club. Ada insisted that he turn down the invitation because they were simply inviting him so that they could be considered for an upcoming golf tournament. Frederick Jr. was so blinded by arrogance and pride; he truly believed they asked him because of his worthiness. Ada suffered the defeat silently, recognizing many years ago that people see what they want to see and believe what they want to believe.

Cori's voice snapped Ada back to the present as she informed Bobby Lee of their plans. He was pleased that his mother was going out for a change. As the two ladies headed out the door, Barnett Sampson let out a deep and sinister laugh. Ada could not explain the chill that went over her.

After Cori declined the Chicken Biscuit, they decided to go to the Home Place, a restaurant out near the interstate. Ada nearly cracked her side when she listened to Cori explain how Bobby Lee had told her they didn't use real chickens at the Chicken Biscuit. Said they were created in some type of labs, and some of the chickens didn't even have heads. She insisted that her chickens had to have heads, even if they were eventually chopped off.

Ada had eaten at the Home Place, and enjoyed looking at the old-fashioned items. Cori had never eaten there, but she enjoyed the homey atmosphere. She was also captivated by the many familiar items on display, and seemed to recognize everyone in the antique frames that lined the walls.

Their country ham and collard greens tasted more like home cooking than restaurant food. She washed it down with cold iced tea and declared it to be some of the best food she had eaten in a mighty long time. They both ate until they were stuffed, but not wanting to waste anything, requested take out boxes for the leftovers.

After the short drive home, Ada headed to her rooms. Cori wanted to join her to watch some more of the colored TV; suddenly her black and white just didn't seem so appealing. Ada started to invite her in, but she knew it would not be good for them to spend every waking moment together for they would quickly grow tired of each other.

"You know, this TV is a little too large for this room. Do you mind if I put it in the parlor?" asked Ada. "I have a smaller one in the basement that I will keep in my room. I even have a little one that I kept in my kitchen down there also. Would you like to put it in the kitchen?"

Cori couldn't believe her good luck. But then she remembered she didn't have cable in the kitchen or parlor.

"Oh, I think I got a package deal that covered three rooms."

So, that's what he was doing in the kitchen and in the parlor, Cori thought to herself.

Suddenly, she was overcome with excitement. She couldn't believe her good fortune, and quickly called Tator Jones to come over to help with the televisions. Tator came, and soon all three televisions were connected to cable. Even though he had finished his work, Tator sat around the kitchen table sharing tidbits of town gossip and chatting with the women as if the three had been lifelong friends. After he left, Cori shared with Ada a little of Tator's history.

"Tator grew up with his mama, her mama, and his aunt. There just weren't any men around and Tator grew up acting like the women who raised him. Folks make fun of him behind his back, but he has the constitution of an ox and I would trust my soul with him."

Ada knew she had found a new friend, too.

Soon the sun began to set and the women decided to eat their leftovers. Cori went to the oven to heat her food and Ada headed towards the microwave.

"Aren't you afraid of all that radiation?" asked Cori.

"I was at first, but I've been using one for nearly 20 years now, and I figure if it hasn't killed me yet, it won't."

After a minute went by, Ada took her piping hot food out of the microwave and Cori was still waiting for her oven to heat.

"Shucks, I'm at the pearly gates right now! Show me how to work this thing!"

Ada laughed and gave Cori a quick lesson on the microwave. They both sat down and feasted on their piping hot leftovers, while Cori secretly thanked God for letting her experience the ice water from the refrigerator door before answering her death pleas.

Chapter Nine

Wildflowers and Dandelions

The shrill startled Cori and Ada. It was the girls chasing something in Cori's backyard.

"I guess they're home," Cori sadly stated.

"Who?" asked Ada.

"The neighbors. They just let their young'uns run wild, and they seem to take great pleasure in making my life miserable. I've told them so many times to stay out of my yard. They've just about ruined by plum trees. I doubt if I'll have any plums this year."

"Who are they?" Ada asked again.

"On one side are two girls. One is about elementary age I guess, and the other is in high school. On the other side are an elementary school girl and a high school boy. They're scalawags who moved here and took over. Their parents are gone all the time and leave their little heathens here to run wild."

They heard a banging sound this time. Cori headed to the back door and screamed at them to stop throwing rocks at her metal lawn furniture.

Just then they heard Tay yelling, "Lizzie, get your butt home. I'm sick of running after you. Get your butt home now!"

Cori looked up at Tay yelling from the window.

"What are you looking at, old woman?" Tay yelled. Cori nearly ran back inside.

Ada sat listening to the entire exchange. Cori headed back in the house looking defeated.

"I guess you want to move now."

"Why didn't I hear them before? I've been over several times."

"Oh, they don't behave like that whenever a car is in the driveway, only when they know I am here alone. You should see how polite they are to Grace and Bobby Lee. No, it's me. They like torturing me. Maybe you should leave your car in the driveway."

Ada was tempted. She really didn't like the old garage. She thought she pulled a muscle trying to open the door.

"You said their parents are always gone?"

"The Colored, I mean Black, I mean…I don't mean any harm, but what do you want to be called?"

"I would prefer American since that's where I was born. But Black is fine. I've gotten use to that. I know in the South most people are identified first by their race."

"Well, the Black family on the right, she's a lawyer here in town and the daddy is a doctor at the hospital. The White family on the left moved here from Massachusetts, and the parents teach at the university. Most of the time they are traveling around trying to save some animal. It's not against the law to leave your children with someone over sixteen, even if the sixteen-year-old doesn't have sense enough to po' piss out of a boot."

Ada doubled over in laughter at an expression she hadn't heard in years.

"I've never seen such disrespectful, rude young'uns in all my born days. They need a switch on their butts for sure. I broke a switch from a tree and told them I'd cut their legs from under them. Those little pissants called the Sheriff on me, and Old Snoot Snead threatened to put me in jail for child abuse. So here I am with folks I don't even know taking over my yard."

Ada decided to look for herself. As she headed to the back porch, she heard the girls laughing and shouting to the older brother in the window. At a simple glance, they were two adorable little girls who were nearly identical in height and size. Matching ponytails with numerous hair clips bounced in the wind as they galloped around Cori's backyard. They could have easily been confused as sisters; however, the slight difference in pigmentation illuminated the obvious. Their gleeful smiles undoubtedly mesmerized many and blinded others to the true dispositions.

"You shut up, Tay! You can't tell me what to do, you idiot! I'll come home when I get good and ready!" shouted Lizzie.

"If I come down there I'll jack you up, you little crackhead. Now get your butt on in this house right now!" Tay screamed back.

Lizzie and Summer continued throwing rocks at the lawn furniture. Ada stood listening to the racket. The older brother continued to yell obscenities from the window, when the younger girl finally decided to go in, but only after equal remarks to her older brother. After the youngsters left the yard, Ada decided it was such a beautiful evening that she put on a jacket and went to sit out on the screened back porch. She took a seat in an old wooden straw-bottomed chair with peeling paint. Cori, who was weary from the entire exchange, joined her in a matching rocker.

"I told you they were heathens."

"They are somewhat uncontrolled. It's really not their fault though. They're just wildflowers."

"Wildflowers?"

"Yeah. No one nurtures them, but they grow anyway. Amazingly, some of them even turn into some of the most beautiful flowers."

"Dandelions more like it. Just pop up anywhere, destroying everything in their path."

Ada found it easy to laugh at Cori's remarks.

"Do you ever feel like God has you here for a purpose?"

"I used to, but I haven't felt of any use to a soul in a very long time. And if he does, it looks like he's running out of time for me."

Both women laughed.

"Cori, do you pray?"

"Oh, yes indeedy. Why, I don't know what I would do if it wasn't for the good Lord."

"Do you think he brought us two together for some reason?"

"I have to admit. I was against this idea from the very beginning. I was tired of living and simply wanted to die. I didn't like the idea of sharing my house with anyone, and I never thought I'd be living under the same roof with a Colored, I mean a Black person.

"I am not going to lie to you. I have tried to be fair and good to the Colored, I mean Blacks, all my life. But your people just seem to be so angry now. Some are just downright mean…like I did something to them. I don't even know half of these folks who are in town now, and I know I haven't done a thing to them. But they just seem to have something against me for being white. It's worse than it was in the sixties. So, I was against you moving in.

"But something happened that day you came here and I saw you struggling with the cane. When I looked at your eyes, it was like I was staring at my own eyes in the mirror. I found myself saying what wasn't on my mind, and actually wanting to share the house with you. And I know that's not how I was feeling. So, I guess that was God."

"I had similar feelings," added Ada. "I wanted to walk out the first time I heard you refer to me as Colored. But I also felt drawn here. I believe it was God drawing us together for some reason only He knows."

They both sat in silence for a while taking in the moment. It was a nice evening. It felt so good to sit and enjoy the beautiful evening, listening to all the sounds of the long-awaited spring.

Chapter Ten

A Village

———————————○———————————

The banging of the rocks against the lawn furniture alerted the ladies to the exact arrival of the young girls. When the girls heard the door open, they assumed it was Old Lady Jacobs, as they called her, and proceeded to throw rocks at the screen.

"You really need to be careful with those rocks. If they do any damage to Mrs. Jacobs' screen, she could have you arrested for vandalizing her home."

Both girls' hands stopped in mid-air at the unfamiliar voice that came from the porch.

Slowly they headed a little closer to get a better view.

"I'm your new neighbor, Mrs. Passmore."

"Where's Old Lady Jacobs?" asked Summer.

"Did she die?" asked Lizzie.

"Oh, no. Mrs. Jacobs is just fine."

"Oh, man," stated Lizzie disappointedly.

"I am her new housemate."

"Are you two gay?" asked Summer.

"What? Gay? Oh my, no," laughed Ada. "We're just too old to live alone, so we thought we would share the house."

"You mean you gonna live with that mean old bat?" added Summer.

"She's not a mean old bat. She's a kind lady. One who likes her house and her yard. Don't you have favorite games or toys that you want to keep nice because they are special?"

"Yeah, my Little Lady collection," said Summer.

"Yeah, mine too," added Lizzie.

"You have the entire collection? Even Marisol?" asked Ada.

The girls were shocked that this elderly lady was familiar with the Little Lady collection.

"Yes, every one of them. I get one every Christmas," Summer replied proudly.

"Me too," Lizzie joined in.

"You two are very fortunate. That is quite a collection. I only purchased one. I purchased the Albertine doll for my granddaughter, Kenya, when she was about your age."

"I had to send my Albertine to the hospital. Tay, my evil brother from hell, broke her arm off. It cost nearly fifty dollars to repair the arm, but my parents made him pay for it."

Tay sat in the window listening to the exchange and with the mention of his name had heard enough.

"Lizzie, you have ten seconds to get your black butt in this house. I am tired of getting in trouble because of your little nappy-headed self!"

Lizzie and Summer looked at Tay and stuck their middle fingers up at him.

Tay left the window, and Lizzie started towards her house.

"I better go."

Ada stared at Tay's window with concern on her face.

"Oh, he's just a punk. He fusses, but he knows he better not touch me. He knows I am not afraid of him."

"That's for sure," added Summer. "One time, she hit him so hard in the face, his eye was black for an entire week."

Lizzie and Summer continued towards Lizzie's home just as Tay threw the back door open.

"No, Summer, you can't come over. Go home! I'm not putting up with you two tearing up the house, and then I get blamed for everything. Go on home!"

"I hope a cannon ball lands splat on you!" shouted Summer.

"You are a conceited, black-hearted varmint!" added Lizzie. Both girls, who had memorized most of the lines from *Gone with the Wind*, laughed hysterically.

"You better go, Summer. You know how wacked he can get." Plus, Lizzie remembered her parent's stern instructions that no one was allowed in the home when they were not there.

Lizzie headed to her house, and Ada could hear the siblings arguing and calling each other some of the most awful names. Summer headed back across the yard to her own backyard. Just as she left Mrs. Jacobs' backyard, she turned to Mrs. Passmore and waved. Ada smiled and waved back.

***

The transition went more smoothly than Cori and Ada's children had dreamed. The ladies ate breakfast around the same time, each preparing her own meal. Bobby Lee still came by on his way to the store. Ada always found a reason to excuse herself when Bobby Lee stopped by, with his constant chatter about the wonders of the Republican Party. As the weather began to warm, they went for a daily walk to the post office. Dr. Lacy was right about walking being good for her arthritis, which seemed to get better each day.

They watched *The Price is Right*, *Little House on the Prairie*, and *Murder, She Wrote* together. After visiting several of the local churches, Ada decided to join the Blessing AME Zion Church, since she had been a member of the AME Zion church in Detroit. It was a small church, but had a strong Religious Education Program, which she enjoyed. She joined the weekly Bible study group, and helped at the food pantry and clothes closet. She was amazed at the pockets of poverty that were still so prevalent in a town that appeared to be prosperous and progressive. Cori attended the First Church of Blessing, where she had taught Sunday school for nearly 50 years.

Ada also decided to get involved at the Senior Citizen's Center. Cori had been approached several times about joining the group, but always had an excuse. Deep down, she knew she could not afford some of the trips and extracurricular activities. But now that she had a little income, she warmed up to the idea. So, three mornings a week they went to the Senior Citizen's Center.

Cori was very quiet on the ride home from the Senior Citizen's Center. She was still angry about the changes. She had been looking forward to the visit all week because they were going to learn a line dance today.

"Who told them to bring that Spanish teacher anyway?" Cori asked angrily.

"They say we need to know Spanish since so many have moved here."

"Well, that still doesn't give them the right to cancel our dance class."

"They just wanted to introduce her to us and let us know that they were going to start the class."

"Well, I just think that if they come over here, they ought to learn English. If I go to Spain, they gonna expect me to know Spanish."

"I agree, but it helps to be able to communicate with them until they learn English."

"Well, I'm not going to take it. Anybody talks to me needs to know English."

So, the next week Ada was a little surprised to see Cori ready to go to the center.

"I thought you weren't going," Ada said.

"I got to thinking that every time I go to town, those children are running around wild and knocking things over. Seems they don't have any control over their young'uns."

"All children need discipline, not just the Spanish."

"Well, I figured I'd go and learn how to say 'stop running around tearing up the place.' Then next time I catch them in the store acting like wild heathens, I'll tell them that in Spanish."

Ada shook her head at Cori's reasoning.

Chapter Eleven

"In the early twentieth century, Parrish Street in Durham, North Carolina, was the hub of African American business activity. This four-block district was known as 'Black Wall Street,' a reference to the district of New York City that is home to the New York Stock Exchange and the nation's great financial firms. Although other cities had similar districts, Durham's was one of the most vital, and was nationally known. National leaders W.E.B. DuBois and Booker T. Washington both visited the city in 1912 and 1910, respectively, and praised Black entrepreneurship and the tolerance of Whites."

– NC Digital History: Durham's Black Wall Street

As the days warmed, Cori and Ada gravitated to the front porch and engaged in their new hobby: people watching. The ladies' living arrangement was not questioned, since Bobby Lee had led everyone to believe that Ada had been hired as a companion and driver for his mama. As townspeople passed Cori's home, she informed Ada of the person's history. Ada was amazed at the elderly lady's memory and her talent for storytelling.

"Now that's a bad combination," Cori stated. Tay was walking down the street with a young man about his age.

"Who is that young man?" asked Ada.

"That's Amanna Dove's boy, Jabo. His real name is Jereboam. You know how everyone 'round here has a nickname, so he's called Jabo.

"Amanna was a good girl," Cori continued thoughtfully. "Her folks raised her right, and she had a kind disposition. Jabo was a nice young fellow too, but he changed like so many others. Walks around here with that diaper on his head like he's mad at the world. In and out of trouble all the time."

Cori paused, her eyes distant, recollecting another time.

"Oh, his mama was the sweetest girl. It still saddens me to think about what happened to her."

"What happened?" asked Ada.

"It was the strangest thing. Like I said, Amanna was the sweetest child and everybody loved her. When she finished high school she went away, but a few years later she moved back and had little Jereboam with her. The story she told was that she was married, and her husband had been killed in an accident, so she came back home with Jabo. Nobody doubted her word because it was Amanna Dove. Says she kept her name like Hillary Clinton. Umph!

"Apparently, her husband left her in good shape, for wasn't long before she built a nice fine house for her and Jabo. She went back to her old job at the Sampson Industry, and when that closed, she moved out to the Sampson's company out near the interstate. Things seemed as normal as pie.

"Then one Saturday morning, Jabo, who had been watching the Saturday morning cartoons, went in to jump on his mama's bed like he did every Saturday to wake her up, 'cept this time she didn't move. Lord knows how that poor boy survived.

"He shook her and shook her and she still didn't move. He pulled the spread back and she was covered in blood. That girl had been beaten to a pulp. It's a wonder that poor boy ain't half crazy. After that, all kinds of stories came out about her, that she had a boyfriend in the mob, that she was a kept woman, and she was involved in drug selling.

"Jabo's grandparents, Jim and Eliza, moved into the house to raise Jabo. Well, you know how daddies are about their daughters. Jim just grieved himself to death. About a month later he dropped dead of a heart attack. Jabo's been living with his grandmother since then.

"She's done the best that she could, but I imagine it's been real hard being old and trying to raise a teenage boy. The town was just stunned. Like I said, everybody loved Amanna and the town hadn't had a murder in twenty years, not since the H&H murders."

"The H&H murders?" asked Ada again. Cori had an uncanny way of telling just enough to make you want to know more.

"Yeah, the H&H murders. Wasn't really but one murder though."

Ada, intrigued, pressed Cori for more.

"Lammy Jones and his mama, Leafy, lived out on the outskirts of town in a little log cabin that had been on her family's land for years. Lammy was born with 'half a mind,' as the old folks say. He hardly ever opened his mouth, and did everything Leafy said, just like a robot. That's why they started calling him Lammy. Said he was just like a little lamb and Leafy was the sheep dog. I reckon the part of his brain that makes you mean and rebellious just never took shape.

"He wasn't a real big fellow, but was strong as an ox. I 'spect what God didn't give him in mind, He gave him in strength, and boy could he chop wood. He could swing an ax by the age of five. So, Leafy would say, 'Go chop wood, Lammy', and he would chop and chop until she would say, 'Come drink water, Lammy' and he would stop and drink water. Then she would say, 'Come eat lunch, Lammy' and Lammy would sit down and eat lunch. After he rested, she would say 'Go chop wood, Lammy' and he would go back to the woodpile. She bought an old truck and Lammy loaded that truck with wood, and they went through town selling it. Had a good little business going."

"Leafy was a good looking gal and could've gotten just about any man. Nobody could understand why she took up with that shiftless, beady-eyed Meshack Pounds. He was just a no-account, but with Leafy, the sun set and rose by him. Must've had a gold pickle or something."

Ada spit her Dentyne probably five feet with her outburst of laughter.

"What's so funny? You act like I don't know nothing about sex. Shucks, folks today act like they invented sex. Anyhow, Leafy married sorry Meshack Pounds, but that didn't stop him from chasing after everything with a skirt. Lost his leg in a car accident and got him one of those wooden ones. Every time he got the hankering to go wandering, Leafy would hide his wooden leg, God rest his soul.

"He took sick with some stomach ailness and died when little Lammy was a youngun'. Some folks said she poisoned po' Meshack 'cause she got tired of taking care of him and little Lammy. After Meshack passed on to Lord knows where, most men stayed away 'cause they thought Lammy was crazy.

"Well this Colored, I mean Black, salesman, Lester Lark, came through town selling insurance and encyclopedias. Now, most of the Black families couldn't afford them, but this fellow was slick. He came over from Durham and musta been well-off. There were plenty of well-off Black folks in Durham around then.

He worked at the big ole insurance company over in a part of Durham called Black Wall Street and peddled encyclopedias on the side. He drove into town in a fine car, jet black wavy hair parted on the side and slicked down, and before you knowed it, he had sold those encyclopedias to just about every single woman on Pearl Harbor. It took most of them about ten years to pay them off. Course by then, Lester Lark was long dead."

"Oh, I bet I know the rest of this story," said Ada. "He was messing around with some of the women, and one of them killed him."

"Close. Folks started noticing Lester's car over at Leafy's cabin on Saturdays about once a month and figured Leafy was the one who caught him. I sure hope she didn't buy those encyclopedias for Lammy. He couldn't read *cat*.

"Anyway, one morning Lammy was cutting wood when a fancy-dressed lady drove up in a car that was just as fancy. Lammy, of course, kept chopping wood since Leafy hadn't told him to stop. Leafy opened the door and thought the lady was selling Avon or something. Come to hold, that lady was Lester's wife. She spread pictures of her, Lester, and their three children all over Leafy's kitchen table. She went on to tell Leafy how Lester was a Deacon in their church, how they had a fine home over in Durham, and how she had no plans for her life to change. She got up, gathered her pictures, got in her yellow Buick and drove off.

"Leafy was beside herself with anger, and when Lester drove up that next Saturday, she let him have it. She ranted and raved 'bout how he said he wasn't married, and how he said he traveled the country selling encyclopedias, and how she ought to get the ax and chop his head off. The screaming woke Lammy and as he found his way to the door, he heard his mama say 'chop your head off.'

"Lammy walked out the bedroom and walked right by his mama and Lester. She was still screaming, and Lester was grabbing her, trying to calm her down. He never knew what hit him. With one swipe, Lammy chopped Lester Lark's head right off. Well, Leafy went plum crazy, and Lammy just stood there waiting for his mama to tell him what to do next. Leafy just kept screaming, and I guess all poor Lammy could figure out was 'police' and 'head,' because he grabbed Lester's head by his jet black wavy hair and walked to the police station.

"Hoss Tatum was on duty that night. He was a big ole fellow who never missed a meal and had the gut to show it. Folks say he had a 'moment of silence' and made that sign that the Catholic folks make when they enter the Catholic Church every time he passed the Pig Out Palace. You know, he's the only person I know who asked for a refill of a baked potato.

"The folks out there at the Pig Out Palace established a new rule in his honor after his passing: *The Hoss Tatum Rule*. They put a two-hour time limit on how long a person could stay at the Sunday buffet, stating that no one would be able to stay longer than Deputy Hoss Tatum.

"Nobody really knows what happened next, but the best they could figure was Lammy took Lester's head to the police station and Hoss Tatum was probably rod back in his chair sleeping as usual. When Lammy dropped the head on the desk, Hoss apparently woke up, took one look at Lester's head with eyeballs bulging out, and died instantly of a heart attack.

"Now, Hoss was a walking heart attack anyway, but there were some who said Lammy caused Hoss's death too, so they tried him for chopping off Lester's head and for causing Hoss's heart attack. Some reporter called the trial the "Head and Heart Murders," or the "H&H murder trial" and the title stuck. Wasn't much of a trial. Only lasted about 30 minutes. Not a soul doubted that Lammy was crazy, and they sent him straight to Camp Butner.

"Poor Leafy just about went crazy, herself. She drove that piece of a truck to Camp Butner every Sunday until it broke down. Then friends took her as often as they could. But one winter, we had a freak ice storm. Things stayed frozen for nearly a week. By the time folks were able to check on Leafy, she was frozen dead in her bed.

"Their Pastor went to tell Lammy but po' thang couldn't understand. The hospital folks kept his routine just like his mama, and let him chop wood for a while. Last I heard, they had given him a big push broom and told him, 'Go sweep Lammy'. Folks say you can eat off the floor, cause if Lammy's been sweeping, there's not a speck of dirt anywhere."

"Well I never." Ada said. "Cori, you are quite the story teller."

"Oh, folks say I just ramble on and on."

Chapter Twelve

"On January 18, 1922, Canadian officials ordered Matthew Bullock's deportation. Newspapers covering the case sympathized with Bullock, and the editors from Buxton to York unleashed a steady stream of articles that attacked mob violence. Moreover, many suggested that even if North Carolina officials protected Bullock from lynching, the unwritten legal code of the South would ensure his death."

– Lynchings in North Carolina

It was a beautiful spring morning, and Ada and Cori had completed their morning walk to the post office. Cori needed to stop by the General Store for a few items, and as they entered the store, they saw Bobby Lee, whose head was nearly conjoined to Barnett Sampson.

The vein in Bobby Lee's neck bulged and his face was as red as the apples in the basket on the counter. Just as the women approached the two men, the previously strained voices faded to whispers.

"Good Morning, Miss Cori, how are you feeling today?" Barnett Sampson asked.

"I'm nearly a hundred! How do you think I feel? My bones ache and my body's tired!"

"That's the thing I love about you, Miss Cori. I never have to guess what's on your mind."

"Well, if you know what's on my mind, you know I don't feel like wasting what time I got left on this earth talking to you. Bobby Lee, we are going out to the Home Place for dinner. We'll be back directly."

"They got a chocolate cake that'll knock your socks off," Barnett added.

"Do you see any socks on my feet?" responded Cori.

Ada found the entire exchange somewhat humorous; however, the moment was brief.

She could not explain the uneasy feeling that came across her each time she saw Barnett Sampson. He was polite, although he always avoided looking directly at her.

Even though slavery had ended nearly 150 years ago, there were many Whites, especially in the South, who found it difficult to look directly into a Black person's eyes. Often, they looked at the floor, the sky, or anything other than the person's eyes.

Memories of her visits to town as a young girl flashed through her mind. After the Civil Rights movement, when Blacks received more of their equal rights, many Whites still refused to look into their eyes. This had annoyed Ada throughout the years, and her veins swelled each time it happened to her.

Often, she brought the matter to their attention by making statements such as, *I'm over here,* or *Are you talking to me?* When Barnett spoke directly to her, his eyes shifted to the floor or to Cori. After standing with them for a moment, Ada saw PM in the back of the store, excused herself, and headed towards him.

"Have a good day, Ada," Barnett said.

Ada turned abruptly to Barnett, who was standing there with a sneering grin on his face. What had he said? It wasn't what he said, but how he said it. He seemed to take pride in calling her Ada, not "Miss Ada" or "Miss Passmore" like everyone else in town. It was his subtle way of letting her know that he was superior to her. For the first time, she saw what it was that had troubled her about this man.

She looked at the tall man with hair as white as a cotton ball, and skin that apparently had never seen a day of sun, because it nearly matched his hair. She looked directly at his eyes. They weren't gray or blue, but clear. It was if she could look right through them. She had read that "eyes were the window to the soul." Then she recognized it. Barnett Sampson had no soul. She was standing directly in front of pure evil. Her entire body shook with a chill.

On the walk home, she questioned Cori about Barnett.

"Who exactly is Barnett Sampson?" Ada asked.

"He's the head of the Sampson clan. Now some folks are mean, but then there's some who are mean all the way to the bone. Meanness is in their blood. Their great-great…I disremember how many greats, but their grandpappy was head of the Klan back in the day. I remember the stories my grandfather told of how he and his brother ran things around here after the Great War."

Ada had heard World War I and World War II referred to as the Great Wars, but she wasn't sure if she had ever heard the Civil War described that way. *I guess it was great in its own way, after all it ended slavery,* Ada thought to herself.

Cori continued, "Yeah, my Granddaddy said Barnett's folks raised such a ruckus, until the Governor sent in troops to settle things down. They played a part in most of the lynchings in the area and never served a day, even bragged about them.

"I guess it came to a boil after this big-shot Colored preacher's son was lynched, when he and his brother started a ruckus over some apples over near Henderson. My granddaddy said that Barnett's grandpappy and his mean ole brother, Lusky, really went on a tirade after the Preacher's other son escaped the lynch mob and fled to Canada.

"Then Lusky went missing. They searched for days for the body, then they discovered that he had another family over in Chatham County, so folks just stopped looking for him until they found him floating in the Dan River. Barnett's grandpappy tried to say that the Colored did something to him, but folks were just about tired of the burning and the killing by that time. Plus, they couldn't find anyone to pin it on, so they figured he just fell in the Country Line Creek and drowned.

"Barnett went to school with Bobby Lee. When the boys went off to Vietnam, his daddy paid off some doctor to say one of Barnett's legs was shorter than the other, so he didn't go to war. He just stayed around here raising hell. He had a couple of mills, but one closed down, and now he runs a company out near the interstate, and he opened that S-Mart that's killing Bobby Lee's business. He's chairman of the City Council and Head Deacon in our Church.

"His dumb ole son, Wallace, is the Principal at the high school. He went off to school somewhere and came back and married some white trash who thinks she is the first lady of the United States. Barnett's got two other boys named Bedford and Forrest. He always bragging that he named all three of his sons after some ole Ku Kluxer and the great governor of Alabama.

"Bobby Lee never did care too much for him. He and his kin are trying to buy up every piece of dirt in town, plus he was head of the Republican Party until your son took over, I reckon. He seems to be hanging around quite a bit. I guess it might have something to do with the election."

Ada listened but couldn't help but feel that there was more to it than that.

Chapter Thirteen

"Although many people remain staunchly in favor of homework, a growing number of teachers and parents alike are beginning to question the practice. These critics are reexamining the beliefs behind the practice, the wisdom of assigning hours of homework, the absurdly heavy backpack, and the failure that can result when some students don't complete homework. There's a growing suspicion that something is wrong with homework."

— *Rethinking Homework,* Cathy Vatterott

Cori could not believe how much she enjoyed the Senior Citizen's Center. Although one of the oldest in the group, she looked much younger than some of the younger ones, who were in awe at her energy level. They exercised, took computer courses, got regular blood pressure checks, played Bingo, went to the mountains to enjoy the early spring blooms, and visited different restaurants.

Cori didn't care for the computers, the aerobics made them both a little sore at first, but she loved Bingo, the restaurants, and the trips. She could never understand how a person could view the majesty of the mountains and see the white waves of the oceans and not believe in God.

Lizzie and Summer continued their assaults on Cori's backyard, but now they ceased the attacks whenever Ada joined them in the backyard. Ada soon realized their attacks on Cori's furniture were their way of letting her know they were out back. They still were somewhat cautious of Cori, but they were not as disrespectful to her. One day, as Ada sat on the back porch with the young girls, they began discussing schoolwork and their grades. Ada was surprised that such intelligent and bright young girls had such low grades. Later on, she discussed it with Cori.

"I bet they don't do their homework. I saw it when I was teaching. The students who didn't have anyone at home to motivate them to do their homework often had the lowest grades. What do you think about me offering to help the girls in the evening with their homework? It's nice now. We could sit right out on the back porch and work. We wouldn't bother you at all."

"Suit yourself. Just make sure they don't break anything."

Ada looked around at the splintering chair and the chipped what-nots, and wondered what the girls could possibly break. The old metal table with the peeling paint surely couldn't be hurt.

"Oh, I will make sure they are careful," Ada said.

So, that night when they heard the rock hit the storm door, Ada excitedly went to meet the girls to discuss the tutoring idea. It was arranged that they would come to the backdoor, politely knock, and Ada would meet them and supervise them as they completed their homework.

Ada suggested that they inform their parents, but the girls casually stated that their parents didn't care where they went as long as they were home by six o'clock. This statement did not surprise Ada, because her own students had told her the same thing. She still found it astounding that professional, progressive parents could be so smart about everything but raising their children.

Cori stayed in the house when the girls came the first few days, however, the lively banter of Ada and the young girls was magnetic, and she soon found reasons to venture out to the porch. At first the little girls eyed her suspiciously and avoided her with Cori responding in kind. Ada feigned ignorance with some of the girls' assignments and solicited Cori's assistance.

The girls slowly warmed to her, and with Ada's coaching, eventually apologized for their disruptive behavior. Cori remained somewhat skeptical, but joined the group and was quite adept at helping them with their vocabulary skills. Apparently, all the days of working crossword puzzles had turned her into quite a linguist.

She also had a story about everything, and was such a masterful storyteller that the girls, who had a fascination with old movies, hung on her every word. It was amazing how much a little structure and order changed the atmosphere, which surprised even Cori, who secretly enjoyed her former enemies.

The routine was established. Each evening, as soon as the girls arrived home, they came straight to Cori's home. Ada was surprised at their promptness and faithfulness. The ladies prepared a little snack for them, and after going over their homework and preparing them for any upcoming tests, Cori told them a story from the "olden days."

It wasn't long before Bliss, Summer's teenaged sister, started dropping by also. At first it was to check on Summer, but the visits became more and more frequent, and the previous tensions between them and Cori simply evaporated.

She loved Cori's home. "It is *so* vintage!" she squealed. Soon her friend, Unique, joined the growing group.

"Unique, that a 'unique' name," said Ada one evening.

"That's why my daddy chose it. He said there was no one on earth like me."

"What do your parents do?" asked Ada.

"My mom does hair, and my dad used to work at the mill, but he's in prison now. After he got out of the military, he went with my sorry, trifling uncle to the store. While he sat out in the car waiting, my dumb uncle robbed the store and ran back to the car. Of course, my daddy had no idea his brother was robbing the store, but no one believed him but his family. So now he is in prison for armed robbery. My mama spends all of her money on lawyers who say they are trying to get him out, but he's still in, and she stays broke."

Ada was once again saddened by the dichotomy of the justice system, African American males and mass incarceration. She was proud of Unique and amazed that she wasn't embarrassed by her dad's imprisonment. Resilience was how it was described in one of her education books. Some children persevere and overcome challenges regardless of their circumstances.

Although they were exhausted at the day's end, Ada and Cori's lives were fulfilled with the antics of the elementary girls and the trials and tribulations of the teenagers.

***

The ladies had just left the post office one morning when they were nearly knocked down by a young man in quite a hurry.

"That Hoopoe Cokey is a mean rascal. Whole family mean as snakes. They're probably the only family in town meaner than the Sampson's. They've gone from pillar to post for as long as they've been alive 'cause no one can stand to live near them. They'll fight a tree. The only one who doesn't fight is that oldest gal, and the only reason that she doesn't fight is 'cause her mama keeps her holed up in the house. She's got some disease where she is just about covered up with hair.

"They say Pansy, her mama, was marked by a monkey at one those traveling circuses. One got loose and ran up in the benches where Pansy was sitting and scared her half to death. Po' thang was pregnant and that young'un came out looking just like that monkey. Now, she don't fight like the rest of them, but she can cuss worse than any sailor. Most of them are in jail for fighting, or cutting, or beating some po' soul half to death.

"I never could figure out how a family got so mean. Seemed like the more young'uns Pansy Cokey had, the meaner they got. They fought each other as well as every neighbor they've had. One time, after they had beaten everything that was breathing, they went out to their daddy's hog pen and started having wrestling matches right in the pen with the hog. Beat that po' hog to death. It wasn't hog killing time, but they fixed him up anyway. Had fresh sausage and tenderloin for breakfast the next morning.

"Had a duck which was just as mean as they were. They had a mangy dog who would eat you alive, if he hadn't been chained up. But since he was all tied up, folks thought they were pretty safe, until that demon duck came around the corner flapping his wings like a bat out of hell. He chased everyone who came to the house back to their cars."

"Now how did they come up with Hoopoe as a nickname?" asked Ada.

"Shucks, that ain't his nickname; that's his real name," answered Cori.

"What?"

"Seems Pansy got so tired of them fighting that she decided to give Jesus a try and went to one of them traveling tent revivals. Her husband had just run off with one of the hoochie-coochie girls at the fair, and she was at her wits end. They say by the time that Preacher finished preaching about the evils of cussing, fighting, and killing, Pansy screamed so loud she woke up Persimmon Cartwright's baby in the trailer park next to the revival tent.

"Next thing you know, she was running around the church shouting and thanking Jesus for saving her. The Preacher was preaching at a fever pitch, when suddenly Pansy headed in his direction.

"Now, he tried to stand there 'bold in the spirit of the Lord', but when he saw Pansy heading toward him full speed ahead, and weighing about 300 pounds, he took off running, too. She caught him though, over in the corner by Sister Sara, who was on the piano.

"It took four deacons to help get Pansy off the Preacher. But after that she swore she had religion, and when she found out she was pregnant with her ninth young'un, and even though she no longer had a husband, she said she knew he was a gift straight from God, and she was going to name him from the Bible. So, when the baby was born, she named him after the first name she saw when she opened the Bible. That's how Hoopoe got his name, straight from the Bible."

"I don't remember a Bible character named Hoopoe."

"Neither did I. So, I asked Pansy one day in town about Hoopoe's Bible name. She stated proudly that Hoopoe name came straight from Deuteronomy 14. When I got home, I looked it up, and sho' nuff, there it was. I don't remember the exact story but it's in there. Look for yourself."

So as soon as Ada returned home, she grabbed the Bible from the middle of the table and looked up the scripture reference.

"You may eat any clean bird. But these you may not eat: the eagle, the vulture, the black vulture, the red kite, the black kite, any kind of falcon, any kind of raven, the horned owl, the screech owl, the gull, any kind of hawk, the little owl, the great owl, the white owl, the desert owl, the osprey, the cormorant, the stork, any kind of heron, the hoopoe and the bat." (Deuteronomy 14:11-18)

Ada couldn't contain her laughter. "You mean she named him after one of the animals!"

"Sure did. I didn't even know what a hoopoe was so I looked it up. Some kind of bird.

"Well, I never," said Ada.

"She said he musta been a mighty special bird that God didn't want him ate up. And she didn't want to name him bat or horned owl, so Hoopoe it was. Didn't matter anyway that he was named from the Bible. He's still mean as a pit bull. But say what you want, Pansy kept going to church and is in church every Sunday, praying for those heathen young'uns of hers. Then she leaves church and goes to visit the ones in prison. It's right sad."

"It's nothing like a mother's prayer, and it's no telling how those children might end up. The fact that they're still living is an answer to her prayers."

"I reckon so."

Chapter Fourteen

Homecoming

Sunday afternoons were normally a time for relaxation at Cori's, but the ladies had just returned from their churches when they heard a knock at the door. Cori, although several years older than Ada, still moved much more quickly, and was at the door beckoning Damaris and a distinguished dressed young man through the door.

Cori showed her best hospitable skills, but quickly exited the parlor, because on previous visits, Damaris did nothing to hide her disdain for Cori, who Damaris viewed as the devil incarnate. She had convinced herself that White women were the source of all evil to African Americans. Ada once again was baffled as to how her children had acquired such viewpoints.

As soon as Ada joined them in the parlor, Damaris began her verbal assault.

"Mama, please move out of this oppressive, degrading, depressing, destructive environment. This is an insult to our entire race!"

"And how are you, Damaris?" Ada stated in a calm, expressionless tone.

"I told you not to call me Damaris. My name is Naana Yaa. I will not be called by the name of a White woman who kept my ancestors in bondage and deprived them economically, socially, and emotionally."

The young man sat silently as if under a spell, until Ada spoke directly to him.

"Hello, my name is Ada Passmore. I am Damaris' mother."

The young man politely introduced himself as Kedar Mukhtar. Ada was impressed at his exquisite manners and eloquent speech. She immediately recognized the attire of the young Muslims who often worked tirelessly on the streets in Detroit. He also had a calming effect on Damaris, whose expression warmed as the young man spoke; however, the harshness returned when she spoke to her mother.

"This is insanity. We really need to have you evaluated. There is no way you can be happy living here."

Kedar could not remain silent.

"Naana, you must remember that this is Mother, the first to envision your earthly presence. Our Father chose her as His vessel for the creation of life, so she must be cherished as the rare treasure that she is."

Ada saw Damaris' stern expression soften again, and was amazed at the effect this young man had over her daughter. What he said was very beautiful, and such words would bring tears to any mother's eyes, yet she found it troubling. But if it meant a peaceful visit with Damaris, she'd take it. They had fought for too many days, and it was honestly wearing on Ada, who simply wanted peace in her life. So, she was happy when the rest of the visit continued somewhat civilly.

When the conversation shifted to the upcoming election, Damaris began challenging her mother's sanity again as they debated Ada's support for Hillary Clinton. Damaris' voice rose to a fever pitch when she declared that she would vote for the devil himself before she voted for a White woman over a Black man.

"I thought you didn't believe in God or the devil," Ada stated.

For some reason the small group found this statement humorous, and Ada was glad to laugh again with her only daughter. She realized how much she missed the laughter. Cori trembled as she listened intently from the kitchen. She was very glad to hear the young couple leave, and secretly hoped they would never return.

The visit overall was pleasant in comparison, but Ada was mentally exhausted after Damaris and her friend left. She retired to her room where she lingered the entire afternoon.

The girls were busy with their families on the weekends. Lizzie spent Sundays out in the country with her mother's family, and Summer's family crusaded for the "cause" of the day in their camper. The more time the girls spent with Ada and Cori, the more the women learned about their personal lives.

It seemed both girls were very well provided for financially, but the support ended there. Bliss and Summer's last name was actually Winthrop. Their parents Abigail and Stephen, who preferred to be called Abby and Steve, had grown up together in upper class families in Boston, and rebelled against money, class, and power, and became teachers. They were zealous supporters of PETA and spent much of their time advocating for animal rights.

The ladies missed the girls' company and anxiously awaited their return. Lizzie talked about her extended family in such detail that Cori and Ada felt they knew the entire family personally. There were her grandparents, Grandma Elizabeth, "Ma Liz," for whom Lizzie was named, and Papa Simon Taylor, who was Tay's namesake. They had four sons and four daughters, each named after a famous African American. '

There was Uncle Booker, named after the great educator, Booker T. Washington, Uncle Thur, named after the well renowned attorney, Thurgood Marshall, Uncle Jessie, named after the track star, Jessie Owens, and Uncle Louis, named after the singer Louis Armstrong.

There were also Aunt Béthune, named after the educator, Mary McLeod Béthune, Aunt Harriet, named after Harriet Tubman of the Underground Railroad, and Aunt Marian, who was named after Marian Anderson, the opera singer. Some years later, when they thought they were past their childbearing years, Lizzie's mother was born and they named her Lena, after Lena Horne. All the children except Lena had built homes on the family land.

Summer was right, Lizzie was quite the actress, as she imitated her many relatives from the country. Today they were having Homecoming at her mother's church, and they knew that she would have quite a tale to tell. It was getting late and the ladies began to worry, when they heard the screen door open and Lizzie's feet sprinting across the back porch.

"I didn't think we were going to ever get out of church!" Lizzie stated out of breath.

"That preacher just went on and on about opening the doors to the church. I kept turning around looking to see if they were ever going to open the doors so we could leave, but the ushers just stood there guarding the door like we were prisoners about to escape. He started screaming about the blood running warm in your veins, and I kept looking at Miss Jade, the Mother of the Church, waiting for her to start shouting.

"I knew once she started shouting, then the Preacher would feel as if he had done his business and sit down. Jesus had already bled, hung, and died on the cross, so the only thing left was for Miss Jade to shout. Finally, she yelled, 'Yes!' I knew it was coming. 'Yes, Lord!' Then she screeched so loud, I heard the birds fly from the roof.

"She started flapping her arms and knocked Miss Fanny Grayson's Sunday go-to-meeting hat off, and the ushers left their posts at the door, ran to her, and started fanning rapidly. I started to make my escape, but I knew I would have to answer to Ma Liz.

"Then the preacher started getting quieter, and I knew that it was almost over. But I didn't want to get my hopes too high, because sometimes he psyched me. Just when I thought he was done, he would start screaming again to the top of his lungs as if God had a hearing problem.

"When I got home, my mama said it was too late to come over, but I told her you wanted to hear about the Homecoming, and since both of you were so old, that you might die tonight, so I couldn't wait until tomorrow."

Both ladies laughed at Lizzie's candor. Just then, Summer came entering very much the same way as Lizzie.

"I've been waiting! What took you so long?" asked Summer.

"Well, it was Homecoming, and that takes forever," replied Lizzie.

"Who came home?" asked Summer.

"Nobody. Everybody lives right around the church."

"So why do they call it Homecoming?"

"I don't know and I don't care. I hate it. It lasts forever."

"Many of the Black churches still have Homecomings," Ada began, seeing every moment as a teachable moment.

"It was a tradition that started after the Great Migration North," Ada continued. "Many Blacks moved North after slavery, in hopes of a better life. They would often come back during the summer months, and churches would have a big celebration that they called 'Homecoming'. I believe some churches call it 'Friends and Family Day' now."

"I didn't know if we were going to make it at first. You see, Mama had bought this brand new suit, because she likes to show off when she goes to the country. It was bright yellow with a hat to match it. Well, she let Papa Simon drive because he likes to drive up in the parking lot in one his children's fancy cars. Ma Liz sat up front with him, and Mama and Ma Liz were fussing as usual. Papa says they fuss so much because they are just alike. Ma Liz says he just spoiled my mama rotten.

"See, my mama was what Ma Liz said was a 'change' baby. Most of my uncles and aunts were just about grown when my mama was born. Ma Liz says they all spoiled her rotten except for her. Anyway, Mama and Ma Liz were fussing because Ma Liz said the air conditioner made her legs ache. So, Papa Simon rolled down the window and Mama started fussing because the wind kept blowing her hat off.

"In the meantime, Papa Simon, who chews tobacco, spit some 'bacca juice right out the window and it came right back in the back window on Mama's new suit. She started crying like a little baby. Ma Liz mumbled something about 'that's what happens when you so vain'. That made her cry even more. Papa Simon felt so bad I thought he was going to cry too. Ma Liz finally calmed her down.

"Lord child, if I had that shape of yourns, I wouldn't have that jacket on anyway," Lizzie began imitating her Grandma. "Done had two young'uns and still got a better figure than some of them teenagers running around looking like dey thirty. Shucks, I bet that big butt Jauntice Kimbro will be pea green with envy when she sees you coming looking like you stepped out of an *Ebony* magazine.

"Well that saved the day. And of course, when we got there, everyone raved about how beautiful my mama was, and all was forgotten."

"Were all your uncles and aunts there?"

"Of course, they didn't want to answer to Ma Liz. Papa Simon says she's the meanest woman he knows."

"I doubt that, or he wouldn't have married her," Cori said smiling, remembering that her Robert used to say the same thing about her.

"He says that's what drew him to her," Lizzie continued.

"Papa lived on the farm that he and Ma Liz live on right now. He tells the story, 'I was in town one Sat'day for my weekly supplies and I spied this pretty little thing sitting on the back flap of a truck. I waved and she paid me no mind. For three Sat'days I waited in the same spot, and there she sat on the back of the truck.'

"You see, my Ma Liz's leg was broken when she was a baby. She didn't get to see a doctor and her grandma set it the best she could, but it never did heal right, and she just dragged it behind her. So, when they went to town every week, she sat on the back of the truck with her legs hanging over the edge, waiting for her uncles to return with their supplies.

"Each week my Grandpa would stand there and wave to Grandma. After a while he finally got the nerve to talk to her. He just walked right over to the truck and said 'Hey.'

"'Hey yourself,' she said.

"They exchanged names and then he asked her if she'd like a cone of ice cream. He was so surprised that she said yes, that he tripped and fell as he ran to get it.

"He had just gotten back with it when her uncles returned. Her Uncle Morris was a teaser, and started singing, 'Lizzie's got a boyfriend, Lizzie's got a boyfriend.' My grandma took her left hand, balled it into a fist, and knocked him flat on the ground. She got up then and went to the truck cab dragging her leg behind her. My granddaddy said he knew right then and there she was the one for him. She was tough as nails.

"You see, her mama died carrying her, and her grandma raised her right along with her seven uncles. She may have had a limp, but she fought those uncles just like a man. Her grandma was very protective of her, and didn't want people teasing her. Never did let her go to school, just taught her what little bit she knew, which wasn't much."

"Her grandma talks just like Mammy on *Gone with the Wind*. It is so cool!" added Summer.

"Yeah, Mama doesn't like for me to spend too much time out there. '*You come back talking and acting like a little slave. Running around sticking forks in the yard trying to hear the devil beating his wife,*'" said Lizzie mimicking her mother. "My grandma is very superstitious."

"But all the uncles, aunts, and cousins were there?" asked Cori.

"Of course, they didn't have to come far. The church is built on family land. Ma Liz had cooked enough food to feed the entire church. And of course, everyone was lining up at her table because she's the best cook in the county. She spread her food out in a section by itself, because she didn't want anyone else's food getting mixed up with hers.

"All day long you'd hear, 'Miss Liz, I couldn't leave this ground without a piece of your sweet potato pie,' or 'Miss Liz, I didn't have to even chew your green beans, they just melted in yo' mouth,' or 'Miss Liz, that has got to be the best potato salad ever made.' Ma Liz would just smile and stick her chest out and act like the best Christian woman on this earth. As soon as we got back in the car, she'd start.

"'Lord, how mercy! I think I saw a pine needle in Serendipity's turnip greens. That sho' nuff is one nasty lady. Did you see Jerutha Mae's runny mashed potatoes? Looked like pancake mix. Some folks just ought not to try and cook.

And Stella Stanton, with her stingy self, ought to know that nobody wants that 25-cent macaroni. T'aint fitting for a dog. Pastor said my chicken was better than the chicken at the Chicken Biscuit. It sho' nuff was a good day. Sho' nuff was. It would've been a better one, though, if Gertrude would wear a girdle. She knows she is too big to go without a girdle, going around shaking like jelly. Turned my stomach.'"

Ada and Cori were so amused by Lizzie's story that they nearly forgot about Summer.

"How was your day, Summer?" asked Ada.

"Boring, as usual. I wish I could have gone to the Homecoming."

Chapter Fifteen

"Red and yellow, black and white, they are precious in his sight..."

Daisies and Buttercups lined the paved driveway, and tiny sprouts of Vinca began to poke their heads in the stone pots that adorned Cori's porch. The streets were alive with activity, as young mothers pushing strollers the size of Volkswagens and small tykes on tricycles filled the sidewalks. After the first phase of young mothers, there was a series of middle school cliques huddled closely and so intense in their "need to belong" that they were oblivious to anyone on the outside of "their" world.

The next group consisted of the lovebirds, who were totally enamored with each other, the bookworm walking solo already transformed to the world held in her hands, and the teens who had not managed to get the coveted "ride" to school. The last group appeared to be angry at everything and everyone. Tay and Jabo belonged to this group.

Cori could not help but notice how much her small town had changed. This multicultural group represented more nationalities than she knew existed in her once predominately white community. She was mesmerized by the different attire, speech, and cultures, although it was still unsettling.

Though they viewed the camaraderie from the porch, the ladies felt a sense of connection with the groups.

Some waved their hands at the "Golden Girls," as they were called out of earshot. Some eyed them suspiciously, and occasionally a young mom would seek their wisdom about the habits of an energetic toddler.

The local advertisements began to blow through the yard. Cori had protested on more than one occasion about the package that she received weekly. Ada spied the flyers blowing freely in the wind, and decided to gather them before Cori popped a blood vessel.

Ada giggled like a young girl as she tried to catch the loose leaflets, which managed to avoid her every grasp. As soon as she bent over to catch one, it skipped away with the wind. She nearly lost her balance trying to capture the one leaflet from Ed's Furniture Mart. Just as she caught herself from tumbling, she heard the snicker of small children. Realizing what a humorous sight she was, she too joined in the laughter. Ada smiled at the two golden children with coal black hair and matching eyes.

"Buenas tardes," Ada said, glad she had remembered how to say "good afternoon" in Spanish. The children's faces lit up as they heard their native language spoken to them.

"Buenas tardes," they replied.

"¿Como esta ud?" asked Ada.

"Estoy bien, gracias," said the little boy.

"Me llamo Ada, como se llama ud?"

"Maria," said the little girl shyly.

"Jesús," responded the little boy.

Ada, realizing that was nearly all the Spanish she knew asked, "¿Habla ud ingles?"

"Si, si," they both responded in unison.

Just then, Lizzie and Summer approached the trio and immediately began a conversation with them.

"Hey Jesús, hey Maria."

They continued their conversation in Spanish and English, laughing at an amusing event that happened at school. Watching the children communicate so freely and in each other's language touched Ada's heart. *If only adults could be so care free,* she thought.

"So, you met Miss Ada?" asked Lizzie.

"Si, si," answered Jesús.

"We come here every evening after school, and she and Miss Cori help us with our homework. You want to come too?" asked Summer.

Ada saw their little black eyes light up with excitement at the idea, but Jesús, being the older of the two, quickly reminded Maria that they must head home. Seeing the dejected look on their faces, Ada, who glimpsed Cori standing stoically on the porch, suggested that they ask their parents if they could come for help with their homework too. The joy instantly returned as two smiles graced their faces.

Later on that evening, after Ada and Cori had finished tutoring Lizzie and

Summer, they heard a knock at the door.

Standing on their porch was Jesús, Maria, and an older version of Maria. Ada quickly and correctly surmised that the older lady was their mother, who she learned was Carmilita.

Carmilita spoke broken English, but Ada clearly understood that she approved of the children joining the others for tutoring. Ada hoped she interpreted accurately that the mother would pick them up around 5:00 when she left her job at the dry cleaners. Carmilita began searching her purse and handed Ada a small package wrapped in tissue paper. Ada, somewhat confused at first, realized that Carmilita was attempting to pay her.

She explained as best she could that there was no charge, but Jesús responded that it was a gift. Ada slowly unwrapped the package and found the most delicate linen handkerchief, with small pink roses embroidered on it. Carmilita said only one word. "Ma Ma's." Ada felt tears form in her eyes as she realized that Carmilita was giving her a gift that belonged to her very own mother. She reached and hugged the small woman and the little children, knowing without a shadow of a doubt that this was a God thing.

Cori, who had been listening on the other side of the door, didn't say a word. She hoped they wouldn't tear up the place.

***

Word of Ada and Cori's tutoring spread like wildfire. Before long, they outgrew the kitchen table and divided the sessions into two groups. The young children arrived and sometimes brought additional friends, such as Casey.

Cori caught herself staring at the talkative young girl, who had difficulty staying in one room. It saddened her as she imagined her little Tara as a young bubbly teenager like Casey. Then there was Shaira, whom Cori eyed with suspicion, even though she was a small and quiet child. Shaira's mother arrived one afternoon with the children, inquiring as to whether her daughter could receive tutoring. The mother, who was wearing a hijab, nearly gave Cori a heart attack.

Cori continued to be very firm with the children, but the children had a way of softening her hard exterior. She even made a more conscious effort in her Spanish class so she could communicate better with Jesús and Maria. The small group still broke out into laughter each time they recalled Jesús explaining his name to Cori.

"What is your name again?" she asked Jesús for the umpteenth time. "Hayzeus, is that H-a-y-z-e-u-s?"

"No, Miss Cori, J-e-s-u-s."

J-e-s-u-s? Cori spelled the name over in her head. "Wait a minute! J-e-s-u-s is Jesus! Who in the world named you Jesus! Lord, Ada, we got us a Spanish Jesus!"

All the children and Ada laughed hysterically. Cori, looking puzzled at first, joined in.

As the evening progressed, the energetic and lively teenagers Unique, Bliss, Nevaeh, and Sinclair arrived, anxious to share what Cori considered were the most bizarre tales of high school.

Chapter Sixteen

"Testing children until they cry is a bad idea. It is an educational malpractice."

– Diane Ravitch

The end of the school year was approaching, which normally excited children; however, the young girls came home with distressing news. They would be administered an end of grade exam, and if they didn't pass the test, they would have to repeat the third grade. Ada was certain that the girls were misinformed. Both had B's and C's in all their subjects, so she found it difficult to believe that if the girls didn't pass the one test, they would have to repeat the entire grade.

She knew that No Child Left Behind had brought several changes, but she was not aware of a policy which retained children based on the results of one test, especially if the students were passing their courses. She was sure the young girls misunderstood the testing requirements, so that evening Ada decided to pay a visit to Grace to inquire about the end of grade exam.

Grace stated very much what the girls had said.

"I agree with you. Too much is based on one test. There have been students who were honor roll students but experienced test anxiety, failed it, and could not go to the next grade unless they took a remedial course and were re-tested. Plus, there is a cost for the remedial course, which adds an additional hardship for low-income students. There was one student in the eighth grade who failed it three times and repeated the eighth grade three times. He eventually turned sixteen and quit school.

"But that's not the worst part. Many schools not only reward the students who passed the test with an elaborate party, but the students who fail the test stay in their classrooms and continue with regular class assignments while listening to the festive activities and celebrations."

"Why is this allowed?" asked Ada.

"Money," Grace stated.

"What do you mean?"

"The teachers are given a bonus based on the school's results, which can be as much as $1,500. In addition, the superintendent is given a bonus based on his school district's results. Our superintendent was given a bonus of nearly $40,000. That's more than most teachers' salaries."

"And this is allowed?"

"Oh, parents have complained; some have formed a group that petitions the lawmakers in Raleigh, but test scores are the driving force in education now. Eddie teaches at the high school, and when parents come to register students at his school, Wallace immediately looks at their previous test scores. If the student has failed the test, he identifies a 'technicality', confuses parents with regulations and district rules, and the student is sent to another school. Plus, if a student has a low test score, he is held to higher discipline standards than the student with the high test score."

"I don't understand," said Ada.

"The students are scored 1 through 4, with 4 being the highest. Say John has a 2 on his reading test, and he skips school. He is immediately sent to the alternative school; when Justin, who has a 4 on his reading test, skips school, he is sent back to his class. It's a common practice, especially at the high school. The most appalling thing to Eddie is the cheating."

"Of course, the children cheat with this type of pressure," replied Ada.

"I'm not talking about the children. I'm talking about some of the teachers. The 'sacred tests,' which are held in a high security vault that rivals something at Fort Knox, mysteriously make it to certain schools. And mind you, these schools are not in the poor neighborhoods. He said there was a history teacher at his school who showed movies every day. About a week before the test, he reviewed some test questions and all of his students mastered the end of course test.

"A friend of mine teaches middle school. The reading and math tests are in the same booklet but are given on separate days. She said she walked in on a math teacher copying problems from the test, which was going to be given on the following day."

Ada looked as if a dear friend had died. "I taught school for over 30 years, and I have never heard of such unethical practices in my life."

"The teachers are under an enormous amount of pressure and unfortunately, that's what happens when money is involved. There are some great, hardworking, dedicated teachers in the schools. But Wallace Sampson, Eddie's principal, protects the teachers who cheat to bring up the scores, and the superintendent protects the principals who have good test scores.

"Eddie has nearly lost his job on several occasions for speaking up against his principal's unethical behavior. He would have been fired a long time ago, if it was not for the fact that his family has a history here in town. And in the South, history still holds a little power.

"I don't know how much longer he is going to be able to take it, though. He feels that they are always looking for some reason to fire him. It's like the gangs. They protect their own and attack anyone who goes up against them. But to make a long story short, Lizzie and Summer are right. They will have to repeat the grade, if they do not pass the test."

"It seems that since their parents are educated, they would be a little more concerned about the test," said Ada.

"They're fairly new here. Lizzie's mom was raised over in Caswell County, but they just moved here a few years ago, the same with Summer's family. Fortunately for them, the test didn't carry the same weight last year. It counts towards promotion in the third, fifth, and eighth grade. The high school students must pass before they graduate.

"It's good that you are helping them. I have a friend who teaches at the elementary school, and I know there are a lot of test prep materials available now. I will give her a call and see what she recommends. Those two little girls are sharp though. I wouldn't worry too much about them."

"Well, thank you so much. This has been a learning experience. I guess I am a little shocked. I've prided myself on being caught up on the latest educational trends, but this one slipped by me. I was a supporter of testing, to hold students and teachers accountable. But this is to the extreme. I guess I know the reason now."

"Excuse me?" said Grace.

"Oh, I'm sorry. Cori and I were wondering why God put us here together. He wants us to help those children."

"I'm sure he does. But they are the lucky ones. They have parents, and although they are absent parents, they are still much better off than most of the children in this town. And on top of everything, now they have you and Mother Jacobs. There are hundreds who are falling through the cracks, and failing because they don't have anyone as advocates for them. I'm sure you are already seeing that Lizzie and Summer aren't the only children who need you two."

"It's something else for me to pray about."

"I'll pray too.

"How about now?"

The two women, who were years apart in so many ways, sat at the table and petitioned God for help, guidance, direction, and protection. Ada felt rejuvenated after the prayer, and had no idea how God would answer, but was excited about the fact that she knew He would answer. Her steps were a little lighter as she headed back across the street.

Chapter Seventeen

Alamance County, circa 1930

It was three days before the older girl began to talk. Damaris put them in the small bedroom that she had hoped would one day be a nursery. She fixed a warm bath for them and let them bathe together. The older girl bathed them in silence, while the younger one delighted in the bubbles.

She examined their caramel skin, with a hint of red, and wavy long hair, and determined they were part Indian. She rubbed their little blistered feet in lard and again, shook her head at what those little ones had possibly experienced. She rubbed their legs in cream, but as she looked at the numerous insect bites and abrasions from life in the woods, she was sure some of the wounds would leave permanent scars.

She dressed them in old gowns that she cut to fit them, and placed them under the quilt she had made over one long winter. Then she knelt beside them and prayed for the little lost souls who had found their way to her home.

They had hearty appetites and loved Damaris' pancakes. The smaller one, although sticking very close to her sister, warmed up to Damaris first. She didn't have many toys but Damaris did have some dolls that she had kept from her childhood. The younger one squealed with delight at the sight of them, and began to carry one with her always.

They had apparently been raised well, because each morning Damaris would enter the little room and find the bed made and pajamas properly folded. At the end of each meal, the older one politely removed the dishes and began to wash them. It was the third night that she prayed when Vivian finally spoke.

"My mama prayed with us like that," she said as the tears began to flow.

"Where is your mama?" asked Damaris as she passed her a handkerchief.

"I heard her scream! I heard some gunshots. I don't know."

"Can you tell me what happened, dear?" Damaris asked softly.

"She told me to run and don't stop.

"She gave Georgia to me and told me to keep running, so I did. But I did stop. I heard my mama scream, and I stopped and looked back. I heard the guns and then I saw our house on fire. Then I kept running and running and running. Just like my mama said."

Rehashing the details created a fresh torrent of tears, and of course the little one, who Damaris assumed was Georgia, started crying too. Damaris did as she did on the first night. She held them both and let them cry as she tried to absorb the terrible story. Her mind began to race as she tried to put the pieces together. She thought back to the story she heard in town and couldn't help but think that the two stories were connected.

Could these girls belong to the family that was murdered? Surely these little girls didn't walk all the way from Caswell County! But Caswell is the next county over, and we actually aren't that far from the county line, so I guess it is possible. These poor little angels.

She continued to hug them and sing to them and the girls gradually calmed down. It was at that moment that she vowed no one would ever hurt those little girls again if she could help it. She decided she would keep them, and she would tell whatever lies necessary. Damaris began making plans as to how she would raise those little girls as her own.

Damaris told the girls to stay in the house, and of the course the girls were obedient, considering they were still frightened half to death. She prayed and prayed and at one point decided to turn the little girls over to the authorities. But the racial tensions were at an all-time high.

She started fearing for the little girls' safety if the murderers knew they were alive. She had heard stories of the Kirk Holden War, when the atmosphere in town was just as volatile. Although Damaris felt chills up her spine, she was determined to keep the girls.

She told the little girls that they would play make believe. They would pretend that they worked for her, and they would have pretend names. Georgia became Ada and Vivian became Mary. Since Damaris lived out in the country, there weren't too many questions.

Damaris kept them solely in the house for about a month. She made them a playroom in her attic and they seemed content playing with her childhood toys. She had always been an excellent seamstress, and made them beautiful little dresses.

Then one day, one of her workers showed up and wanted her to help deliver a baby, and Mary and Ada were sitting at the table. Damaris calmly informed them that she had brought the little girls from some property she had on the other side of the county. Their mama had died in childbirth, so she decided to bring them to help her in her house. This was not unusual, because many of the southern families still maintained some of the old traditions of having little "pickaninnies" around to help with light chores.

When her nephew came by one day unannounced, she told them they belonged to one of her people who had died in childbirth, and they were helping her at her house until they could find some of their kinfolk. He, having believed that slavery was the best thing that ever happened in South, was pleased that she had some young help that she could mold and shape.

As far as anyone in the community was concerned, Ada and Mary belonged to some of Damaris' sharecroppers. To make it look authentic, she had them do chores around the house, especially when she thought she was going to have company. Otherwise, Damaris believed that God had sent her these two children.

She was fully aware of the atmosphere in her community, and played to the stereotypes that were prevalent during those times. The girls were dressed somewhat shabbily when she went to town and rode in the back of the truck. Before she left, she would talk to them and tell them she loved them like they were hers, but bad people would hurt them if they rode up front with her. When they returned home, she dressed them in the beautiful dresses she made for them, and loved them as if they were her very own.

***

Both the girls were very bright students and quick learners. Damaris taught them from old school books and soon Mary was reading to Ada, who had practically memorized every story by heart. She considered sending Mary to the Colored school, but decided against it. It met in the church and had very little supplies, and the teacher was a former student who had completed the seventh grade. But deep down, Damaris was afraid someone might find out their secret. So, she began to order more books and continued to teach Mary at home.

Eventually, the talk of the murders died down and as usual, no one was arrested. Their lives continued, and with the exception of occasional nightmares, little Ada appeared to have forgotten her former life completely. She often caught Mary staring blankly into space, and as she approached her teenage years, she wasn't giggly or bubbly like the other teenagers who lived on her land.

Damaris had noticed on more than one occasion the stares Mary received from the young men on her land and when she went to town. However, she did not think any of them was good enough for her Mary, who had the heart of an angel. Not only did Mary have the physical beauty that drew attention, Damaris didn't think there was a sweeter child on this earth.

The girls on her property all vied to be Mary's best friend and the women on the land often commented on her quiet, sweet personality. Damaris reluctantly began to search for schools for Mary to attend when Coy Healey made his intentions of "calling" on Mary.

Coy was from "Tiller Town," the Colored section of town, and was quite a handsome young man. The fact that he didn't look like any of his brothers and sisters and was the spitting image of Josh Caldwell, his mother's employee, was not lost on anyone.

However, Damaris learned long ago that good looks don't always make a good person. Coy was several years older than Mary, and already had a reputation with the women. So no, she did not think even the handsome Coy Healey was good enough for her Mary, and she was even more determined to find a school for her to attend.

She had heard of a school for Colored girls which wasn't too far away, so one day she and the girls drove to Guilford County to Bennett College. As much as she hated to see Mary go, she felt strongly that Mary should continue her education. After talking to the dean, and after Mary had completed some preliminary tests with perfect scores, Damaris made arrangements for Mary to attend Bennett College.

But Mary had other plans. She informed Damaris that she was getting married to Coy Healey. Damaris felt as if she had been hit by a two-by-four, but Mary was unrelenting. Mary argued that most girls her age were already married, and she didn't want to leave and go to the school with all those strange people. Damaris pleaded with her and told her she didn't have to go to school, but it wasn't enough.

One day, when Damaris drove to town to buy the weekly supplies, Mary, after saying she didn't feel good, ran off and married Coy Healey. Damaris was devastated, but didn't want to make too much fuss for fear their secret would come out or Mary would come and take Ada, who was around twelve. So, Damaris tried to act supportive, and even threw a little reception for Mary at the Reverend Jones' home.

Mary left the comfortable farmhouse and moved into a small three-room shanty in Tiller Town. Damaris could have taken it better if Coy hadn't been so possessive and domineering over Mary. The few times they saw her, she seemed timid and afraid to speak. Then one time Damaris thought she saw a bruise on her face. It kept her on her knees, for she truly loved this sweet child like her own and had vowed years earlier that she would never let anyone hurt her.

She and Ada had turned in early that night because of the terrible thunderstorm that blew through, when they heard the pounding on the door. It was Reverend Jones. According to Reverend Jones, Coy found Mary on the floor. Apparently, she had fallen off a stool and hit her head on the corner of the table. By the time Coy got her to the doctor, the doctor said she was dead.

Damaris felt her knees give out and Reverend Jones helped her to her sofa. She felt like someone had ripped her heart right out. She knew right away that Coy had done something to her sweet, beautiful Mary. Ada was hysterical, and Damaris couldn't calm her down. Reverend Jones prayed without ceasing while Damaris held Ada, both sobbing.

He didn't appear to be concerned that Ada had come out of the bedroom beside Damaris instead of the one out near the back, where most people's servants lived. He also didn't seem fazed by the beautiful cotton nightgown Ada wore. However, he knew there were some in the community who would not respond in kind.

"Miss Damaris, I think it be best to take Ada on down with me and my missus for a few days until after the funeral."

"What?" shouted Damaris. "You can't take Ada! She's all I've got!"

"Miss Damaris, I know youse upset right now, but I don't know how it will look you grieving like you is, and Ada sitting here like she yo natural born daughter. My missus will take good care of her. Matter of fact, won't look strange a'tall if you came visiting and took part in the burial, since the girl 'worked' for you so long. But the grieving best be done with her people. You understand Miss Damaris?"

"You think I want Ada down there with the very people who killed her only sister? Do you think I am that crazy?"

"Nome, not a'tall. But folks will think you is crazy iffen you try to plan a Colored girl's funeral, as if she is yo blood when she got a husband and everything."

"I don't care what folks think. Mary is my daughter and I will take care of her. I should have put my foot down and never let her marry that low-life. It's all my fault. I promised her I would take care of her and never let anybody hurt her." Damaris continued to sob uncontrollably while screaming something about taking her double barrel shotgun and blowing Coy Healey's head off.

"Now, Miss Damaris. I knows better than anyone how you feel about that child. I know she's more than a housekeeper for you. Many folks know but don't say nothing, 'cause they admire the way you took 'em in as yo own. But you can't be calling Mary your daughter. There's some folks here that don't feel like you do. They might want to cause trouble for the other one. Now I knows youse upset right now, but you got to think about the other girl."

Reverend Jones' words began to sink in. She knew he was right. She had to keep their secret. So even though her heart felt like it had been ripped out, she had to think about Ada, who had already lost so much. She continued to sob as she packed Ada the shabby little clothes she often wore into town. She collapsed on the floor as Ada reluctantly left with Reverend Jones.

Planning the funeral was not as much a conflict as Reverend Jones had thought, because no one had seen Coy since he left his dead wife at the doctor. His family was totally crushed by the events, for they too had fallen in love with the sweet spirited girl. But they left the funeral plans totally to Damaris, who planned a simple funeral in the Colored church.

She spent as much time as was considered proper at the Reverend's little home, and promised Ada each night that she would be there when she awoke the next morning. Ada seemed to withdraw back into the little shell she was in when Damaris first saw her. They brought Mary's little body back to the Preacher's house, and Damaris prepared the body herself.

She dressed her in the prettiest dress she had, and declared if someone said something about her being dressed too well for a housekeeper, she would take her double barrel and shoot them herself. She had begun to take that double barrel with her everywhere, and folks believed she actually did intend to kill Coy Healey. They all knew that Miss Damaris could have killed Coy Healey in broad daylight in front of everyone in town, and no one would have touched a hair on her head.

The funeral was a sad day for the entire community. Mary's dress was nicer than what most white women owned. Her long, shiny black hair lay over her breast and Ada thought she looked like Sleeping Beauty. Miss Damaris sat right up front, with Ada on one side, and with her double barrel shot gun on the other side. Coy was nowhere in sight. If folks thought it was strange, no one mentioned it.

Damaris sat in silence with tears running down her face, and with her clinched fists twisting the drenched handkerchief so tightly that it had nearly become a thread. She watched the procession of mourners pass by Mary's body, sobbing and crying at the loss of such a young and sweet soul. How she wished she could sob and scream right along with them.

Her entire body trembled as she tried to consume her pain, and just when she thought she could take no more, May Juba Healey, Coy's mama, approached the pine casket wailing like a lame coyote. But that wasn't enough. She threw her entire 300-pound body over poor Mary, sobbing and drooling all over Mary's beautiful dress. It took every bit of Damaris' energy not to get up and smack May Juba Healey.

After the necessary mourning period, she took Ada back to her home to continue being her "maid." They mourned together for their precious sweet Mary. Damaris didn't know how she could go on with her life. She felt even worse than she did when her husband died.

One Sunday morning, Reverend Jones stopped by on his way to church and told Damaris that Coy Healey was dead. A man caught Coy in bed with his wife and cut his throat. Damaris thanked the Reverend for the news, went to her bedroom, got on her knees, and thanked God that "whatsoever a man soweth, that shall he also reap." She quietly got up, picked up her double barrel, and hung it back on the gun rack.

A few weeks later, Damaris dropped Ada off at Reverend Jones' house while she went on a trip to see her nephew. Everyone was fully aware of Damaris' nephew's views about the "Colored," and couldn't blame Damaris for not wanting to take Ada around him.

Damaris' nephew lived in Person County, which happened to be the same county where Coy Healey was killed. On the way, Damaris made a brief stop at the local county jail in Person County, and had a private conversation with the Sheriff concerning "types of crimes." After the brief exchange, she continued her journey to visit her nephew.

The following week, the county had the trial for Jessie Thomas, Coy's killer. It was a quick trial, in that the courts determined that the murder was a "Crime of Passion." Jessie was released to go home to take care of his five young'uns, and the next week the sheriff department received a new patrol car from an anonymous donor.

Chapter Eighteen

"At least fifteen Palmer graduates are principals of high, elementary, or county training schools in North and South Carolina. Four are county demonstrators in agricultural projects; five are builders and contractors; and some are successful ministers, dentists, and physicians. Several of the young women graduates have achieved distinction as Jeanes Fund workers. One of the girls became a leading soloist in 'Blackbirds,' and another is a member of the chorus in 'The Green Pasture.'"

– Sadie Iola Daniel

Slowly Damaris and Ada's lives returned to some sort of normalcy, but their home and hearts were empty. Damaris continued to teach Ada just as she had taught Mary, but as Ada approached her teen years, Damaris began to have panic attacks. What would happen to Ada if something happened to her?

She never worried before, because she knew Mary would take care of her. She was constantly thinking of Ada, who was a smaller version of Mary, and Damaris was determined that Ada would not go down the same path as her older sister. She was consumed with the realization that she needed to get Ada away before some magnetic young riff raff became a more powerful force than she could handle.

She knew the wealthy Whites often sent their children away, and although she wasn't wealthy, she knew she could afford to send Ada somewhere. She decided to discuss it with Mrs. Jones, who although not formally trained, was the teacher for all the children on her property. Damaris was surprised when Mrs. Jones informed her of Palmer Memorial Institute, a boarding school about 30 minutes away.

Mrs. Jones spoke highly of the school, where many of the wealthy Coloreds in the country sent their children. Damaris couldn't believe her ears. Just 30 minutes from her home; why, she could visit Ada all the time. Mrs. Jones thought Ada might be a little young, but Damaris was not swayed, and decided to find out more about the school.

Damaris knew Ole Man Johnson at the Mercantile would have questions about her getting mail from a Colored boarding school, so she decided to drive over to the Institute one Sunday afternoon. Damaris was elated that such a fine school existed and was so close. How could this school be so close and she not even know it existed? She was baffled that people so intertwined with each other were worlds apart.

She made up her mind that she would send Ada to the Palmer Memorial Institute as soon as possible. A few weeks later, she made another trip to the school, but this time she took Ada with her. The founder of the school, Miss Charlotte Hawkins Brown, was the epitome of professionalism and knowledge.

Several tests were administered to Ada, who passed with flying colors; however, both women agreed that Ada would not begin until the following year, when she celebrated what Damaris had determined to be her fourteenth birthday.

Even then, she would be one of the younger students. Ada didn't want to go to the school, but being the compliant child she was, she quietly accepted it as part of the game she had played for so long. After Mary's death, she never fully returned to the happy joyful child she had once been.

Over the next year, Damaris taught Ada as much as she could. She also spent hours preparing an adequate wardrobe, because the impressive quality of the students' wardrobes did not go unnoticed. She was keenly aware that some of the wealthiest Negroes in the country sent their children to this prestigious school, and she was determined that her daughter would fit right in. She used her expert seamstress skills, and soon Ada had a wardrobe that was as classy as any of the other students.

Damaris was beside herself with excitement about the school, and was elated that Ada would have this wonderful opportunity. If she knew the inner turmoil that tormented her young "daughter," she would never have been able to take her to the Institute.

Damaris' home was all Ada knew, and she also struggled with the fact that she was leaving Mary behind. Even though Mary was in the little cemetery out back, she still felt close to her sister. If only Mary was alive and could go too. But just as she had learned to do early in life, she stored her feelings away and continued to play the game.

Soon the day of Ada's departure arrived. The last night before she was to take Ada to school, Damaris kneeled beside Ada's bed in prayer, as she had done since she first took them into her home. Knowing that the God they had prayed to every night would be with her at the unfamiliar place brought Ada comfort, and knowing that as she knelt beside her bed and prayed each night, her "Mother Damaris" would be doing the same thing.

"Maybe things wouldn't be so bad," she thought to herself.

Mother Damaris promised her that she would come to the school every weekend to see her.

Chapter Nineteen

The Wednesday Night Special

The highlight of the week for the two elderly women was their weekly visit from Robert Edward Jacobs, IV Eddie. Cori truly adored her grandson, who was the spitting image of a young Robert Edward. He had the same caring personality of her late husband, and made a conscious effort to keep this date with his grandmother. Ada was equally impressed with the young man, and admired his devotion to his grandmother.

Every Wednesday when Eddie's wife, Lindsay, worked late, Eddie spent the evening with Cori. They worked crossword puzzles together, and Eddie had even gotten Cori interested in Scrabble. Secretly, he worried about her getting Alzheimer's and had read that word games were good exercises for the mind. Soon Ada joined in the board games, and looked forward to Wednesdays too. It was also relaxing and therapeutic for Eddie, who stayed until it was time for his church's family night, where he worked with the youth.

He attended A Blessing, the new church that met in the old elementary school. It was an energetic church with lots of loud contemporary music. Cori had gone with him on one occasion, but was turned off by the dancing, and found the people waving their hands in the air distracting. The church was initially a satellite of the church Cori attended. The people who preferred the traditional worship continued at the old church, and the younger couples with young children attended a Saturday night service.

They met as a large group once a month, which seemed to satisfy everyone. But at some point, Pastor Johnny and the young Reverend Basley began to disagree about the direction of the church. Reverend Basley wanted to start an after-school tutorial program for children in town, but some in the church balked when they found out that the majority of the children were from the low-income community nearby.

Reverend Basley stood his ground, and argued that they had no problems sending money to Africa, but refused to help African Americans who lived on the same street as the church. Then Reverend Basley accused Pastor Johnny of being pro-birth. He argued that there was no way that Pastor Johnny could be pro-life, because he cared nothing for the children's lives after they were born.

This was the final straw for Pastor Johnny. Reverend Basley left First Church and started A Blessing, a non-denominational, multi-cultural church that soon had close to five hundred members, with new ones joining weekly. First Church happily maintained its traditions, and became a church in sync with its aging and dying congregation.

Although Eddie appeared to enjoy the Scrabble game, he missed some easy opportunities and was obviously distracted. After the second game, Cori, noticing her grandson was simply going through the motions, put the game away.

"What's wrong Eddie? You have something on your mind?"

"Grandma, I honestly believe you know me better than anyone on this earth. I didn't know it was that obvious. Just the same old thing, I keep bumping heads with Wallace."

Wallace Sampson's name immediately caught Ada's attention. Wallace Sampson was the high school principal Grace had mentioned, and the son of Barnett Sampson.

"I don't have any proof, but I think he goes through my desk when I am not there."

"Why would he want to go through your desk?" asked Cori.

"I think he's trying to find a reason to fire me."

"But you and Wallace grew up together. What could he have against you?" Cori asked.

"It's not that he has anything against me, he's just trying to protect himself."

"Protect himself against what?"

"Wallace didn't get his position based on what he knew, but because of who he knew. Now he wants to keep it and will do whatever it takes."

"Is it those test scores?" asked Ada.

"That's just part of it. Because he wants the highest test scores, he will do anything to get them. He has surrounded himself with teachers who have no ethics or morals and are willing to cheat, steal, or lie, whatever it takes. Those are the ones he protects and he tries to force the ones out who believe in truth, fairness, and justice.

"Just today two students came to me because they were upset that Cathy Jarvis was openly flirting with the coach. When they went to tell Wallace about them, he threatened to suspend them for spreading vicious rumors about teachers."

"Are they rumors?"

"No, they are not. They are having a full-blown affair, and right in front of the students. One night I returned to school to do some work, and I spotted their cars parked out back near the Coach's office."

"Why, in my day they would have been fired on the spot," stated Ada.

"Oh, they wouldn't dare fire either one of them. He has a winning team that brings in lots of money to the school and she has high scores, which guarantee job security. Shucks, she only teaches two classes a day."

"What does she do the rest of the time?"

"You tell me. There are several of the 'chosen ones' who teach two periods a day instead of four."

"Do they get the same pay?" asked Cori.

"Of course they do. Wallace manipulates the student enrollment numbers each year to show that we have more students than we actually have, and when the data shows that we have more students, we get more teachers. Then he rewards his chosen teachers with small classes, high achieving students, or a few classes. It's a win-win for those teachers, while others have large classes and low achieving students."

"And he gets away with this?" asked Ada.

"Sure. The Sampsons run everything. They are situated in key positions throughout the county and protect each other fiercely. I don't know. Maybe I am imagining things."

"Maybe you're not. You need to trust your instincts," added Ada.

"It just seems as if a black cloud is hovering over this town. What is right is frowned upon, and what is wrong is glorified. The good are persecuted and the bad are rewarded, and the children are the ones who suffer. Children today are very bright and these deceptions are not lost on them. Many of them have so much potential but are steadily falling through the cracks."

"Well, it's just something else we need to take to the Lord in prayer," stated Cori in a matter of fact manner.

Eddie was somewhat surprised at his grandmother's new zeal for the Lord.

"Have you ever been scared to pray?" asked Eddie.

"Scared to pray?" responded Ada.

"Yes ma'am. It seems lately the more I've prayed, the worse things have gotten. Like today, when Unique and Fabulous came to me about the teachers' affair, I prayed with them and told them to talk to the principal. They came back to me in tears, afraid they were going to be suspended."

After Ada's brief distraction by the name Fabulous, she found her voice. "Fear is just a tool of the devil," she stated firmly. "Have you thought about how things would have gone without prayer? Perhaps Wallace wouldn't have threatened them, but gone ahead and suspended them."

"I guess that's one way to look at it," stated Eddie.

"I've known that Wallace Sampson all of his sorry life," Cori began. "He's just like the other Sampsons, a bunch of ignorant skunks who wormed their way into positions of power. Crazy fools seem to think the name 'Sampson' makes them powerful. They were po' as Joe's turkey growing up. Shucks, they were so po', they stole Joe's turkey and ate him.

"One of his old grand pappies claims to have founded this town. He told the story that the great General Robert E. Lee was passing through and stopped, and rested on his property. He had an old trading post, no more than a stable and a well. Well, he claimed that General Lee and his men rested right there in his field. Said the great General felt that the place was a *blessing* from the violent and bloody war. So, that's how the town got its name.

"A few years ago, the Sampsons tried to have one of those historical markers put up near their land. Some of those fools even wanted to change the name to *Sampson's Blessing*, but when the Civil War historians came through, they couldn't find any record of the great general being anywhere near old man Sampson's land.

"Of course, by that time the town was called *Blessing*. There were still some from the Sampsons' camp who wanted the name of the town changed, but most folks didn't want a new address, so we are still called *Blessing*.

"They didn't have a pot to pee in, but they stole everybody else's pot that wasn't nailed down, and finally wound up having more than most folks in town. When his little snot-nosed brats grew up, he sent them to college where they majored in cheating, butt-kissing, and brown-nosing.

"Then they came back here like they were somebody, worming their way into offices, businesses, and now they walk around putting on airs like they are better than most folks in town.

"I taught that Wallace in Sunday school when he was little. Dumb as a rock. Put a nickel in the offering and tried to get five pennies back. Now that numbskull is principal of the high school."

"Grandma you are a mess."

Ada laughed along with Eddie.

"You always know how to make me feel better."

"Do you want me to go that school and talk to that Wallace Sampson? I'll just give him a piece of my mind."

"No, Grandma. I can handle Wallace. I just get tired sometimes."

"Do not grow weary of well doing, for in due season you shall reap if you faint not," Ada said with fervor. "You hang in there, Eddie, and we will pray for you every morning and pray for you during the day too. Wallace won't know what hit him."

"Thanks Miss Ada. Somehow I feel as if your prayers make it through better than mine."

"God hears all of his children's prayers. Sometimes we just can't see it right away. I know I didn't feel like God was listening to me for nearly 30 years," Cori stated. "Can you imagine that? I felt like God hadn't heard a prayer of mine since Robert Edward died. Now I look back over the years and don't know how I would have made it without the Lord. I didn't feel him, but He was just like air. He was there all the time."

"Thanks. I needed that," stated Eddie. "Sometimes I feel like I need a good old fashioned tent revival. I went to one when I was in college, and accepted the Lord right there on the spot."

"What do you mean you accepted the Lord?" asked Cori. "You been a Christian all of your life, had your Christening right after you were born."

"I know, but I really didn't know the Lord. He was like a giant king sitting on a huge throne looking down on us. I didn't want to make Him mad and tried to do what was good because he was watching everything, and I would wind up burning eternally if I didn't. But one night when I was in college, I went with a friend to a tent revival. I didn't have any major problems like some of the folks there. They were sick, broke, living in sin.

"Shucks, I was in college, on the Dean's List, came from a good home and life was good. But that night I felt so worthless. The preacher started talking about all the sacrifices the Hebrews had to make, and how the lambs had to be perfect without blemish, and how sacred the sacrifice was. They had to do that every time they did something bad. He went on and told us how Jesus was perfect, how he never did a thing to a soul, except to love them. That he loved me so much that He offered Himself as that sacrificial lamb and died on the cross for my sins.

"The preacher went on to say that some of us felt that we had never done anything wrong, but each day that went by and we didn't acknowledge Christ as our Lord and Savior was just as bad as killing and stealing. That when we were critical, or envious, or jealous, that we were just as bad as the murderer. He went on to say that all Jesus wanted in return was our love and obedience. When we went through the day and not thank God or honor Him, it was like we were nailing Him to the cross over and over.

"It was like he was talking right to me. I no longer felt so good. I felt like what I actually was...a sinner. I nearly ran up to the preacher on that night. That was when I felt like I truly became a Christian. I had never read my Bible, except for when I was in church. I began to read my Bible every day, and talk to God every day, and I felt like He was truly like the song said, 'He walked with me and talked with me.' I felt so close to God, it was like I could reach out and touch Him. But I haven't felt that way in a while. I still read my Bible every day, and I still pray every day, but it's like it is routine. I don't feel His presence and I don't feel the closeness I once felt."

"It sounds like you're having a good ole desert experience to me," said Ada.

"Yeah, I felt that way for thirty years," Cori added.

"Whew, Grandma! You wandered in the desert almost as long as the Hebrews. I sure hope my desert experience doesn't last that long!"

"The fact that you are longing shows that you are on the way out," stated Ada

"I sure hope so. I better get going. We are going to play Bible Bingo tonight and the kids love that game. We'll probably have a large group tonight."

Eddie hugged both women and reminded them to pray for him. They both assured him they would.

Chapter Twenty

"After climbing a great hill, one only finds that there are many more hills to climb."

– Nelson Mandela

"I told you, I want no part in it," said Bobby Lee.

"You might want to think again, and this time, think hard," Barnett replied.

Barnett Sampson smiled a slimy smile that made you feel as if he was chewing you slowly before spitting you out. His gray eyes narrowed until they were barely visible.

"I was over at the city manager's office visiting my boy, Bedford, and he was just telling me about the new city codes for businesses downtown. It seems like the crooks in Washington are sending out a new bunch of codes and regulations every day."

Bobby Lee continued stacking the bags of salted peanuts on the counter, seeming uninterested in what Barnett was saying. His feet automatically shifted from one to another, a habit he developed as a youngster to deflect the nervousness from his face.

He had just finished paying the painters, who charged him an arm and a leg to paint the front of the building, because the city had a new code that required all businesses to be freshly painted. Since his building was so old, he had to have the place treated for termites and much of the old wood replaced before the painters could even attempt to paint it.

"Bedford said that these new codes would require all merchants to purchase licenses to even sell soft drinks and potato chips now. Some liberal sued a storeowner because he choked on a peanut that was purchased at his store. Anyway, Bedford said it's right around the corner. Of course, now Bedford works with people to make sure that they are able to continue running their stores, and I'm sure he would be willing to work with you, considering you've had this store going for so long."

Bobby Lee's mind raced faster than he had run down the field against Southern Alamance in the Conference Championship game. How in the world was he going to keep up? First, he had to have a liquor license to sell beer and wine. Then, he was forced to stop selling slices of bologna because he didn't have a license to sell food. Then they took the gas tanks away because of the new EPA regulations, and now he may have to stop serving snacks all together.

Barnett continued, "Cade Kannart was having the same problems at the mini-mart, but he and Bedford were able to come to sort of a 'gentleman's agreement,' and his business is now flourishing. He sells fast food, has the video rentals, and he and his wife go on the Saved Saint's Cruise every summer with their church. Good Christian hardworking folks deserve to prosper. It's in the good book."

Bobby Lee's chest pounded so hard, that he felt as if it was about to rip wide open.

"Bedford's brother-in-law just has some merchandise that he would like for you to sell in your store. Not much, just a few bottles of finger nail polish remover, cold medicine, batteries, nothing illegal."

Bobby Lee rolled his eyes as Barnett carefully chose his words.

"They gonna buy the stuff anyway; you may as well benefit from it."

That was it for Bobby Lee, and he finally found his voice.

"Get out Barnett! Get out right now! I've told you I will not turn my daddy's store into a crack house."

"Now, who said anything about crack? You know, it's sad when people are ignorant to innovation. Your daddy's store is going down, Bobby Lee, and you are going down right with it."

"You don't scare me, Barnett!"

"Yeah," smiled Barnett. "That's what Amanna Dove said."

The crash caused them both to jump at the same time. Bobby Lee headed down the cluttered aisle, with Barnett in step behind him. They saw the cans of tomatoes scattered across the floor, and PM lay sprawled across the floor, rubbing his head.

Bobby Lee let out a bunch of words he hadn't used in quite a while.

"PM, what in the world are you doing back here?"

PM continued rubbing his eyes. "I guess I musta really tied one on last night. When the boys and me finished playing cards, I headed home, and I guess this is as far as I made it."

"I swear PM," ranted Bobby Lee. "You and your friends are gonna be the death of me yet. I'm gonna move that ole barrel away from my place and close that basement up for good. I am getting sick and tired of you bums hanging out at my place anyway. Now git on up and get on home. Your Mama's probably worried sick about yo' drunk butt."

"Oh, Bobby Lee, I didn't cause no harm, just caught a few winks. Look here, I'll stack your tomato cans up just like they were."

"Just leave 'em PM, and go on home. I'll take care of them myself."

PM continued rubbing his eyes and began brushing himself off. He stumbled through the backdoor down the cinder block steps.

Barnett grinned his steely grin. "You got yourself a ready-made clientele."

He let out a guttural laugh and continued laughing as he exited the door. As he stepped out on the sidewalk, he spotted PM wobbling down the road. The laughter stopped abruptly. Barnett stared at PM and if looks could kill, PM was as dead as Amanna Dove.

Chapter Twenty-One

Palmer Memorial Institute, circa 1945

Damaris kept her word and visited Ada every weekend. At first it broke her heart to leave the young girl in a strange place, but she was convinced that this was what she had to do to keep her from a tragedy like her sister's.

Ada was very withdrawn at first, but each week Damaris saw progress, and left confident that she had made the right decision. The reports from the teachers indicated just what Damaris knew. Ada was exceptional in all her courses and was soon at the top in all her classes.

She loved learning, but what Damaris didn't know was that as much as she loved school, she loved her Mother Damaris even more. When they were alone, she called her Mother Damaris, and the sound caused Damaris' heart to melt even more.

They continued their charade that Ada was her hired girl when she returned to rural Alamance County, but when the doors were shut, they were as much mother and daughter as anyone. Ada worked hard in her classes because she knew it brought happiness to the woman she had grown to love. Her heart overflowed when she watched the older woman's face as the professors informed her of Ada's progress.

As Ada grew older, Mother Damaris planned special trips, mainly up North, where there wouldn't be as many questions. She drove to the school, picked up Ada, and they continued their special adventures.

It was Thursday, and Ada was already excited as the weekend approached. As much as she enjoyed school, she longed for the time with Mother Damaris. They sewed, read, and simply enjoyed each other's company. The weekend never ended without a visit to the mound in the backyard with the roses blooming.

She was surprised when she was summoned to Miss Steepleton, the Dorm Mother, in the middle of the day. When she arrived, the atmosphere reminded her briefly of the time Mary died. Miss Steepleton was very strict, never smiled, and she had been the butt of many jokes by the other girls. Ada smiled at some of the jokes, but as she looked at the plain but somewhat attractive lady, she thought her eyes looked sort of sad.

"Ada, come on in," smiled Miss Steepleton. Ada had never been in the Dorm Mother's room. She found it simple, but quite comfortable. There was a small parlor with a bedroom to the side. In front of the sofa was a coffee table with a beautiful china teapot and teacups on it.

"Please have a cup of tea with me," Miss Steepleton stated softly.

Ada tried to remember everything she had learned about manners and etiquette. She sat down and politely accepted the tea, hoping her hands didn't tremble too much.

Miss Steepleton began, "Ada, I have been in contact with your guardian, Mrs. Gilliam, since before you arrived here at Palmer Institute. I am fully aware of your home circumstances and your history."

What is this about? Ada thought to herself. *Why is Miss Steepleton having tea with me and talking about Mother Damaris?*

Miss Steepleton continued, "Mrs. Gilliam gave me instructions about your care while you were here, and instructions for you in case anything ever happened to her."

Ada felt the air being sucked from her body, finding it difficult to breathe.

"I am so sorry," Miss Steepleton's voice cracked. Tears formed in her eyes. "I am so sorry to have to be the one to tell you, but Mrs. Gilliam was found in her bed yesterday. Apparently, she had a heart attack in her sleep."

Miss Steepleton's mouth was moving and a sound was coming out. The clock ticked loudly on the wall, but for Ada, time stood still. She sat paralyzed, motionless, and for the first time in her life, she was totally alone.

"Ada?" Ada heard her voice but could not respond. Miss Steepleton walked over to the young girl and put her arms around her.

"Ada, you can cry. You can scream. You can run around my little parlor until your legs give out if you want to."

As Miss Steepleton continued talking, Ada's body began to tremble and a soft, inaudible sound escaped from her mouth. Miss Steepleton held her tight, and the trembling became more prevalent as well as the sound, which was now a pain-wrenched sob. Miss Steepleton didn't know how long she held the young girl, but sometime later in the evening, Ada's sobs ceased and silent tears trickled down her face.

"You said she had a heart attack," asked Ada.

"One of the men who sharecropped on her land had been given instructions, that in the event something happened to her, he was to bring this package to the school," Miss Steepleton explained. "Poor fellow jumped in his old wagon and drove straight here." With that comment, more tears trailed down Ada's face.

"He said it looks like she fell asleep and woke up right where she belonged, with the angels. You weren't the only one who loved the kind lady."

Ada nodded in agreement.

"He said her funeral is this Sunday, and he'd come back to get you if you wanted to attend. I can drive, and I am sure Mrs. Brown will let us use the school car to take you to the funeral."

Ada remained motionless in the woman's arms for a few more minutes. She wanted to stay there and never leave, because she truly believed that once Miss Steepleton's arms left her, she would be totally alone in the world. They sat in silence, and Ada knew that she had imposed on the kind lady long enough. It would be bad manners to stay any longer.

"I guess I need to go back to my room now. I have a lot to do."

"I can help you pack, if you'd like, Ada."

"No, I think I can handle it. It's just one thing though. I don't know where to go."

Miss Steepleton looked at Ada somewhat confused. "The man, I believe his name was Wilson, gave me directions, and we should not have any trouble finding the church."

"I know how to get to the church, Miss Steepleton, but I'm talking about after the funeral. I don't know where to go after the funeral. I have no other family."

"Dear girl, you will come back here, of course."

Ada thought about that statement. She knew there were some girls who worked on the campus to pay for their schooling.

"Do you think I could? Do you think I could get a job like Mearlee and Darle to pay for my school?"

"Ada, I'm so sorry, I haven't finished telling you everything. Mrs. Gilliam was not only loving and kind to you and the people who worked on her land, but over the years she became a dear friend to the people here too. The entire faculty and staff are grieving with you right now."

Ada's mind wandered back to the times Mother Damaris visited. Often, she walked across the campus with one of the faculty members, or sat on the veranda having tea with Mrs. Brown as if she belonged right here.

"She was a wise woman and one of the most generous people I've ever met, Colored or White. She arranged through an attorney in Greensboro to continue to take care of you. She put money aside for your care and education, and money for your life after school ends.

"She also left money for the school. She shared with us how her nephew would have a fit if he wasn't left anything, so she left him her properties on the other side of the county. She had titles to the little homes on her land drawn up in all her employees' names, and she donated her home as a Parsonage for her pastor. She loved his wife, and knew that she would take care of her home and the people nearby.

"So, Ada, you don't have to worry about a thing. We love you here and we will continue to take care of you as long as you need us too."

A fresh waterfall of tears ran down Ada's face, when she thought about the angel God sent to take care of her and her sister. Not only did she love them and take care of them while she was on earth, but she was an angel in heaven watching over her now.

Through her tears, Ada smiled.

Chapter Twenty-Two

Palmer Memorial Institute, circa 1950

"Often functioning as superintendent of the black schools, the Jeanes teachers worked to improve education, public health, and general living conditions for their students and community. They raised the quality of teaching, pushed for resources from the school board, raised money from the community, and built schools. Mostly female and all black, the Jeanes teachers' voices were marginalized so that, in spite of their pioneering work, documentation of it is scant."

– The Women Who Ran the Schools

Ada vacillated from grief to worry. She missed her Mother Damaris terribly, and worried constantly about what would happen to her when her schooling ended and she was no longer a student. She knew the pastor and his wife had moved into the farmhouse. It was even more obvious when all her belongings were sent to the school. Little did she know that the request that her personal items be sent to the school had been made by Mother Damaris.

Ada was a popular student and had just been crowned May Queen prior to Mother Damaris' death. Mother Damaris had been notified that Ada was on the court and arrived with the most beautiful white dress for the celebration. Many of the students grieved right along with Ada, and some even asked their parents to adopt Ada.

Miss Steepleton's prayers were answered. After graduating from Hampton Institute, Joann Steepleton arrived in Durham, North Carolina, as one the Jeanes teachers. Although she loved the people in rural Durham County, she was delighted to receive the offer to become a part of the Palmer Memorial Institute staff. She told herself repeatedly that she was the mother to hundreds of children, but even that did not satisfy her longing to be a mother.

She was elated to learn that Mrs. Gilliam wanted her appointed as Ada's guardian. She loved the company of the kind lady, but had no idea Mrs. Gilliam considered her as anything other than one of the staff members. Now she had her very own "daughter."

Ada continued to live in the dorms as other students whose parents were part of the faculty and staff. Once the summer arrived, Miss Steepleton informed her that she would be joining her on the train ride to Hampton, Virginia, to spend the summer with the Steepleton family.

As her graduation approached, Ada expressed her desire to become a school-teacher, and her interest in attending Bennett College, the girl's college that was nearby. Miss Steepleton liked the idea of having her "daughter" close, but also secretly hoped she would attend her alma mater, Hampton Institute. They had visited it on several occasions and she knew Ada's "aunts" would keep an eye on her; however, the decision would be Ada's.

Miss Steepleton was completing some quarterly reports when Ada surprised her with a visit. She glanced at the grandfather clock and was surprised that Ada had completed her dishwashing duties so early, but was happy to have her company.

Ada was not aware she was wealthy and wanted to know the cost of an education at Hampton Institute. Some of her friends were planning to attend Hampton, and had mentioned that it was one of the best schools in the country. She knew her Mother Damaris would want her to go the best school, and stated that she could live with "Grandmother Steepleton" and get a job. Miss Steepleton restrained herself from doing a cartwheel.

Hampton proved to be exactly what Ada needed. The distance from her childhood home was beneficial for her grieving process. It was both intellectually stimulating and inspirational. Each year she blossomed more and more, and the sadness slowly disappeared from her eyes.

When she was crowned the school's homecoming queen and graduated at the top of her class, no one was surprised. Some thought she was driven, but if they only knew that everything she did, she did for all her parents: the parents she never knew and the ones who loved her as if they had given birth to her.

Ada was shocked when Miss Steepleton explained her finances to her shortly after her graduation. She had no idea that Mother Damaris was a wealthy woman, and had left most of her fortune to her.

As she examined the detailed ledger, she realized that Miss Steepleton had never compensated herself for one day of Ada's care. The expenses for her education at Palmer Memorial Institute and Hampton Institute were the only monies that had been deducted from the account. Miss Steepleton had taken care of her as if she was her very own child. Once again, she cried for the many angels God had sent her way.

One of the first things that Ada did after graduating was to purchase a home for Mother Steepleton, so she could be near Grandmother Steepleton, who was ailing. Also, she knew how much Mother Steepleton wanted to become a member of the Hampton Institute faculty, and now she would have the opportunity to do so.

Everyone was excited when Ada was hired as a teacher at an elementary school near Palmer. Even though she knew she could afford to purchase a home, she decided to live in the teacherage with the other young teachers.

However, there were days when she second-guessed her decision. Sometimes the record players were turned too loud, and some of the teachers didn't adhere to some of the "expectations" of the educators. But deep down, she knew she didn't desire the alternative. Being alone.

They joked with her and teased her, calling her the "nun" in the group. She smiled and laughed right along with them as she curled up in the chair with her date, a good book.

Even her introverted lifestyle did not hinder the looks and gestures from the young male members of the faculty. She had been told all her life that she was beautiful, although she thought herself to be rather plain compared to the other stylish and glamorous teachers. She responded politely to the attempts at her attention, but when the new principal arrived her second year at the school, she couldn't explain the flutter in her chest or the chills that raced through her body.

Mr. Frederick Douglas Passmore had taught briefly at a school in Durham after completing his degree at the North Carolina College for Negroes. He believed that the field of education was a calling, just as a preacher was called to preach, so he ventured north for further education in hopes of becoming the most effective educator for his people. After completing his master's degree at the University of Michigan, he returned to the South, excited to fulfill his calling to motivate, educate, and inspire young minds.

Ada couldn't explain it. He was handsome in his own way, but it was more than his looks. The entire staff hung on his every word and even teachers who were normally reserved, gushed all over themselves at the least bit of attention from him. She felt silly joining the rest of the ladies in their giddiness, so she hoped her voice was even, when on the last day of school, he finally asked her out on a date.

The summer was a whirlwind of long walks, reading books together, and dinner with his elderly parents who lived nearby. That August their engagement was announced, and after a short engagement, she became Mrs. Frederick Douglas Passmore. Miss Steepleton beamed with pride and excitement as Ada walked down the aisle at the Palmer Institute Chapel, wearing a revision of the white May Queen dress her Mother Damaris had purchased for her shortly before her death.

Their lives were busy with educating and nurturing young children while devoting all their extra energies to the local NAACP and Civil Rights movements. They had just returned from Selma, Alabama, where they had participated in the Selma to Montgomery March.

The brutality and the cruelty had left them both shaken, so when Ada discovered that she was pregnant, Mr. Passmore, as she called him, informed them that they would focus on creating future leaders. He stated that they needed people on the frontlines at the present, but they also needed people to ensure that there was a future for their race also. Secretly, the brutal murders of Harry and Harriette Moore were never far in his thoughts. They not only lost their jobs as teachers, they lost their lives.

So, when he was asked to become a part of the leadership in a school district in Detroit, Michigan, he shared with Ada how he believed the move would be a good one for their growing family. She had grown to love the people she met at the little Congregational Church in Montgomery.

The images on the television of her dear friends being beaten, sprayed with water hoses, and bitten by police dogs, still brought her to tears. Ada, having only imagined living in an integrated world, and after the hostility she experienced in Selma, was anxious to get away from a world that disliked her for one sole reason, her color.

Chapter Twenty-Three

"In the long run, we shape our lives, and we shape ourselves. The process never ends until we die. And the choices we make are ultimately our own responsibility."

– Eleanor Roosevelt

The nightmare had haunted PM in his dreams for nearly 10 years. It never changed, and it was as clear today as it was the first time he had it.

The party had been a good one. The club was having a Jackson 5 night, and a lot of young folks showed up dressed as the Jacksons. He was too old to cut a step like he could when he was younger, plus his crippled legs couldn't move even if he wanted them to, but he enjoyed watching the younger ones moon walk and spin to Michael Jackson's "Bad."

He sat at the table drinking and smiling at the young folks on the dance floor. After a while of soaking in the liveliness of the younger generation, he headed to the back room with folks more his age. There was a good poker game going and plenty of weed for everyone. He played a couple of hands, and felt his body melt away with the atmosphere.

Pot always had that effect on him. He just floated as if on air, without a care in the world. Still in a daze, he headed in the direction of home. After each experience, he headed to the little house at the end of the road that he shared with his aging mom.

He had gotten accustomed to walking on the path near the road, because if he walked on the main road, he was often harassed by bored teenagers, or some of Barnett's cronies on the police force. He knew the path even in his drunken stupor.

It was late and there was no traffic on the road, until he heard wheels squealing. PM stooped down by some brush, hoping to remain unseen. There was a truck that was weaving all over the road and as PM looked closer, it looked like one of Sampson factory trucks.

As it got closer to him and just before he ducked, it looked like there was a struggle, and as the truck approached the light on the corner of Pine, a person was trying to get out of the speeding truck. He wasn't sure but the person looked like Amanna Dove.

PM woke up on the path and couldn't remember how he had gotten there. His head was spinning and the pain reminded him of the previous night of heavy drinking and smoking pot. He looked around dazed, got up out of the damp grass and headed home to face his mama, who probably worried about him all night.

***

Bobby Lee couldn't explain why he dreaded the morning coffee visit with his mama so much. It wasn't that he didn't like Miss Ada, but he felt so uncomfortable around her. She was always courteous and kind to him, but there was an unsettling feeling. And now Grace had started joining them in their little prayer meetings in the mornings. He knew they tried to time it to finish before he arrived, but occasionally he still interrupted it.

They're all turning into a bunch of holy rollies, Bobby Lee thought. *First, it was Eddie coming home from college a Jesus Freak and marrying that missionary's daughter. Why don't they ask Jesus to give them some children? All my friends are going to see their grandchildren play little league, and visiting with them on Sunday afternoons, and I have nothing.*

He briefly thought of Tara, but dismissed the thoughts of her as quickly as they entered his head.

Bobby Lee opened the back door just as Ada was placing her coffee cup in the sink.

"Good Morning, son," Cori began. "Got your coffee right here just the way you like it."

"Good Morning, Mama, Miss Ada."

"Good Morning, Bobby Lee. I'll give you two a little private time," said Ada, and excused herself just as she did each morning.

"How are things at the store?" asked Cori.

"About the same," answered Bobby Lee. "Seems the harder I try, the harder times get."

"Well, I just know things are going to work out. I pray to the good Lord every morning and he ain't never let me down yet. You got to pray too, Bobby Lee."

"Now Mama, don't start preaching to me."

"I ain't preaching to you. I'm just telling you the God-in-heaven truth. Prayer helps. I've been around long enough to know that for a fact. Now you can keep on being stubborn and trying to do things your way, but you just gone wear yourself right into the ground. Look at you. I don't know the last time I saw you smile about anything."

"What's there to smile about?" asked Bobby Lee sarcastically.

"What in the world has gotten into you, Bobby Lee? You healthy, you own a business, you got a family, what else do you want? Don't sit there whining about what you don't have like I did after your daddy died. The next thing you know, you'll be over ninety years old like me, and in the same spot. Time ain't waiting for nobody, boy."

"I gotta go, Mama." Bobby Lee gave his mama her courtesy peck on the cheek, feeling just as he did when he went in. *If Mama only knew.*

***

It wasn't the marriage that she dreamed she would have. It wasn't the life that she giggled about with girlfriends on sleepovers in high school. A slight smile went across Grace's face as she thought of all the nights she swooned at the sight of Bobby Lee Jacobs. Bobby Lee Jacobs, the big man on campus, the high school quarterback, voted most likely to become famous. He could have had Opaque and any girl on campus, but he chose her.

Her return to town didn't seem to affect Opaque's continuous visits to the store. Opaque, having recognized a stress fracture, held on to the possibility that fatigue and weariness would cause a full break.

Even though she exuded confidence, Grace knew her marriage was in serious trouble. But worry wrinkles converted to a smile when she thought about Mother Jacobs' response to the rapidly spreading Opaque-Bobby Lee rumors. *"Opaque's just a boll weevil looking for a cotton ball to land on."*

She was reminded of her high school fear and anxiousness. Oh, she was pretty enough, but she never felt she measured up to Bobby Lee Jacobs. She really wanted to go to college, but when Bobby Lee's daddy dropped dead in their basement and he decided to run the family store and proposed to her, she knew there was no way on earth that she would leave him in Blessing. So, she married him, the man of her dreams, right out of high school and planned for a fairytale life of happily ever after.

Grace really couldn't pin point what happened in their marriage. It seemed she went from being the apple of Bobby Lee's eye and he her Prince Charming, to them coexisting in their home barely passing two words between them a day. She could honestly say she tried to be a good wife and mother, but at some point, that just wasn't enough. Then things started going downhill at the store, and they could barely make ends meet.

I guess he never did like the idea of me going back to school. It seems like that started it all. But as I think back, there were problems even before then, Grace thought to herself.

When the children came along, things just changed. First, there was the disagreement about Eddie's name. I could understand that Bobby Lee wanted him named after his dad and him, but I just didn't want to name him after a confederate soldier, no matter how much he was loved. Bobby Lee was adamant that his son would be named Robert Edward Lee V, but I insisted that we call him Eddie.

From the time he started walking, Bobby Lee was hard on him. Eddie was such a sweet and caring child, and didn't have a rough bone in his body, and the more he played his grandmother's piano the angrier Bobby Lee got. Even though he was good in sports, his heart wasn't in it. Then Eddie decided to join the marching band. Bobby Lee got so mad and took it out on me as if it was my fault. Said I cuddled him and pampered him too much. I guess that was the beginning.

Things were better with Tara, at least at first. She was truly a daddy's girl. She went with him everywhere, fished with him, played football with him, watched the games on TV with him, and even worked in the store with him. As far as Bobby Lee was concerned, Tara walked on water, and she thought the sun set and rose on him. How things could have gone so wrong is still a mystery to me.

A tear drifted slowly down her cheek. *How could love turn to hate so quickly? I guess that old song "It's a thin line between love and hate" is true. So here I am, married to a man who totally ignores me, doesn't speak to his son, and has totally disowned his daughter.*

***

"When will we see Grandma again?" asked Robbie. "I love Grandma. Do I have a grandpa?" Tara hugged her little boy tightly. How could she explain to her little three-year-old that he had a grandfather who despised him? Just then she heard the key turn in the door.

"It's Daddy! It's Daddy!" Robbie left his mother's arms and quickly ran to the door, into the arms of the man waiting with the brightest smile on his face. Tara joined the two.

Chapter Twenty-Four

"The birth of Fontana was not without sacrifice and controversy. Almost 70,000 acres of land were taken through the federal government's power of eminent domain to support the project. 1,300 families were relocated—some elderly, some widows with children, and many that had never lived anywhere else. Hundreds of homesites, dozens of small communities, and more than 20 cemeteries were rendered inaccessible or flooded by the new lake."

– Digital Heritage

Cori stood at the backdoor, dreamily mesmerized by the garden spot. *I still remember the first time I saw my Robert. He came into my Papa's store looking like a ragamuffin, telling the strangest tale. Claimed he had just come in on the train, and was looking for a job and a place to bury his kinfolk. Said his family owned a store under a lake. I figured he was touched in the head.*

Then he went on to tell how he owned a store in a town called Judson that was flooded to build a dam. Said the government paid him a little money for his land and even dug up his Ma and Pa so their graves wouldn't be under the new lake. The strangest story I'd ever heard, but I fell in love with him. Shucks, most folks thought I was gonna be an ole maid, but I showed them. My Papa thought he was too old for me, but we worked side by side inside this house, in the store, in the yard, and we just loved watching the vegetables grow.

The weather turned warmer and the topic of the garden spot came up more than once. They mentioned it to Bobby Lee again, and he promised he would plow it as soon as he found time, but he never found the time as far as they were concerned.

One day while watching *The Price is Right*, both ladies gasped in sync at the image on the television.

"THE PLOW!
THE NEW LIGHTWEIGHT TILLER!
WEIGHS ONLY 20 POUNDS! USED BY MILLIONS.
EVEN GRANDMA CAN USE IT!
Found at most hardware stores for the low price of $199!"

And right before their eyes was an elderly lady plowing a garden. Both ladies jumped up at the same time.

"Are you thinking what I'm thinking?" asked Ada.

Cori was already heading for her purse. "I believe I might have $200 left over from my deposit yesterday. I was going to use it to pay my bills. Why, I'll just buy it with this money and pay my bills later."

"Why don't I pay half? After all, we both have been craving that garden for some time."

"Suit yourself. When ya wanna go git it?"

"How about now? They may not have it at the hardware store, so we may have to look around."

Cori and Ada headed to the hardware store, but were sorely disappointed to find that they didn't carry "The Plow."

"Why don't you check over at the S-Mart? They carry just about everything," the clerk said.

Cori's face was even more downcast. "Bobby Lee would have a fit if he knew I purchased something at the S-Mart," she voiced her concerns to Ada.

"I tell you what. I will buy it. He shouldn't have any questions about me making purchases with my own money."

"I reckon that'll be all right."

"Do you want to ride with me? You can wait in the car if you like."

Cori hated to pass up an opportunity to go. She loved more than anything the rides they took in Ada's big fancy car. "I don't see much harm being done with me walking around in a place, long as I don't give them any of my money."

"Well, what are we waiting for?" asked Ada.

Cori never dreamed such a place existed. There was a grocery store, restaurant, a beauty salon, a nail salon, an eyeglass store, a place that sold telephones, plus just about everything else that you needed all under the same roof.

"Lord, have mercy, Jesus! I've never seen such the beat! How in the world did the Sampsons get a place like this? I knew they had money, but I didn't know they had this much! It's no way Bobby Lee can compete with this store," Cori said in astonishment.

She continued to walk down the aisles, as enthralled as a child in the toy store before Christmas. "Heavens to Betsy, there are tires in here, too!"

Finally, they arrived in the gardening section, and were excited to not only find "The Plow," but also other variations of "The Plow." But since they saw the grandma using "The Plow" on TV, they decided to purchase it.

The clerk had to help them load it into the car, because even though it supposedly weighed only 20 pounds, it was in a box nearly as big as Ada's car. Thankfully, the clerk provided twine to secure the trunk door after it refused to close.

The ladies were anxious to try "The Plow," but were exhausted after unloading it from the car. They decided they would set it in the backyard, have lunch, rest awhile, and begin plowing the garden in the afternoon before the youngsters arrived.

After finally getting "The Plow" out of the box, the ladies faced the obstacle of assembling it. Cori was ready to give up in exasperation.

"Remember, the clerk said we would have to do a little assembling," Ada said.

"I guess I was too busy looking around to hear him," replied Cori.

It took the ladies the entire afternoon to get the handlebars in place and just as they finished, they heard the children arriving for their tutoring session.

"Well, that's about all we will be able to do today," said Ada.

Both ladies, although saddened at the thought that their garden spot would have to wait another day, met the girls and headed to the kitchen for snacks. The girls informed them that Bliss and Unique would be late because they went to the cheerleading meeting. That was music to Cori's ears. While Ada tutored the small children, she thought she would venture to the backyard and give "The Plow" a try.

She stepped unnoticed down the back steps and grabbed the shiny handlebars. She pushed the start button again and again, but it didn't make a sound. After quickly scanning the directions, she soon realized the problem.

"Shucks! It needs gas." Cori chuckled to herself. She went around the side of the house, hoping to find the lawn mower gas can. She was ecstatic to find the gas can with enough gas to get the plow going. She examined the plow, searching for a place to put the gas, when Tay, who had been watching the entire scene from his window, appeared.

He grabbed the gas can from Cori, poured the gas into an area that Cori had not seen, placed the gas can on the ground, and walked away without a word. Dumbfounded at what had just transpired, Cori stared at his back, but was excited about the possibility of finally getting to use the tiller.

This time she pushed start and "The Plow" started. It went somewhat faster than Cori had anticipated, and Cori began to weave crazily around her backyard. Tay appeared again, this time rescuing Cori from the runaway tiller. Totally oblivious to Cori, who stood speechless, Tay proceeded to go up and down her garden spot making perfect rows.

After her feet were finally able to move, she robotically walked up the steps to the back porch. Ada stood at the door watching in amazement. The children joined the women as Tay expertly handled the plow, cultivating the now freshly plowed garden.

It was Lizzie who broke the silence. "Dumb ole Tay. That's all he wants to do is farm. He helps my Papa Simon all the time. My parents say nobody's farming now, and tell him to forget about it. But Tay loves working with Papa Simon in the fields and taking care of the animals. Papa Simon says he's a natural born farmer."

Tay continued plowing the garden spot, totally captivated by his new world. Ada grabbed some of the sugar cookies and lemonade, and took them to him just as he finished. He stopped, drank the lemonade, and ate the cookies.

"These are good. They taste like my grandmother's." With that, he walked off and left a mystified Ada holding the plate and glass.

Chapter Twenty-Five

"Family is not an important thing. It's everything."

– Michael J. Fox

It couldn't be ignored anymore. Something was definitely wrong with Uncle Booker. Ma Liz cooked her Sunday dinner as usual, and family members arrived after church for the Sunday dinner and began the weekly ritual of eating until they had to be rolled from the table. Each family member piled their plates with fried chicken, mashed potatoes and gravy, sweet potato soufflé, potato salad, turnip greens, green beans, and macaroni and cheese, and Ma Liz's famous cornbread.

It was Ma Liz who noticed it first.

"What's wrong with you, Booker? You barely touched your food."

"I guess I ate too much homemade ice cream last night. Stomach bothered me all night."

"I told him he needs to go get himself checked," said Tricia. "I think he's lactose intolerant. Everything he eats gives him an upset stomach."

"Yeah, son. I noticed your butt's not filling out yo' pants no more," Papa Simon added.

"Now, one thing the Taylor family is known for is their big butts," Uncle Thur added.

"You got that right," added Harriet. "Never have to worry about any of us Taylors getting butt implants. God gave 'em to us when we were born."

The whole family laughed at that, everybody but Ma Liz. She was studying Booker closer.

"I know one thing. Booker, you never passed up a piece of fried chicken in yo' whole life. I reckon that's 'cause I gave you a drumstick to suck on when you was teething. I 'spect you better call Dr. Grant first thing in the morning."

"Oh, Ma, I am not going to call old Dr. Grant. Shucks, that man probably delivered you. The last time I went to see him, he fell asleep during my check-up. My annual physical is coming up at the Air Force base. If anything's wrong with me, they'll find it."

"Well in the meantime, let me get you a dose of castor oil. That'll sho' nuff flush out what's ailing you."

As Ma Liz began to push away from the table, Booker nearly shouted.

"Naw, Ma Liz, I sure don't want no castor oil. My stomach's already empty. Ain't nothing the castor oil could flush out if it wanted to."

"That's right Ma Liz. He was in and out the bathroom all night," Tricia added.

"I'll be all right. Just some bug going around. Seems like every time I turn on the news there's some new sickness that the medicines can't treat."

"That's cause the medicines just a bunch of mess themselves," Ma Liz began. "Folks fine 'til they go to the doctors and get all them fancy expensive medicines. Now, I remember a time when all you had to do was go out into the field and you'd find something for whatever ailed you. Didn't cost a penny, and you perked up right fast after taking it too. Now of course, there were some sicknesses that even the best roots and herbs couldn't heal. I remember when my Uncle Morris got sick."

Ma Liz's talking ceased as she was summoned to another time and place. The family knew that Uncle Morris was more like a brother than uncle to Ma Liz. She sat in silence, and as she looked at Uncle Booker, the sadness showed in her eyes. She pushed her chair from the table and left for the kitchen.

"Ya'll ready for some lemon meringue pie?"

The family continued eating and enjoying the banter between each other as much as the food. Ma Liz was in the kitchen, leaning on the sink as tears left her face and joined the dish bubbles in the sink.

"Lord Jesus, no. Please, precious Jesus, no," Ma Liz cried softly to herself.

Suddenly, she was at a dinner table fifty years earlier, when someone mentioned that Uncle Morris hadn't touched his food. Her grandmother enticed him with all his favorite dishes. He would take a bite and declared himself full, only to run to the outhouse minutes later. This kept up for about three months as his health continued to decline.

Soon, Ma Liz took her young children and moved in to help her grandmother take care of her Uncle Morris. They spent many hours in the field searching for roots and herbs used in remedies that had been passed down for hundreds of years. Nothing worked, and soon Uncle Morris was a bit more than a skeleton and his skin took on a yellow tone.

There wasn't a doctor around for miles, and the nearest hospital that would take Coloreds was too far away. Ma Liz spent all her waking hours sitting by his bed, telling him old stories and quoting all the scriptures she had memorized. She was in the middle of a story about Uncle Morris taking her grandma's bloomers off the clothesline and running around the backyard with them on his head, when he smiled at her.

He just sat there smiling without blinking. She kept talking to him and he never took his eyes off her, just sat smiling without blinking. She called her grandmother, who ran to the room and let out a spine-chilling wail that told Ma Liz what she didn't want to know. Her Uncle Morris was gone.

Oh, dear merciful and precious Jesus. I know we all gots to leave this here earth one day. You have been so good to me over the years, and I don't have a right to ask you for one more thing. But I got to, Lord. I just got to. My baby's in there and something's wrong with him. I just know it in my soul.

I am pleading to you, Lord Jesus, to let this sickness not be unto death. I don't think I can bear to bury one of my young'uns, Lord. I know you gives us strength that we don't know we have, but I am asking you just like Jesus asked you before he died, please let this cup pass by my Booker.

I know I'm as ornery as an old rooster, and don't deserve to come before your throne, but I am here Lord, and I need you. Now Jesus, I got to go back in there and be strong for my family, when right now all I want to do is curl up in your arms and cry to you to have mercy. So, I am asking you for strength, Jesus. Strength is what I need right now.

"Ma Liz, where's that lemon meringue pie?" shouted Uncle Booker. Ma Liz smiled, trusting that God was already answering her prayer.

***

"How are your relatives out in the country?" asked Ada.

"Everybody's doing fine. We all went to church. It was the Philathea Class anniversary."

"What is the Philathea Class?" asked Summer.

"I don't know. They all dress up in white dresses and sing twenty verses of their song."

Ada laughed at Lizzie's description of the club. "I belonged to the Philathea Class at my church in Detroit. 'Philathea' is a Greek word meaning 'Lover of Truth'. We studied the Bible and taught it to the younger women in the church."

"Well, I don't know about that. All I know is their song has more verses than 'The Twelve Days of Christmas.' After that we went to Ma Liz's for dinner.

"At first, I didn't think we were even going to get a chance to eat. As soon as we sat down at the table, the uncles and aunts started arguing about the election. Half the uncles and aunts are for Hillary Clinton, and the other half are for Barack Obama. They started shouting and screaming, until Ma Liz stomped her one good foot so hard, it shook the plates on the tables.

"*I mean it, not another word about this election in my house! Just don't make a lick of sense. Getting mad at folks you know over folks you don't even know!'*

"The uncles and aunties thought that was about the funniest thing they had ever heard, and after the laughter died down, began eating like they had never seen food before.

"Everybody did except Uncle Booker. He hardly ate anything. Of course, the whole family thinks something is wrong with him since he didn't eat. If someone skips a meal in our family, they are rushed to the hospital. Anyway, Uncle Booker has a doctor's appointment at the Air Force base next week and that calmed everyone, either that or Ma Liz's lemon meringue pie."

Chapter Twenty-Six

Time Out

It was a dream come true for Booker. Even when he was serving in the Air Force, he dreamed of going back to his community and doing something for the young people. Of course, there was the brief moment that he thought about moving to Soul City, North Carolina. He had read about Floyd McKissick's proposed planned community, and thought this would be the perfect place to retire. But after the model city faced numerous setbacks, he stuck with his original plan.

"An idle mind is the devil's workshop" is what Mama always said, thought Booker. *Our minds never had time to get idle because we always had something to do on the farm. But folks aren't farming like they used to, and these kids have the deadly three: time, money, and lack of supervision.*

Most of their parents work either on one of the campuses, or at the Research Triangle. They have good salaries, but the jobs often require long hours, and many of their children spend much of the time without supervision. Then their absentee parents compensate them with fat "allowances" and elaborate sixteenth birthday parties where most of them are presented with a car.

Tricia called it a "Sugar Shack," but Booker was proud of his Rec Center, which he called "Time Out." True, it wasn't much; a simple pre-fab building with a couple of bathrooms and a small kitchen, but his heart nearly burst with pride when he saw the kids dancing on the floor, or sitting in the make shift booths playing checkers. His brothers combined their resources and purchased a pool table, and his dad even chipped in a ping-pong table.

Louis, who had a little concrete business, poured concrete on one side of the building and put up two basketball goals. Grilling was Thur's thing, so during the summer he grilled hot dogs and hamburgers for the young people. They didn't charge an admission, but entry was one canned good, which was taken to the church for their food bank.

With the little profit they made from the snacks and soft drinks, they invested in a couple of video machines and a giant screen television, which was always turned to an ACC game. During March Madness, it was standing room only.

Tricia was totally against it at first, but she even started working the snack bar, and made sure the girls' bodies were completely covered. They kept it open until 11:00 and required all the young people to be in Sunday school and on time. If anyone failed to make it to church on time, they were not allowed admittance the following week. Amazingly, most of the young people were at church the next day.

The church balked at the idea at first, and there were some who wanted Booker off the Deacon's Board for playing heathen music. Some even requested that he ask the church's pardon, as they made the unwed mothers do. It was one of the saddest times of Booker's life. No matter what they said, Booker was steadfast that he was not begging the church's pardon.

"We just don't think it's right for a deacon to run a devil's den," said Deacon Patterson.

Booker tried to remain calm and not focus on Deacon Patterson's DUI that Lena had handled at no charge.

"Young'uns rubbing all up against each other, just fornicating with their clothes on," added Deacon Baldwin.

It took every ounce of control for Booker not mention Deacon Baldwin's son by Sister Saphira. "It's probably good that Daddy made Mama stay at home, although she did put up a fight."

"I know those trifling good-for-nothings are not gonna sit in judgment of my son," she argued. "You is better than all of them, Booker. I know them all. Kaleb Patterson ain't nothing but a drunk, and old Reverend Limberson would have never let him on the Deacon Board.

"I like the old ways when the deacons had to go through a preparation period. Now young Reverend Limberson just gets an inkling, and the next thing you know, there they sit right up in the Amen corner with your God-fearing daddy. And Lord have mercy, everyone knows that ho-mongering Rory Baldwin chased everything with a skirt on. Got young'uns scattered all over North Carolina.

"When he prays, I just close my eyes and think about my Sunday dinner. Now they think they gonna sit in judgment of my son. Not if I got anything to do with it. I'm going to that Deacon's meeting and I'm giving every one of them a piece of my mind. Even young Reverend Limberson."

Booker smiled at the mention of young Reverend Limberson, who was over 60 years old. He was the third Limberson to pastor the church. Old Reverend Limberson pastored even after he was so blind that he preached with the Bible upside down. Folks just sat there saying amen to everything he said.

Old Reverend Limberson's daddy was the first Limberson to preach there. Booker was shocked to see that he was still alive when he retired from the Air Force, and was even more mortified to see that he was still preaching. He literally preached himself to death; dropped dead right there in the pulpit. He said that's the way he wanted to go.

Now I personally think it was not a good idea to get a third Limberson, but I had been gone a while and didn't want to start World War III. Booker felt a little guilty for listening to Charles Stanley before he went to church, but he needed something more than just whooping and hollering.

It's a good thing Daddy put his foot down. Mama's got a pretty big bark, and Lord knows the sun rises and sets with her as far as Daddy is concerned, but he has the last word, and Mama respects his word. Now of course, she stomped her one good leg something awful and called him all kinds of nappy-headed buzzards, but Daddy didn't pay her no mind. It may be a while before he gets any bread pudding though.

Papa Simon usually sat quietly in the meetings, and let the new deacons run the show most of the time. He believed and was often heard saying, "It's time for me to step back and let the younger ones do some leading." The newer deacons didn't have any problem stepping up to the leadership plate, and tried to ignore him most of the time, so they were caught off guard when he announced that he supported the opening of "Time Out," and he even planned to donate a ping-pong table.

He went on to share, "Every day I reads of a young person who has gotten caught selling drugs or is in some kind of trouble with the law. My Booker has always been responsible. When that fellow came by when he was no more than six or seven to start the Cub Scouts, Booker was one of the first to join. But when he saw that they paid their dues every week and all they did was sing 'I love my wiener man, he owns a hot dog stand,' Booker went and asked the man for his money back. Even at that young age, he knew what was right.

"At least we will know where they are and what they are doing. Plus, all of us have been young and had our own ways. Some of them were probably not pleasing to God either. I imagine some of those young folks would be shocked at some of the things we did when we were their ages."

There was dead silence. The vote was unanimous that Booker would stay on the Deacon's Board. Booker was happy, but still somewhat angry at the archaic methods of the church.

Chapter Twenty-Seven

"A mind is a terrible thing to waste."

– United Negro College Fund

Ada could not shake the feeling. She had been feeling this way since the meeting with Principal Eugene. Although she still found it hard to believe, the girls' information was accurate regarding the incentives for good test results. The girls normally arrived for their afternoon homework sessions full of excitement and anxious to share the stories of their elementary school day.

However, this particular spring day was different. As Cori and Ada sat calmly on the faded wicker furniture, surrounded by the budding red geraniums that Cori had recently planted, they knew immediately that something had happened at school. Maria and Jesús walked in pace with Lizzie and Summer as they headed to the ladies' home for their after-school snack.

The End of Course exams were over and the ladies felt their little minds needed a break, so after the snack, they prepared board games for them to play. Ada knew the results of the test were due to arrive this week and each day she paced the floor and prayed that all the children would do well on what she believed in her heart was an unfair educational tool that bordered on mental torture.

Summer and Lizzie were not overly concerned initially, because even though they didn't make the best grades in class, they always scored a four, which was the highest on the test. Little Maria, whose English was getting better and better, had scored a three her first year, but Jesús barely scored a two, and that was not considered passing.

But this year the standards became even more challenging for the children. A four was no longer good enough. The students would have to show that they had improved on the test, or they would not be able to attend the Mardi Gras festival, which the school had planned for students who showed a growth of plus two points in their scores.

This was great news for Jesús, but Lizzie and Summer would practically need to make a perfect score to show growth. Ada initially thought the girls were confused, so she felt it was necessary to talk to the principal herself. Mrs. Eugene was very cordial and had been very supportive of the ladies' assistance with her students, but on this day, the atmosphere was quite different.

"I'm just a little confused," stated Ada. "It seems the girls believe that they have to make a perfect score on the test, or they won't be able to attend the Mardi Gras."

"That is true," stated Mrs. Eugene. "Some of our students are making the same score every year and are not showing any growth. It is important that we show that our students are improving."

"Growth in what?" asked Cori. "It seems to me that a 98 percent is plenty enough growth."

"We simply want to push our children, and want them to use all of their abilities, and we find that once some students reach the four, they don't put forth 100 percent."

"But what about the ones who do put forth 100 percent and still miss one question? Shouldn't they receive some incentive?" asked Ada.

"They will receive an incentive. We will provide a movie and popcorn for them in the classrooms. It's not like they will be punished."

"I reckon if I had to choose between a movie and popcorn in a classroom, or a Mardi Gras with carnival rides, I would choose the rides. What child do you know who would not think they were being punished by having to stay inside?" Cori asked.

Ada kept an eye on Cori's feet. She had noticed in the past that Cori began patting her feet rapidly before "blessing someone out." One foot was beginning to pat.

"All of the students will be receiving incentives. They are just different incentives."

Cori had heard all she cared to hear. "That's about the dumbest thing I have ever heard. Johnny Dumbo, who scored a one last year and scored a two this year, will be out on the football field riding the Ferris wheel, and my girls will have to stay in, eat stale popcorn, and watch a movie that they probably have seen fifty times."

"I am sorry you feel that way. We are all under pressure to achieve high scores, and we do the best that we can. Legally, I should not even be discussing the children's academic progress with you. I do not see your names on their cards, so please excuse me but I have another appointment."

The entire conversation disturbed Ada so much that she tossed and turned, something she had not done very much since moving back down South. She never liked the standardized tests, even when she taught school.

Now schools were rewarding students, and teachers and superintendents received bonuses based on scores. She had even heard that prison systems used third grade reading test scores when projecting the number of beds needed in the next decade. It seemed that nothing mattered anymore except for the scores.

She didn't have to ask the girls how they did on the test. Their dejected faces spoke volumes. As soon as the girls spotted Ada and Cori on the porch, they immediately ran towards them as the tears raced down their faces. They didn't need to say a word. The ladies knew, but the girls couldn't help spilling it out through sobs.

"We both made fours, but we didn't show growth!" the girls cried. "We can't go to the Mardi Gras!" Cori held one and Ada held the other. Maria and Jesús stood silently with tears in their eyes also.

Ada reached out to them and held both the little ones as tight as she could.

Maria said, "I made a three but I didn't show enough growth, so I don't get to go, either."

Jesús jumped in, "I made a two again, but I showed growth. I get to go." But he started crying harder than the other three. "I want Maria and Summer and Lizzie to go, too."

So, Ada and Cori tried to comfort all four children, who were devastated because of a school test, as they wondered what the world was coming to.

Cori was the first to break away. "I got a good mind to go to that school and give each of those teachers and that principal a piece of my mind. Something's got to be done about that foolishness. Lord Jesus, I see why so many young'uns are dropping out of school! I probably would have dropped out too, with that nonsense. Why, I am making me some signs and I am going right down to that school and walk up and down the streets, and let everybody know about this unfair system that is mistreating and abusing our young children."

Ada was about to agree, when she had another thought. "You know what, children, this is not over. We are going to go get your snacks, and we are going to talk to the good Lord. But this is not over."

Cori didn't quite know what Ada had up her sleeve, but she had seen that look before, and she knew that somebody had better watch out.

There was a dour atmosphere over snack time, but even Cori had to admit that the children were good troopers about the entire event. She noticed when Grace's car pulled up into her driveway that Ada immediately headed across the street. The kids were engrossed in a game of Trouble, and didn't even notice that Ada had left. When she returned, she had a pep in her step.

All four of the children looked up when they heard the creaky screen door open.

"I am sorry, but the four of you will have to miss the school movie and popcorn. We are all going to Carowinds!" Ada shouted.

"What!" The children yelled.

"You know Miss Grace is a contact for each of you, Summer and Lizzie, so she just got permission from your parents, and she is taking a day off and is driving all of us in her van down to Carowinds. She contacted your parents too, Maria and Jesús.

Jesús, you earned the Mardi Gras, but your mother said she would leave the decision up to you. We will be stopping at Old Salem and visiting the historic town, so it is also an excused absence because it is an educational trip. So, what do you think about that?"

The children could not hide their excitement. The trip was planned, and to their surprise, there was a caravan of vans heading to Carowinds and Old Salem on the day of the Mardi Gras.

Unknowingly, the ladies started a movement that not only began with the trip to the amusement park, but also led to several parents marching outside the schools with signs protesting the incentive program that punished the high achieving children.

So many parents showed up that the local media covered the event. The principal did not show her face that day, but she was seen on the local news that night, stating that the school would revisit their incentive program.

Chapter Twenty-Eight

A Natural Born Farmer

Tay was a complex young man, too complex for one so young. The anger and disillusionment were attributes that Ada had seen in many of the young men who found a corner and barrel as their only source of pleasure throughout the day. These young men usually came from broken homes, fatherless homes, a parent on social assistance, and lived in government housing.

Tay was quite the opposite. He had both parents who were successful, a beautiful home and security, yet the same self-destructive characteristics of so many of the young men in Detroit haunted him. It was a mystery to Ada. Nevertheless, something drew him to that freshly plowed mound of dirt in the backyard.

The metamorphosis became evident the moment he left his own yard and entered through the rickety, fragile gate. There was a brightness in his eyes and determination in his steps as he approached the soil, touching it with the care of a doctor examining a newborn baby. He said very little to Ada and Cori as they provided the seeds and the small plants for him. He answered them mechanically at first, but as little shoots began to break through the soil and little blooms sprang to life, so did the life in his eyes.

The passion that this young man showed for the earth was astounding, especially for someone so young. He had a natural gift for bonding to the earth that reminded her of the Native American's love for nature. With each day of progress in the garden, the ladies shared in progress with Tay. Ada remembered the words of Lizzie's grandfather, "A natural born farmer."

Tay's parents had even stopped arguing with him about his desire to be a farmer, because he was so much more pleasant since he began working in the garden. Plus, Ada had discussed with his mother the crisis of farmers in America, and how someone with Tay's skills could be very beneficial in the field of agriculture. It was a long way from being a doctor or a lawyer, but it was still a professional degree. His mother accepted this, but secretly harbored the thought that farmers needed lawyers too.

Ada enjoyed the company of the young, aggressive mother. She was as smart as she was beautiful, and seemed to have it all. She was assistant DA, married to an orthopedic surgeon, had two beautiful kids, and was part of a big loving extended family who lived nearby.

True, Ada felt that she neglected her own children at times, but it was evident that she truly did love them and wanted the very best for them. It was also very evident that she loved her extended family very much, even though it was obvious that they had very little in common.

Each week she went to the country to worship at her home church with her family. She shared how she really needed more than what the country preacher offered and there were other churches that met her needs, but there was something about the big family dinner that she missed when she was away. Plus, she wanted her children to have the wonderful memories she had of family Sunday dinner.

She was always warm and friendly with Cori and Ada when they met at the mailbox, and she was extremely thankful for the attention that they gave the children in her absence. She reminded them so many times that it truly does take a village.

Cori balked at that comment since she didn't care too much for Hillary Clinton, but she was glad to be of help too. Lena had only been to their home a couple of times, and then it was to retrieve Lizzie. So, when the doorbell rang, the ladies thought the sound came from the *Family Feud* game on the television.

Ada knew right away that something was wrong. Lena's eyes and face were swollen from crying and as Cori opened the door, she collapsed in Cori's arms, sobbing.

"Child, what is it?" Cori asked. Lena kept right on crying, so Cori just held her limp body until the wrenching ceased.

"I'm so sorry," Lena cried. "I didn't mean to break down like this."

"What in the world is the matter, hon?" asked Cori.

"It's Booker, my oldest brother." Lena was not aware that even though they had never met Booker, they knew exactly who he was. They felt as if they knew the entire family because of Lizzie's detailed accounts of the Sunday dinners.

"The doctors say he has colon cancer. He had surgery this morning and they came out and told us it didn't look good."

With that she began sobbing again. "All seven of us children and Ma Liz and Papa Simon sat in that waiting room for six hours and they came out, huddled us into a room, and said they would begin chemotherapy and radiation, but it was already in stage four." She broke down in sobs, and Cori continued to hold her.

"I haven't told the children yet. I just don't know what to do. Ma Liz just walks around saying, 'Lord, have mercy, Jesus!' Papa Simon, who is the strongest man I know, broke down and cried like a baby. I have never seen him cry. My sister-in-law, Tricia, just fell to the floor and Aretha, his daughter, screamed to the top of her lungs. All the time, Ma Liz just kept saying, 'Lord, have mercy, Jesus!'"

Ada felt hot tears stream down her own face and Cori, whose eyes sparkled with unshed tears, continued to hold Lena.

"I don't know what to do. I just don't know what to do. Booker is more than just my oldest brother. He's like a father to me." She began telling the ladies the story, unaware that they already knew it.

"He was grown and married when I came along, and I am just a couple of months older than his daughter, Aretha. His wife was a city girl and never wanted to move to the country, but he always wanted to return home. After he finished his time in the service, they built a beautiful home beside the family farmhouse.

"He made sure that I went to every dance class, took every piano lesson, and went to every musical and amusement park, right along with Aretha. Sometimes I think Aunt Tricia didn't like it, but Booker didn't care. I just don't want to lose him."

Ada could stand it no more. She moved towards Lena. "We just have to pray. We just have to pray."

"Lord, have mercy, Jesus," she began, sounding just like Ma Liz. "We need you right now. Lena's entire family needs you. They need your strength, they need your love, they need a miracle. They need your peace. Lord, please help them through this valley. Only you can help them right now. Be with Booker. Give him a peace that passes all understanding.

"I know that you know every hair on his head. I know that you know every cell in his body. I know you knitted him together, and now I ask that you would be with this family. Only you can help them right now, Lord. Help them, Lord. Help them, Lord."

Ada didn't say amen, because she knew that this was a prayer that would need to be continued over the next few days. Her prayer had a calming effect on Lena, and for the first time since she came through the door, she was calm.

"Thank you so much Miss Ada. Lord, Miss Cori, I just slobbered all over you. I am so sorry."

"Hush child. Don't you worry none about this ole frock."

"I'm thinking about taking a leave of absence from my job. There's a new young attorney in the office who can handle my cases. He needs to get some practice anyway. I need to be with my family. They have always been there for me. All my sisters and my niece work, and my sister-in-law is going to need some help.

"I can afford to leave my job and I plan to do just that. Ma Liz can help, but her leg is starting to give her more and more trouble the older she gets. She's walking with a cane now. I imagine it won't be long before she will need a walker and then a wheel chair.

"Papa Simon is still a strong man physically, but I don't think he will be able to stand watching his oldest son so sick. He is real tenderhearted. I heard him on the back porch pleading to God to take him instead. That he had lived a full life."

"Whatever decision you make, we pray that God will be with you in it," Cori added.

They heard the screen door open and Grace walked through. The ladies filled Grace in on the situation, and once again they prayed. All four ladies sat around the table, hand in hand, petitioning to an Almighty God for help.

Chapter Twenty-Nine

Give Me a B!

Cheerleading tryouts were to be held the following week, and Bliss and Unique decided they would try out for the squad. Each evening they met in the backyard to practice their cheers, cartwheels, flips, dance moves, and splits. Cori loved helping them and informed them that she was a cheerleader once. She even demonstrated a cheer that she did back in her day.

Unique was a natural, and spent most of the evening helping Bliss perfect the cheers. Cori and Ada felt that both girls were good enough to make the squad, and were looking forward to going to watch them perform. They were surprised to hear that Unique had tried out two previous times and never made it.

"The coach doesn't like me."

"What do you mean, the coach doesn't like you?" asked Cori.

"She doesn't. She hates me," said Unique.

"But surely she doesn't let her opinion of you affect the outcome of the tryouts," Ada said.

"Oh, yes she does!" replied Bliss.

"Don't they have a panel of judges to pick the cheerleaders?" asked Cori.

"No. She handpicks them, and she normally picks her niece and all of her friends," added Unique.

"You have got to be kidding me. Surely she doesn't pick her own niece," said Cori.

"Not only does she pick her, she made her the captain of the squad, and she received the Most Valuable Cheerleader Award," explained Unique.

"It's true," Bliss added." Her niece has been captain both years of the JV squad, and she received the MVC Award both years."

"And the principal allows this?"

"Of course he allows this. It's his brother Bedford's daughter." Cori interjected. "Plus, I told you he was as dumb as a rock."

"I am surprised that parents have not complained," Ada added, somewhat astonished.

"They have, but nothing ever happens. The principal says that the basketball coach picks the basketball players, the football coach picks the football team, and the cheerleader coach should be able to pick the cheerleaders."

"But in the case of the cheerleader advisor being an aunt, common sense would tell you that you need a panel of unbiased judges," Ada stated as a matter of fact.

"You said the magic words, common sense. There is a definite shortage of that in these schools," Cori added.

On the day of the tryouts, the girls met with Cori and Ada and asked them to pray for them. The request nearly brought both the ladies to tears. They watched them heading down the sidewalk, repeating the chants that they had rehearsed so many times over the past few days.

Around 2:30, Cori and Ada began pacing the floor. They unconsciously took turns looking in the direction of the school. The young children came home with their usual din and headed for the after-school snacks. Cori was making another trip to the front porch when Bliss made her appearance at the door. They could not tell from her face if she had made the squad or not, but it was very unusual for her to be alone. Ada held her breath.

Cori could not wait any longer. "Did you make the squad?"

Bliss began crying. "I did, but Unique didn't. I don't want to cheer without her. I can't stand those other girls."

"Where is Unique?" asked Ada.

"She went home. She was so upset, she didn't even want to walk with me, even though I told her I wasn't going to cheer without her. She said something about Mrs. Sampson only picking me to hurt her. I know she didn't mean to hurt my feelings, but it did, and I know she is right. She still hates Unique because she beat her daughter, Ariel, for eighth grade queen. We had a penny drive, and even though Mrs. Sampson gave money to Ariel to put in her own jar, Unique still beat her because all the students love Unique. I don't want to cheer anymore."

"You know what I think?" asked Cori. "I think it's time to make some more signs. Who are some of the other girls who didn't make the squad? I am going to call their parents tonight."

Not only did Cori get the names of girls who didn't make the squad, but the list grew longer and longer. That evening the phone rang off the hook with girls who were in college, but wanted to come back and protest the unfair selection process of the Blessing High cheerleaders. Of course, once again someone tipped off the press, and they were there for the picket.

That evening, the lead story for the news was "90-Year-Old Former Cheerleader Leads Picket Against Unfair Cheerleader Selection Process." Wallace was on the six-o-clock news defending his stupid decision. Bliss decided that she didn't want to cheer for a school with a principal who couldn't make the best decisions for the students.

It was not long before the phone was ringing for other reasons. Ada and Cori were becoming quite the celebrities. There were television, magazine, and newspaper reporters wanting interviews with the ladies. They were modern day Robin Hoods to some, but a pain in the butt to a few. Ada and Cori appreciated the accolades, but refused all offers. They were just doing their civic duty, as far they were concerned. Not everyone thought so.

Chapter Thirty

"North Carolina has the largest population of Montagnards outside of Southeast Asia, estimated at 20,000."

– Center for Asian American Media

The school year was rapidly coming to an end. The young children were anxious to rip and run freely throughout the day, with no hassles or concerns. The older girls were looking forward to their senior year of school, and Tay was concerned about nothing other than the garden that was a beautiful and welcome sight to the ladies.

Thanks to Tay's natural and gifted gardening skills, the garden was full of healthy thriving plants, which would provide more vegetables than the families could possibly use. As the dirt and seeds flourished into a thriving garden, so did Tay transform into a young man with a purpose in life. Even though he was still somewhat reserved, his entire disposition had changed. He even joked with the women as he taught them his gardening techniques.

Ada and Cori were amazed at his knowledge of soil, fertilizer, weeds, the moon, and the sun. He knew exactly what to plant, what plants needed to be planted near each other, which ones needed more space, and when to plant them. He treated each plant as a child, and nurtured the garden with tenderness and love. Both the plants and the elderly ladies were also the recipients of his loving care.

There was a growing hodgepodge of young men who joined him in the back, hoeing weeds or watering the plants, each showing genuine interest in the garden. These were the same guys who Eddie said stayed in trouble at school, yet there was a transformation in the garden.

Cori concluded that every nationality on earth had taken an interest in her garden. Tay, Jabo, and Ray Rock were soon joined by Jesús and Maria's older brother, Juan, plus two new regulars, Musafa and Jarai. Jarai shared in Tay's enthusiasm for farming, which he acquired from generations of Montagnard farmers who settled nearby after the Vietnam War.

Ada was always ready with the homemade sugar cookies that Tay loved. Cori was initially suspicious of the young men, but slowly began to warm up to them, especially after they raved over her homemade lemonade. Some of them had never tasted homemade lemonade, and Cori blushed when they declared it to be the best thing they had ever drunk in their lives. The ladies laughed right along with them when they argued over which alcoholic beverage it rivaled.

But surprisingly, the older boys were serious about the garden as well as the young girls, who constantly searched for weeds, which had been declared the enemy. The teenage girls laughed hysterically at any and everything, as they constantly attempted to get the young men's attention. One of the teenage girls ran and whispered something in Ada's ear, who joined them in the laughter.

It was this scene that Ada's granddaughter, Kenya, found in the backyard. Kenya had driven into town to show her grandmother her new candy apple red Honda Civic that she had received for her sixteenth birthday. She rang the doorbell, and when no one answered, she headed to the garage to see if her grandmother's car was parked inside, when she heard the commotion in the backyard.

Ada was elated to see Kenya, and was surprised at how fast she ran to her granddaughter. She grabbed the young girl, who was perplexed by the weird feelings that she experienced when she saw her grandmother with the young people. Ada introduced her to everyone, forgetting that Kenya went to school with them.

Kenya almost forgot why she was there, but excitedly told her grandmother about her birthday present. All shovels, hoes, and rakes dropped as everyone ran to the front to see the new car. Ada made over the car, even though she thought it was too expensive for someone so young. Of course, the other girls squealed and screamed while the young men eyed it with so much pride, you would have thought it belonged to them.

Kenya insisted on taking her grandmother for a ride, and Ada gladly went along. This was the most attention she had received from Kenya since she had moved from Detroit. The rest of the crew cheered as her granddaughter drove off with Ada smiling beside her. The gardeners headed back to their garden, faces still glowing from the proud moment.

***

Lena took the leave of absence and made the 30-minute journey to the country each day after the children departed for school. She dedicated her days to her family in the country, and timed her return home with her children's return from school. She even joined them for snacks and board games.

There were only a few more weeks left in school. Cori and Ada decided that they would have the children over each day for a couple of hours for lunch and games during the summer. Lena was especially glad to hear this, because she didn't want them under foot while she was trying to help with Booker, who was doing remarkably well. The entire family was optimistic.

Chapter Thirty-One

"Despair is a narcotic. It lulls the mind into indifference."

– Charlie Chaplin

Cori could not put her finger on what was bothering Bobby Lee. He was preoccupied, distant, and at times downright angry. She knew that he was concerned about the store losing business to the S-Mart, but that was old news.

She constantly prayed for Bobby Lee. She especially became concerned when he began missing the morning coffee time. At first, she thought he was uneasy with Ada, but it was more than that. She planned to talk to Eddie about it that Wednesday evening.

The store was all that Bobby Lee had. He felt like the home belonged to Grace, because even though he would die before he let his mama know, Grace's income had made the payments for the past 20 years.

If he lost the store he would not have anything, since Grace had moved into Tara's bedroom years ago. Eddie was caught up in his religion, and his daughter had not spoken to him in six years. Then there was Mama, who worried him to death. It hurt him so much that he could not take care of her and she had to take in a boarder, although he had to admit that the boarder turned out much better than he anticipated.

How did it come to this? I played by the rules, I went to church, I took care of my family, and I worked hard. I paid my taxes, and now I am on the verge of losing everything.

I tried to do the right thing. I gave up my football scholarship to run the store for Mama. How could I leave her after she lost little Tara and Dad a year later?

His hardened face was numb to the tears that trickled down his face. *I thought if I had stayed here, married Gracie, and had children, then maybe some joy would return.*

Gracie…when was the last time he had called her that? It was his own special name for the woman whose smile once caused his heart to stop.

How did it go so wrong? Things were good for a while. The children did bring joy to the family, and the business was going well.

If only people knew. They think since Mama lives in that big home, we own the store on the square, and Grace has a state job, that we are rolling in dough. At least that's what they insinuated when I tried to get money to go back to school.

Mama's home costs a fortune to maintain, and the little that I make at the store barely keeps it open. I guess I should be grateful Mama stood firm about using the properties as collateral, because the way things are now, we would definitely be in foreclosure.

I just couldn't compete with those bigger stores. I tried everything, records, CDs, videos, and each time, a bigger, better, and cheaper business moved right on in and took over. I even continued the lines of credit that Dad had with the Black community, but they went to the better deals and ignored my phone calls about their debt. I see them on Sundays with their new outfits and shiny cars as they drive by me, some not even turning their heads.

When the Mexicans arrived, I offered them the same lines of credit and could depend on their business for a while. Now they have their own stores with their own merchandise and cell phones plans.

I tried to live within the law, and now I have the choice of losing everything or living outside the law. Sure, I won't be selling the drugs, but having the ingredients readily available in the store is just as bad as selling the drugs.

How can I look myself in the mirror and see my father's eyes knowing that I was part of a drug cartel? I just don't know what to do. I don't have anybody to talk to, either. Not Grace, not Mama, not Johnny, and definitely not Opaque, even though she is willing and able.

So yes, I stay angry.

Who wouldn't be?

Chapter Thirty-Two

Reaping What You Don't Sow

Tay truly was an expert farmer, and the garden was proof. Ada and Cori watched the garden with the excitement of little children awaiting the arrival of Santa Claus. As each plant formed and began to resemble the long-awaited vegetables, the ladies made daily visits to the garden.

Tay carefully examined each plant. It was not unusual to see someone other than Tay in the garden, because it had become a community garden. Tay continued to bring his "homies," as he referred to them, to assist him in the tending of the garden. Young men who roamed the streets aimlessly came to life in Cori and Ada's garden.

This confirmed Ada's belief that the school districts made a huge mistake when they dissolved the vocational education track. These young men would flourish in a hands-on vocational education class. But someone, probably someone who had never set foot in a classroom, made the decision that the emphasis needed to be solely on academics, and eliminated the vocational classes. She had witnessed many of the young men fail the academic track and join the large number of high school dropouts in Detroit.

Jabo, Amanna Dove's son, and Ray Rock never missed a day, and there was now a competition forming as to whose plants were the healthiest. Jabo was a handsome young man. Cori said he had the good looks and disposition of his mother. Often tears invaded Ada's eyes as she thought about him finding his poor mama dead in her bed. Even though he seemed to have gotten over the tragic event, Ada was sure something so traumatic was bound to have lingering effects.

Ray Rock was actually Jamison Young. He was the grandson of Mr. Raymond Young, a pillar in the African American community. Apparently, the new trend was to take the name of the grandfather. Ada thought that the young men finally found a trend that was meaningful. Whether they knew it or not, they were paying their grandfathers a great tribute and honor by taking their names.

As the young men pulled worrisome weeds from their respective rows, Ada noticed that the tone of their voices showed more than just the normal friendly banter.

"But you were with me and he didn't do anything to you," said Ray Rock.

"Look, you knew you weren't supposed to be on third hall during lunch, but you went anyway. Don't blame me 'cause you got caught," replied Jabo.

"It's not right that I get suspended and you get in-school suspension and we both were caught on the same hall. Is it Tay?"

"Don't go trying to get me in your mess. I don't know how you do it, Jabo, but you can talk yourself out of anything."

"If you've got it, then you got it. What can I say?"

"It's still not fair."

"As my grandma says, 'Favor ain't fair'," Tay added.

At this comment, Ada felt that she needed to inquire about the situation. Just as she was questioning Ray Rock, Cori joined her in the backyard to hear the disturbing story of his suspension. Apparently, they were hanging out in the bathroom on third hall during lunch.

It was lunch break for fourth hall and they were supposed to stay on the fourth hall, but Jabo forgot his book, and his locker was on the third hall. So, he and Ray Rock went to get it, and stopped to use the bathroom while they were on that hall.

While they were in the bathroom, Mr. Franks, the math teacher, walked in and asked for a hall pass. When they could not produce one, they were escorted to Mr. Sampson's office. Mr. Sampson took Ray Rock in his office first, and according to Ray Rock, did not give him an opportunity to explain anything, but gave him one day of suspension from school.

This suspension would cause him to get a zero on his history test, and his grade would drop to failing. Mr. Sampson then called Jabo into his office, and Jabo came out smiling, stating that he was going to ISS.

"That don't seem fair at all. What did Mr. Sampson say when you asked him why you weren't getting ISS?" asked Cori.

"He told me to get my books and go to class, or he would have me escorted off campus. The man hates my guts."

"I've told you to leave his niece alone," said Tay.

"What?" asked Cori. "You going with Bedford Sampson's girl?"

"I can't help it if the women are crazy 'bout me," said Ray Rock.

"Listen, son. Now I know you young folks don't thank nothing about dating outside your race, but you need to leave that Sampson girl alone."

"To be honest with you, Miss Cori, I don't call her or nothing. She calls me or shows at my house in her new car."

"What did he tell you, Jeroboam?" asked Ada.

"He asked me why I was on the third hall, and I told him that I needed my book, plus I had to use the bathroom. Then he wanted to know why I didn't use the bathroom on fourth hall. I told him that I didn't like to use the bathroom when others were in it.

"He started laughing and told me that I would get ISS. It was sort of weird. I just figured it was because my grandma worked for them a long time ago or something."

Tay interjected, "Jabo does have a way of talking himself out of trouble."

"You need to tell your parents what happened, Ray Rock," Ada stated emphatically.

"My momma can't take off work or she'll lose her job, and my daddy is deployed. He's in the National Guard, and he's been in Afghanistan for nearly a year. She says if I get myself in trouble, I have to get myself out of trouble, because she's not bothering my dad. He has enough on his mind."

"Do you mind if we talk to her? It seems that you two should have gotten the same punishment," said Ada.

"You can try, but she may not talk to you," said Ray Rock.

"Well, it won't hurt to try," Cori added.

Ray Rock gave the ladies his mom's phone number, and Ada quickly made the phone call. Mrs. Young was defensive at first, but soon saw that the ladies only had her son's best interest at heart. She not only agreed to them visiting the school, but also planned to accompany them.

"Now, I'm not saying the boy should not have been punished, but I don't understand why he didn't receive the same punishment," Mrs. Young said to Wallace Sampson.

She wanted to say, "No. I do understand." It took everything she had within her to keep from telling him to keep his trashy niece away from her boy.

"Each case is unique and we treat it as such," Wallace said. "As I recall,

Jamison was very defensive."

"According to Jamison, he didn't have the opportunity to say a word," Mrs. Young said.

"Well, we all know how children lie when they are caught," Wallace said.

"Are you calling my son a liar?" asked Mrs. Young.

"I call it as I see it," Wallace replied.

"How many times has Jamison been suspended?" asked Ada.

Wallace thumbed through his record. "This is his first suspension."

"Has he ever been in ISS?" asked Cori.

"Uh…uh…no," stumbled Wallace.

"Has he ever been in trouble at all?" Cori continued.

"Miss Cori, I don't even know why you are here," Wallace complained.

"Don't you worry about why I am here, just answer the question. Has he ever been in trouble?"

"Well, it says here that he has a problem with authority. That he is always talking back to teachers."

"What is the punishment for that?" asked Cori.

"It depends on the situation."

"Don't you have penalties for certain actions? Shucks, I ain't been to college, but even I know that!" shouted Cori.

"Miss Cori, again, this is between Jamison's mother and me."

"Boy, do you think we would be here with Jamison's mother if she had not asked us to come? You just as dumb as you were when I taught you in Sunday school, and you put a nickel in the offering and wanted five pennies back!"

Wallace's face was past red, it was more of a purple.

"I am going to have to ask you to leave, Miss Cori."

"You can ask all day long and I ain't going nowhere 'til I get good and ready."

Ada knew she needed to say something, and say something really quick.

"According to your handbook, you have a list of infractions, and it says right here that based on what Jamison did, he should have been given a minimum of a school service project or a maximum of one day ISS. Since you have already stated that he doesn't have any serious prior infractions, the suspension seems somewhat excessive."

Wallace's face was so red that it reminded Cori of the apples on the tree that grew in her yard as a child. His voice was shaking, and his Adams apple was a volcano about to erupt.

"If you notice the asterisk, it says that the principal has the right to levy whatever punishment he deems necessary for the violation."

"Then why do you have this here rule book if you get to make the rules yourself?" Cori asked.

"The decision is final. Is there anything else?" asked Wallace as he opened the door.

"Yes, there is something else," Cori said.

"Well, take it up with the school board," Wallace smirked confidently.

"Cori, let's go," said Ada. "We don't want to make things worse for Jamison."

"Well, I never!" shouted Cori.

As the three ladies walked to the car, Mrs. Young began crying. "It just doesn't make any sense. If he is suspended, he will get a zero on the test. He is already struggling in history and this will probably cause him to fail.

"He doesn't need an F on his report card, plus it will break his daddy's heart. If he gets an F, they won't let him run track, and he really is good in track. It's the only thing that he seems to enjoy since his dad left. It just doesn't seem fair. Wallace is just taking it out on our son."

"What do you mean?" asked Cori.

"You see, Ken and I went to school with ole Wallace. Do you remember my husband, Miss Cori? Ken, Eddie, and Wallace and I were all in the same class. Wallace and Ken played football, and every year Wallace was awarded the MVP award just because his uncle was the coach at the time. Everyone knew that Ken should have gotten the award.

"Then Coach Jethro finally retired, and they brought in a new coach who took them to the state championship. Apparently, this coach didn't care anything about the Sampson family or the Sampson name, and that year the award finally went to Ken.

"Wallace was livid, and tried to claim that the coach did something unethical. But the coach simply let the students vote, and he had all the paper ballots. Ken got all the votes except one. At the end of the year, the coach's contract was not renewed, and Wallace has hated Ken's guts ever since.

"And now his slutty niece is running after my boy. That girl is only 16 and already has a reputation. He's probably mad because she wants Jamison to take her to the prom, but I've put my foot down, and he is not taking her."

Cori's disgust was not lost on Ada, and she knew it was more than disgust with the Sampson's.

"It's not fair, and I'm going to do something about it too," Cori said.

Ada was often in awe at how spry Cori was, especially when she was angry.

When Eddie stopped by that night, the women were still on edge about the encounter at the school.

"Yeah. That's his normal response. Take it up with the school board. He knows that the school board is made up of Sampson cronies and they side with Wallace on every case. There was this one time, though, when a CEO at one of the new industries out near the interstate moved here.

"His children were very smart and were very active in school. Soon they were winning competitions, and that didn't sit well with some of the local folks. Outsiders are treated with the same contempt as the poor and the minorities. They were getting ready to suspend their son for some stupid reason, I can't remember what, and the parents challenged them.

"Wallace responded with his same remark about 'taking it to the school board.' These parents consulted a friend of theirs, who was a school board attorney, and he explained school law to them, that if Wallace took it to the school board, they would lose. They would have to take it out of the local school board's hands and file a civil suit in federal court. This would be very costly, but this family had the resources and followed through.

"Of course, the school was willing to work with the family after that, and the suspension was 'suspended'. Sadly, that is the only case that I know of that Wallace lost, and he lost it because the family had resources. The poor children don't stand a chance unless the parents are bold enough to go to the press. They hate bad press more than anything."

That evening, Ada heard Cori on the telephone.

"Hello, is this Channel 3? I want to talk to the folks at the 'Help's On the Way' Segment."

The next week there was a segment on "Help's On the Way" about teachers and administrators who abused their power and authority. Even a national news network picked up the story, and soon Blessing High School was in the national news.

After some investigation, reporters found that punishments were not distrib-uted fairly at Blessing High School and several other schools around the country. There was no method to the distribution of the punishments. African Americans, Hispanics, and poor Whites topped the number of punishments, with African Americans making up 35 percent of the population, but with 95 percent of the punishments.

Most of their punishments were solely at the principal's discretion and did not follow the school code of conduct book at all. The principal was not available for comment, and the school board was forming a committee to examine school discipline. Ada summed it up. In other words, nothing would be done.

Ray Rock arrived that evening with a smile as wide as the Mississippi. His suspension had been changed to one day in ISS. He eyes glistened as he thanked the ladies for their prayers.

Chapter Thirty-Three

"Listen to your elder's advice. Not because they are always right, but because they have more experience of being wrong…"

– Unknown

Cori smiled admirably at her much longed for garden. On one of the many glances to garden, Cori was surprised to see an elderly man with Tay. As she looked closer, she recognized the man as a regular visitor to the Vessey home. Even though she had never officially met him, she assumed he was Tay's grandfather.

The man walked the rows with Tay, nodding with pride at each perfectly plowed row. Cori watched as he pointed at vegetables, paused, studied, and made comments. She could not help but notice the illuminated smile on Tay's face, also. It was hard to believe she was once afraid of such a fine young man.

She didn't even hear Ada's approach, but the sound of the screen door caught her attention. She watched as Ada went and introduced herself to Mr. Taylor. While the two were in the midst of embarrassing Tay with deserved compliments on his gardening skills, Cori decided to venture to the garden too.

The thought that she had lived beside this family for several years and had seen Mr. Taylor many times, but had no desire to meet him, never entered her head. As the ladies continued to shower Tay with praise, they were moved by the boy's adoration for his elderly grandfather.

"Papa Simon taught me everything I know about gardening," Tay added.

"Yeah, as soon as the young'un started walking, he followed me everywhere I went. Most of the grandchildren did, but as they got older they stopped. Not Tay. I don't farm like I used to. The boys have taken over, but Tay hangs right with them, when I can talk Lil Lena into letting him come out to the farm. His mama don't think farming is good for him, but I don't think I've ever met a farmer that's a bad person."

"Come to think of it, I don't either," said Cori.

"And you ought to see him swing a bat. I taught him using a 'bacca stick. I imagine he could play on any of the college teams around here. How's that going?"

"Oh, Papa Simon, they still ask me to play on the team, but I hate that school. I wish I could go to the school out where you live."

"Now buddy, you can't go around hating school. Education is a blessing straight from God. In my day, we would have given our right arm to get an education. Shucks, I went as far as I could in my school, and that was the seventh grade. So, you can't go throwing God's blessing back in his face. You hear what I say?"

"Yes sir, Papa Simon."

"And he also gave you that gift with that baseball bat. You need to think about that gift too. Now, I know your Mama got her ways and those are her ways. She's just like yo' Ma Liz. But what about your ways? Is she keeping you from working this garden?"

"No sir."

"Do you like to play baseball?"

"Yes sir."

"Then what's keeping you from playing? Do ya think ya hurting her by not playing?"

"No sir."

"Then who ya hurting? The coach?"

"A little."

"What's he done to ya?"

"Nothing."

"Well, I spect you don't need to try to hurt him, either."

"Yes sir."

Ada and Cori were amazed at the relationship that this young man had with his elderly grandfather, and the respect he showed for his wise elder was refreshing. It was so rare to hear young people say "yes sir" and "no ma'am."

Grandfather Taylor did not see the need to "wait until the right moment" to discuss these issues with Tay. He did not see the need to "talk to him in private." It was simple to him. These were life lessons, his grandson needed direction, and it was his place to offer it to him.

It was simply beautiful to witness the loving wisdom naturally passed from one generation to another generation. If only society could see the benefit of generational love and wisdom.

***

The girls were more animated than ever when they entered the back porch. The younger ones had completed their homework and were enjoying their cookies when Bliss and Unique rushed in. Fabulous and Neveah soon joined them in the parlor, where they discussed the upcoming prom.

Ada saw Cori's expression each time Bliss mentioned how she wanted to go to the prom with Tay. They were both in their junior year and would be able to attend for the first time. Their excitement was contagious. Each day they poured through magazines looking for the most "awesome and amazing" dress. Ada wondered if they had more than two adjectives in their vocabulary.

"I still haven't found the perfect dress. I spent the entire night looking at gowns on the internet, but none of them are just right," Neveah said.

"I'm wearing the one I wore in my cousin's wedding last year," said Unique. "My mama said I had to get my money's worth out of that dress. It's pretty, though."

"When exactly is the prom?" asked Ada.

"It's in two weeks, right before we get out of school, so we don't have too much time left."

"Do you have dates?" asked Ada.

"Dates? You girls are much too young to go out on dates," interjected Cori.

"Oh, Miss Cori, you are so funny," said Neveah.

Cori looked perplexed. She didn't see what was so funny about what she said. Bliss continued giggling at what she apparently thought was a joke.

Unique and Fabulous joined in with the giggles, and Cori and Ada both realized at the same time, that there was more to the story.

"Bliss still wants to go with Tay," said Summer.

Lizzie interrupted, "You want to go with my dumb ole brother? You really must be desperate."

Both teenagers began giggling again.

Unique began, "Bliss thinks Tay is so hot."

Ada looked at Cori and saw the same expression she witnessed when Ray Rock's mother mentioned the Sampson girl wanting to go to the prom with him.

"What?" asked Cori. "Okay. I just don't see why you can't find someone from your own race. Now I said it."

All the girls began laughing again. "Miss Cori, you are so 1950s. But we love you."

Ada joined in the laughter too at that last response. It was refreshing to see how simple things were for young people.

Cori looked at the magazines with the girls.

"Why, these are just rags!" said Cori. "You gonna look like a floozy, sho' nuff, if you wear that trashy mess."

"Oh, Miss Cori…you crack me up! This is the style now," Fabulous said.

"Style, my foot. If you wear that trashy mess, you're just asking for trouble."

The girls burst out laughing, and Bliss stomped in disgust.

"No stomping in my house young lady," Cori said. She was still trying to figure out what was so funny, when she heard a chime or a ring.

"Is that you, Unique?" asked Neveah.

"No girl, you know that is not my ringtone."

"Is that you, Miss Cori?" asked Sinclair.

"No, I don't ring."

"Oh my gosh, it's me!" Bliss said. "I just changed my ringtone and forgot I changed it. Let me take this."

Bliss exited to Cori's living room, and the group was startled by a scream. Ada, Cori, and the younger girls ran to the living room.

"I found it! I found my dress!" shouted Bliss.

Mystified, the ladies looked around for the dress, and were confused as to what Bliss was talking about.

"This is it! The dress I've been dreaming about," Bliss continued ecstatically.

Then they realized that Bliss was looking at the wedding photo of Cori and her Robert. The dress was beautiful. It was white lace that fitted the waist snuggly with a slight flare at the bottom. The lace stopped right above the bosom, which consisted of white sheer.

"This is it! Where did you buy it, Miss Cori?" asked Bliss.

"I didn't buy it. I made it myself for my wedding."

"Do you still have it?" asked Bliss.

"I do." Cori paused. "I hoped my daughter would wear it in her wedding." Ada saw the familiar sadness overshadow Cori's face.

Bliss continued, totally oblivious to the pain Cori was experiencing.

"I will buy it from you. How much do you want for it?"

"It's not for sale," Cori repeated defiantly.

Bliss, totally ignoring Cori, began dialing her little phone, screaming once again about the dress into the phone and muttering something about vintage. She looked at Cori and said, "Grandmother said she will pay you $500 for the dress."

Cori, although shocked beyond words, stood firmly, "I told you it's not for sale."

"Grandmother!!!!" shouted Bliss. "She said she will pay $1,000 for it."

As tempting as it was, five months ago she would have sold just about anything for $1,000, but she simply could not part with the dress.

"Listen, child, I told you it's not for sale, but if you want to wear it that bad, I will let you borrow it, but you have to be very careful. The lace is nearly 100 years old, and the dress is very fragile."

With that, she dropped the phone, and ran to Cori, nearly knocking her down with a hug.

"All right now, calm down child. It's no need to get so tizzied up. Come by tomorrow evening and I will have it down for you."

Suddenly remembering her phone, she ran back and picked it up.

"Grandmother did you hear? She's letting me borrow it. Wait 'til you see it. It is the most beautiful dress I've ever seen."

That night Cori stood staring at the picture. She thought the same thing when she finished it. She looked forward to seeing it on the young girl.

The next day right on time, she heard the girls. It sounded like a hundred people, but it was only Bliss, Unique, Fabulous, Neveah, Calamari, Casey, and the younger girls. Cori's excitement matched the girls' as she unpacked the dress from layers of tissue paper, inspecting it for any signs of moths or defects.

She expected it to have faded after so many years, but she was surprised at the quality of the dress. It wasn't as white as it was on the day she wore it, but overall it was in pretty good shape.

"May I try it on?" asked Bliss.

"Don't you want me to have it cleaned first? It's been packed up for nearly a hundred years."

"I don't care; I'm just dying to try it on."

"Well, be careful. It's pretty darn fragile."

"Use my room," Ada said, joining in on the excitement. "I'll help."

They made the short steps to Ada's quarters. Cori tried to hide her excitement, but it rivaled the younger girls. Within minutes, Ada stepped out. "The moment we've all been waiting for!"

More squeals. Even the younger ones joined in. Bliss did look pretty in the "vintage" gown. The dress wouldn't need many alterations. It was nearly a perfect fit, except Cori was taller than Bliss when she was younger. She had shrunk some, but not as much as Cathleen Corbett, who was stooped over a foot. The girl's beautiful complexion accentuated the color of the lace, and her dark hair made the dress even more elegant.

She pranced and danced around the room, only stopping long enough to catch a glance of herself in the hall mirror. Smiling, she began to tuck the top under, revealing the top of her cleavage.

"Oh no you don't," Summer began. "You can't sho your bosom before three o'clock!" she added, mimicking Mammy on Gone with the Wind.

"Stop it, Summer!" said Bliss. "Just wait until Tay sees me in this."

Lizzie joined Summer.

"I ain't seen Mr. Tay as'ing to marry ya!" Lizzie joined in the Mammy imitation.

With that, both girls fell on the sofa, laughing hysterically. Ada and Cori tried to contain themselves, but joined the younger girls. Bliss even found the two girls' annoying imitations somewhat funny.

"Laugh all you want, Tay is going to love this dress."

"He hasn't even asked you," Unique said.

"I don't care; I'm going to ask him."

"I still don't know why you want to go with that idiot," said Lizzie.

Cori knew it was no use mentioning her thoughts again about their race differences. It was obvious that it wasn't an issue to them, but she couldn't contain herself.

"I just don't understand why people choose to date outside their races. There are some folks in this town who still don't take lightly to interracial dating, and they can make life very hard."

Ada surprisingly nodded in agreement.

"I don't see why you can't go with your own kind," asked Cori.

"Oh, Miss Cori, you could have been in that gray movie about the mockingbird," Bliss added.

"I might be 1950s, but I know you are just asking for trouble. Folks round here might pretend like they've changed, but they haven't."

Unique entered the conversation. "I hear you Miss Cori. I'm going to stick with my own race. All my life I've heard 'marry someone like you.' Plus, I could never see myself dating a white boy, too many fine brothers walking around here."

Fabulous nodded in agreement with Calamari then added, "However…I would date Mark Wahlberg any day."

"Oh my gosh! Mark Wahlberg! Now that is one white dude I would date in a heartbeat!" added Unique. All five girls screamed in union.

Ada and Cori gave each other a puzzling look.

"Now, not crazy psycho stalker Mark Walberg in *Fear*. I'm talking about hot Bobby Mercer in *Four Brothers*!"

Another shrill from the girls.

Fabulous continued, "Oh my God! When Bobby Mercer comes swaggering across frozen Lake Saint Clair, shoots Victor Sweet, and dumps him in the fishing hole in the middle of the lake, I thought I would pass out. That's the Mark Walberg I'm talking about."

Another shrill.

Ada and Cori sat there wide-eyed with their mouths hanging open.

"Did they just get excited about a murder?" Cori wondered.

That evening, as the ladies were getting ready to head for bed, there was a knock on the door. It was Bliss.

"Well, I did it. I asked Tay to take me to the prom. He said he didn't plan on going but I got him to change his mind. Then he came back and said that his mom thought he was too young to date, and thought it would be good if we went as a group.

"So now his mom is renting a party bus that is taking Unique, Ray Rock, Jabo, Juan, Musafa, Fabulous, Neveah, Casey, Calamari, and me to the prom. We will all go to dinner first at the new restaurant out near the highway and then to the prom. Unique is ecstatic, so I guess it's cool."

When Bliss left, Ada smiled at Cori. "I guess your prayers are answered."

To which Cori responded, "I guess *our* prayers are answered."

Chapter Thirty-Four

"Sometimes you will never know the true value of a moment until it becomes a memory."

– Dr. Seuss

Cori and Ada were exhausted after the children left for the prom. Stern, emotionless Cori began to cry when she saw Bliss in the dress that she wore in her wedding to her precious Robert. Silently, she prayed the girl would be careful.

She had just finished going over her Sunday school lesson when she was startled by a commotion. When she arrived at the bottom of the stairs, she met Ada, who was heading to the front door.

"Don't open it!" Cori whispered.

"I'm not. I was just trying to see what was going on."

Cori headed to the picture window and peeked through the side of the curtains.

There was the entire prom party, exiting the party bus.

"My word!" Cori began. "Surely, the prom ain't over already."

Ada started unlashing one of the three lashes on the front door when the knock on the backdoor caught their attention.

It was Lizzie dressed in her pajamas and nearly out of breath.

"They're back! Tay called from the Prom! They got kicked out! Well, actually, Ray Rock got kicked out, but the rest of them left too!"

"What happened?" Ada asked as Summer, who was sleeping over with Lizzie, crashed through the backdoor, still in her pajamas too.

"They were all on the floor dancing in a big group," Lizzie began out of breath, "and the principal wanted them to dance the old-fashioned way, one boy and one girl. So, he kept trying to break up the group.

"Then the DJ started playing Bow Wow's 'Bow Wow.' Ray Rock got down on the floor and started dancing like a dog on all fours. He then danced over to Principal Sampson and lifted up one leg like a dog and pretended to pee on Principal Sampson's shoe. That was it. He threw him out. So, everyone left with him. Not everyone, but just about!"

"So, when Tay called Mama, who was about to crack her side laughing, she told them to come home and they could have a party here. She told me to come tell you and Miss Cori not to call the police if they get a little too loud. Miss Grace is on her way over to help."

With that, both girls ran down the steps headed to the prom sequel, totally oblivious to the fact that they still had on their pajamas.

"I don't know why she thought I'd call the cops," Cori said turning to Ada, who had disappeared.

"What you say?" Ada shouted from her room.

"What are you doing?" Cori asked.

"Well, you know Lena is going to need more chaperones!"

"Wait for me!"

Once again, Ada was astounded at the speed and agility of this 92-year-old woman.

It was just as Ada imagined. She was energized as she witnessed the young people, of all shapes, sizes, and colors, enjoy their house prom as if they had never been kicked out of the official one. She couldn't help sniggling as Lena danced in and between the teens, who were content to dance as close as possible.

Cori had to admit to herself that she was a little shocked at the different races getting along as if they were the same color. But laughter interrupted her confusion as they reminded her of the apples bobbing in a tin tub.

Then a song came on and they instantly broke apart and began doing the same steps in sync. Lizzie, Summer, Lena, and even Leigh joined in.

Ada could contain herself no longer. Those arthritic legs were soon in sync with the rest of the folks.

Both Cori and Grace's mouths fell open, but not for long. Lizzie and Summer ran and grabbed Cori's hands and dragged them to the floor.

Cori, being the quick learner, was soon in step with the other ones, and the young people cleared the floor, leaving just Cori and Ada, while shouting "Go grannies!"

Around 2:00 in the morning, the ladies finally lay down with identical smiles and identical thoughts running through their heads: they hoped they would be able to move the next day.

Chapter Thirty-Five

"'For the first time in decades, it's a wide-open race,' says Tim Storey, senior fellow at the National Conference of State Legislatures. 'Both parties have many legitimate candidates, and there is no incumbent candidate, so the primaries really count.' When you cast your vote for one of the candidates in your chosen party, you are participating in a winnowing process—from up to dozens of candidates down to one Democratic candidate and one Republican candidate—that will determine our future President, arguably the most powerful leader in the world."

– Lindsey Palmer

Although exhausted, Ada made it to her church on time. She could not believe how much she enjoyed the Blessing AME church. She had visited her son's church, and thought the folks were a little pretentious. She even visited Cori's church. The congregation was extremely kind, and nearly everyone invited her to come back. She wasn't surprised, as this had happened to her and Mr. Passmore on numerous occasions.

When he was appointed to a leadership position in the city, they often visited the churches in his district. They were always extended an invitation to return, and cameras were constantly snapping. She and Mr. Passmore surmised that they graced the halls of many White churches that lauded their progressiveness and diversity.

She was still ashamed of her arrogance in thinking that the Blessing AME church would be less satisfying since it was in the South and the pastor did not have an advanced degree. She was reminded of the scriptures that warned against *thinking more highly of yourself than others*, and was once again reminded of her own clay feet that slipped and slid into sin so easily.

She enjoyed this time of the day on Sundays. Cori arrived home first because her church started on time, ended on time, and lasted the customary one hour.

Since Cori taught Sunday school, she was drained after both Sunday school and church and looked forward to the time of rest after church. She knew Cori would probably need additional rest after chaperoning the prom party.

Ada used this time for meditation on the message; plus, she wanted to be well rested when the girls came over for their visit. They would probably be late this evening because Lizzie's church was having another special service that Lizzie dreaded. Her church had numerous programs and anniversaries that the entire family always supported.

Before integration, the church was the source of the social life in the African American communities. Many churches continued the traditions, but Ada preferred churches that focused on social justice and community outreach. Plus, she detested how too often tradition trumped scripture.

This was also her prayer time for her children. Many mornings, she awoke to a tear-stained pillow. Her tears often lured her to sleep as she pondered over some of the choices her children had made. She tried to console herself with the fact that all her children were law-abiding citizens, which was a blessing, but how she longed for them to walk with the Lord and have a personal relationship with Him.

She wondered if she and Damaris would ever have a loving mother-daughter relationship. The day she slapped her was one of the lowest in her life. Oh, she had spanked her kids on numerous occasions, but this was different, and that slap not only bruised Damaris' face, but left a permanent scar on their relationship.

The visits were short and tense, and no matter what Ada said, Damaris interpreted it another way and the visit ended just as it began. This appeared to be a common trait with this generation. Reality was simply what was perceived by that individual, even when the evidence of truth was lacking.

Her mind flashed back to her recent birthday celebration at Denise and Frederick's home. She was surprised that Damaris attended the party since she no longer spoke to Frederick, whom she considered a sell out to his race. As exciting as it was to have a woman and an African American vying for the Democratic Nomination, Ada thought the 2008 election would permanently destroy her family.

Frederick, of course, was firmly for John McCain, while Damaris and Martin for once were on the same side and were staunch supporters of the young Barack

Obama. The political debate got so heated that Ada thought the three children would come to blows.

"How you could give a thought to supporting John McCain or any Republican is a mystery to me. But I should not be surprised," stated Damaris emphatically.

"Barack doesn't have enough experience. After all, he hasn't even completed his first term in the Senate," said Frederick.

"And John McCain is as old as Methusala. Yet, you have no problem voting for him just because he is a Republican," Damaris replied.

"I'm surprised that a feminist like you isn't supporting Hillary." Frederick added.

"I've had enough of the Clintons. Eight years should be enough for anybody," replied Damaris. "They hate losing. She knows she will never get the nomination, but she refuses to surrender. Just plain power hungry."

"That's why we need someone with fresh ideas who wants to take this country in another direction," added Martin.

"Yeah, we just had eight years of hell under your guy, Frederick," Damaris added.

"Can we please change the subject?" Ada asked, the conversation completely draining her of energy.

"What you think, Mom? Which Democrat are you supporting?" asked Frederick.

Ada knew a trap when she saw one, and she was not about to fall into this one. She recognized the cynical sarcasm from her oldest son and refused to take his bait.

"Who I vote for is my business. I will pray as I always do, and I will vote for whom I believe God wants me to vote for."

"Oh God, not another sermon," Damaris began. "Will someone please tell me what God has to do with the 2008 election? It was our 'Christian' president who lied about weapons of mass destruction and sent our young men to die in Afghanistan and Iraq."

Frederick jumped in, "The Democrats are completely void of values, simply use the African American race for votes, and totally discard them after the elections. They claim they care so much about African Americans but put policies in place that rewarded families with welfare checks only if the father wasn't in the home. Your party glorified the broken homes. Don't even mention their hand in mass incarceration and for-profit prisons!"

"What have the Republicans done for African Americans except stick tokens like you in key positions to say that they are diverse?" asked Martin.

"And don't even talk about welfare," Damaris added. "Your man Reagan preached about a Welfare Queen and conveniently neglected the fact that the Welfare Queen that he was referring to was White. Plus, let's not forget about the greed of big business and all the corporate welfare!"

Ada knew where this discussion was going, and before she wound up in the middle of another heated battle between her children, she simply got up from her seat, picked up her purse, got in her car, and drove off with the unlit green and yellow "7" and "9" still on the birthday cake.

As she drove up in the driveway of Cori's home, her three children stopped arguing long enough to notice that she was gone.

She didn't try to control the tears as she replayed the event in her head, and once again she knelt on her arthritic knees in prayer for her splintered and divisive family. The heart-wrenched prayer left her emotionally drained as she lay across the bed.

Lord, I will be so glad when this election is over. It is tearing my family even further apart. And to be honest, I couldn't answer Frederick's question if I wanted to.

I thought I'd never live to see the day when this country would elect a Black president, and I must admit he is inspiring and is smart as a whip.

But Lord, I just don't know if the country is ready. I know a lot of people like him, but Cori is right. There are some people who say one thing, but deep down they believe another.

Ada smiled as she reminisced about her Mr. Passmore.

He was so proud when they made him principal, and everyone knew it was well deserved, but poor Frederick just couldn't win. The Blacks thought he wasn't Black enough. He was stuck up...tried to act white...talked 'proper'...thought he was better than the rest.

And then there were the Whites. I guess it was our first real lesson about the paradoxical desires of White people.

A pained, worrisome demeanor replaced her brief proud loud.

Oh, they smiled and gave numerous verbal accolades about his scholarly attributes and exceptional leadership skills, but no matter what he did, it was not good enough.

High academic achievements, state competition victories, superior building maintenance, outstanding school climate, superior safety records, exceptional parental support…all received, "That's good" when White principals received 'Principal of the Year'. He always had to run faster and jump higher, only to stay in the same place.

But the most painful part was the very people who we thought were our closest friends; our biggest supporters provided our greatest challenges. Misty and Andy Barkley were hired the same time as Frederick and I were hired. We babysat for each other, our children had sleepovers, and we thought this was a real example of what life could be like in America. But all that changed when Frederick was made principal. Every decision Frederick made was met with skepticism, and criticism replaced camaraderie.

So, what would happen if a Black man got the biggest prize of all, the White House? Would that be too much for White people? Would they turn against him too? What would it do to this country, which is already too divided? Would the vile divisive tentacles of jealousy and envy stretch from the pits of hell? No, Lord, I just don't think we are ready. But if not now, when?

She tossed and turned as she usually did on Sunday afternoons, which were still the hardest for her. It was their time. Even when the children were home, they found things to do in their rooms, and she and her Mr. Passmore usually relaxed, reading the Sunday paper or working the crossword puzzle together.

But long before she even met her Mr. Passmore, Sundays were special to her. Her sister and her Mother Damaris worked on jigsaw puzzles or made homemade ice cream, which they shared with all the other little children. Her eyes glistened once again as she thought of her sister Vivian and Mother Damaris.

Mother Damaris was a good cook, but Vivian had been their mama's helper and would tell Mother Damaris little tips to make her food taste even better. Vivian loved cooking and Mother Damaris was amazed at how much the young girl knew about cooking and baking.

She deserved so much better.

Ada quietly sobbed into her pillow.

How long had it been? 60, 65 years. It still seemed like yesterday. So many losses. Vivian, Mother Damaris, Miss Steepleton, and her Mr. Passmore.

They say time heals. She guessed she needed some more time.

Chapter Thirty-Six

"The 1960 Greensboro sit-ins sparked a national movement but were not the first such action. A protest in 1957 in Durham had wider consequence, as it led to a court case testing the legality of segregated facilities. The Royal Ice Cream Company had a doorway on the Dowd Street side with a 'White Only' sign and, on Roxboro Street, a sign marked 'Colored Only.' A partition separated the two sections inside the building. On June 23, 1957, Rev. Douglas Moore, pastor of Asbury Temple Methodist Church, and six others assembled at the church to plan the protest. The young African Americans moved over to Royal Ice Cream and took up booths. When they refused to budge, the manager called the police who charged them with trespassing."

– Dennis Daniels

She and Cori awoke from their afternoon naps feeling as tired as they did when they lay down. Cori could not put her finger on it, but church seemed to drain her recently. Johnny always had good sermons, but lately the sermons sounded more like a political rally.

She was so tired of hearing about voting and the upcoming elections, and she would be glad when the whole thing was over. Plus, instead of feeling rejuvenated as worship had done for her in the past, she left church feeling angry about something.

Today Johnny informed the church of more details of the Muslim who was running for President. She just could not believe that her country would be this close to electing a Colored man, and a Muslim Colored man on top of that. Johnny was passionate about it, and rightly so, but he was downright angry about it this day.

You couldn't blame him. When they put that Muslim's preacher cussing up a storm right there in his own pulpit on that giant TV, I got chills right to my bone. And Johnny was right. You can't listen to evil that long, I believe they said 20 years, and it not set in your mind. Lord, have mercy, Jesus!

Scared po' Geneva Albright so bad, they had to rush her out. What in the world has become of our good God-fearing country? Everybody's on edge, and angry, and such. Lord, I sho hope we ain't headed back to those dark days.

Cori was old enough to remember many, many dark days, but some were much darker than others.

Some of her earliest memories were of her parents talking in hushed tones of how soldiers once walked up and down the streets in some cities in the state to keep folks from killing each other.

They heard stories of how things had had gotten so bad somewhere on the coast that about 100 folks had been killed. Then a family was killed in Salisbury and there were more lynchings. So, Governor Glenn sent soldiers to keep an eye on things. The grown-ups were always talking in hush-hush tones and Papa bought extra bullets and had rifles in every room.

Even after Cori was older, her folks still referred to the hottest December on record, and they sho won't talking about the weather. Eventually Cori learned what caused all the tension.

Apparently, a White woman was raped by a Colored man, and when the Colored man was put in jail, the governor had him released. This really riled folks up and no sooner than you could blink your eye, the most God-awful thing happened.

A little five-year-old was raped by another Colored fellow. Well, this was the last straw. Good Christian folks had had enough. When they took that Colored man to court, some good Christian folks led by the president of the college over in Burlington decided to take matters in their own hands. They found that sorry rascal and took him in.

Some others decided they were done trusting the justice system. They stormed that courtroom and that Negro was killed dead as a nail. They were mad enough to kill the governor himself. Things eventually calmed down, but not for long. That poor Colored family was murdered over in Caswell County and things got real tense again.

Cori shook her head slowly.

By this time the Coloreds' good friend, Governor Bickett, had left office and died of a stroke, so not too much happened. Colored folks were plenty angry, but the soldiers didn't come in and take over the town, after all it was a Colored family.

I guess things were back to normal after a while. There was a preacher and some college students over in Durham who thought they could just walk in an ice cream store and get a cone of ice cream. They knew they were not supposed to sit down, but they did anyway. Not much came of it, then those fellows wouldn't get up from that lunch counter in Woolworth and folks started going crazy all over.

Her face turned an ashen gray as her mind scurried back to a time she prayed many nights to forget. She felt the tears swell up in her eyes as they always did when she thought of that time.

Robert Edward was as kind a person as he could be, and he thought the sun rose and set on little Tara's head. Lord, we thought for so long that Bobby Lee would be our only child and then we had little Tara. She was the sweetest child on this earth…a pure angel if I'd ever seen one. Tears began to roll down her face.

Never once complained, no matter how much she suffered, and Lord I never will understand how you could let such a sweet child suffer so. When she was born, I looked at that baby and God forgive me, but I knew I had never seen such a beautiful baby. After she got so sick and we were told she wouldn't live, some of the old folks said she was too beautiful for this ugly old world.

Robert Edward was always making her something…a dollhouse, a little table and chair set, a little desk. When she'd cough so hard it looked like her little lungs were coming out, he would hold her so tight I thought he would squeeze her already strained little breaths right out of her. What was it called? Cystic Fibrosis or something. How many trips did we make to the Chapel Hill hospital or to the Duke hospital? We had just decided to try that new Danny Thomas hospital that had just opened, when the whole world seemed to fall apart.

It seemed after those boys refused to get up from the lunch counter in Greensboro, folks just started plopping their butts everywhere, refusing to move. Now Robert always treated the Colored the same as the Whites, so he didn't have anybody plopping down in his store. So, he was just as surprised to have a cross painted on the store door. Apparently, folks wanted him to stop selling to the Colored. Of course, he wouldn't hear of it. I was busy taking care of little Tara and didn't have time to fool with no crazy crackers. I just let Robert handle it.

She closed her eyes tightly, willing the memory back to a place of forgetfulness.

That night we were busy packing for the trip to the Danny Thomas hospital, when a rock came crashing through my picture window. It nearly gave me a heart attack, but that won't the worst of it. Those Ku Kluxers were out in front of the house, dressed from head to toe in their robes, and they had the nerve to light a cross right in our front yard.

I ran to get the shotgun, but Robert stopped me, telling me they had made their point and don't make things worse. He urged me to go back to Tara, and just as I approached her door, I heard her scream. The burning cross was nothing compared to what waited for me.

Little Tara apparently tried to see what had happened and had gotten out of her little bed and gone to the window. She lay on the floor beneath the window, covered in her own blood. I picked her up and rushed down the stairs. Robert nearly passed out at the sight of his little angel fighting for her life. We barely made it out to highway 70 when I knew she was gone.

Robert was driving like a maniac and I was more afraid of telling him that she was with the angels than I was of those Ku Kluxers. I kept talking to Tara because I believed in my heart that he would drive that car over a cliff if he knew she was dead.

When we arrived at the Alamance hospital, the hospital folks took her, and Robert and I just prayed for a miracle. The doctors had warned us that she would probably drown on her own blood, but we just could not give up on our precious little girl.

It wasn't long before the doctor came out and told us what I already knew. Poor Robert Edward just collapsed on the floor, sobbing. I didn't know what to do. I was so angry that I prayed to God that the Ku Kluxers would return so I could blow every one of their heads off.

What did Tara do to deserve such a tortured life and awful death? What did she do to the Ku Kluxers? I was even mad at the four students who sat at the lunch counter, because as far as I was concerned, they started the whole mess.

I know my Robert loved Bobby Lee and me, but he adored his little Tara. It won't a year before I found him in the basement. He started going down there every day after we lost Tara. I would hear him down there just a bawling. One day I noticed how quiet it was and went to check on him, and he sat there with the most beautiful smile on his face. He hadn't smiled like that since Tara was with us. I guess he just decided to join her.

Cori wiped the tears with her apron.

Life didn't mean a thing to me after that. I didn't care about a soul except for Bobby Lee and his young'uns and to be honest, sometimes I didn't care about them either. I used to help and volunteer in the community, but the community could all go to hell as far as I was concerned.

Just when it seemed like things were getting somewhat better, folks started going plain crazy, talking about integrating the neighborhoods and schools and everything. I trusted President Johnson, but I never thought he would turn his back on good God-fearing White folks and sign that Civil Rights Act. I swore I would never vote for another Democrat after that.

Now they got that Muslim running and some folks think he just might win. I know the world is coming to an end. I wish I could talk to Ada about it. She's pretty level headed, but I know she's a Democrat even if she never says it. Plus, I couldn't help but hear that nutty daughter of hers singing the praises of that Muslim. She looks at me as if she wants to spit on me.

I imagine that trifling, lazy son is gone vote for him too. I don't know about that uppity one who lives out there in the Country Club. He claims he's a Republican, but I know some of the Colored who claims they are Republican will still vote for that Bama because he black. That's the way they think.

***

Ada tossed and turned in her bed.

You would think church would put you in a good mood, but Cori seems to have a chip on her shoulder every Sunday when she gets home from church. I don't know for sure, but I believe it's the things Johnny preaches at that church.

That column in the newspaper is so right-winged and so full of hate, it gives me chills. He even stopped speaking to his own daughter, who said she was voting for Barack. I heard he said that anyone who is a registered Democrat will be asked to leave the church.

Even Bobby Lee challenged him on that. Who would have thought that Bobby Lee would be the voice of reason? I just may lie in here the rest of the evening because I don't have the energy to deal with Cori's sharp abrupt responses today.

Just then she heard a knock at the door. *Who could that be? It's too early for the girls.*

The knock startled Cori, who was tossing and turning over the morning's sermon. She rarely got visitors on Sundays unless Ada's kooky kids stopped by. But they had visited the previous Sunday, so it wasn't like them to visit two Sundays in a row. She quickly pinned her hair in the back of her head and arrived at the door just in time to see Ada peeking through the blinds.

"She looks familiar, but I don't know who it is." Cori joined her at the opening in the blinds and gasped.

Chapter Thirty-Seven

"If I had known about grandchildren, I would have had them first."

– Unknown

"Are you going to let us in, or are you just gonna let us stand on the porch, Grandma?"

Cori continued to stand frozen in her spot, when Ada decided to take matters into her own hand. She opened the door and just as the door unlatched, a little boy quickly ran past her and grabbed Cori's leg.

"Grandmatoo! Grandmatoo!" Ada looked down at the golden little boy with thick, black wavy hair and the bluest eyes, thinking it had to be one of the prettiest children she had even seen. Ada saw Cori struggle to contain her composure, but each cry of "Grandmatoo" chipped away at the elderly ice statue.

Cori looked down into the sky-blue eyes of the little boy and saw the eyes of her precious Robert Edward. The tears poured down her face as she knelt down with the little boy jumping into her arms yelling, "I give you a big hug Grandmatoo! Mommy! I give Grandmatoo a big hug!"

As Ada watched the adorable great grandson nearly squeeze the life out of her housemate, the young woman finally spoke through her own tears.

"Hi, I'm Tara. You must be Miss Ada. Mama told me all about you."

"Yes, I am Ada, and you must be Bobby Lee and Grace's daughter, Tara. It is so good to meet you."

"Yes, I am their daughter, and this is Robbie, their grandson. He's been dying to see his two Grandmas. We pray for both the Grandmas every night, but lately he's been praying that he could go see them. So here we are."

Cori finally found her voice and managed to speak through little Robbie's chokehold.

"Robbie, you named him after Robert."

"Yes ma'am. Just like Daddy named me after Aunt Tara."

It sounded so funny hearing her little girl referred to as Aunt Tara.

"And you are Grandmatoo. As Robbie got older, I began showing him your pictures as we said his bedtime prayers. Somehow, when I explained that you were his Grandma too, that's what he began calling you. I thought it was so cute, I didn't try to correct him."

The look on Cori's face showed that he could have called her Magilla Gorilla and she wouldn't have cared.

Ada took over the role of hostess, since Cori was totally mesmerized by her little great-grandson.

Tara continued the conversation with Ada, explaining how she went to see her parents but found the house empty. She was awestruck as she witnessed the loving encounter between grandmother and great-grandson. Ada was caught up in the event also.

She had seen pictures of Tara in Grace's home, and Grace had shared through tears how Bobby Lee had forbidden her to return to their home. The subject upset Grace so much, Ada never pressed her for more information, but once she laid eyes on little Robbie, she quickly surmised the reason. It was obvious that the little boy was biracial.

"Grandmatoo, can I stay at your house? Grandmatoo, do you have some toys? Grandmatoo, do you have some cookies?"

"I've decided that he should be a reporter, because each question has a follow up."

"Of course, you can stay here. I bet I still have some of your grandfather's toys around here. Let's go up to his room and see what we can find."

Tara watched the two disappear up the stairs, gave Ada a look of disbelief, as tears glistened her smile.

Squeals of delight trickled down the stairs as Tara joined Ada in the kitchen for a glass of iced tea. Except for the new refrigerator and the small television, very little had changed…there were the same gingham curtains, the same chrome table and chair set, the same fading tin canister set.

"I prayed for this reception, but I am still amazed at Grandma Cori's response to Robbie. I shouldn't be surprised, because he seems to have that effect on everyone who he meets."

"He is a little angel."

"Children are truly a gift straight from God. I didn't realize that so much until we nearly lost little Robbie. When he was born, I found him in his crib and he wasn't breathing. The doctors thought for sure that he would have some brain damage, but look at him. Michael and I are so grateful for this little miracle.

"I wanted to come home so bad. I miss my parents so much. I talk to Eddie and visit with him some, but it's so hard with the tension in our family. Even though Michael worked in the store with Daddy after school for many years and we knew his family, we were surprised at both families' responses when they found out we were dating.

"I've known Michael nearly forever. We went to school together, he was captain of the boys' basketball team and I was captain of the girls'. We had most of our classes together and were friends. We really didn't start dating until we were both in Charlotte. He played basketball for Johnson C. Smith and I played for UNC-Charlotte girls' softball team.

"You know, we actually thought both families would be happy for us, but they exploded when they found out we were dating. Daddy even told me I was no longer his daughter. That nearly killed me, because Daddy and I did just about everything together.

"I know he wanted Eddie to show more interest in sports and Eddie was good, a natural athlete. He just didn't have the passion for it that is needed. He was more caring of people like Mama, but I was a Daddy's girl. He taught me how to play baseball and basketball right along with Eddie, and I loved working in the store, when Eddie preferred 4-H and playing Grandma's piano.

"Daddy was so disappointed in him that he poured all his attention and affection into me. Eddie played sports in middle school and excelled in them, but I could hear him crying through the walls some nights after Daddy ridiculed him for wanting to play in the marching band in high school. Then Daddy turned on Mama and blamed her for everything.

"But the family survived, and Daddy just continued to coach me as I excelled in sports, too. Eddie left for college and returned home one summer a born again Christian, and for some reason, that made things even worse.

"Daddy barely spoke to him after that and accused him of joining a cult. I was still the apple of Daddy's eye until the summer after my graduation from college, when Michael and I announced that we had been dating during college and would be getting married.

"I guess we handled it wrong and should not have sprung it on them so suddenly. Both families reacted so hostile, until we didn't even have the dream wedding we wanted. Daddy disowned me and Grandma kept screaming something about the tower of Babel falling on us and something about children with mice tits on their heads."

Ada tried to restrain her laughter at that comment.

"Michael's family basically gave us the silent treatment. We found a pastor in Charlotte, got married, and decided to build our own lives together. We have a good life and Michael's family has slowly begun to come around, but I miss my family so much that I just decided to drive up.

"Mama always visits when she is in town for business, but I want Robbie to really know and belong to a family. I knew I was taking a big risk by just showing up, and Michael was against it, but I decided to come anyway."

Just then Cori reappeared, holding Robbie and an antique red fire truck.

"Grandmatoo said we can sleep in Grandpa's room. Can we Mommy? Can we?"

It was at that moment that Cori finally looked at her Granddaughter. She didn't have to say a word. Her eyes spoke all the words Tara wanted to hear.

Chapter Thirty-Eight

Going Up the Rough Side of the Mountain

Bobby Lee didn't usually work on Sunday, but he knew he needed to check on the store. He wasn't sure if he was imagining things or not, but occasionally things were not exactly where he left them.

The lid was left off the cookie jar one morning. He couldn't believe he had been so careless; that was an outright invitation for ants. Then one day the sliding door to the ice cream freezer was not completely closed. He reminded himself that he needed to be more careful.

He could not get Barnett's threatening words out of his head. He wished he could afford one of those alarm systems, but he could barely pay the regular monthly utility bills. His water bill and electric bill had nearly doubled with no explanation.

Bobby Lee climbed up on the wooden bareback stool that his father used every day while working at the store. He could still hear the friendly banter of the men finishing the first shift at Sampson Industries as they munched on fried bologna sandwiches and Tom's potato chips, while washing it down with cold Pepsis.

Just as Walter Cronkite told the world that "that's the way it was," they grabbed their lunch boxes and headed down the paths to part two of their lives. Even though they had homes, families, and warm dinners waiting for them, this brief stop was a much-needed halftime break between work and life.

Even as a young boy, he looked forward to this part of the evening as the men argued, debated, and solved all the problems of the world. He smiled at the memories of that period, when the wrinkles in his forehead reappeared.

Voted off the Trustee Board. I've been a member of the Trustee Board for over 25 years, and held the position of chair for the past 10 years. I expected to lose the chairmanship, but I never thought I would be voted off completely. I should have expected it. I was the only one who stood up to Johnny when he wanted to use church funds to support campaigns.

Shucks, I should be glad. Now I don't even have to go. It's been like a never-ending political rally for the past year anyway. I don't know the last time I've heard a real sermon. Every message is about the election. What I would give to hear a good ole fashion sermon where you came away feeling good and encouraged instead of angry.

I guess I could give Eddie's church another try. I don't know. They sing so loud and the music sounds like a rock band, and I still don't get all that dancing and prancing around twirling ribbons and stuff. I guess this is why so many folks long for heaven, because this world is a downright mess.

He glanced around the store and even though everything else appeared to be fine, he double-checked the old lock on the back door.

"PM, what in the world are you doing back here? You scared the living daylights out of me. You gonna mess around and get yourself shot!"

"Oh, I didn't mean to scare you, Bobby Lee. I sit out here some Sundays and listen to the singing from the church."

"Why don't you go on in the service?"

"Naw, do you know how many times I made the sinner's walk up to the altar? Shucks, I've been baptized about four times. After I served my time, I went up and I really meant to turn my life around, but I can't seem to stay on the straight and narrow. So, I just sit out here and listen to the singing. With those new speakers they got, I can hear real good."

Bobby Lee sat down on the opposite stoop and listened too.

He thought back to when PM was sentenced to a year with no parole for pot. He tried everything to get the sentence reduced, but to no avail. Something about him being a habitual offender, since they counted a couple of public drunkenness offenses against him.

So what if he smoked a little pot? As much as he had gone through, they ought to have paid for it. Nearly killed his po' mama. But here he sat, smiling his snaggle-toothed smile, with not a bit of hatred or bitterness.

"Barnett's got you over a barrel, don't he?"

"Yeah, he's holding all the cards."

They sat quietly, listening to the words resounding from the church.

I've done my part, but it's darker than dark.

I tried to climb, but I'm left behind.

My spirit's weak and I'm losing my will.
but I know in my heart,
There is no pit so deep, that God is not deeper still.
"I've never heard that song before. Must be a new one," said Bobby Lee.
"Yeah, those are the young folks singing now. They sing a lot of the new songs. Now watch this. The Senior Choir is gonna bring it on home now."
When you're down in trouble, you need a helping hand…. Ain't nothing…ain't nothing going right. Close your eyes and meditate on Him. Soon you're be there, God will brighten up, he'll brighten up your darkest hours…Precious Lord, Take My Hand.
"Mama sang that song for as long as I can remember."
Bobby Lee smiled as some of the members began wailing.
"You see, Pastor John believes in letting the young and the old participate in the service each Sunday. Says each group has something to offer. Now the young folks get people up on their feet moving to the beat, but when the old folks get to singing, people really start feeling something deep down in their souls."
Bobby Lee pat his own feet as the pace of the song picked up.
"How does your mama keep up with her bad legs?"
"Oh, she's passed the song on to June Sadler, even though you can still hear her singing over poor June. She's on her scooter now, riding up and down the aisles waving her handkerchief in the air. She said she ain't gonna let no bad legs keep her from praising God. Ran over Ezekiel Boney's foot a few weeks ago and broke two of his toes. He has a habit of falling asleep during the sermon and stretching his long legs out in the aisle. Mama was so caught up in the spirit, that she didn't even see his feet."
"I bet he doesn't fall asleep anymore."
"Yeah, he does. Just moved to the center of the pew."
Precious Lord, lead me on let me stand. I am tired, I am weak, I am worn. Through the storm, through the night, lead me on to the light, take my hand, Precious Lord and lead me home.
Sitting there on the stoop of his broken-down business, with the town drunk, Bobby Lee didn't know the last time he had felt such peace.

***

What am I doing? Daddy said he never wanted to see me again. I should have let Mama know that I was coming. Where could she be? At least it hasn't been a total waste of time. I still am shocked at Grandma's response. Even asking me to stay with her.

Of course, little Robbie has that effect on people. Her heart just melted the instance she laid eyes on little Robbie. Am I asking too much to hope for another miracle?

The store looks just as it did the last time I saw it. Tara's mind drifted back to the days of working behind the counter after school with Michael.

Michael and Eddie had been best friends since elementary school. Who would have thought that we would one day fall in love and marry? It's so funny now. I went to his games, he supported me at mine, and we were each other's therapy during doomed relationships.

It was during our senior year after being best friends all through college that we realized that we had feelings for each other. It never crossed either of our minds that our families would react as they did. We had practically grown up together.

The "closed" sign was on the door, but Grandma said that Dad often went to the store after church. She knocked softly, but there was no answer. She took a deep breath and quietly turned the doorknob.

Nothing had changed except the refrigerator with the glass door that stored the packages of bologna and cheese was gone. Oddly, there weren't too many items in the store except a jar of cookies, a few canned goods, some boxes of Tide, Clorox, and a few bags of Wise potato chips and peanuts.

"I don't know how Daddy is even able to make a living with these few items." She walked down the nearly empty aisles and was about to turn to exit the store when she heard the music. Glancing at the back door, she noticed the door was unlatched.

She was about to open the door when fear froze her steps. She would soon be face-to-face with her own father, a man she had not seen in nearly six years. She took a deep breath and was about to open the door, when she pulled the curtain back instead.

There they were…a truly odd couple, her dad and Mr. PM sitting on opposite stoops, in total silence, listening to the gospel music echoing from the Blessing Missionary Baptist Church. She didn't know how long she stood savoring the moment. As she stepped through the rickety old door, her father's stunned eyes caught hers. "Daddy."

Bobby Lee could not believe his eyes. It was as if an angel appeared right on the back steps of the store. There was no hatred, no anger, just gratefulness for the opportunity to see his beautiful little girl again. She didn't stop.

She didn't think about how he would respond, she didn't think about the harsh things he once said to her, she just saw her daddy, her hero, and she ran into her arms. Bobby Lee didn't know how, but he knew at that moment that things were going to get better.

There was no need for words. Their actions spoke the necessary volumes. Bobby Lee learned that she was in town just for the day, and had driven up on the spur of the moment with his grandson, Robbie.

He nearly fell off the back steps when she told him that Robbie was with his Grandmatoo, and she wanted her to fetch him and bring him back to the house to see his grandson.

"Grandma Cori saw little Robbie's resemblance to Grandpa and that was all she needed. She's invited us to stay the night, and Robbie is dying to sleep in Grandpa's room and play with Grandpa's toys. So, I guess we will be staying the night.

"You should see him. He is the spitting image of Grandpa and Aunt Tara. He is so smart and just loves everyone just like the stories I heard of Aunt Tara. Plus, he is a natural when it comes to sports. Do you know he can already catch a football at three years old?

"He plays on a tee-ball team, and the rest of the players' dads stand behind them, coaxing them to hit the ball. Robbie walks fearlessly to the mound, hits the ball way out near third base. He hits a home run each time he goes to the bat. Now, mind you, this is tee-ball, and most of the players are tripping over weeds, bases, and each other.

"We bought him a little Fisher Price goal and made a little three-point line. He only wants to shoot from there, and he makes most his shots. Folks say he is a prodigy."

PM, who was relishing being a part of the reunion, spoke up then. "He's got good genes. His grandpa, Eddie, Michael, and you. He couldn't help being good at sports."

"And the best part of it, he loves sports. It's fun for him!" Tara continued. "I see so many of the parents trying to make their children play, and it's obvious that they don't want to play." Tara caught herself and stopped. Things had gone so well; she didn't want to bring up the memories of her dad forcing Eddie to play sports. She quickly changed the subject.

"I hope you can come to some of his games. I know he would love that."

They could hear the people exiting the church, and PM knew this was his cue.

"PM, let me drive you and your Mama home," Bobby Lee said.

"No, it's the only time I can get her to move the entire week. I know if she moved more, her arthritis would get better."

"Please tell Mrs. Inez I said hello, and I will bring little Robbie over to see her the next time I am in town."

Chapter Thirty-Nine

"God of our weary years."

– James Weldon Johnson

The stoop had recently become a blessing and a respite for PM. His mom's health was steadily declining, and he practically waited on her hand and foot when he was home. He still frequented the old sugar shacks that were still in operation, but they had a new crowd. An angry crowd who had guns of all sizes and shapes, and men who had no problem coming in with two women, one on each arm.

The girls wore outfits that probably were too little when they were in elementary school and seemed to think nothing of being part of a threesome. They played music that was just as angry, and full of cuss words that even embarrassed him. The dancing would be raunchy behind bedroom doors but seemed to be acceptable to this crowd.

When he was younger, pot was the rave, but this stuff the young folks were on now made pot seem like an aspirin. Plus, they called him some of the most awful things. Now, he'd always gotten some teasing and ribbing from kids, but these young people today appeared to hate him for being crippled.

He had heard on the news about some young men beating up on crippled or homeless people just for fun, and he really believed that some of these young folks were capable of hurting him. They had no conscience, especially that Breeze.

He was the ringleader. He and his family moved here with nothing but the clothes on their back when his dad was sent to prison for drugs. He came and just took over the streets, and that mean Hoopoe and some of the other ones trip all over themselves trying to be part of his posse.

I ain't never done a thang to him, and he acts like he hates my guts. I just go in the other direction when I see him 'cause that boy is a fool…a hateful fool at that.

Then there is Barnett and his flunkies on the police force. No matter where I am standing, I get a warning for loitering, or I am threatened of another stint in jail. Sometimes, I am as sober as a jaybird, but they say I'm drunk anyway.

It's gotten to the point that I don't like to leave the house anymore. But if I stay there, Mama will drive me completely nuts. So, I walk her to church on Sundays and make my way to this stoop for the service. I don't know what I'm going to do when it gets cold. I guess I'll climb in the basement window and listen from down there.

Bobby Lee knows that I climb in there occasionally. He's really a good soul, like his pa. I guess if I was a real friend, I would tell him that he needs to put a new lock on that window. I might be imagining things, but I don't think I am the only one who is using it.

Things are really getting bad. I don't understand the Sampsons. They have more money than God, they own nearly everything, and yet they are the meanest folks I know. Now they are having all these political rallies, scared to death that we might have a Black president.

Shucks, I am the way I am today because I went to war for this country, so they would have the right to vote, when Barnett's parents fixed it so their sorry son was exempt. Now they are running everything and ruining the lives of anyone who is different from them. Not just different, but anyone who thinks different from them. And they sho got Bobby Lee over a barrel.

'Just a few bottles of cough syrup, some Clorox... I will bring it from my store and you sell it here. What you make, you keep.' I heard every word Barnett said, even though I let him think I was sleeping off a bender.

They're shutting down every store in town if the owner disagrees with them. Stores that were barely making it are now flourishing because the owners gave in to them and are letting them use their store as a front for the Meth supplies.

I don't know what Bobby Lee is going to do, but I sho hope he holds out. His family are the last good White people in town, as far as I am concerned. Oh, his ole mama ain't all bad, she's more bark than bite. But the thought of a Black president is running some White folks stone crazy, though. And I don't put anything past the Sampsons.

I know I was drunk as a skunk, but that sho looked like Amanna Dove in that Sampson truck. Then the next day, lil Jabo finds his po' mama as dead as a door-nail. I guess I should have told someone, but when I sobered up and thought about it, what was I going to say? "Last night when I left the Sugar Shack drunker than a sailor, I saw Amanna Dove fighting someone in a Sampson truck." Who would have believed me, the town drunk?

But I ain't drunk now, and I know what I saw and I know what I heard in Bobby Lee's store. I played it off as if I didn't hear anything, but Barnett's evil eyes seemed to look right into my heart. I swear that man is the devil himself. So, I just keep laying low playing the role of the passive, crippled ole town drunk, and I guess that's as good as it gets for me. A pitiful life. But it sure was good to see sweet little Tara again.

***

Bobby Lee felt more excited than he had felt in several years.

Why in the world did I waste so many years being angry at Tara? He thought to himself. *Why, I am just as bad as the folks in the church. Mad at people because they have different views or look different. I missed the first three years of my grandson's life, and it's no one's fault except mine.*

He knew Grace had gone down for visits, even though she never mentioned it to him. He knew that Tara had a baby and all he could think of was having a Black grandson. The thought of that just sickened him, and now he couldn't see him fast enough.

Little Robbie was sitting on the floor playing with some wooden blocks when Tara entered the room. "Look Mommy, Grandpa's building blocks," he yelled.

Tara hoped her face didn't show her concern about the blocks that were probably on every possible recall list. Then Bobby Lee stepped in behind Tara, and the yell immediately went to "Grandpa! Grandpa!"

The little boy ran across the floor and practically leaped in Bobby Lee's arms. Ada could not believe her eyes.

Big, stern, Bobby Lee literally melted as the tears drenched the young boy. No one could get a word in as Robbie talked endlessly about Grandpa's toys, sleeping in Grandpa's bed, Grandmatoo this, and Aunt Ada that!

In the midst of the excitement, Grace appeared. She had been at a co-worker's baby shower and found Tara's note on the door. Little Robbie was so ecstatic that Tara thought that he would make himself sick. He ran from Grandma to Grandmatoo, to Grandpa, to Aunt Ada.

Bobby Lee wanted to kick himself each time he thought about how awful he had been. He felt something he hadn't felt in many years. Happiness.

Tara had packed an overnight case in anticipation that things would go well. They went far better than she ever imagined. It was decided that everyone would have a late dinner at Grace and Bobby Lee's.

Grandma called Eddie and told him that he was needed at home immediately, but didn't tell him why. Cori and Ada fixed a couple of salads using some of the vegetables from their garden and made the little trek across the street.

Uncle Eddie arrived with Lindsay. The warm and adoring banter between Robbie and his Aunt Lindsay revealed a closeness between the two. It was obvious that she had spent time with little Robbie, and for the first time, Cori saw the emptiness of being childless in Lindsay's eyes.

If a stranger had entered the home, no one would have ever known that one day earlier, this family who sat laughing around the dinner table, were strangers. Cori had them in stitches as she described all the potential renters who showed up on her step.

"Then there was the Colored one, I mean Black one. Ada told me she wanted to be called Black. Anyway, I went to the door and there she was with long hair…I couldn't tell if it was plaited or braided. It was all tangled and looked like it hadn't been washed in a year."

"They are called dreadlocks, Grandma," said Tara.

"Well, I don't know a thing about no dreadlocks. She was real mannerly, but I couldn't help staring at her nose. First, I thought she had a booger hanging out, but as I looked closer, it was some kind of earring. Right in her nose! I said child, how in the world do you blow your nose! She was still laughing as she walked down the steps."

Ada felt all eyes on her and she laughed right along with them. The blurred lines of ignorance and innocence stopped shocking her long ago.

Chapter Forty

Crowns of Glory!

Both ladies turned in early. Bliss and Summer were with their parents on the coast, investigating a puppy farm that was abusing animals. Lizzie's family arrived home late most evenings now because they wanted to spend as much time as possible with Uncle Booker.

The slamming of the old screen door startled both the women, and the hurried steps only added to their alarm. Soon, the door slammed again, and frantic knocking nearly gave both ladies a heart attack. It couldn't be good news.

Ada arrived at the door first, attempting to maneuver the old latch. With her arthritis hindering her efforts, the girls began yelling in unison. Finally, Cori made it to the door and quickly unhooked the rusty lock.

The girls nearly knocked them down. Ada was on the verge of hyperventilating, dreading the possible unfortunate news of Uncle Booker's decline or even worse.

"Now y'all just need to settle down. You give us both a fright. Calm down and tell us what's got you all riled up," Cori began.

"Lizzie called me on the way in, and I was waiting in the solar room," Summer added. "Go ahead Lizzie, tell 'em about it."

"I don't know where to start. It's just so much."

"Well, how about starting at the beginning," said Ada.

"Okay," Lizzie began breathless. "I guess it started last week, when they announced they were going to have Praise Dance group for the old folks and Ma Liz said she was going to join. Of course, all the children started telling her about her leg, and how she didn't need to try to be a part of everything that happened at the church.

"Now, I 'spect I knows my legs better'n ya'll do," Lizzie began mimicking her grandmother.

"When I was young I wanted to dance so bad, but my Grandma never would let me go to dances. Said the folks would make fun of me. Wouldn't let me go to school for the same reason. Well, I'm a grown woman now and I'm gon' dance in that group. You hear me."

"Nobody said a word after that. When Ma Liz said 'you hear me,' that was usually the end of the conversation.

"When we got to church, everyone was in a tizzy waiting to see the old folks dance. But just before the church service started, in walked Uncle Booker. He had not been to church since his operation. Everyone in the church stood up and clapped. Of course, Ma Liz was in the back with her group.

"Everybody was happy for a change. Most of the time it seems like they're mad about something, but it was different today. Then it was time for the Crowns of Glory. That's what they called themselves. They had the front set up like a church. Then the music started and a song called 'How I Got Over' started playing. A woman who was pretending to be an usher walked in ushering an old lady in with a cane.

"When the woman faced the audience, it was Ma Liz who was fanning with a Poteat Funeral Home fan. She was fanning right in rhythm with the music. Then the rest of the old women marched in waving their church fans right in sync with Ma Liz.

"Each time they said, 'My soul looked back and wondered,' they would look back. Well that's about all they did, except make a few more moves with the fans, but you would have thought it was the greatest thing that ever happened in the church.

"Then the last time Ma Liz looked back over her shoulder, she caught a glimpse of Uncle Booker, who was sitting over in the amen corner with the deacons. She kept moving her fan in step, but with heavily glistened eyes. By the time the song ended everyone was crying, even me.

"Reverend Limberson jumped up and started praising the Crowns of Glory. He called them all back in, and started preaching about folks not letting age keep them from praising God. Then he started preaching about Ma Liz and how she never let her leg keep her from doing anything, how she never let it stop her from visiting the sick or fixing a meal for a needy family. Then he started on Uncle Booker and how the Lord had laid his healing hands on Uncle Booker.

"I wasn't sure if it was the Lord, or if it was the rabbit tobacco pillow Ma Liz made him sleep on, or the possum Papa Simon killed and made him eat, or the lock of hair they had cut and put in the tree out front, but folks just kept hollering and screaming and carrying on. I couldn't get in to this too much because I was wondering if this was his sermon or if he planned on preaching again when it was time for him to preach.

"But it didn't stop there. Just when I thought the folks' shouting had scared the angels in heaven, the door opened and it was my cousin Emmett, Aunt Marion's son who is in the Army. He walked in sharp as a tack in his Army uniform! Everybody started clapping and screaming again. I even got excited because Emmett is my favorite cousin."

"Now, just who was Emmett named for?" asked Cori. "I know most of you are named after a famous African American."

"Yes, ma'am. That's right, all the uncles and aunties, and most of the cousins except for those who are named after relatives, like me and Tay. I'm named after Ma Liz and Tay is named after the Taylor name, since my mom said her parents are the greatest African Americans she knows. Emmett is named after a little boy who was killed a long time ago."

Cori gasped, "Emmett Till, I remember when they found that little boy. Another awful time." She shook her head. "Too many awful times."

"Well, I don't know much about him, except my best cousin in the world is named after him. Before he left home he was always bringing home some stray animal, or was trying to fly off the roof with a cape tied to him, or working on some fancy go-cart made with old wagon parts.

"But just when it seemed as if things couldn't get better, there was total silence. Cousin Emmett went to the door and motioned for someone, and I soon realized why there was silence. He was not alone.

"He reached through the door and grabbed the hands of someone and ushered her in…a very pretty girl. A very pretty girl with long blonde hair, and eyes as blue as the sky. I could hear Aunt Harriet's commentary five rows back. Something about the blue-eyed devil.

"Seems like the Holy Spirit just evaporated, and I thought Reverend Limberson's false teeth were going to fall out of his mouth if he didn't close it. He soon found himself and welcomed Emmett up to the front. He didn't say a word about the girl.

"Emmett walked all the way to the front and hugged Aunt Marion and Uncle Wayne, then went over and hugged Ma Liz. He nearly ran over to Uncle

Booker, and they hugged for the longest time. Emmett always said he wanted to be like Uncle Booker, and that was why he joined the Army. I think Emmett forgot about the girl, who just followed him all over the front of the church.

"Persimmon Sinclair grumbled something about she didn't come to church for a family reunion, and Reverend Limberson asked the choir to sing. Well, they must have been distracted by the spectacle, because the piano player started playing 'Glory, Glory, Hallelujah.' Half of the choir started singing that, but there were some who apparently were not at the choir rehearsal, and they started singing 'Will the Circle Be Unbroken.'

"It was an honest mistake, since there are about ten songs that have the same tune. But they just started hunching each other, with one half trying to get the other half to sing with them. But neither side would give in, and they just kept singing, elbowing and rolling their eyes at each other.

"Some in the audience snickered, but I didn't dare, because I knew if I did Ma Liz would be able to determine that it was my snicker, and I didn't want her wrath. Not today.

"The service finally ended, and I don't know why Reverend Limberson didn't just let his first sermon be his only sermon, since the second one didn't make any sense. But I couldn't be worried with that. I had to find Ma Liz and volunteer to be her helper at the family dinner.

"There was a tradition that each Sunday one of the grandchildren would help the aunties in the kitchen. That person would sit next to Ma Liz and would be her legs for getting things from the kitchen.

"Young grandchildren think of it as something special, but usually by the time they hit elementary and middle school, they see it as more work than fun, and quickly begin passing on the task as something sacred and honorable to the younger ones.

"None of that mattered right now. I was determined to be the helper at the Sunday dinner today and get the coveted seat of honor beside Ma Liz. I didn't want to miss any of her 'under breath commentaries' as Mama called them.

"I spotted her walking down the handicap ramp and I hurriedly ran to her, complimenting her performance with the Crowns of Glory and asked if I could be her Sunday dinner helper. It was set.

"It wasn't long before the entire family arrived for dinner. Ma Liz was standing by the stove, taking corn bread out of the oven, when Emmett walked in with Brittani."

"Ma Liz," Emmett began, "I want you to meet my girlfriend."

"Hi, I'm Brittani, like with an *i*."

Ma Liz looked at her from head to toe and said, "Hey, Brittani-like-with-an-*i*."

Emmett laughed nervously. "No, Ma Liz, she spells it with an *i,* not a *y*."

Ma Liz mumbled, "Why should I care if it's spelled with an *i* or *y*? You still say it the same way. Anyway, take that chair in there. We're just about ready to have grace."

Emmett took a deep breath and took the worn straw bottomed chair toward the dining room, pausing as he listened to the rowdy exchange through the door. He couldn't help thinking of the hogs they killed each year on the day after Thanksgiving.

For the first time, he knew just how the hogs felt as they exited the hog pen on the way to their slaughter. He entered through the door, feeling as if he was part of a real-life video with someone hitting the pause button.

Lizzie sat straight up in her chair, because she knew whatever had happened in her life prior to this would never measure up to this moment.

"Hey y'all," Emmett began.

Lizzie felt sorry for him, sort of like she felt sorry for the caged animals she saw at the Pet Store.

"This is Brittani."

Brittani repeated the explanation of the spelling of her name, as if it added some value to her worth.

Lizzie was not surprised when Aunt Harriet was the first to respond.

"It seems like it just got a little brighter in here."

Some of the family snickered softly.

Emmett took the empty chair and set it beside another empty chair.

Lizzie held her breath as Aunt Harriet cleared her throat. This aunt made it no secret how she felt about White women. She believed that they were the causes of most of the world's problems. She blamed them for the Civil War, Jim Crow, WWI and II, Emmett Till, the mass incarceration of the African American male population, and even for the death of King Kong.

She worked in the elementary school, and believed the little White girls were favored over the other children. She swore that all they had to do was bat their blue eyes, swing their blonde hair, and let a few tears fall, and humankind melted. Then they grew up and had affairs with students, and were suddenly declared too pretty for jail. So, Lizzie kept her eyes glued on Aunt Harriet.

Lena hoped her thoughts did not betray her. She did not share her older sister's views, and still had a close relationship with her roommate from Elon College, who was the matron of honor in her wedding. She thought about challenging her on more than one occasion, but believed that she would be fighting a losing battle.

"Seems somebody didn't learn a thing from O.J.," Harriet began.

Ma Liz stopped everybody cold. "Now y'all might be grown, but you is in my house and we got company, and we treat company with kindness. Now act like you got some sense, and if you ain't got none, I will smack some in you."

With that, everyone began eating and laughing about the Crowns of Glory, and even Brittani with an *i* seemed to enjoy the meal.

The ladies knew that Brittani with an *i* would be the topic of the conversation this week. Lena provided daily updates about the new Taylor addition. She was sweet…she adored Emmett…tried to help, but didn't know how to do much…was smart enough to avoid Harriet…and the visit seemed to go well, overall. Just as they thought, Bliss saw this as justification that she and Tay could have a relationship.

Chapter Forty-One

"When hope unborn had died."

– James Weldon Johnson

PM knew exactly what he had to do. Bobby Lee would be at church, even though they had kicked him off the Trustee Board. He could have had the latch fixed on the window, but he was aware that PM often sneaked in there and slept on the old cot his father kept in the basement.

But this time he didn't want to sleep. He knew what he had to do, and the time was now. He had wasted too much time already, and Bobby Lee needed him. He had just put the cigar box back, when he heard a noise.

PM knew it wasn't Bobby Lee, because Bobby Lee always entered through the front or side door. He never came in through the basement because the door was nailed shut, and the only entry was through the broken window. He looked for a way to escape, but the steps were getting closer and closer.

Just as he attempted to squat beside the trashcan, he heard the hate saturated voice sneering, "Oh snap, look what I've got here. It's you and me now."

The first blow knocked him backwards against the floor. After the second one, the pain he had felt in his legs for over thirty years was finally gone. As a matter of fact, he felt no pain at all.

He lost count of the blows and didn't even realize they had stopped. It was now quiet, and quite peaceful. He lay there savoring the moment listening to the choir...*Precious Lord, take My Hand...*

***

Cori could not remember a time when she felt such peace in her heart. She thought of all the times she prayed to God to let her die in her sleep, and tears flowed freely down her face as she thought of having missed the opportunity of meeting her adorable great grandson. She honestly never thought of herself as prejudiced. Even though she still struggled with the idea of mixed marriages, those thoughts simply dissolved with just the image of her grandson. She didn't think she could love a grandchild as much as she loved Eddie, but the heart's capacity for love amazed her.

Her lonely old house suddenly burst with energy and love. At first Tara brought little Robbie for a weekly visit, but since Michael had decided to take a coaching position at the Blessing High School, they would be living directly across the street with Bobby Lee and Grace until they found a home. This was much more than she ever dreamed.

Lizzie and Summer spent most of their afternoons with the ladies, especially since Lena spent so much time in the country with her brother Booker. Unique and Bliss worked at the Frozen and Fries, but always found time to stop by with a cool treat. Cori and Ada were happy that Bliss's family recognized the value of Bliss having a summer job.

She hoped she didn't wake Ada with her laughter at the silliness of Bobby Lee. The younger girls bought the cutest little toy over for Robbie. Cori wasn't quite sure what it was. It looked like a squirrel's tale with a head, and it just ran around chasing a little ball. Little Robbie chased it all over the place, tripping over himself laughing. *I guess when they were called to their homes for dinner they forgot the little creature.*

She and Ada were just about ready to turn in, when they heard what nearly sent them both on to glory. They both jumped, but before they got to the door, Bobby Lee met them.

"I saw this thing in your garden after your vegetables, and I took care of him."

There Bobby Lee stood, holding the tail of the girls' gift to Robbie in his hand. She laughed every time she thought about it.

She even had a newfound appreciation for Summer and Bliss's parents. Since school was out, they spent a lot of time helping the ladies with their garden. Cori still snickered each time they referred to her garden as an *organic* garden and commended her on her recycling skills.

Who would have thought saving jelly jars and plastic milk jugs for plant seedlings was called recycling? Cori thought about the girls and how they rushed over with the little puppies her parents had saved from a puppy farm on the coast. When she saw the story on the news about the cruel puppy mill and saw the girls' parents on television, she suddenly admired their efforts, even though she still felt they neglected the girls.

They compensated during the summer by spending as much time as possible with their daughters. She watched how the parents interacted with the girls in a playful and carefree spirit and saw their obvious, genuine love and devotion for each other.

Jesús and Maria also made weekly visits. They had little jobs with their mother at the dry cleaners, and stopped by often to see if the ladies had anything that needed to be taken to the dry cleaners. Ada and Cori were touched by the kind gesture and how their mother taught them responsibility at an early age.

Cori had made up her mind. She definitely was not going to sell her house. She was going to leave it to Tara and Eddie. She knew that as long as they lived, they would take good care of her home. It was decided and she would discuss the legal stuff with Lena that evening. She couldn't wait to tell Ada.

Things had been sort of tense with them since all that election business started, but even Ada's mood was a little better since Tara arrived. Her children were still weird as far as Cori was concerned. She sometimes found it hard to believe that they could even be related to Ada.

Just as Ada walked in the kitchen and Cori began to share her decision with her, the phone rang. Ada watched Cori practically prance to the phone.

"What did you say? Speak up! Someone broke in the store! Hello! Hello! Something about the store being broken in. I better call Bobby Lee."

***

Bobby Lee opened the door and everything looked fine. Maybe someone was just playing a practical joke on his mom.

As he walked around the counter he saw a puddle, and just as he knelt to inspect the mysterious liquid, he saw the source.

"Oh my God! PM!" He ran over to PM just as he heard someone kick in the front door.

"Police!"

He jumped up and the police shouted, "Freeze! Don't move!"

Chapter Forty-Two

The Pits of Hell!

Cori, who sat anxiously waiting to hear from Bobby Lee, quickly grabbed the phone just as it began to ring. It was little Robbie planning his next visit. As soon as she placed the phone on the receiver, it rang again.

How this 92-year-old woman could move so quickly still mystified Ada. As Cori answered the phone, her face contorted painfully. Ada knew the news could not be good, and a prayer instantly escaped her lips. Cori's strong vibrant legs were noodles, as her body collapsed to the floor in a dismal heap.

Ada had witnessed tears from Cori, yet these were not tears, but torrents. Ada tenderly approached her as she heard the muffled names of PM and Bobby Lee.

***

Ada could barely hold the steering wheel as she tried to grasp that PM was dead and Bobby Lee was in jail for his murder. Sweet PM. Ada surrendered to her own barrage of tears. His face lit up with the brightest smile each time he saw her.

Even though he didn't seem to have anything materially, and could barely walk, he never hesitated to carry her groceries to the car and always refused any money. How anyone could even think that Bobby Lee could harm PM was insane. Sure, he fussed and griped about him, but it was evident to everyone that he cared deeply for PM and it was more than an old war debt.

They arrived just as Snoot Snead was returning from telling PM's mother what happened. Fortunately, she was at her church and had the support of her church family. Ada always felt that the jail was a sad place, but the sadness today was unbearable.

Once they entered the small lobby, they could hear sobbing and moaning coming from the jail cells down the hall. As they approached the lobby of the jail, they saw Grace, whose face looked even more tragic than Cori's. She raced to her mother-in-law and collapsed in her arms. Only God knows what kept them vertical.

Even though Bobby Lee was only allowed one visitor, Snoot Snead, who normally was void of compassion, let all three of the ladies in to see Bobby Lee. Ada was totally unprepared for what awaited her. Bobby Lee was crumbled up on a cot, in an infantile position, sobbing uncontrollably.

Ada could make out very little, but PM's name was inarguably clear. There was no concern about his new dwelling. His only concern was for PM. He was alone in his world of grief, unaware of the women's presence. They stood immobile until a crack in his anguish alerted him to their presence. He quickly grabbed his mother and began sobbing again like a little boy.

"Mama, please go tell Miss Inez I didn't hurt PM. I never would have hurt him. Please go tell her. He was all she had. Lord, help her! Lord, help her! Lord, have mercy! Go Mama, please go tell her." He paused. "I'm all right. Go help her, Mama!"

It took a minute for Cori to realize that he meant for her to go at that very moment. Cori's grief and mercy became one, and before Ada could process the transformation, she and Cori were headed down Main Street to PM's house.

As they headed toward Pearl Harbor, Ada brought the car to a sudden stop at something that never occurred in Blessing, a traffic jam. There were cars lined up on both sides of the street and there were hordes of people on the sidewalks in parallel to the cars. Ada wasn't aware that Blessing even had that many people.

Cori was still sobbing so Ada knew that it was a waste of time to consult her as to what they should do. As she glanced past Cori, she saw Tator approaching the car carrying two Red & White grocery bags.

"Hey, Miss Ada." He didn't say anything to Cori, who was still sobbing. He placed the bags on the ground and grabbed both of her hands. "This sho is something."

Cori searched for a handkerchief.

"What is going on Tator? We are trying to get to Miss Inez's house," asked Ada.

"Well you see, this is the line of folks trying to get there. Snoot came by the church and summoned Miss Inez and Reverend John to the back of the church and told them about PM. Miss Inez's po' legs just plumb gave out and she fell to the floor. She is still at the church. The brothers and sisters at the church are taking care of her right now. She ain't got nobody now. Pastor said they will just receive visitors at the church and someone will take her home and stay with her at night. How's Bobby Lee, Miss Cori?"

Cori sniffled, wiping tears.

"He's just a mess. He wants us to tell Miss Inez that he didn't kill PM."

"Now Miss Cori. I don't think nobody in their right head believes Bobby Lee done killed PM, 'specially Miss Inez. Shucks, Bobby Lee fussed and all, but folks know Bobby Lee loved PM like a brother."

With those words, Cori began sobbing uncontrollably again.

"Y'all mightest well relax cause all these folks are trying to get to the church to pay their respects to Miss Inez. Reverend John asked folks to bring food, so that's what I did. This is about the worst day I ever did see. What is the world coming to?"

As Ada sat behind the wheel, her mind tossed with emotions. She hurt for the mama who had lost her only child, she hurt for Cori, whose son was innocent but was suffering an injustice, and she hurt for the loss of a dear friend. But she was also moved.

She was moved by the fact that the death of a man with no education, no job, and no earthly wealth had touched the lives of so many. Not only was there a line of cars that snaked as far as she could see, but the steady stream of people, Black, White, Hispanic, old, young, carrying bags, pulling wagons with food, had the same effect on her as PM's snaggle-toothed smile. She wondered how poor Miss Inez would be able to sustain the outpouring of sympathy.

Tator had gone on ahead, and Cori and Ada continued at a snail's pace, but eventually got close enough that the walk would not be too unbearable for Ada. As she parked the car and Cori exited, she noticed the sudden hush that came from the crowd.

More tears added to the trail that lined Cori's face. Cori didn't know how she would find the strength to put one foot on the ground, much less face poor Miss Inez. Her hand was shaking uncontrollably as it attempted to wipe the evidence of her sorrow away.

As they began to make their way to the church, they could hear shouts from the people. "How's Bobby Lee? Don't worry, Miss Cori! He's gonna be all right! Don't nobody here thank Bobby Lee did nuthin' to PM! Here Miss Cori, let me help you."

The help and strength from the people seemed to give Cori the energy she needed to take the necessary steps. Her body automatically responded to the kindness in the voices of the people. Then she heard the pastor of the Blessing Missionary Baptist Church over the church speakers.

"Miss Inez wants to thank all of you for your support and prayers. She's tired right now, but she will be receiving visitors right here tomorrow from 10-5. Go home and pray for Miss Inez. Pray for Bobby Lee and his family. God help this town. Now before we go, we want to say a word of prayer."

"Dear Merciful Lord Jesus, we need ya right now."

As the prayer began, she immediately recognized the voice of Reverend Slaughter, the pastor emeritus of the church. Ada learned that he had been the pastor of the church for nearly 50 years before the new pastor arrived. Even in his senior years he was a force in the town, with his weekly column in the newspaper challenging everybody and everything that he felt was going against God's plan.

"We need you in this church. Miss Inez needs you now. Bobby Lee's family needs you now. The devil done showed his face here in this town and we need you now."

Ada squinted as she tried to hear him through all the "Yes, Lord's" and "Yes, Jesus" that vibrated louder and louder with each word from Reverend Slaughter.

"We don't know why thangs happen, but you do Lord, and we trust in you. Lord, we need ya to be with Miss Inez. Lord, only you know the pain she is feeling right now. Lord, she done lost her only son and I know you know how that feels. Please help her, Lord. Please comfort her. You know how faithful she has been, but Lord, even the strongest need you during times like this. So please be with her. Give her your strength. Surround her with your love. Please hold her in the palm of your hand and heal her broken heart.

"And Lord, please be with Bobby Lee. We know how good he's been to this church. We know we wouldn't have that ramp for the crippled if it hadn't been for him. We know we wouldn't have this good microphone system if it hadn't been for him. How many of our light bills has he paid? How many of us got food at the store when we didn't have a penny to our name? Lord, be with him right now. Lord, his heart is broken in half. We knows how much he loved PM.

Be with him Lord. Stop by, Lord. We need you to stop by."

With these words, Ada's eyes were no longer closed, but opened, opened wide to Bobby Lee. She glanced at Cori, whose face was smothered with tears. She scanned the crowd and saw faces that mirrored Cori's. There were hands lifted up to the heavens, pleading to God, and people hugging in support of each other.

"Lord, this may have caught us by surprise, but it didn't catch you by surprise. Naw sir. You knew the day that PM was born, the day that he would come to be with you. But Lord, we is just human, and we don't understand. So, Lord, stop by. We need you, Lord. We is confused, Lord. PM didn't bother a soul, Lord, and there is so many evil folks running around here, so Lord, some of us is confused. We need you to stop by. We need you to give us some direction, give us some understanding, give us some peace. Only you can do it."

The praises and cries were at a fever pitch. Ada felt that if he continued to pray like that, Jesus really would come down in the flesh and walk among the crowd. And for that she would be so grateful, because as bad as her legs hurt, she would be the first one in line asking for His healing touch.

Then he stopped. The crowd continued to moan and cry and then Reverend Slaughter began singing.

"Precious Lord Jesus. Take my hand. Lead me on, help me stand."

The crowd joined in.

"I am tired. I am weak. I am worn.

"Through the storm, through the night. Lead me on to the light. Take my hand, Precious Lord and lead me home.

"When my wait draweth near, Precious Lord, linger near. When my light is almost gone. Hear my cryyyyyyyyy!!!!!!"

Ada thought she felt the earth tremble.

"Hear my call. Hold my hand, lest I fall. Take my hand Precious Lord, lead me home."

The crowd slowly dispersed and spoke in hushed tones. As Ada and Cori slowly made their way back to the car, Reverend John's car passed with Miss Inez and Reverend Slaughter in it. Ada could not move her car, so she and Cori just sat waiting for some of the crowd to leave.

The townspeople slowly filed by the car, offering their prayers and concern to the two ladies. Cori continued to cry even more, but this time the tears were not for Bobby Lee. The tears were tears of gratitude.

These dear people were not only kind, she felt something else. She felt a genuine love and concern from them. She didn't know where the tears came from, for it seemed as if she had cried a lifetime of tears. Just as Ada started the car, Tator approached and informed them that Miss Inez wanted them to go to her house. Cori's face revealed her thoughts.

"Don't worry Miss Cori. Miss Inez knows Bobby Lee didn't hurt PM. She just wants to tell you herself."

"Can you ride with us Tator?" asked Miss Cori. "I don't know the last time I've been to Pearl Harbor. I don't know if I remember which of those houses she lives in."

"Sho thang." Tator went to the crowd and spoke to a few men in the crowd.

The men who Tator had addressed immediately moved from the crowd and cleared a path for Ada. They began directing the people and stopped all the traffic until Ada could maneuver her car into the open.

Tator sat in the back seat.

Mary Lou Janston elbowed Puddin Sims and summed it up best.

"Look at Tator. You'd think he's riding with George Bush in the presidential motorcade."

Several in the crowd burst into laughter.

Tator couldn't believe his good fortune. He would have a front row seat to the juiciest news in town. Even though he was glad to be a part of the somber summit, he knew that he would never share one word that was spoken in that house.

These were his friends, the only true friends he had in town. He knew what the people were probably saying about him but he didn't care. This was the proudest moment of his life.

Chapter Forty-Three

"Dr. Pauli Murray is hardly the household name that Supreme Court Justice Ruth Bader Ginsburg is, but a recent profile in *Salon* argues she should be. As *Salon's* Brittney Cooper explains, Murray, who graduated from the Howard University School of Law in 1944, was one of the first lawyers to argue that the Equal Protection Clause's approach to racial discrimination should apply equally to gender-based discrimination. She was arrested in 1940 for refusing to move to the back of a bus, protesting a Virginia law requiring segregation on public transportation—15 years before Rosa Parks' similar protest sparked a bus boycott in Montgomery, Alabama. In 1944, Murray graduated at the top of her class from the Howard University School of Law, where she encountered gender discrimination from faculty and fellow students. It was there that she coined the term 'Jane Crow' to refer to sex discrimination—the sister of Jim Crow."

– Kenya Downs

It only took a couple of minutes to get to Miss Inez's house. They could have walked the short distance, if they had not been so emotionally spent. They arrived to a street with a row of tiny, cookie cutter homes. Ada hoped her surprise at the "transition" of the Pearl Harbor community was not evident. People of all races gathered in yards, attempting to absorb the shock and sadness of the tragedy.

Tator gave a little history for Ada. "Mr. Ledbetter, who owned the Hosiery Mill, had these homes built, I reckon back in the fifties. Most of the folks over here worked in his mill or in his house. They used to be stucco with no running water. There was an old pump down at the end, but some time back, I disremember exactly, Mr. Ledbetter died and left this property to his children, who sold it before he was cold in the ground.

"Some of the folks who lived in them were able to purchase them. A company bought the rest and continued renting them to the others. PM used his military benefits and purchased their home for his mama."

Ada was appalled that people were still living in these conditions in 2008. Most of them hadn't seen a coat of paint in decades. Some had grass, but most of the yards were bare dirt. Then they approached PM's home.

"This is it," said Tator.

Ada thought it looked like a cottage that her family once stayed in at Inkwell Beach on Martha's Vineyard. *I wonder if Black families still vacation there*, she thought to herself.

It had what looked like aluminum siding. The yard was a lush green and freshly mowed. There were beautiful flowers planted on both sides of the side-walk, with a few tomato plants intermixed. The porch had green metal lawn furniture with a small porch swing in the corner.

When they entered, they were immediately met with the crisp coolness of air conditioning. Miss Inez was sitting in one of those lift chairs that Ada had priced once and decided was too expensive. The house was modestly but tastefully decorated.

As they entered the house, there were pictures of a young PM in his cap and gown, and one of him in his military uniform between portraits of President Kennedy, Dr. King, and Jesus. On the opposite wall was a portrait of a striking couple that looked as if it was taken in the late forties or fifties. Beside it was a distinguished looking woman in a beautiful ornate robe.

"Come on in, Miss Cori, Miss Ada," said Mrs. Slaughter.

Miss Inez blew her nose. "Here Miss Cori, sit here beside me." She bowed her head as if summoning for strength. Cori began crying again as soon as Miss Inez spoke to her. She began muttering, trying to convey Bobby Lee's concern, but each word was met with body jerking sobs. Miss Inez reached out her hand to Miss Cori and both women cried tears for their beloved sons.

Ada felt the tears stream down her own face. Tator and the Slaughters sat quietly, giving the moment the solace that was due.

Finally, Miss Cori wiped her nose and began, "I don't know what to say. I can't tell you how sorry I am. PM was like a son to me. He saved my boy's life. Bobby Lee is a wreck. He wants you to know..." The tears began again. She blew her nose and continued, "He wants you to know that he wouldn't hurt a hair on PM's head."

Miss Inez sat rocking and nodding, with tears dripping down her white dress.

"I wish I could go to that jail right now and tell Bobby Lee that don't nobody with an ounce of sense believe that he hurt my Paul. Lord Jesus, give me the strength." She let out a guttural scream that was so painful it felt as if the house trembled in grief.

"First, dear sweet Mr. Robert. When them boys came home and Paul Murray was broken up like he was, and Mr. Robert found out that he got that way saving yo' boy, it won't nothing that we needed that Mr. Robert didn't try to get for us. Then when that angel went on to glory, Bobby Lee kept right up with it. He and his wife are just like my own young'uns. That pretty white stuff on the outside of the house…I forget what you call it. He had that put on a few springs ago. When they put that new air condition and heat in yo' house, he had the folks to come on over and do the same thing here. And when they sent my boy over to the Blanche prison, your boy didn't miss a Sunday driving me to see him. And sweet Grace is always helping us with getting what the government owes us. She did the paper work for me to get this fancy chair and my scooter. Lord knows as soon as I am able, I am going down to that jailhouse and see Bobby Lee. I hope to God they find out who did this to my boy…" She began crying again. "…Who did this to our boys."

They sat in the room wiping tears and trying to console each other during sporadic sobbing.

"That is such a beautiful portrait," Ada interjected during a brief lull.

Mrs. Inez sniffled, "That's me in my heyday. That was made on the day I married Roosevelt."

Ada smiled at Mrs. Inez's attempt to lighten the melancholy mood of the room. The love vibrated in her voice each time she called her Paul Murray's name. His kind eyes on his Army photo seemed to be smiling at her as they did in life; so young and handsome with his whole life in front of him. Ada's mind began to wrestle, as it often did when trying to decipher the difference between injustice and fate.

"Well, it sure is a lovely picture. Now, who is the lady beside Paul Murray?"

"That's Pauli Murray. She went to high school with my older sisters and made quite a name for herself. When I had my boy, I named him Paul, after her."

"I thought she looked familiar. I remember meeting her at a NOW meeting back in the '60s…an amazing woman. I never made the connection. I guess I just always thought of Paul as PM. He told me his friends called him that, so of course I called him that also."

"Oh, he was right proud of that nickname. He loved to dance back before he was injured in that ole war, and he could out dance just about everybody on the dance floor. One of his buddies started calling him PM because he didn't show his face on the day of a party until that night when he made his grand entrance."

The ride home was quiet. Cori laid her head back in such a stillness, Ada slyly checked to see if she was breathing. She wondered if this wouldn't be what took her on to glory. So many thoughts raced through Ada's head. Her mind flashed back to the March on Washington, and she distinctly remembered Pauli Murray being upset that there were no women speakers. So many years ago, yet she could still remember her profound and inspiring words. Plus, all this time living right across the street from Bobby Lee, him in and out of the house on a daily basis; yet, she realized she didn't know him at all. Apparently, the people in Pearl Harbor knew Bobby Lee a lot better than she did, because from what she witnessed that day, there was not an African American in Blessing who believed Bobby Lee had killed PM.

***

It was a mournful group that gathered at Cori's the next morning. Lena listened to Cori and Grace as she scribbled notes. She hated not making the trip to the country to see Booker, but Lizzie was nearly hysterical, and Booker told her that she needed to be with her own family. He assured her that he would be fine, but Lena wasn't sure. True, he had been gaining weight and had even gone to the Rec center the night before for a fish fry. The family was convinced he had beaten the cancer, but Lena had heard the stories about Uncle Morris from the time she learned to comprehend. Plus, Ma Liz's eyes seemed to darken each day.

Grace's question brought her back to Miss Cori's kitchen table. The four women bowed their heads as Ada led them, pleading to God for help. Grace's normally radiant face appeared ashen and aged. Ada's arthritic walk was more labored but the normally spry and vibrant Cori's countenance almost caused

Lena's own legs to buckle. Even though she knew Cori to be over ninety years old, Lena never thought of her as nearly a hundred. But today, Cori looked every bit her age, plus some. Lena doubted that she had gotten any sleep, and wondered if she had eaten anything at all since Bobby Lee's arrest. There was a cup of coffee in front of her, but it obviously had not been touched.

"Bobby Lee really needs a criminal attorney. I know of one who is very good, but he is from New York. He could only assist an attorney who is licensed to practice in this state, but I have to tell you, he is very expensive."

"How expensive?" Grace asked, with her voice cracking. "The judge set Bobby Lee's bail at a million dollars. Both of our homes, plus Eddie's, would not be enough to get him out on bail. Eddie and Tara are working trying to see what they can do to help, but I don't know how we are going to come up with that much money."

"That is excessive and puzzling. According to the paper, they are saying it was pre-meditated, a hate crime, plus the victim is an invalid and a Vietnam Vet."

Lizzie and Summer, who sat quietly, got up and left, apparently bored with the legal discussion.

"How could anybody believe Bobby Lee would harm PM?" Cori began crying again.

The once stone-faced Rock of Gibraltar cried so much, until she was oblivious to the tears that trailed her numb face.

Chapter Forty-Four

The Scales of Injustice

Lena had not been back to the office since she took her leave of absence to help with Booker's care. She was surprised when she opened the door to a new face at the receptionist desk. She was even more surprised at the new black and glass lacquer desk with a matching black leather chair.

The young lady didn't look much older than a high school student but was sharply dressed, and seemed to be quite comfortable in the lobby, which now consisted of sleek modern leather furniture that matched the receptionist chair.

"Wow! This place looks great! Did someone hit the lottery?"

"Excuse me, may I help you?" asked the receptionist somewhat annoyed.

"Oh, I'm sorry, I am Lena Vessey. I work here."

"Uh...I'm sorry, but I don't see your name on the roster."

"Well, you see, I am on a leave of absence. Where is Judith?"

"Please be seated, and I will see if Mrs. Gaston can see you."

Lena, ignoring the receptionist, headed back to her office. Just as she entered, she heard Judith on the phone and stopped instantly in her tracks.

"Thank you. I'll take care of it," said Judith.

"By it, do you mean me? What is going on and why are you in my desk?"

"Hi Lena, have a seat."

"You're in my seat."

"We weren't sure if you were coming back, and we really needed the office space. I have been moved up to office manager, and we hired a new receptionist. I packed your things up for you. What can I help you with?"

"Where is Doug?"

"He's busy with the Jacobs' case. Can I help you with something? Did you want to come back to help with the trial? It's going to be big. I just finished talking to CNN and CBS. White Businessman kills African American Veteran in a hate crime. NBC will be running the story tonight."

***

"None of this makes any sense."

Lena sat across Grace's kitchen. They thought it was best to meet in private to discuss her visit to her law office. The million-dollar bail was unprecedented, and was grossly excessive, and she argued that point with her co-workers.

They were unyielding and the bail remained as it was. They would not even listen to reason, and they quickly reminded her that she was on a leave of absence and it could easily become permanent.

They also reminded her of her loyalty to the office, and how she was either with them or against them. She had always had a good rapport with her co-workers, but their response to her simple questioning of the bail was more than hostile.

Suddenly, Bobby Lee was not the only one on the defense and in typical Ma Liz fashion, Lena quickly responded to their unreasonable and vicious attack with an attack of her own. She reminded them that she didn't need the job and told them what they could do with it.

She exited her legal office with confidence and pride, but under the surface, the encounter left her feeling blindsided and hurt. She had poured herself into the job and into the relationships in the office, but she suddenly realized that though she felt a kinship with the staff, it was obvious that the feelings were not mutual.

She was discarded as quickly as fast food that had been left out overnight. She was shaking when she called Grace and asked her to meet with her.

Grace had spent the morning trying to find answers to help with Bobby Lee's case and she too ran into one brick wall after another. Bobby Lee insisted that she forget about trying to make bail; he would be fine in jail until the trial.

Grace had money left from her sister's life insurance policy, but that plus what Eddie and Tara scraped together wouldn't put a dent in what they required for the bail. On top of that, the media camped out in front of her house and Mama Jacobs' house.

Lena had to make her way through a maze of reporters to join Grace in her kitchen. Nothing made sense.

"You would think Bobby Lee is famous or something. There has to be more to this."

"You mean PM's death is not bad enough?" asked Grace.

"No, no. That's not what I mean. Sure, we are all saddened by PM's murder. There wasn't a kinder soul in this town than PM. No matter what life dealt him, he always had that smile on his face."

"I know. I know." Grace wiped the tears as they began to fall again.

"Was Bobby Lee in any trouble or anything? Did he owe anybody any money?" asked Lena.

"I hate to say it, but I just don't know. We lived in this house, but we had separate lives. He was always so angry and seemed as if he blamed all his problems on me. We didn't talk at all until recently, when Tara returned to town. Things had actually gotten much better between us, then this happened."

"What kind of problems did he have?"

"I don't know, really. I know the store hasn't been doing well since the S-Mart opened. Plus, he tries to take care of his mama, and he was always trying to help Miss Inez. He felt like he owed PM so much for saving his life in Vietnam. That's what's so confusing. The newspaper says that Bobby Lee caught PM stealing. Everyone knows that PM would never take anything from Bobby Lee."

"I contacted my friend in New York, and since I am no longer employed, I can serve as lead attorney and he can assist me. Now of course I am going to waive my fee, but like I said yesterday, he is very expensive."

"I guess I can sell the house and ask Mother Jacobs to sell hers too. I know she loves that old house, but I know she loves Bobby Lee even more. I keep praying and praying, but I don't know what to do."

"At times like this, I wish I had the faith of my parents. They always had it so hard, but simply trusted that God would work things out. I called them and asked them to be praying for us. Papa Simon started praying on the phone and Ma Liz said she would be praying too, but of course she had to add her own commentary.

"I'm gonna pray…but you needs to be praying too. God'll answer your prayers just like he answers mine. You need have a little faith yo'self."

Chapter Forty-Five

A Bridge Over Troubled Water

"Bobby Lee doesn't want me or Mother Jacobs to put the house for bail," Grace shared with the group around the table. "He says he's gonna stay in jail until the trial. He mumbled something about not trusting the system and them just trying to get our homes from us. I am just so confused. It seems the more I pray, the worse things get. I don't even know how to pray anymore."

Lena looked at the eyes of the kind lady who came over the first day they moved into their home with baked cookies for the kids. She had been the emergency contact for her children, and on many occasions, picked a sick child up from school when she herself was stuck in court and didn't want her own parents to make the drive from the country.

Her warm smile melted whatever mood a harsh day in court had created. But now the dark circles under her eyes told the story of a sleepless pillow-drenched night.

Mrs. Jacob, who Lena had long ago decided would be here when Jesus returned, seemed so weak that Lena feared each breath would be her last. She guessed Mrs. Ada's arthritis was acting up, because steps which normally came without thought, required deliberate focus. Each labored step reminded her so much of her own disabled mother.

They sat in silence, pondering the disappointing updates, when the doorbell startled them.

Were Grace's eyes deceiving her? Summer could not contain her excitement. She nearly did a cheer right there on Cori's steps. A very weary looking Bobby Lee even found delight in her enthusiasm. He was a little embarrassed as the young girl pulled him and a distinguished looking lady into a group hug.

"This is Grandmother Winthrop," shouted Summer.

Although puzzled, Grace could not contain her joy. With no inhibitions, she grabbed Bobby Lee and hugged him with the passion she exhibited as a young high school girl.

Grandmother Winthrop got straight to the point. "I came to help. When Summer and Bliss called, I flew right down and paid Bobby Lee's bail."

It took a moment before any of the ladies responded. What was it? Was it her elegant 1950s Grace Kelly look, or was it the fact that she mentioned the million dollars as if it was one cent? Did she actually fly herself down? Somehow Cori imagined if she didn't, she could.

"Hearing my precious angels sobbing on the phone nearly broke my heart. How could anyone believe Bobby Lee killed PM?"

"I promise I will pay you every penny, if it is the last thing I do," Bobby Lee said.

Once again, the speechless ladies stared at this new marvel.

For probably the first time in her 92 years, Cori was speechless. "I'm sorry, but have we met?"

"No, I haven't had the privilege of meeting you in person, but I've known all of you for a while."

"You some kind of hoodoo woman? Now, I want to help my Bobby Lee, but I ain't in for no devil stuff."

"Hoodoo? Devil stuff?" With this, Victoria Dent Winthrop broke into a boisterous laugh. Her laughter was contagious, for the other ladies joined in, even though they secretly shared Cori's concern.

"Oh no. I am not a hoodoo, or witch doctor, or fortuneteller. It's funny, I feel as if I know each of you and have known you for some while, but you don't know me, do you? Let's start over.

"I am Doris Winthrop, the grandmother of Summer and Bliss. I don't see the girls much except for summer visits in Boston, but I talk to them every day, and Summer and Bliss give me a daily update of all the happenings in Blessing. How is Uncle Booker, Lena?"

Still caught off guard by this stunning woman, Lena, who had been trained to answer quickly and with precision, stuttered, "He's fine...he's actually doing a little better."

"Oh, that is great news. I have been praying for him every day. I know it must be hard on Ma Liz and Papa Simon."

"It is. Sometimes I don't know how they do it. I hope that one day I will have their faith."

"You have a strong, solid foundation. You will be all right. You've grown up in an environment of love and faith in God. I am 70 years old and just prayed my first prayer a few months ago, and it was my little Summer who told me that I needed to pray."

"She told me about the two of you and the afterschool sessions, and I must confess, at first I was a little jealous. Then I found myself looking forward to the evening calls from my grand darlings with the updates on all of you wonderful people."

Cori was somewhat distracted at the notion of the children she knew being referred to as "grand darlings," but decided to disregard it in light of the fact that this stranger had freed her only child from jail.

"I contacted my attorney and he is promising to come down here and straighten this mess out himself. He said he would need to work with a local attorney. Lena, I know you are busy with Uncle Booker, but I am sure you could recommend someone."

"Actually, I went by my office and found that I no longer have an office. So, if it is all right with you, I would like to work with him."

"That's just right as rain. I tell you, God is amazing, isn't He?"

"Where is that precious little Robbie, Tara?"

Tara stuttered, "He...he's with his other grandparents."

"I can't wait to meet the little angel. The children just adore their new little brother."

Just then the doorbell rang. Cori didn't know if her heart could take anything else good or bad. It was little Maria and Jesús holding a little rosary.

"For Mr. Bobby Lee," said little Maria as she handed Cori a Ziploc bag of dollar bills.

At this gesture, Bobby Lee had to leave the room. A few minutes later, after regaining his composure, he returned and was astounded at the vision before him. The children had pulled up chairs and joined the older ladies around the table. Unique's family had sent over sausage and ham biscuits and Grandmother Winthrop, who had never eaten one, was enjoying her second one when she noticed Bobby Lee enter the room.

When the rest of the group became aware of his presence, the youngest girls quickly broke into applause, with the older women joining in. It was a small group, but Bobby Lee had an unnatural resolve, and he was confident now with his life in the hands of this coalition. Even though he was probably facing the death penalty, Bobby Lee felt like the luckiest man on earth.

With his voice cracking, he began, "I can't thank you enough for everything. One day I hope to be able to repay each of you for everything you have done for my family and me." Grace jumped up and hugged him, with Tara joining in.

"Have you tried these little things?" Grandmother Winthrop began. "I don't know if I have ever tasted anything so good. There are two kinds! They say they come from the pig. I don't know if I've ever eaten pig before, but this is some of the best food I've ever eaten."

The group broke out in laughter and Bobby Lee even joined in.

"No, thank you. But I agree with you, it doesn't come much better than pork. I'm just gonna grab a cup of coffee and go see Miss Inez."

"Do you want me to go with you?" asked Cori.

"No ma'am, but Gracie if you have some free time, I really would like for you to go with me."

Grace didn't say a word, just ran to get her purse.

Bobby Lee was somewhat nervous as he knocked on the door. Reverend John was already there to pick up Miss Inez for the drive to the church.

Her next-door neighbor opened the door. "She's getting ready to head to the church, but I know she wants to see you. Have a seat."

Miss Inez entered the tiny living room, holding on to the side of the walls for balance. Each deliberate step seemed to carry with her the weight of her world. The sight of Bobby Lee revived her tragic countenance, while her presence released the temporary pause of his tears.

She sat on the sofa and motioned for him to join her on one side, and for Grace to join her on the other side. Bobby Lee not only sat beside her, but lay his head on her bosom as she stroked his hair in such a motherly, loving way. Grace let them have their moment.

It's strange, thought Grace. *Somehow things have gotten mixed up. We came to offer comfort to Miss Inez but instead she is comforting us.*

This was the picture the preacher found when he entered the room. There were no scriptures he could offer, no words of encouragement. There was no need. This was the personification of the power of the love of Jesus.

Chapter Forty-Six

A Time to Mourn

Cori hoped her face would not betray her feelings. *I reckon I've gone to a thousand funerals, but this sho' nuff beats all. A limousine to a funeral. It's one of those things I've never understood. Why do folks spend so much money on a person after they have died?*

It makes more sense to spend it on them while they are living so they can enjoy it. And Black folks are the worst. They may be broke as Joe's turkey, but that doesn't stop them from having the most elaborate funerals.

Cori tried to quiet her thoughts before they escaped her mind. She glanced at Bobby Lee, who sat across from her. Cori didn't think she had ever seen his face so broken and downcast, even when his own daddy died. Grace sat beside him, constantly dabbing her eyes. Ada sat beside her with her head thrown back against the cushioned car seat, eyes closed, obviously in deep prayer.

As they drove closer to the church, Cori spotted the television crews. They had been ruthless, downright harassing the family ever since PM's murder. At least they stayed on the other side of the street after Cori's "baptizing" with the water hose, as she called it.

Mrs. Inez insisted that they ride in the family car, which was shocking to the media and many in town. She said they were family to her and PM, and she wouldn't have it any other way. On top of that, she asked Bobby Lee to give a few words.

I wonder how they will report this, thought Ada. *Accused Murderer and Family Ride with Victim's Family to the Funeral.*

As they approached the church, Cori heard Ada gasp. They still had a couple of blocks to go, yet there were people in line snaking blocks away. Miss Inez sat amazingly stoic in the front of the limousine. Even though the people could not see her through the tinted window, they waved at the cars, some of them crying as they waved.

The church was soon in view; however, the grounds were carpeted with people. Cori shivered with nervous anticipation. Even though she knew that Bobby Lee was innocent, she could only hope that the throngs of people who awaited them felt the same way.

The driver parked the car and opened the doors for the funeral party to exit. There was a still hush as they headed to the ramp. "We love you Miss Inez!" someone shouted, which was soon joined by more chants of "We loved PM!" and then Cori heard it.

"Hang in there, Bobby Lee! We love you, man! We love you Miss Cori!"

Cori's felt her knees give way, but Ada, who worried so much about her own knees giving out, grabbed her around the waist, giving her the support she needed to take the necessary steps to the church. Her Robert Edward had said it on so many occasions, "Black folks are forgiving people."

Ada had been to funerals of educators, dignitaries, and politicians, but she had never experienced anything like this. PM, broken in body, broke financially by worldly standards, probably could count on one hand the times that he had been out of the state of North Carolina since returning from Vietnam, yet the entire town, probably most of the county, were here to pay tribute to his life.

Although Cori chaffed at a service that went beyond one hour, two hours passed without her even noticing it. The energetic spirit-filled singing caused her to pat her feet. *Clapping at a funeral...well, I never,* but soon Cori could no longer control her hands as she clapped along with the others.

She lost count of the speakers, each telling a memory about PM. PM as the little league umpire, PM planting flowers at elderly homes, PM taking in stray animals, PM running errands for the sick and elderly, PM the once super star athlete in high school, PM cashing his disability check to pay someone's utility bill. Cori no longer tried to wipe the unending tears.

She took a deep breath because it was Bobby Lee's time to speak. Bobby Lee first said no, when asked by Miss Inez, but she wouldn't have it. The loud lively atmosphere of singing and praise was still silence as Bobby Lee approached the pulpit. Cori held her breath and trembled as her spirit intertwined with her son's.

Bobby Lee looked out at the audience. He looked down at PM's body, his face smiling even in death. He stared at the projection screen of PM's pictures. PM smiling with missing teeth. PM in an umpire's get-up, PM in his Army uniform. He grabbed the pulpit and started sobbing. Someone from the audience yelled, "That's all right!" Another one… "Take your time brother!"

Cori prayed so hard…"Lord, help my boy. Please help my boy." She didn't even realize she was praying aloud. Ada grabbed her hand and squeezed it.

Bobby Lee took a deep breath and began. "I didn't kill PM."

Someone from the audience shouted, "We know you didn't, brother." Cell phones clicked in sync as some in the audience began taking pictures.

Someone is probably hoping to make some money off the pictures, Ada thought.

Old Reverend Slaughter stood up, didn't say a word, and gave the audience a steely look. Slowly, all the cameras disappeared.

Bobby Lee began, "PM was my best friend. I hardly knew him when we went to Vietnam. I just knew we were from the same town. I'd seen him in the store from time to time, but I didn't really know him. Everybody hung out with their own back then, and PM and me did too, but for some reason we searched each other out. Both of us got it from our boys. 'Why you always talking to that Negro? Why you always talking to Honkey?'"

Some in the audience snickered.

"I guess we were both scared, and just seeing a familiar face seemed to make things a little better. We'd see each other and yell, 'Hey Blessing!' And the other one would respond, 'Hey Blessing!' Folks thought it was some kind of prayer."

Bobby Lee paused again.

"I didn't even know what happened. I was walking and then I felt like I had been tackled by a lineman. After the shooting stopped, I turned over, spitting out dirt, and saw PM. I thought he was dead. It wasn't until some of the fellows behind me told me that PM saw the sniper in the woods aiming at me and knocked me out of the way.

"Who does that? Who takes a bullet for someone? What type of person sacrifices his life for someone he hardly knows? PM did that for me. PM didn't stop to think about himself, he simply thought about me."

He started sobbing again. "That's the way he was. Always thinking about others. He didn't care about things, he cared about people. He wasn't perfect but his love for others was. I don't deserve to be here, but I am because of PM. I don't know how anyone could have harmed him. It had to be pure evil to destroy something so good. My mama used to say, 'These are praying times.' People, these are praying times."

"Yes, Yes!"

"I ain't always been a good Christian. I went to church, was a trustee, but I wasn't a good Christian."

"Yes, Yes."

"I was raised in the church, but I wasn't a good Christian."

"Tell it brother!"

"I prayed in church but I never prayed outside the church. My mama, Miss Ada, and my wife, would be sitting at the breakfast table praying and I would get disgusted at them. My son came home a born-again Christian and it made me mad. I wasn't a good Christian.

"God gave me a good wife, but I didn't appreciate her. I drifted from her. She didn't deserve the way I treated her. When women, women in my own church, started throwing themselves at me, it was PM who told me, "You got a good thang, Bobby Lee. Don't throw it away."

"There were so many days I felt alone, felt no one cared, even in my church, but PM was always there smiling that snaggle-toothed smile, wanting to know how he could help me. Help me? I should have been doing what I could to help him."

"You did brother, you did."

"When my church kicked me off the Trustee Board, it was one of the lowest points in my life. I didn't think a soul really cared about me, that no one understood me.

"Sometimes," and his voice broke again, "Sometimes, I took it out on PM. I'd yell at him, curse at him, and tell him to leave." Bobby Lee paused, grabbed hold to the podium with his body trembling.

"That's all right. Let go!"

"He'd leave, but the next day, he'd be right back smiling that big smile as if I had never mistreated him. I didn't deserve him. I didn't deserve his friendship; I didn't deserve his forgiveness. But because of PM, I can stand here right now and tell you, I know there is a God."

Folk started standing up. "Preach brother, preach!"

"I know there is a God, not because of anything I learned in my church. Not because of how I was treated in church. I know there is a God because I felt His love and forgiveness every time I was around PM.

"I know there is a God because I saw the strength of God in PM's smile, even when his broken body caused him to grimace in pain. I know there is a

God, because I saw God's love in the love that PM had for others.

"I know there is a God because right now at this very moment, I know His power and I know His forgiveness! I would be dead right now if it was not for Him stretching His hand out and upholding me in the darkest of days."

Members of the congregation rose to their feet clapping and shouting, "Amen, Bobby Lee!"

"It was PM who showed Him to me. We were sitting on the steps, listening to the choir singing, listening to the preacher preach, and PM sat out there worshiping God with such awe, I swear his face glowed like an angel. I thought to myself, *I wish I had that peace.*

"The choir was singing a song, 'There is no pit so deep, that God is not deeper still.' I had never heard the song, but the lyrics jumped out at me. Cause that's where I was. I was losing the store, losing my wife, losing my children. A few days later, PM, the best friend I ever had, someone who loved me unconditionally, was dead, and I was in jail for his murder.

"I was stretched out on the floor of the jail cell crying." His voice broke again.

Ada felt Cori's body trembling. Grace started to him, but the minister held up his hand.

"I don't know if you can get any lower than I was that day. But I cried out to the Lord, Lord, have mercy on me. Somehow, I heard the choir singing that song that I had only heard that one time. *There is no pit so deep, that God is not deeper still.* I cried and begged God to forgive me.

"Forgive me for thinking I didn't need Him except for on Sunday mornings. Forgive me for not being a better husband, son, father. Forgive me for not being as good a friend to PM as he was to me. I prayed that God would forgive me of my sins, so that one day I could see PM again, because if anybody made it in, I know that PM did.

"I thank y'all for loving me even though I didn't love you. I thank you for showing me true Christian love and I want you to know I love you. I love you Grace, I love you Mama, I love you Eddie, I love you Tara, I love you Miss Ada, I love you Miss Victoria, I love you Miss Inez, and I love you Blessing Missionary Baptist Church."

The entire church was on their feet now, shouting and crying. Miss Inez was on her scooter riding up and down the aisles waving her handkerchief, shouting praises to God. All the preachers surrounded Bobby Lee hugging him, offering words of encouragement, when Reverend Slaughter came to the podium.

"The eulogy has been preached. God has spoken, let the church say Amen."

Ada hoped her gasp was not too loud. She had never seen a preacher turn down the opportunity to preach in front of a crowd that huge.

Reverend Slaughter said it again. "The eulogy has been preached and God has spoken. We want to pray for our brother Bobby Lee. I want to ask all the pastors to come around and let's lay hands on our brother. Those of you out there, stretch out your hands toward him.

"Lord, Jesus, we come this day as humbly as we know how. We come here today to celebrate the life of Paul Murray, who is in your presence right now. Because the scriptures say 'to be absent from the body is to be present with the Lord.' So, Lord we thank you."

"We thank you that PM is with you, PM is running around heaven with a whole body, not a broken body, PM is smiling that smile with the angels right now and we thank you. We thank you for his mother, who has been such a witness to each of us, a pillar of strength who has not once questioned you, but knows that you are a God of love who is too just to do wrong, and is too wise to make a mistake.

"We thank you for our brother Bobby Lee, who even though he has been falsely accused and everybody in this place knows he has been falsely accused, he has stood before us today seeking your forgiveness, and is an example of the power of the love of Christ. Lord, he summed it up, these are praying times, and I pray right now that you would undergird him with your strength. I pray right now that you would be with each of his family members right now and uphold them with your hand.

"Lord, evil has touched this town. Lord, evil is tearing this town apart. Lord, we don't trust each other. Lord, we slay each other, maybe not with physical weapons, but we slay each other with our cold, callous words. We slay each other because of jealousy and envy. Lord, evil done touched this place. Lord, we are a broke town, people are without jobs but can find money for drugs and alcohol. Lord, I pray right now that you would send your angels down just as you did for Joshua to take on the evil that is taking over this town. I pray that what is done in the dark will be brought to light.

"I pray that your justice will roll down, and I pray that you restore this town that is so divided and broken to the blessing that you intend for it to be.

A blessing for the hurt, a blessing for the homeless, a blessing for the broken in body, mind, or spirit, a blessing for the less fortunate, a blessing for the helpless. I pray this in the mighty name of Jesus. Amen."

Cori didn't know if she had the strength to stand. She had never experienced something so powerful, and she felt spiritually, physically, emotionally, and mentally drained. She hoped her legs would hold her up. She believed she felt her spirit leaving her body when Miss Inez kissed her only son and covered him up. How that poor woman will make it, she didn't know. She wished she could have a fraction of her faith.

The church's repast after the funeral was another celebration, but the Jacobs' finally declined the invitation. They were emotional skeletons. Bobby Lee thought his mother had the strength of Sampson, but he could see the toll this had taken on her body.

She excused herself and went straight to bed. The rest of the immediate family went to Bobby Lee's and Ada tried not to show her appreciation, for she was bone tired too. Somehow, she knew this was just the beginning.

Chapter Forty-Seven

"'If, by... looking at a person in a leering manner, or watching and then following, one causes another to become frightened and run, then he is guilty of assault,' said the judge to the jury in the superior court in Yanceyville, North Carolina, last November. The all-white jury promptly found Mack Ingram, a Negro farmer, guilty of 'assault' against Willa Jean Boswell, daughter of a neighboring white farmer—even though everybody agreed that Willa Jean had safely run off across a cornfield, and Ingram was never closer than 50 feet to her."

– TIME, July 23, 1951

The mood was light at the table. Klein Jude, the defense attorney from Boston, would be arriving that afternoon. Lena had tried to rent office space in town, but ran into a brick wall each time she inquired about a vacancy. She had a room converted into a bedroom with a bath in the event her parents would need to move in with her, so it was decided that they would use it as their office.

Bliss and Summer's parents had wanted to take a trip to Africa, so Grandmother Winthrop surprised them with a trip as an anniversary gift, and she would be staying with the children for a month. The attorney, a high school buddy of her son, would stay in the basement apartment that was used for visiting professors.

The evidence was staggering. Bobby Lee's fingerprints were on everything, and the blood-covered shirt didn't help. According to Snoot, there was an anonymous tip called in that there was a fight at the store. When the police arrived, Bobby Lee was leaning over PM's body.

The wrench that PM often used to open the downstairs window was covered with blood and was laying beside the body. It was the only tool missing from the tool box that Bobby Lee kept in the basement.

A number of people said they had heard Bobby Lee yelling at PM on several occasions about hanging out at the store. Even though Lena and Klein knew Bobby Lee was innocent, they had a hard time coming up with a defense. They just knew that he was not guilty.

The elderly ladies continued to meet every morning for their daily prayer, but also began watching episodes of *Matlock; Murder, She Wrote;* and *In the Heat of the Night.* Cori believed that if anybody could figure out what had happened, Matlock, Jessica, and Chief could.

They tried to stay in the house after Cori was on the evening news giving one of the reporters a piece of her mind. Lena and Klein were not even successful in getting a restraining order keeping them from camping out in front of the ladies' home. But even the town justice system could not stop Cori from watering her lawn every night and giving them a good drenching.

Bobby Lee had a lot of time to think.

I know how Mac Ingram must have felt. Being accused of doing something you didn't do. Not just Mac Ingram. Black folks have been enduring this for years, shucks…centuries. I never really thought about it before.

Just figured the justice system was fair for the most part, and figured most of those folks were guilty of something, or they wouldn't have been suspect in the first place. I guess that's the way folks feel about me now.

I thought most folks around here knew that I would not have hurt a hair on PM's body. But they quickly turn their heads now when I go the post office. Some of the same folks who worshipped with me all of my life act like they don't see me.

Now of course the black people still check on me and drop food off at the house. He smiled when he thought of all the different dishes they had received.

They seem to think the answer to everything is food. They're always having some eating function at the church and would send a plate over to PM on the stoop. If I was around, they'd run back and get me one too. They're hard to figure out sometimes. He continued to smile as he reminisced over a conversation he once had with PM.

"Yeah, they dog each other out, but let something happen to one of them, they'll have the grandest funeral and have enough food to feed the entire town. It don't matter how big a scoundrel the person was, by the time Reverend Slaughter finishes with them, he'd been preached right through the pearly gates."

Bobby Lee had to admit PM was right. No matter what crime they committed, once they left prison, they'd throw the biggest cook out and the folks from all around would come out to celebrate the return. Many of them believed the person to be a victim of an unjust racist legal system anyway. "I imagine they were right. But as Daddy always said, they are a forgiving people."

Even though he had heard his papa say this many times, Bobby Lee never saw that in them. All he saw was that they showed up for church with hats the size of umbrellas and bright suits and shoes on Sundays, but never seemed to be able to pay their bill at his store. But none of that mattered to Bobby Lee now. He was glad to have them on his side.

Chapter Forty-Eight

The Valley of the Shadow of Death

Since the murder, the girls had moved from *Gone with the Wind* to *To Kill a Mockingbird*, so they headed to Summer's home to watch it again. There was lighthearted chatter as Ada, Cori, Lena, Tara, and Grandmother Winthrop sat around Cori's old kitchen table.

They almost didn't hear the knock on the screen door, as they laughed about Grandmother Winthrop eating two sausage biscuits and one ham biscuit. Lena walked to the door still laughing and was totally surprised to see her husband, Leigh. The look on his face nearly caused her to faint.

"Is it Booker?" asked Lena.

"No, some soldiers arrived at Marian's door. It's Emmett. He was killed yesterday in Afghanistan."

Emmett had surprised all of them on the Sunday that the old ladies at the church did their now one and only dance. It seemed that the dance woke up their arthritis, rheumatism, and everything else that ailed them. But Emmett's visit was the real highlight of the day. He wanted to see all his family before he deployed to Afghanistan.

They were worried about Booker, and even though they knew Emmett was in a war zone, they believed he would be okay; he was Emmett, after all. All the childhood mishaps, the car accidents, the hunting accidents; it was as if he had a guardian angel watching over him.

The drive to the country seemed longer than ever. Lena sat in the back, holding Lizzie, who was crying hysterically. She could not begin to imagine the pain her older sister Marian was enduring. She couldn't find words to pray. She hoped the ladies' prayers would carry her through.

The family thought they had beaten death one more time. They were practically the only family around who had not lost an immediate loved one. This was the beginning. The family unit would forever be broken, and from now on it would be one after another. An elderly man once told Lena when she told him she was from a large family, "Big families are great until they start dying one at a time."

When they arrived at her sister's home, they were not prepared for what they found. There were people everywhere. People were parked on the side of the road, and nearby fields. Cousins and high school friends were huddled together, sobbing.

Neighbors arrived with picnic tables, chairs, and grocery bags. There were men assembling a big tent. Lena was exhausted by the time she made it to the front door. The entourage in uniform was going over official documents and Ma Liz sat in the corner cradling a sobbing Brittani with an *i*.

Papa Simon, who had always been tenderhearted, was being consoled by her brothers. As Lena heard the group of military officials giving their final goodbyes, Lena and the older sisters rushed to their sister's side. She began screaming at the top of her lungs, and Lena didn't know if she had the strength to bear one more thing.

Ma Liz went to console her daughter and Brittani with an *i* just passed out on the floor. Marian's husband, Wayne, just walked back and forth not knowing what to do. It was Lizzie who ran to him and threw her arms around him.

Emmett's funeral was more than just sad. The military informed the family that the coffin should remain closed. Apparently, he had been part of an explosion. This only added to the pain, because the family had hopes of seeing the physical body just one more time. The young people who had not experienced very much in life except love and laughter were devastated by this tragedy. They didn't know what to do with their grief.

There were so many sobs, screams, and anguish at the loss of this high school star athlete, most popular boy in the school, and genuine friend. Amazingly, Ma Liz seemed to hold up better than anybody. After burying her grandmother and grandfather who had raised her, and all seven of her uncles with whom she was raised as a sibling, her old heart must have become somewhat tough. Either that or she had the faith of Job.

It was decided that the funeral would be in the high school gym where Emmett had led the basketball team to the state championship. There were two huge screens displaying slide shows of Emmett's life. A few of his friends attempted to say words, but had to be carried from the podium.

His military leadership spoke highly of his brief career in the army and presented the family with several medals and citations on his behalf. His parents just rocked and held each other. Young Reverend Limberson said some words that should have been encouraging, but were more for the television cameras.

"This is not a time to be sad. This is a time to be happy! Emmett is with his maker!"

Lena didn't feel happy and thought she just might get up and slap him.

Papa Simon's white handkerchief was soaking wet, and Ma Liz just rocked back and forth, back and forth. It was the worse day of Lena's life. She caught a glimpse of Booker and her heart just broke. Through all the cancer treatments, the side effects, the diagnosis, he had never shed a tear. But he looked at the flag draped coffin and tears ran down his thin face on to his loosely fitted suit.

They say God doesn't put on us more than we can bear, Lena thought. *I just can't imagine having to bear more than this.*

All the cousins loved Emmett dearly. He kept them in stitches and entertained them, from the youngest to the oldest. It was Emmett who organized the baseball games with the cousins, the fishing trips with the oldest, and the Easter egg hunts for the smallest ones. Lizzie grieved especially hard.

Each of the older cousins had a younger cousin as their "pet," and she was Emmett's pet. Ever since his death, she slept with her parents. Tay did just as Tay always did. He withdrew and stayed in his room. The ladies prayed fervently for this loving, hurting family, for they knew that only God would be able to help them through this difficult time.

Chapter Forty-Nine

"Courage is the capacity to meet the anxiety which arises as one achieves freedom. It is the willingness to differentiate, to move from the protecting realms of parental dependence to new levels of freedom and integration."

– Rollo May

Working on Bobby Lee's case was therapeutic for Lena. The children, who had never experienced grief, were quiet and withdrawn. She thought it best to keep their minds as active as possible.

Lena enrolled Tay in an SAT prep course at the high school. She was appalled when she read the study of how the number of prisons were determined by the number of young boys in second grade. She was encouraged that the NEA had taken steps to end the school-to-prison pipeline, but she knew she had to do her part too.

Tay balked at first, until he learned that his mother had enrolled Ray Rock and Jabo, too. Lizzie was excited to learn that she would be participating in a cheer clinic with Summer. Miss Victoria even enrolled Bliss and Unique in the high school cheer camp.

Emmett's death was too painful for her to think about. Her sister had aged ten years since his death and Wayne was simply a zombie. She knew this was not healthy, but she just tried not to think about it.

The trial was a great escape. The trial date was set for one month, which gave them little to no time to prepare. This too was very unusual, and they challenged it, although unsuccessfully. It seemed that all their challenges met with defeat. Klein was convinced this was just small town injustice rearing its ugly, power-hungry head, and it would take time and skill to outmaneuver them. The prosecutors had everyone in the town on their side.

Each night the case was the top news story, with quotes from unnamed sources. If someone didn't know Bobby Lee, they would think he was a skinhead, racist, right-wing Klansman, and his attorney was only down here because a millionaire was bankrolling his account.

Every spare moment was spent out in the country with Lena's family. The Sunday dinner was not the same. Occasionally, someone would tell a joke as an attempt to lighten the spirit, but it usually fell flat.

In all honesty, everyone would rather have stayed at their own homes, but Ma Liz insisted that they continue the family tradition. Sometimes a cousin told an Emmett story, which normally caused the family to erupt into laughter; instead, a fresh deluge of tears emptied the moment of any joy.

It was one such moment when someone knocked at the door. The entire family was there, so it was a mystery as to who was at the door. To everyone's surprise it was Brittani with an *i*, a very pregnant Brittani with an *i*. This same girl, who had once been the butt of ridicule and criticism, was suddenly the best thing since sliced bread.

Marion and Wayne grabbed her and it looked like they would squeeze the baby right out of her. After everyone hugged her nearly to death, she told them about the baby boy that was due in a few months.

She cried as she told the family how happy Emmett was about the news, even though they didn't know that it was a boy at the time. She cried even more as she told them how they planned to get married when he returned. The entire family joined her as the tears of sadness transformed to tears of happiness.

***

The ladies knew the young people needed to grieve, and assured them that they were welcome to stop by anytime. The girls continued their daily visits to the ladies' kitchen table and the boys continued to meet in the garden.

After his cousin's death, Tay spent all his spare time in the garden, which was therapy for his downcast spirit. He was a serious farmer, and when it came to gardening, he made sure that anyone who assisted him was just as serious.

Ada watched as he and Jabo huddled over a hoe almost whispering to each other. At first Ada thought they were just discussing a young lady, but as she walked closer she sensed the concern.

"You gotta tell somebody," said Tay.

"Tell somebody what?" Ada asked startling the young men.

"Come on man, tell Miss Ada. You gotta tell somebody," Tay repeated.

"What is it Jamison? What's troubling you?" asked Ada.

"Well, yesterday, me and Ray Rock were at the school for our SAT test prep class and we stopped by Mr. Sampson's office," Jabo began. "You see, I wanted to borrow some money to go to the movies. He says if I ever need anything, to let him know, on account of my grandpa working for them so long. So, whenever I need money for a field trip or a game or something, my grandma tells me to talk to Mr. Sampson. So yesterday during a break, we headed to Mr. Sampson's office, but I stopped in the bathroom and Jamison kept walking towards the office."

Ray Rock took the story up at this point. "I should have listened to my mama and stayed away from him. I was just going to wait for Jabo outside in the hall by the office door, but as I approached his office, I heard him fussing with someone. I heard someone say, 'Look, I did what you told me to do.' Then Mr. Sampson said, 'Listen, you stay away from me. Don't call me or anything. I'll get back with you.'"

"I ran and hid around the corner, and Breeze walked out."

"Breeze?" asked Ada, "I don't think I've ever heard you mention him."

"Oh, he moved here about a year ago from somewhere and he walks around like he's the king of the world or something. He hangs out with Hoopoe and some older guys, guys who are always in trouble. He didn't say PM's name, but I think that is what they were talking about. I heard him leaving and ran around the corner."

"After he left, I came from around the corner, and he must have forgotten something, because he came back and walked right into me. He didn't say a word, just stared at me. I went straight and told Mr. Jacobs. You would have thought I had an ankle bracelet or something on me because no sooner than I finished telling Mr. Jacobs, Mr. Sampson walked in. He didn't even knock. Mr. Jacobs excused me and I came over here and told Tay, who says I need to tell somebody."

"Tay's right," Ada said. "We have to tell Lena about this. It may mean something. But for now, let's just keep this between us." The four of them walked across Cori's backyard to Lena's office, and Jabo told Lena what he had just shared with Ada.

"Jabo, I'm glad you and Ray Rock shared this with us," said Lena. "I don't know what it means right now, but you be very careful. Don't go anywhere by yourself. That goes for you too, Tay. As a matter of fact, I will be driving you wherever you need to go until this thing blows over."

"Aw Mom," groaned Tay. "We'll be alright."

Klein began, "Young man, a man is dead. Your mom is right. We need to be very careful. Small town injustice is the worst kind of injustice. Townspeople circle the wagons and it's hard to penetrate the boundaries."

Jabo looked at his friends and for the first time, he looked fearful. He toyed with his necklace, his eyes darkened to another time and place.

Lena noticed the solemn expression on Jabo's face. "Jabo are you all right?

Startled, Jabo answered, "What? Um, yes ma'am…just thinking about my mom."

"Is that her locket?" asked Lena.

"Yes ma'am, she gave it to me the night before she died."

"It's beautiful. May I see it?"

"I never take it off. It has a picture of my mom and dad in it."

He opened it for Lena and it held a picture of an attractive young couple.

"It looks like some writing is seeping through."

"I guess I never looked at the back of it. I've never even taken it out of the locket."

"Let's see." Lena gently took the picture out of the locket and she was right. *To my little Jabo, I love you with all my heart.*

Then at the very bottom was the word *Beloved*.

Lena gently touched Jabo's arm. "Jabo, how are you doing? I understand you found your mother."

Jabo's eyes darkened. He stared at the locket longingly. "I don't like to talk about it."

"That's fine. You don't have to talk about it if you don't want to. Here, let me put the picture back again and let's keep all of this between us. Not a word to anyone."

Lena felt bad for bringing up the subject of Jabo's mother's death. The pain in his eyes nearly brought tears to her own eyes. From what she read about his mother's murder, it was a wonder the boy was not stone crazy.

Chapter Fifty

The Merging of a Rock and a Hard Place

Eddie was running late. Once Ada moved in, the Wednesday date with Eddie was anxiously anticipated by both women. They both fiddled around the kitchen cooking Eddie's favorite dishes and getting the board games ready. The young girls had been reminded that this was a special time, so they made sure they were gone by the time Eddie arrived.

Both women kept their eyes on the clock and when the five o'clock hour arrived, they took turns looking out of the window. Even if there was an unannounced faculty meeting, it should have ended by 4:30.

Cori was scanning the list of phone numbers by the phone when they heard Eddie's car in the driveway. Ada knew from the look on his face that something was wrong. Eddie was always a source of optimism. He and Lindsay had tried to have children for years, he had been constantly belittled by his father, and Wallace was forever antagonizing him on his job, but he never seemed to let it get him down. He was definitely his mother's child.

"What's wrong?" Cori began.

Eddie laughed. "Grandma, what makes you think there is something wrong?"

"It's not like you to be late without calling, so I know something's wrong."

"I could never fool you, Grandma, so I might as well tell you. I was fired today."

"What do you mean 'fired'?"

"Just what I said. Wallace came in this afternoon and fired me. Said something about budget cuts, and gave me until the end of the day to get my things out. He said that there was not going to be a marching band this fall." Eddie didn't dare share what Jamison had told him.

Ada was startled as Cori jumped from the table and stormed out the backdoor. It caught Eddie off guard too, but he knew his grandmother and she was on a mission.

"I'm not having it! I'm not taking this crap anymore. I am sick and tired of them bullying my family. Enough is enough. That no-good sorry rascal will fire you over my dead body, and as I am living and breathing, he is going to give you your job back. This ain't got nothing to do with no budget cuts."

"Grandma, please calm down. You're going to make yourself sick. I'll be all right. Please come back in the house."

Ada frantically called Lena, who met Cori's rants in the yard.

Lena joined in, "Please Miss Cori, let the legal system work."

"What's wrong Cori?" asked Victoria. "I could hear you as clear as day."

"They keep messing with my family and I ain't gon' take no more. I mean it. Eddie is as good a soul as they come, and now they done fired him. That's the last straw."

"Grandma, I told you I will be all right. Please calm down and come back into the house."

Cori looked at her grandson's eyes and saw the eyes of her Robert, and just crumbled into his arms.

He and Victoria had to help her back into the house. All her family's struggles were really taking a toll on her.

***

The press was right on time, and all the major networks were represented. Everyone loved a story about a millionaire. It was front page above the fold news, the generous $100,000 donation to the Blessing High School marching band program and their band director, Eddie Jacobs.

Mrs. Victoria Dent Winthrop gave a lovely speech about how her late husband was a member of the marching band in high school, and she had heard that many schools were having to cut their music programs. She expressed how she had recently moved to the lovely town, and how her granddaughter and many of young people spoke so highly of Mr. Jacobs, and how he was such an advocate for children. She wanted to ensure that the Blessing High School music program would not suffer from any of the cuts.

If the Superintendent knew of Eddie's firing and the dissolution of the marching band, he didn't let on. Cori looked at Wallace standing beside the superintendent and summed it up best.

"Always was dumb as a rock."

Chapter Fifty-One

"Someone has said that there is nothing permanent in the world but change. For instance, just a few years ago there was no high school for Negroes in Caswell County, not to mention such things as buses or an ideal classroom. Nevertheless, time has a way of changing things, so in May of 1934 C.C.H.S. had its first graduating class of seven. Since that time, classes have grown larger and larger. Now I am put in the sad position of not only saying farewell to the class of 1969 but to C.C.H.S. As your principal, it is my sincere hope that you will always remember that old C.C.H.S. may not ever graduate another senior class, but it will live on. The 35 classes, including yours, which have graduated from C.C.H.S. will never allow this to happen. For in years to come they and you will be making their contributions to this country, state and nation. Brick, mortar, even steel decay, but the spirit of good character, honesty, love, faith has a staying power that outlives steel and stone. So, face life with courage and a determination to succeed. Write your names on the pages of time. It really doesn't matter from whence you came, but it matters where you are going. Old C.C.H.S. has just really started to live and make its contribution to history."

– Nicholas Longworth Dillard

One cold case in Blessing, North Carolina...the case of Amanna Dove. The case had baffled Lena from her first day as assistant district attorney. A young woman found dead by her little son. There were no witnesses, no clues, and the little boy didn't hear a thing; just a young woman murdered.

She had poured over the police records several times herself. Because of the amount of blood on the victim and the lack of blood in the bedroom, it was concluded that the murder had taken place somewhere else and the body was brought back to the home.

Lena pictured the beautiful young woman in Jabo's locket covered with blood. The violence of the crime indicated a possible state of rage or hatred.

"Sounds like a jealous woman to me," thought Lena. "But it had to be a strong one to do all of that and not leave one clue."

From the newspaper article, it was obvious that she was popular and was well thought of by the community. She volunteered at the Senior Center, coached her son's tee ball team, taught Sunday school, and was in the midst of trying to get a rec center opened in the old African American school, so that young children would have a place to expend their energy.

Her husband had been killed in a hit and run in Queens, New York, and there was speculation that it was no accident. That was it. No more investigations, and Amanna Dove's case was placed in the cold case file.

She had talked with Miss Eliza on several occasions. It was the one home she allowed Tay to visit. She could tell that the old lady in tattered clothes had been a vision in her day, but on most days it appeared as if it took all of her energy to simply put one foot in front of the other.

She was always so appreciative that Lena included Jabo in their family's activities. Even though she claimed she was too old to raise a young boy, she had done a remarkable job. Jabo had not ventured too far out of Alamance County and his world was very limited, but he made up for it with manners and respect. He tried to be cool and hang with some of the rougher young men, but it just wasn't his nature.

She didn't know what she was looking for with this unannounced visit. She took a deep breath and knocked on the door. She knew to wait because Miss Eliza moved slower and slower with each visit. It was hard to believe the short, wrinkled, stooped woman was the same age as her brother Booker. Her body was not beat down with a sickness, but was trampled by a harsh and cruel life.

Lena saw the fear on her face as she pulled the curtains back at the door. She could hear "What's wrong?" even before she opened the door.

Lena yelled through the door. "Nothing's wrong. I just wanted to stop by for a little visit. I'm not working anymore and I have more time to visit."

"Lord, child, you nearly gave me a heart attack. I thought something had happened to my Jabo. You know he's all I got in the world."

"I'm sorry, Miss Eliza. I should have called first. I didn't mean to alarm you. I just have a lot of time on my hands right now, so I thought I would visit some. I really haven't gotten to know many people in town, since I went to work as soon as I got here."

"Come on in and sit a spell," Miss Eliza began. "I don't get much company. Pastor stops by ev'ry once in a while. I send my salary in, but I don't go to church no more. Folks stopped visiting after my Amanna passed. Seems someone put out that her husband was involved in some mob stuff and that's why she was killed. I guess it scared them away. I don't mind much. They were just being nosey anyway. It's just me and my boy."

"How are you doing?" Lena asked.

"I do fine most days, but I have my days. Amanna, of course, was my baby. Now we had our tiffs like most mothers and daughters but she was my heart, couldn't find a sweeter child. Jabo got ways just like her. Lord, I was so happy when he took with your boy. Them other hoodlums had him headed for the chain gang. But now he studies hard and talks about going to college. I know his mama would be proud of him."

Lena smiled. "Jabo is a fine young man, and you have done an exceptional job raising him. He is always so respectful. That boy will '*yes ma'am*' you and '*no ma'am*' you to death," Lena shared with his beaming grandmother. "My folks out in the country think he's just another grandchild."

"He's talks about them all the time," Miss Eliza added. "I sure hope I can visit with them one day. How is your brother Booker doing? You know we were in the same class."

"I didn't know you were from Caswell County."

"Yes, I was from Yanceyville, the county seat. Lived right across from the school we attended."

"All my siblings attended that school," said Lena. "They loved the school and I have to admit I get a little jealous when I hear them reminisce about their times at Caswell High. They speak of Mr. Dillard with such reverence."

"Yes. He was a wonderful man. It was amazing what he was able to do in our small town. You know, our school was nicer than the White high school, and our school was even accredited when the White school wasn't. Can you believe that?"

"I don't think I knew that."

"Yeah, since we lived right across the street from the school, we were very involved in most of the activities. My mom was the PTA president for many years."

"Tay begs me all the time to let him go to school in Caswell, but his uncles and aunts remind him that Mr. Dillard is no longer there and things are very different now. It was a junior high school when I attended it."

"I had a little crush on Booker in the elementary school. Your mama volunteered there quite a bit, but I doubt if she remembers me, I was just a young'un. I married Claude, who lived out near the county line in Stoney Grove, and then we moved here to Blessing."

"Jabo never mentioned that he had Caswell ties."

"I haven't been out to Caswell in ages, since most of my folks are gone. I can't remember if I've been out there since Amanna and her daddy died. He didn't live much long after her death.

"The sun rose and set on his Amanna. He said when she was born that she was like the manna straight from heaven. I stuck the "A" on the front 'cause my mama's name was Amanda. About two months after she died, her daddy just dropped dead at the kitchen table."

"My God, Miss Eliza, how in the world did you make it?" asked Lena.

"Did I make it? Some days I wonder. Some days I don't think I can get out of the bed. Some days I am so mad at God I could scream. I just lie in my bed crying silent tears so that Jabo don't hear me. Only God knows why that boy ain't crazy with what he's seen."

"Do you mind if I ask you a few questions? Since I'm no longer working at the DA's office, I've been looking into Amanna's case. It has always puzzled me."

"Just leave it alone, please. I don't know what happened or why. We wanted answers and we were riding Snoot Snead's back. We even hired ourselves a private investigator, but one day my Claude came home, face as white as a sheet. He said he was at the hosiery mill where he worked, and they called him and told him he had an emergency phone call. He said someone told him that if he cared anything about his grandson, then stop asking questions or he would be having another funeral. So, we did. We left it alone. Claude said it won't gonna bring her back anyway."

Lena looked at the weary face of the tortured soul. She would not bother her with any more questions. "This is such a beautiful house," Lena stated as she began looking at mementos in the curio cabinet. She saw a larger picture identical to the one in the boy's locket.

Lena glanced through the cracked door to the inside of a bedroom and saw the same photo on a nightstand by the bed. "What a beautiful quilt."

Mrs. Eliza's face beamed with pride. "I made that ole thing. It ain't much."

Lena proceeded to heap praise on the quilt as she quickly surveyed the room. It was simple, but a tastefully decorated room. The dresser looked as if it had not been touched. The comb, brush, perfumes, the pair of shoes on the floor by the dresser…the robe on the back of the door…everything looked as if Amanna had simply stepped out for the day.

"Are these Jabo's parents?"

"Yes, that's my Amanna."

"She is so beautiful. They looked so happy." The bed post was a deeper color than the dresser and the end table. *She must have replaced the bed. I can't blame her.*

Miss Eliza turned and went back in the kitchen. Lena followed, surmising that the room was still a source of pain. She joined Miss Eliza, who was totally engrossed in the Plinko game on *The Price is Right*. Lena tried not to laugh. She had recently made a pleasant discovery and this confirmed it.

Because of its convenience to four major hospitals, Blessing had become a popular retirement area. Although she loved older people, they seemed to take their time. They had no jobs or children at home, so there was no need to rush.

They strolled down aisles in the grocery store, they took their time reading labels, measuring produce, enjoying savoring the free samples, and counting out their change to the last penny. They lingered in the restaurants, enjoying their veggie plates and swapping stories of grandchildren.

Lena had discovered the best time to run errands in Blessing was between 11 and 12 in the morning. Children were still in school, it was too early for the college students, and Miss Cori, Miss Ada, her parents, and most of the senior citizens in Blessing stopped whatever they were doing to watch *The Price is Right*.

"Do you mind if I get a glass of water?"

"Lord, child, I don't have a bit of manners."

"No, you just sit there. I can get it myself."

"The glasses are in the cabinet by the fridge."

"That's okay. These paper cups are fine."

"Jabo uses up so many dishes, I just started buying paper cups and plates.

We mostly eat sandwiches anyway. Can't get the boy to eat vegetables, and he wonders why he stays so locked up," she smiled. "How are your folks doing? I cried with your family when I read in the paper about your nephew. I remember reading about him when he played all those sports, on account I knew the family."

"It's been real hard. Our family has been so blessed, and we had not experienced a death in our immediate family. We're just taking one day at a time."

"That's all you can do. Put one foot in front of another and ask the Lord to give you the strength to make it through each day."

The two sat in silence for a moment, letting the peace strengthen their broken spirits.

Lena finally broke the silence. "Did you do your own decorating?"

"No, my Amanna built this house shortly before she joined the angels. She was real good at fixing things up," Miss Eliza continued. "She left the house to Jabo. We tried to sell it, but no one would buy it. Guess they didn't want to buy the home where a murder took place.

"It was hard, and we didn't want to move in here, but it was the boy's home. Our little home was old, and the boy had gotten used to cable and having his own bathroom and such. So, after the police finished with it, we hired a company to clean it real good and fix it up as if nothing had happened."

Chapter Fifty-Two

The Miracle

Lena replayed the conversation with Miss Eliza over and over in her head while she waited on the boys.

She never imagined that she would be in this place. She was now a stay-at-home mom, sitting in her SUV in the carpool lane at the high school, waiting for the young men to finish their SAT prep course.

She knew when she was in high school that she wanted to be an attorney, wanted a career, not the boring life of her mama and her two eldest sisters. Cooking, cleaning, running behind children, and taking care of a husband was not for her. Yet, here she was.

Even though the words would never escape her lips, she didn't miss the stress and pressure of the life of an assistant DA at all. She could not believe how much she enjoyed being with her children.

The competition cheerleading squad kept the girls busy. Miss Victoria found the entire Blessing High cheerleading debacle unsettling. She insisted that the girls get involved in the recreational cheerleading competition league.

Fortunately, all the girls made the squad; the young girls cheered on the squad for elementary girls and the older girls cheered with a group of high school aged girls. Her continued generosity covered the expenses for all the girls, even after Lena insisted that she pay for Lizzie.

Lena had been a cheerleader in high school and served as their chauffer as well as their personal coach. So, her days were busy and unbelievably fulfilled.

She had always enjoyed the theatrics of Lizzie, but she and Tay bumped heads as he directed most of his anger at her for wanting to move to Blessing. Yet, here she was anxiously awaiting him, Jabo, and Ray Rock. She was surprised at the level of their intelligence.

The way they bantered back with each other injecting humor, sarcasm, and with such quick retorts, she recognized easily the potential for each of them as a successful attorney. There were always several laugh-out-loud moments, which she chastised herself for forgetting that she was the adult in the vehicle.

At first Tay rebelled against being transported to the school, but Lena was firm with him, trying to hide her concern and fear for the boys' well-being. The young men had set up a system, although Lena was never able to break the code, as to who would ride shotgun. She saw the intimate huddle formed before they headed to the SUV. The boys were quieter than usual when they entered the vehicle. Jabo was the first to speak.

"You just don't know him like I know him," said Jabo.

"Naw, that ain't it at all," Ray Rock added. "That man hates my guts. He acts like he is mad at me for even signing up for the course. My mom says it has something to do with my ole man, but that stuff happened before I was born. I swear, he seems like he wants me to hit him."

"He probably does because then he could kick you out of school and have you arrested for assault," Jabo interjected.

"Just stay away from him, man," said Tay.

"I do. It's like he stalks me. I don't care where I am, he shows up. I am about ready to quit all together."

"And do what?" asked Tay. "Wind up on the street? Then he wins again. Another black male, high school dropout."

Lena, sat quietly. It was as if the boys forgot she was in the car. She listened at the surprisingly wise advice they offered each other. Yet, she was angry, about to explode. Children should not feel this threatened at school, and especially by the teachers and administrators who are supposed to be their support and encouragement.

It's exactly what she had heard. The school was being run by a gang, a gang of teachers and principals.

She never had the time in the past, but she would start volunteering at the high school tomorrow. Her mama had always told her how important it was to show her face at the school, and now she knew why. Even with her bad leg, her mom was always at the school taking up tickets at the games and working the registers at the concessions stands.

"If they know you care, then they will care," she constantly told them.

Somebody needed to watch out for the children. Her mind was made up. When she dropped the boys off tomorrow, she would stay and volunteer in whatever capacity.

Lena felt good about her new decision, and was still processing the thought when she walked to the mailbox. This had been a highlight of her day when she worked, because Miss Ada was normally at the mailbox at the same time, and they had their brief and thoughtful conversations. *Her arthritis must be bothering her today. I need to go check.*

Lena thought some kids had set off some fireworks. She didn't remember anything else except feeling as if a brick had hit her chest. When she came to, Tay was crying and calling her name, and the other two boys were hovering over her. There was someone screaming. It wasn't until she was safely tucked into her bed that she fully understood what had happened.

According to Tay, just as she headed to the mailbox, a car sped by spraying bullets all over the place. He, Jabo, and Ray Rock immediately hit the ground, and then Tay remembered that she was at the mailbox.

When he jumped up, he saw a large blue Ford with someone in a hoodie spraying bullets at Miss Cori's house and their home. He looked for his mom and saw her lying on the ground. Miss Ada headed out the door and he yelled for her to get back in inside. Then Miss Cori stormed out the door holding a shotgun, yelling that she won't gonna take anything else from those crackers.

He was trying to pick up his mom, when Jabo and Ray Rock came to help him. There was no sign of blood, but there was a hole in her blouse. She began moaning as they entered her home and began rubbing the back of her head.

Apparently, she hit her head when she fell back on the driveway. They laid her on the sunroom sofa when Cori ordered them to move away from her. As Cori examined her for any other wounds, she found a bullet lodged in her bra. It truly was a miracle bra.

Lena had definitely been shot. Fortunately, the bullet had ricocheted off something and hit her. Her husband gave her a thorough examination, and determined that the force of the shot knocked her down and she hit her head on one of the landscape bricks that lined Miss Cori's flower garden.

This was more serious than Lena imagined. Jabo, Ray Rock, and Tay assured Miss Cori that this was not the work of the Klan. They recognized the car as the one that Breeze rode around in occasionally.

Snoot Snead arrived to Miss Cori's ravings about his incompetence.

"You locked my Bobby Lee up, and these hoodlums are riding up and down the street shooting at folks in broad daylight."

Snoot tried to ignore her, but it was obvious that her words struck a nerve. He took down the details of the car, and Klein felt this was the time to notify him of what Jamison had overheard. If Snoot was surprised, he didn't show it all. If anything, he seemed angrier than ever. He offered his apologies to Lena and her family, and assured Miss Cori that he was only doing his job when he locked up Bobby Lee.

Miss Cori was right, thought Snoot. He was sworn to protect the citizens in this town. The nicest girl in town was murdered, a crippled veteran was beat to death, an innocent man was locked up, and now a drive by shooting at children and elderly women.

Barnett and his crew had done their share of dirt over the years, but they really hadn't hurt anyone. This had gone too far.

Chapter Fifty-Three

"Death can be faced, dealt with, adjusted to, outlived. It's the not knowing that destroys interminably... This being suspended in suspense; waiting—weightless, How does one face the faceless, adjust to nothing? Waiting implies something to wait for. Is there? There is One. One who knows... I rest my soul on that."

– Ruth Graham

It was going to be a busy day. The cheerleading competition and a quick visit with Booker would take nearly the entire day. She refused to let the incident keep her in her house. Ray Rock was convinced it was for him. Snoot hoped the bullets were simply to scare them but warned all of them to be extra careful.

Booker looked frail. Emmett's death had really taken a toll on the family. So many family units had lost loved ones, but their family unit had remained intact. They tried not to think about it, but they knew that one day their circle would not remain unbroken. No one would have guessed that her adorable little nephew would be the first.

Marian and Wayne were vegetative until Brittani with an *i* arrived with the news of their first grandbaby. The baby was due soon, and even though they grieved, they were elated that Brittani with an *i* wanted to go to college. The thought of being able to help raise Emmett's baby boy was the balm that both needed desperately.

Lena never thought of her parents as old, but Ma Liz and Papa Simon finally looked like elderly people. A part of them died right along with Emmett, and they were worrying themselves to death over Booker's sickness. Lena didn't know how much more her family could take, but Ma Liz's words always echoed in her head, "The Lord don't put more on you than you can bear."

She had cried so many tears for Emmett and Booker, she was often surprised that she even had any tears left. Keeping busy with the children distracted her from grieving or even thinking.

Now there was Ray Rock. She worried constantly about him. His parents reported him as missing, but Snoot was treating it as a runaway case. She prayed every day for Ray Rock's safety and protection.

She knew he was tired of the harassments, but she feared that he would lash back and make matters worse. She talked with his mama, who was worried sick about him, especially after the shooting.

"Snoot was right when he told all of us to be careful."

This was a small town and everyone once knew each other, but Lena knew that this was no longer true. Many new people had moved into town and she hated to say it, especially since she was one of the new ones to the town, but the crime rate had also risen.

She had even thought about purchasing a gun. The children were only allowed to visit the neighbors without one of their parents. Lena thanked God for the garden, which was flourishing and kept the children busy with weeding, watering, and picking fresh vegetables.

Lena's phone startled her. She normally kept it on silent when she worked, but with her family's situation, she kept it on full blast and simply offered apologies. When she saw her niece's phone number she knew it wasn't good news.

"Lena, Daddy's gone."

Lena didn't hear anything else. She didn't even remember how she got to her room.

Apparently, she passed out and Bobby Lee and Klein carried her to her bed. She didn't know how long she had been out, but there they were. Her children with tear-drenched faces, her husband feeling her pulse, Miss Cori, Miss Ada, and Miss Victoria standing at the foot with their eyes turned toward heaven.

It was a small and solemn group around the table the next morning. Lena and the children packed a few things and moved out to be with her family.

"Summer and Bliss just cried themselves to sleep last night," said Grandmother Winthrop.

"I finally got them to settle down just enough to learn that neither of them had even met Uncle Booker. They were so hysterical, I thought for sure they had spent quite a bit of time with the Taylor family."

"You know, I was actually thinking the same thing this morning as I dried my own eyes. I never set eyes on Uncle Booker, yet I was crying as if he was my very own young'un," Cori added.

All three ladies dabbed their eyes in sync.

Ada finally found the strength to contribute to the conversation. "I guess all the stories and all the hours of concerted prayer endeared us to him and his family. I feel as if I know every one of them."

"I know," Cori continued. "I feel as if I've lost a member of my own family. And they just finished burying young Emmett. I don't know how they gon' make it. It's gonna take the Lord to get the family through this."

No one had to request it. The ladies bowed their head in silence as tears joined their cold, completely full coffee cups. After the prayer ended, it was decided that the older women would attend the funeral and when Lena and the children returned, they would celebrate Uncle Booker's life with the younger ones.

***

Grace volunteered to drive the ladies and Ada offered her car. Grace suggested they plan to arrive at least an hour before the funeral. She also warned them to be prepared to for a long day. Uncle Booker was well-known, well-loved, and the family was huge.

On the day of the funeral, the ladies departed on schedule. Grace had cases out in that part of the county, so she had no trouble finding the church. As they approached the community, she saw people parked on the side of the road walking up the highway about a mile from the church.

Perhaps they don't want to get caught in the traffic congestion when leaving the funeral, Grace thought to herself.

As she continued to drive, she realized that the people were walking because that was as close as they could park to the church. Grace was soon locked in traffic, and was ordered to turn her car around.

Just as she maneuvered the Lincoln and headed away from the church, someone began running towards the car. It was Tay who opened the door and practically collapsed in Cori's arms. Cori, who normally refrained from public displays of affection, held the sobbing boy.

Apparently, Lizzie was informed of their arrival and soon Ada's arms encircled her body, attempting to calm the rhythmic jerking. A funeral director allowed a brief moment of mourning, and then escorted them to the air-conditioned overflow room. One of the attendants parked Ada's car in a reserved parking space.

Grace did not understate the length of the funeral at all. The ladies watched the emotional and heart wrenching ceremony on a huge screen in the fellowship hall. There were gut wrenching sobs intermixed with complaints that the coffin was not open. Ada couldn't help but smile at some of the comments. She would never understand African Americans' obsession to see a dead body in a casket.

After the funeral, they attempted at a snail's pace to make their way to the family. Ada hoped her legs would not give out on her. As much as they wanted to offer their condolences to the family, the elderly ladies were emotionally spent and decided that they should head on back home. They knew Lena would understand.

The past four days were a complete blur to Lena. They knew Booker was declining, but hoped for a little more time. It had only been six weeks since Emmett's death and they were once again facing death.

Booker was prepared in every way. In typical Booker fashion, he had all his affairs in order, including writing detailed, specific funeral instructions. He had enough insurance that his family would be taken care of financially and he even left some for Ma Liz and Papa Simon, the Rec Center, and each of his siblings.

It was just like Booker to think about everyone, but it didn't matter. Hearts were broken, there was confusion, there was questioning, and you can't have a funeral without a family feud.

It started when head Deacon Baldwin, who loved to put on a show in front of large audiences, wanted to say a prayer. He'd been told that he sounded a lot like Dr. King, so when the church was packed he would go into full Dr. King mode on the audience.

His booming voice would wake the sleeping parishioners and scare the unsaved ones straight. The audience would range from those who shouted amen regardless of what came out of his mouth, to the ones who rolled their eyes so much until they left church with a migraine.

When they contacted Aunt Nyra, she said she didn't care who prayed, it wasn't going to bring her Booker back. So, the pastor accepted Deacon Baldwin's offer to pray. Well, Papa Simon, who was normally very quiet about issues such as those, was not having it.

He said Baldwin was the main one who tried to vote Booker off the Deacon

Board. Lena passed this information on to Aretha, who instantly disagreed, because from their junior high years to the present day, if Lena said it was white, Aretha said it was black. If Lena said it was hot, Aretha said it was cold.

Lena honestly did try to get along with her niece, who was only a few months younger than she, but as they got older, the divide in their relationship widened. Ma Liz said she nearly worried herself into a stroke at the thought of only one of them making the cheerleading squad. She said she didn't think there was a happier person on earth when she learned that they both made it.

The older siblings thought that Aunt Nyra fed this rivalry because she resented how Booker doted on his baby sister. Whatever they provided for Aretha, Booker made sure that Lena had the same thing. I think everyone was happy when Lena decided to go to Elon College and Aretha set her sights on North Carolina Central University.

If Lena had not been so overcome with grief herself, she would have insisted that one of the other siblings pass the information on to Aretha. But grief fogs the thinking process, and she didn't think about the one-sided feud. It wasn't settled until Aunt Béthune went over and had a conversation with Aunt Nyra and Aretha.

Everyone was afraid of Aunt Béthune. She was the oldest girl and had ways just like Ma Liz. She didn't play and she was not about to have any foolishness around her brother's funeral. The thought of Rory Baldwin praying over her brother and best friend nearly caused her to have her own aneurysm. She couldn't stand Rory and he knew it. She had given him a black eye in elementary school when he made fun of her name.

"Bethany is spelled B-e-t-h-a-n-y. Not B-e-t-h-u-n-e."

"It's my name and I'll spell it any way I want to spell it."

Rory continued to tease her and she slapped the snot out of him. Nobody was going to make fun of her name.

Aunt Béthune's name was never discussed in her home. Ma Liz chose Aunt Béthune's name after a relative sent her an article with a photo of Mary McCleod Bethune with President Truman. Ma Liz never had a formal education but could sight read a little. No one had a television and their old radio only worked on good days.

All of Ma Liz's children were born at home except for Lena, so when it came time to name her little girl, Ma Liz wanted her named after the Colored educator in the newspaper article, Be-thu-ne. When the midwife tried to correct the spelling, Ma Liz was insistent that she wanted it spelled Be-thu-ne. She said it looked like Béthune to her and that was the end of any discussion on the matter.

But Aunt Béthune received a lot of teasing about her name. She eventually added the accent to it and knocked the soup out of everyone who felt the need to poke fun at it.

Aunt Béthune and Uncle Booker were only eleven months apart and were as close as close could get. She knew Nyra resented her and Booker's relationship, but far as she was concerned, Nyra would just have to get over it.

She marched across the path, opened the door and told Nyra that it would be a cold day in hell before Rory Baldwin would say words over her brother, turned, walked out, and nothing else was said. It was explained to the pastor that Booker had written his plans and the family wished to honor his request.

Lena just wanted to go home and crawl into her own bed. She knew how important it was to support her parents, but she was tired of trying to be strong for the family. If one more person told her to be strong, or how God needed a flower for his garden, or if one more person asked her why they didn't open the casket, she knew she would go ballistic on them.

Profanity was rarely used in her home. Occasionally, Ma Liz used it, and everyone knew that when she did use it, she meant business. The girls in her college dorm used it freely and it wasn't long before she joined in, but as soon as she hit Taylor Road, the words instantly left her head. Plus, once she met that hot biology major who was turned off by her unladylike language, she turned it off for good. But in the past few days, words that she hadn't uttered in years slowly crept back to her vocabulary, and it was the good church folks at Taylor Road Baptist who were able to revive them.

So yes, she wanted to go home. She wanted to crawl in her own bed, pull the covers over her head, and just cry for her brother. But she couldn't. The family needed her. Her heart broke each time Papa Simon sobbed like a wounded animal. But as at least he cried.

Ma Liz had not shed a tear since Booker died. But what was even worse, she had not spoken. She sat stoically through the funeral. At times her good leg tapped the floor violently as if it alone spoke for her.

As friends and neighbors showed up, she sat in the room while they offered words of encouragement, and simply nodded. When asked a question, she responded with a nod or a shake of the head, but no word was articulated. It was eerie.

Ma Liz set the atmosphere in the home. Her voice had been the one constant in the house; it determined the mood of the home, and the absence of her voice made the pain and grief even more unbearable. The family longed for her voice; they would have paid money to hear her response to the many inquiries about the closed casket.

Leigh said nothing was wrong with her physically; it was just her way of dealing with her pain. But her children and grandchildren needed her voice. Even the young grandchildren knew something was wrong. Her great-nephew, Malcom's little toddler, Honore´ would crawl to her, climb up on her good leg, and just stare at her. She'd rub his little head, but no words would come out.

It was more than Lena could bear. The funeral was hard enough. Papa Simon sounded like a coyote that had gotten caught in a trap. She wished Ma Liz would scream or something. Poor Aunt Nyra fell on the casket and the morticians and Thur had to pry her away. This gave Deacon Baldwin an opportunity to be seen as he assisted Thur in carrying Aunt Nyra to her seat.

The tributes were so special, but most of the people ignored the two-minute limit. Lena felt like screaming and telling them to sit down and shut up because they should have told Booker those things while he was living. Then the mortuary broke the cardinal mortuary rule. They ran out of obituaries, and you would have thought the Japanese had attacked the country again.

Lena sat at the repast wanting to scream at the top of her lungs.

Who has an appetite after just burying a loved one? And whose bright idea was it to feed everyone who came to the funeral? Lena thought.

Booker had requested that Aunt Nyra cater the meal so no one would have to work. So of course, when the folks saw the Soulicious Catering truck, everyone stayed, since they had the best soul food in the area.

Lena sat staring at a plate with fried chicken, ham, collards, potato salad, and sweet potato pie, while people she didn't even remember stopped by to share an elementary or high school story with her.

She smiled, pretended that she knew who they were, and tried to act interested in a silly school story, when all her thoughts were on that wonderful man who they were shoving dirt on at that very moment.

So yes, she was ready to go home. And tomorrow morning she would pack up her family and leave. She was sick of sickness, she was sick of suffering, she was sick of dying, and she just wanted to go home. She would make the drive out every day to visit, but she needed her own home.

***

"It would take time," Ada told Cori.

"Yeah, time and prayer," added Cori.

The two ladies were worried about Lena and the children. Little tough-as-nails Lizzie cried at the drop of a hat, and Bliss and Summer joined the fragile child in the sudden outbursts. Tay had become withdrawn and was very much like the angry young man they first knew.

No one had seen Ray Rock, and they were not letting the children out of their sights. The ladies were thankful that Tay still showed interest in the garden, which had become a refuge for him. Lena made daily trips to the country and then returned home to her bed.

The ladies continued to provide snacks for the girls, and Ada even drove them to cheerleading practice on some days with Cori assisting the coach. Each of them had walked through that valley and knew the agony the family was enduring. They would do what they could as the Taylor family rode these rough waves of grief.

Chapter Fifty-Four

A Full Hand

The police tape still hung over the doorway, but Bobby Lee needed to unplug the freezer. Snoot had asked him to be very careful not to disturb the crime scene. He guessed he meant the bloody spot near the counter. Bobby Lee hadn't been back to his store since that Sunday afternoon, and nothing could stop the tears as he saw the area where PM had died.

What was he doing over by the counter? He usually hung out in the basement; he rarely came upstairs when I wasn't here.

He had to hurry. Snoot only gave him 10 minutes, so he would have to clean it on another day. Just as he headed to the freezer he glanced at the register, when he noticed that his dad's cigar box, where he kept the register key and extra change, was missing.

Perhaps Snoot took it for some reason. He was turning to leave when he saw it. It was on the lower shelf with the unopened boxes of potato chips.

That's weird, he thought. He always kept it near the register. He picked up the box and looked in it for the cash register key, which he found under the deck of cards. He picked up the deck of cards and smiled as he thought of his last conversation with PM.

"Barnett's holding all the cards," PM told him.

He examined the cards that PM and his crew had used many evenings around the table in the basement playing Bid Whist and Spades.

These always stayed in the basement. How did they get up here? These are the same cards, aren't they? He poured the cards out on the table. *Wait a minute… what's this?*

Bobby Lee picked up an index card that had been cut the same size as the other cards. He examined it closer. It was from PM.

"Bobby Lee! Times up! I told you, you had 10 minutes. Now don't make me regret even letting you in here!"

Bobby Lee heard shouting in a distant voice.

"Bobby Lee! Did you hear me? Are you high or something?"

Snoot's shouting alerted him and he quickly stuffed the deck of cards into his pocket, praying that Snoot didn't see them. He grabbed the plug from the freezer, muttered an incoherent and mechanical apology and thank you, and eased past Snoot, hoping his thoughts would not betray him.

He was regretful that he had chosen to walk to the store. The false concern, the inquiring, the downright nosiness, made him retreat behind the front door of his home. But he was getting a little stir crazy and decided to risk answering the same questions for the one-thousandth time. He hoped his near sprint back home didn't cause more questions and curiosity.

He pulled the cards out of his pocket and began examining the little card he discovered before Snoot's yelling nearly caused him to wet his pants. PM's tiny writing covered both sides of the card.

"Bobby Lee, I sure hope you find this card. If you are reading this, I guess I've crossed on over. I hope I made it in. I sure hate to go to a place that is worse than what I've had to endure here on this earth. If it wasn't for my mama and you and your folks, I probably would have killed myself long time ago."

Bobby Lee began crying as he continued to read.

"But this is not about me. There are some folks who have been real mean to me lately. Meaner than normal. Almost like they hate me. Now the only thing I can figure, is they know I know.

"I thought I hid really good, but maybe they saw me. See, I was hiding in the field over on Peedee Path the night Amanna Long was killed. I saw her, Bobby Lee. She was in one of those Sampson Mill trucks. It looked like she was trying to jump out, but someone kept grabbing her. The car was swerving like crazy, but when it slowed down to make the right turn on Pine Road, I saw Amanna's face pressed up against the window. I saw it clear as day under that street light on the corner.

"I couldn't see who was driving 'cause the car was going real fast, but I know it was one of the Sampson trucks. I guess you wondered why I never told anyone, but who would have believed me? The town drunk who was three sheets in the wind. But I know what I saw. That sweet girl was fighting for her life. But she didn't win.

"Now that Breeze shows up nearly everywhere I go. And he is in cahoots with Barnett and that gang. He tried to even sell me some crack one time, but I never cared for nothing more than a little reefer. I think they know I know. I know I told you, Barnett was holding all the cards. But he's not. You're holding all the cards."

Thoughts collided and crashed in Bobby Lee's head.

Poor PM. I never knew he was hurting so bad. He seemed to take everything in stride. He never complained one time, and I never knew he was scared of anyone. I never knew him at all.

The tears traced the now familiar path on his face.

I've got to get this information to Lena and Klein.

He stopped dead in his tracks.

Did I just remove evidence and get myself in even more trouble?

He had to get himself together. The last thing he needed was folks to start thinking he had lost his mind.

He knew he had to get this to Klein. He knew Lena was spending a lot of time with her family and Klein was working real hard on his case, but he seemed to run into one dead end after another.

He went around to the side of the house, and was surprised to see Lena sitting down with Klein in the bedroom turned office.

"Are you sure you're ready?" Klein asked Lena.

"If I don't do something, I will go crazy," Lena responded.

Bobby Lee knocked.

"Come on in, Bobby Lee. I was just getting ready to call you."

"Is something wrong?"

"No, I just wanted to get a little more information from you."

"How are you, Lena?"

"I was just telling Klein that I had to do something or I'll lose my mind."

"We've been praying for your family. You've gone through so much."

"One thing I've learned is that everybody is going through something."

"Now, that's the truth." Bobby Lee looked around the room as if he was looking for something.

"Are you all right, Bobby Lee?" Klein asked. "You look like you've seen a ghost."

Bobby Lee pulled a chair up beside Lena, and in a whisper began telling them of the deck of cards. By the time he finished the story, he was shaking.

"Should we give it to Snoot?" Bobby Lee asked.

The cards were evidence, but how would Snoot respond to this new development? Would he accuse Bobby Lee of tampering with evidence, or would they be accused of withholding evidence? This had to be handled carefully.

"I want to trust Snoot," said Klein, "but for the moment, let's just keep this between us. I don't know, but I think all of this is somehow connected."

"What's connected?" asked Lizzie, who rushed in with Summer.

"Lizzie! Didn't I tell you this was an office, and you just couldn't burst in anytime you wanted?"

"But we won first place again! Miss Cori coached us just like you."

"That's great!"

Lizzie continued, "What's connected?" She walked over to the whiteboard, with Bobby Lee's picture in the middle, PM, and Amanna's name.

"Who's Amanna?" asked Summer.

"That's Jabo's mama's name, isn't it?" Lizzie asked. "Somebody killed her, and they never did find the killer."

"Do you think the same person who killed PM killed Jabo's Mother?" asked Summer.

"You know what Atticus said," Lizzie began. "'They've done it before and they did it tonight and they'll do it again'!"

"Okay girls. Let's go," said Lena. "You've been watching too much *To Kill a Mockingbird*. And remember to knock next time. This is my office and we are working."

Summer continued. "I know, I know. Don't worry. We'll keep this under wrap. It's just like Atticus said, 'There's a lot of ugly things in this world, son. I wish I could keep 'em all away from you. That's never possible.'"

Klein, Bobby Lee, and Lena looked at the young girls, mystified.

Chapter Fifty-Five

"There may be times when we are powerless to prevent injustice, but there must never be a time when we fail to protest."

– Elie Wiesel

Snoot felt as if he could finally breathe. He, as well everyone else, knew that Bobby Lee had nothing to do with PM's death, but all the evidence pointed to him. Now he had the proof that he needed.

It's a shame I had to sneak around to get the evidence, but I don't know who I can trust. Barnett seems to have everyone in his back pocket, and since he's dead set on getting Bobby Lee's property, who knows what he's willing to do.

Barnett's power hungry and greedy, but I still find it hard to believe that he is a murderer.

But one thing's for sure. There is a murderer in this town and until I find the killer, everyone is suspect. I will let the facts speak for themselves and if Barnett had anything to do with PM's death, I will not hesitate to throw him in the same jail cell that held Bobby Lee.

Snoot studied the test results and thought back to the day he approached Breeze's lying mom.

Sure, she doesn't know where he is, Snoot thought to himself. *She's as poor a liar as her son.*

He headed back to the squad car, quickly scanning the premises as he had been trained to do. Nothing looked abnormal, if you considered a LSU flag normal. It was common to see a Carolina, Duke, or State flag, or even a Wake Forest flag.

He looked back at the front door. The sudden movement of the curtains did not go unnoticed, nor the smoke from the barrel in the backyard. Since there was an ordinance against burning garbage in yards, he had every right to investigate the fire.

Just as he headed to the back of the house, Breeze's mom hurriedly exited the front door, while shouting to him about a search warrant.

Now Snoot was really curious, and informed Mrs. Baxton of the town's ordinance.

"But since you think I need a search warrant, hold on a minute." The conversation to his office was as brief as his response to Mrs. Baxton.

"Your search warrant is on the way, and you better hope we don't find anything because you will be just as guilty as your sorry son."

Mrs. Baxton stood frozen in her tracks while Snoot examined the trash. It smelled of lighter fluid, which had been quite successful. Snoot picked up a stick and examined the burned particles closer. It looked like a shirt, which was burned nearly to shreds.

There was also a pair of shoes that had suffered quite a bit. Although the top of the shoes had been torched significantly, the flame fizzled before getting to the sole of the shoes. He was just getting ready to return to his car when he saw another barrel near the back door. This one was sparsely covered with a tarp. As he headed to the barrel, Mrs. Baxton chastised him, reminding him of the search warrant.

It wasn't long before he heard the sirens from the squad car speeding towards the house. Deputy Slade nearly stumbled out of the car. Even Snoot was surprised at the record-breaking speed in which he was able to obtain the search warrant.

Snoot sent Deputy Slade to investigate the barrel by the door while he quickly discarded the singed shoes in the back of his car. As he turned the corner of the house, Deputy Slade summoned him to the barrel. He didn't know what to expect, but he definitely didn't expect to find empty alcohol, Sudafed, and nail polish bottles along with lye containers. He didn't have to ask any questions because he knew the answer. He was standing in the backyard of a meth lab.

As Deputy Slade confiscated the containers, Mrs. Baxton vehemently proclaimed that she was not aware of the items in the barrel and quickly threw her son under the bus.

Snoot could not believe his good fortune. He let Deputy Slade expend all his energy on the meth lab case while he purposely kept the discovery of the burned shoes to himself. He was concerned about the constant leaks from his office, and did not believe the press needed to know everything. Sometimes information helped the criminal, and he was not about to help the person who killed the most harmless person in town. So he waited and prayed that the shoe matched the footprint that he found in the store.

When the report from the police lab finally arrived, it gave him the proof he needed. Now his prayers had been answered, and he could put an end to some of the suffering, if not all of it. He was fully aware that many in town considered him as incompetent as Barney Fife. He knew that they thought he was in Barnett's pocket. He'd known Barnett all his life, and he just did not believe he was capable of murder.

Say what they want, he tried to be fair even though he was guilty of turning his head when it came to some things. Some might call that biased; he simply looked at it as essentials and negotiables. There were some things that were negotiable. But matters of life and death were not negotiable, and somebody was going to pay for PM's death, and he didn't care who was involved.

Chapter Fifty-Six

A Balm in Gilead

Tay and his posse had poured themselves into the garden since Uncle Booker's death, and the garden was flourishing. It even seemed to brighten Papa Simon's face when he stopped by to see his grandson's harvest.

"That man has aged twenty years," Cori observed.

Ada nodded as she joined Cori at the kitchen window. The once tall frame had taken a slight stoop.

"Grief done beat him down," Cori continued.

Ada shook her head in agreement, but could see the pride in his grandson radiating through the sadness.

The ladies spent nearly every spare minute with string beans, black-eyed peas, cucumbers, tomatoes, and squash. Since Bliss and Summer's kitchen was larger and had more up to date appliances, the vegetable duties were relocated to their home.

Every morning Bobby Lee brought Miss Inez by to join the ladies for the morning devotion and to help with the vegetables. He thought it would do her good to get out of the house. At first she balked, but once she got to her chair in Cori's kitchen and realized that Lizzie and Summer would be her legs for the rest of the morning, she could not imagine not being a part of the group. Even though she didn't move much, she could string beans faster than all the other ladies put together.

There was constant activity in Cori's and the Windt's backyards. The Windts had a small herb garden that they turned over to Tay, who expanded it, plus he plowed up his own backyard for a third one. The older boys nurtured the gardens and the little ones picked the vegetables. Casey, Jesús, and Maria had joined the group, also. The older girls helped, although their help was merely attempts to get the young men's attention.

But the biggest surprise was Kenya, who visited her grandmother at every opportunity. Carr even joined her on many of the visits, and they joined the group of young people in the garden.

Tay's garden had been more productive than even he had imagined.

They had eaten strawberries, frozen strawberries, and even made homemade strawberry preserves. The cabinets in both homes were nearly full with not only strawberry products, canned green beans, and tomatoes, but their freezers were overflowing also with squash and apples.

Cori thought her apple tree was finished producing, but once Tay pruned and treated it, they had more apples than they could use. They shared what they had with the parents of all the children, but they still had more apples left.

Cori, Ada, and Victoria had their hands full with slicing apples and supervision. Everyone was so busy that no one even noticed Sheriff Snoot Snead and Bobby Lee with his arms around Grace.

"Mama," Bobby Lee began. "It's over. The charges have been dropped."

Cori dropped a half-peeled apple as she ran to her son.

"Yeah, Mama," Bobby Lee continued. "Snoot just gave us the news."

All the young farmers dropped what they were doing and ran in to congratulate Mr. Bobby Lee.

"It was Breeze, wasn't it?" asked Tay.

"He's the number one suspect right now. I wish I could tell you this thing is over, but it's not. They located him down in Louisiana, and he's been talking and cooperating. But we still need you to continue to be careful. That young man is still missing, and until we put Breeze in prison where he belongs, no one is really safe."

Bobby Lee held Miss Inez and she cried softly. Cori fell to her knees thanking God. She didn't care how it looked. As far as she was concerned, the nightmare was over. She got so excited she even gave Snoot a hug, as well as a basket of apples, some canned stringed beans, a bag of squash, and some corn.

"This is some garden," said Sheriff Snead.

"Yeah, we got two other ones. I guess we got a little carried away," said Cori gleefully.

Ada, unaware she was holding Tay's hand, forgot about her dislike for the local policeman.

"This young man really has a gift with gardening. We have way more than we will ever be able to use."

"Why don't you sell some of it? All these young people who are moving into town are always looking for that *ora-ganic* foods. You might want to think about selling some of it at your store, Bobby Lee."

"I'm sure there's some ordinance or some license that I will need to get."

"I don't know about that. On the first Saturday of each month, all the farmers bring their goods into town for the farmer's market. Most of them sell out before noon. It's one coming up this Saturday."

***

The next days were busier than any of them could have imagined. They picked everything that was ripe and ready. The girls made signs advertising "Granny's Veggies." They scrounged up every table from all three homes, discussed prices, and by Friday night they were so excited, they didn't think they'd be able to sleep.

No one needed an alarm clock the next day. All the young men slept at the Vessey home, and the girls had a sleepover at Bliss and Summer's. Even Ada's grandchildren joined in the sleepovers. Victoria, who had missed out on so much of her grandchildren's lives, was just as excited as the young girls, and even slept in a sleeping bag right along with them.

They packed as much as they could into the vans and Bobby Lee's truck, and decided that they would double back for the rest when Papa Simon and the uncles arrived in their pick-ups. Tay was the star of the show, as the uncles marveled over the results of his farming skills.

With the additional room, the ladies added some of their canned goods. By 11:00 all the tables were empty, all the canned items were gone, and the ladies made more in that day than Bobby Lee made in a month at the store. The ladies were giddy at the success of the sales of their produce.

Tay stood in silence between his parents and his grandfather, but his face said it all. *It doesn't get any better than this.*

Bobby Lee thought he had cried more in the past month than he had in his entire life, so he was surprised by the new surge of tears when the ladies offered the proceeds to him. He insisted on sharing it with the young people, but unbeknownst to him, the "farmers" had met prior to this day and decided that since his store had been closed, the money should go to him. He knew that some of the children could really use the money, but they insisted that he take it. He now knew the meaning of the scripture, "for his cup runneth over."

That night, he and Grace sat at the kitchen table and examined the old green ledgers. The next morning, he walked to the post office with a pep in his step, smiling as he mailed the bills to all his regular customers marked "paid in full."

Chapter Fifty-Seven

"At his best, man is the noblest of all animals; separated from law and justice he is the worst."

– Aristotle

───────────────○───────────────

Klein had made up his mind. There was too much local and imbalanced justice in this town, and he would stay right in Blessing. Bobby Lee offered his basement to him, since Klein's request for rental properties had been denied at all the available properties in town. Grandmother Winthrop stepped right in with financial assistance for renovations.

He would continue working at Lena's until the renovations were complete and until he could obtain his credentials for practicing law in North Carolina. Then the two of them would begin practicing at their own firm. They had even decided which cases they would tackle first. After hearing about PM's sentence for marijuana, they would first aim their efforts at getting sentences reduced, starting with Unique's dad.

"Snoot Snead really wasn't a bad guy," Klein surmised. "He was real understanding when he and Lena explained how they took Jamison out to her parents' farm after the shooting. He cracked his side laughing when they told how they dressed him up in a cheerleading uniform and put a wig on his head and loaded him in the Windt van on a cheer competition day. One of the Taylor aunts picked him up at the competition and drove him out to the farm, where he had been for several weeks."

"That probably was a smart thing to do. I guess you know I don't think this Breeze character was working alone. I'm really glad no harm came to him."

Klein thought about sharing PM's letter, but too many legal ramifications were rushing through his head. He and Lena would have to think the matter through carefully. That afternoon, they decided that Bobby Lee would take the card back to the store. In a couple of days, while they were cleaning and getting the store ready to reopen, they would "find" the letter and call Snoot.

Bobby Lee was nervous when he called Snoot, who read the card over and over. He thought he even saw him wipe away a tear.

"I just don't get it. Barnett is greedy and can be cold-hearted, but it's hard to believe he would be caught up in a murder." He paused, "But power is like a drug with some people.

They begin to crave even more power and will do just about anything to hold on to it."

Chapter Fifty-Eight

"Behind every crime is a story of sadness."

– Enrique Pena Nieto

The relaxed days of summer were quickly becoming late summer, with back to school sale signs hiding windows. The girls were getting excited about their fall wardrobes and the boys had decided to try out for the football team. The ladies didn't know what they would do when they returned to school.

There was still quite a bit of produce left in the gardens and although they enjoyed it, their bodies did reveal their ages on more than one time. The young people were insistent that they leave the picking to them. They were excited about the young men's sports desires, but they were hoping that they would be able to continue to help in the garden after school.

They were discussing this over their morning coffee when Lena joined them.

"I just returned from the hospital."

All three ladies felt their hearts stop.

"Jabo's grandmother fell and broke her hip. She just got out of surgery and is doing fine, but Jabo just broke my heart. She's all he has in the world. That boy crumpled in my arms and sobbed through the entire surgery.

"I told him that I had promised his grandmother that if anything happened to her, I would raise him as if he were my own. That calmed him some, but then he started sobbing again. He told me about that awful morning when he ran in to jump in the bed with his mother, as he did every Saturday morning so they could watch the morning cartoons together.

"She was under the comforter, so he thought she was hiding from him as she often did. When he pulled the cover back, she lay their unrecognizable, covered with blood. His body shook uncontrollably as he recalled that horrible morning."

"Who could have done something so evil and brutal? They had to have known an innocent little child would find her," said Ada.

She wanted to share the information in PM's letter, but even though she didn't, she resolved that she would find who murdered Amanna.

"I just dropped him off at school, and this afternoon he'll pack and come stay with us for a while. His grandmother is going to have to go to rehab for several weeks, so I'm going to run by his home and pick up a few things for her."

***

Snoot was more than helpful, making several stops by the office with reports. Klein and Lena got the impression that he didn't feel as if his office was the most secure place. They went through every detail of the police report, which revealed very little. The only information that was most beneficial was the information on the card from PM.

Barnett had an alibi. Snoot was his alibi. There had been a big fancy gala out at Barnett's business that night, and nearly everyone who was anyone was at the gala. Snoot himself had been at the gala and Barnett was there the entire night. He was sure he saw Wallace, Bedford, Forrest, and their stuck-up wives.

"Suppose they hired someone to kill her," Klein asked.

"But why, and why use a company truck? How dumb is that?"

"Plus," added Lena, "Who would want to kill Amanna? Miss Cori said she was the sweetest girl in town, Black or White. She said everyone loved her and she didn't have any enemies. The report that I saw said that she had been knocked around some, and some of her hair had been pulled out. That sounds like a jealous woman to me."

"This is exactly where we got when we investigated. We checked into Jabo's father. His grandmother showed us an article where he had gotten hit by a car. After doing further research on the father, I found the name connected with some criminal activities up North. Soon it was all over town that Amanna had been involved with a mobster before moving here. I learned then that I couldn't trust the very people who I worked with."

It didn't take long to find the items Miss Eliza needed. Just as she was exiting, she glanced in Amanna's room. She was drawn to the photo on the bed stand, a copy of the one that Jabo had in his locket.

She looked closely at the attractive couple. She thought about the words written on the back of the picture. "Beloved." Just as she turned to leave she had a thought. "I wonder…"

Even though she knew she was alone, she looked around to make sure no one was watching. She had always been suspicious, so she even looked around for what might be some type of surveillance camera. Realizing she was bordering on paranoia, she quickly sat on the bed and began dismantling the back of the photo.

It was a good thought, but there was nothing written on the back of the photo. Deciding to leave the investigating to detectives, she began reassembling the frame, when she noticed something on the cardboard filler. It was Jabo's birth certificate, glued to the cardboard. It looked exactly like the one in the frame on the dresser, except for the father's name. It was filled in with Wallace Sampson's name. At the bottom was the same word that was written on the back of Jabo's photo, "Beloved."

Lena was shaking so hard she thought she would have a stroke. She finally calmed herself down and put the photo back together with the birth certificate in place. She placed the photo back on the nightstand, and was exiting the bedroom when she noticed some VHS tapes on the dresser. Right between *Titanic* and *My Best Friend's Wedding* was the movie, *Beloved*.

Lena's lawyer instinct kicked in and she grabbed the video and inserted it into the VCR that was on Amanna's dresser. She surveyed the room again for cameras, and with her body trembling, she sat at the foot of the bed waiting for the movie to begin, hoping that there would be some clue in the movie. Nothing could have prepared her for what was before her eyes.

Beautiful Amanna sat in the very spot that she was sitting, but on a different bed.

What was it Mama always said? "What a tangled web we weave, once we practice to deceive." Mama hated lying. "If you lie, you'll steal, if you steal, you'll kill." I know what I did was wrong. I learned early that God hates a liar. I pray he forgives me.

Wallace is a good person. He was even willing to run away with me, but I knew he could never disappoint his father. But who could've blamed him. That man is the devil himself. I pretended like I wasn't scared of him when he questioned me about Wallace. I guess that's why he was more than willing to help when Mama approached him about me going to New York to go to school.

Then I met Vinci. I was waitressing and he came in every day and sat at the same table. He was in law school, and it wasn't long before we were in a relationship. That's when the lying started. I knew I was pregnant, but I let Vinci think the baby was his. Then he gets hit by a car and I learn that he is estranged from his family, who is more powerful than Wallace's family.

I was so scared that if the family found out about me and the baby, they would believe that the baby was Vinci's and take it from me. I knew there was some reason that he didn't want his family to know me. I just thought it was my race. After the accident, the story of his family was published in the newspaper. I never believed it was an accident, but I was not staying around to find out, so I left town with nothing but the clothes on my back.

Wallace was so happy to have me back and learn about Jabo. I had no idea he would react the way he did, saying he was going to get a divorce. He wanted to tell the world, but I wouldn't let him, and he was so angry with me. I swore him to secrecy, but Jabo and I never wanted for a thing.

I didn't think a soul knew but Wallace and me. Then Mrs. Sampson, as she insists I call her, orders me into her office today and tells me she knows that Jabo is Wallace's and she doesn't care. She said she will never give Wallace a divorce, and I did her a favor since she never wanted any kids and never planned to have any. Then she looked at me with eyes of steel and said if I cared anything about Jabo, I would never breathe a word of this to Wallace or anyone else.

That woman is pure evil. Now she knows that I know what she is up to, and I don't put anything past her.

The doorbell rang and the camera stopped. Lena felt her heart stop.

That evening she met with Snoot, and discovered that he had never really closed the case. Amanna's mom once cooked meals for the jail, and Amanna made the deliveries to the jail and just lit up the place. So, he was extremely interested in solving the Amanna Dove case.

"It is another piece to the puzzle," Snoot said.

"So, Amanna had an affair with Wallace, and Jabo is Wallace's child. Do you think she tried to break up with him and he wasn't having it?" asked Klein.

"No, I can't see it. Plus, it sounds like he was really in love with her; but it's a thin line between love and hate," said Lena.

"Naw, Wallace doesn't have it in him," added Snoot. "He never would have made a football team if it hadn't been for his dad. Too soft."

"What about his wife?" asked Lena. "It sounds like Amanna thought she was capable of anything."

"But she was at the Gala," said Snoot. "She headed up the entire thing. She does it every year; raises lots of monies for charities and scholarships."

"How long was the event?" asked Klein.

"It lasted several hours. I remembered thinking how long the thing was going. My head was beginning to hurt because the music was so loud. It was still hurting when I got the call about Amanna."

"Was she there for the entire event?" asked Lena.

"I mean, I didn't keep my eyes on her the entire evening. Not much of a looker."

"Is she from around here?" Klein continued questioning.

"No, he met her at the university. She's old money. One of her grandfathers was a US Senator or something way back in the day. Claimed she was named after a great grandmother or something."

"What is her name...I'll get this friend of mine who is a private investigator to check into her."

"Rosalie...Rosalie Brown Sampson."

Chapter Fifty-Nine

The Belle of Blessing

A few weeks went by before they heard from Ty, the PI, and they were pretty discouraged with what they heard.

Just Googling Rosalie Brown turned up 65,000 entries. There was a US Senator from Caswell named Brown, a Bedford Brown back in the 1800's. There was a daughter named Rosalie, but he couldn't find any connection to this Rosalie Brown.

That part of Rosie's story added up, but Ty's PI mind was not satisfied. A few weeks later he decided to take a trip to the university. Since the old newspaper clipping with the wedding announcement indicated that she had been a member of Sigma Phi Pi, he started there.

Ty took his daughter with him under the guise of visiting the sorority that her mother had joined. He timed it during the day when the girls would likely be in class. The housekeeper was disinterested and didn't seem to care what they were doing, as long as they didn't need her to do anything. They studied the old photos on the wall and looked through some albums that were on the shelf, with no success.

"Who y'all looking for?" asked the housekeeper.

"It's been a while, but we are trying to find a relative who was a member of this sorority about 30 years ago. How long have you been here?"

"I'm retiring next week after 35 years."

"You wouldn't happen to remember a Rosalie Brown would you?"

The maid pondered, "Rosalie...Rosalie?"

"Here's her wedding photo." Ty handed the elderly lady a photo of Rosalie and Wallace sitting in a car on their wedding day.

"Oh yeah. Rosie. I remember her. Stuck up little something."

"Yeah, that sounds like her," Ty added, pretending to know Rosie.

"But she won't in the sorority. She worked with me cleaning the rooms, if you want to call it that. Spent most of her time looking through these books. The last I heard, she had transferred to another building across campus. I didn't much mind, since she won't much help anyway."

∗∗∗

Rosie Lee Grundy could not believe her stroke of luck. Her elderly great aunt wanted her to move to her home to help care for her. Her uncle had worked in the tobacco factories and smoked as much as the factory made, until his lungs finally gave out. Now her aunt had retired and needed her help. She always knew she was destined for greatness, and this was her way out of her little backwater town.

Her one small bag was packed before her mom could finish the reply to her aunt's letter. Her family tried to talk her into waiting until the weekend, but as soon as her brothers arrived from their shift at the mill, she practically ordered them to take her to the bus station. With the bus fare and spending change her aunt had included in the letter, she didn't look back as the bus left the Rabbit Shuffle bus stop.

She prepared breakfast for her Aunt Cate and headed to the new job her aunt had arranged for her at the university. Aunt Cate was disappointed that the girl wanted to work; she had hoped Rosie would be content to take care of her, but Rosie insisted on working on the campus.

Since her aunt lived so close to the campus, she had a leisurely lunch with the fragile lady and returned home in the evenings with entertaining stories of the snooty university students. She doted on her aunt, read to her, painted her nails, styled her hair, and watched *Little House* reruns with her.

This was not hard for her, especially after she discovered that her aunt and uncle had saved nearly every penny they had earned. Even with this knowledge, she anxiously looked forward to returning to the campus. Deep down, she believed the campus held the key to her fulfilling her dreams.

The Sigma Phi Pi sorority house was unlike any home she had ever seen: the large rooms, the bathrooms with the huge soaking tubs, the spiral staircase, the sunroom, and soft plush carpet.

She became obsessed with the house, and planned from that moment to one day live in a house like that. She spent more time reading the history on the walls and studying the photos than she did cleaning.

Gertie, the senior housekeeper, argued with her on more than one occasion regarding her slothfulness. Rosie ignored Gertie, and soon began styling her hair and dressing like the girls in the sorority. Gertie tried not to show her excitement when Rosie requested to work in another building. According to records, she quit soon after she moved to the new location.

Ty continued, "When I looked at the date of her departure, I cross referenced it with dates of events on campus that year. There was a big sorority gathering of the Sigma Phi Pi sisters around the time she quit her job. Several of their sisters from neighboring colleges joined them in the celebration of the sorority's 75th anniversary.

"Now, I'm getting to the good part," Ty continued. "The Sigma Phi Pi sorority's brothers are the Alpha Gamma Epsilon fraternity. Who is a member of Alpha Gamma Epsilon? None other than Wallace Sampson.

"We looked at several photos of the sorority, but couldn't find one with her in it, until we saw this photo of the 75th anniversary of the Sigma Phi Pi. With so many of the sister sororities from around the state joining in the celebration, it would have been easy for her to slip in. When we examined the anniversary photo closely, there she was sitting on the front row, dressed in the sorority colors, smiling as if she had been crowned Miss Sigma Phi Pi.

"My next stop was Canary's Beauty Salon, where I had learned that Rosie Sampson was a regular. I told them my daughter and I were passing through and she needed to get her hair trimmed. I casually mentioned I was doing research on an old U.S. Senator from Caswell and heard he had a relative living in the area.

"I hit the jackpot, because Rosie had told them more times than they cared to hear how she was the great-great-great-granddaughter of a US Senator. Every beautician in the beauty parlor knew the story by heart.

"After a visit to Rabbit Shuffle, it didn't take long to track down the brothers. They claimed their parents had a good insurance policy that they invested wisely. Nobody had seen Rosie Lee in about twenty years. Just left and never returned. Heard she was up North somewhere.

"The next stop was the small coffee shop, where I learned that there were two other brothers who are in prison. The other two live in their deceased parents' little mill home, and are hauled in for questioning every time there is a crime in the area. About ten years ago, the mills left town, but when most of the town hit a depression, their luck seemed to change for the better. According to the waitress, they get a spank brand new Ford F-150 every two or three years."

Lena felt a chill go through her entire body. Amanna was murdered ten years ago.

Ty continued, "From my conversations with the locals, Wallace Sampson was smitten with Rosalie and her rich heritage. He proposed to her shortly after a brief courtship. Rosalie had the entire Sampson family wrapped around her fingers. Jessie had always wanted a daughter, and Rosalie doted on Barnett so much he thought she was Princess Diana. After living with them for about a year, she used her trust fund to build a huge plantation-like home on some of Barnett's land. It's probably the biggest home in the town, and the Sampsons couldn't be prouder."

They knew the rest of the story. Wallace became the principal of the high school, and Rosalie runs the Sampson Foundation and hosts a big gala every year.

Chapter Sixty

The Needle in the Haystack

Amanna's words palpitated through Lena's head. She imagined so many scenarios that she needed a break and decided she needed some Ada, Cori, and Victoria time. The ladies were sensible, practical, and just plain wise. The young people were in the garden and the ladies were busy shelling black-eyed peas.

She sat down, grabbed a bowl, and was surprised at how relaxing shelling peas was.

"Tell me about Rosalie Sampson," said Lena.

"Oh, let's see. There's not much to tell," Cori began. "Wallace met her in college or something, and she came here acting like she is the Queen of Sheba. They got a big ole house right outside of town. She comes from money 'cause it's no way they could have built that big house on Wallace's salary, unless his folks helped."

"I understand she chairs the Sampson Foundation."

"Yeah, they have a big ole party or something, what is it they call it…a gala. Every year they honor somebody in the town. Even honored Bobby Lee one year 'cause he has one of the oldest businesses in town. That one lasted a long time, lasted so long until Eddie had to take me home."

So even Cori remembers her being at the Gala too, Lena thought, somewhat dejected.

"Yeah, they had a live band that played while we ate dinner. The music was so loud, I thought my head would split, plus I had on an old girdle that was killing me. But soon as Bobby Lee finished thanking them, I asked Eddie to take me home. She was all over the place, nearly knocked us down as we left. Said she had to go in the basement to get more wine or something."

Lena nearly dropped her little bowl of peas. "I am sorry, I just remembered something I needed to tell Klein before he leaves."

**

They weren't hopeful, although blood residues had been recovered from ancient relics.

Rosalie was quite warm and friendly when Snoot and his deputy showed up with the luminol and the search warrant to search the basement.

Snoot, who normally was calm in most circumstances, was quite shaken when the lights were turned off and blood was found in the corner of the room.

Barnett was not as calm as Rosalie, though. He was offended that Snoot was insinuating that he was involved in a murder.

Barnett, Rosalie, and the entire Sampson clan were at the gala. Just about everybody in town could vouch for that, and the Sampson family had employed Amanna and her parents at some time or the other.

The news reported that the blood found in the industry basement matched Amanna's, and the amount indicated that the murder could possibly have taken place there.

Wallace didn't show up for work the next day. His staff thought the news report was too embarrassing to the family. Little did they know, he had been in his bed sobbing uncontrollably since he heard it. Fortunately for him, Rosalie's restless leg syndrome caused her to take a suite at the other end of the hall some time ago. He didn't like the idea at first, but he was glad to be able to grieve alone in private.

Snoot was so close, but still so far away from solving Amanna's case. They had the murder site, but no weapon, no witnesses, no motive, and the interested parties all had alibis. So, he was back where he started.

Snoot was relieved that Breeze was safely behind bars after they tracked him down in Louisiana. When they found him, he admitted to killing PM, but claimed it was an accident, that he was just trying to scare him a little bit. That part Snoot believed.

He believed Breeze was trying to scare Bobby Lee into selling his place, but he had no proof.

"Unfortunately, Breeze now appears to have amnesia," stated Snoot, "and is not as cooperative as he was in Louisiana. He has a high-powered attorney who has a reputation for defending White supremacists. His mama visits him every day, and returns to her brand new doublewide out on highway 119, so I imagine he will remember even less. I hate to admit it, but this has Barnett's hands all over it."

Lena listened quietly. She hoped the guilt of assuming that Breeze was Black didn't show. She had heard that his dad was in prison for drugs, that he stayed in trouble, and she made the very false assumption that he was Black. She was as bad as the people she quickly judged and criticized.

Tay and the guys had never mentioned his race, and she thought he was called Breeze because they thought he was so cool. They, too, were surprised that *Brees* was his real name. Leigh was a New Orleans Saints fan, so Lena was familiar with quarterback, Drew Brees. She was sorry that this young man chose to dishonor his name.

That evening, they sat in front of the white board again.

"Okay," Klein began. "We have Amanna, the Sampsons, and the gala. How are these connected? What did she discover?"

Ty arrived just as they brainstormed, trying to connect the dots.

"I did find out a little about the foundation. Besides honoring a citizen and giving out a few scholarships, I could not find any record of any other donations or beneficiaries of the monies.

"The bank for the foundation is a small bank near Chapel Hill. Now get this. It's right around the corner from where Rosalie's aunt lived. I know this is cliché, but we need to follow the money."

"Barnett was appalled that his industry had been used in a mob hit," the paper stated. Rosalie reiterated the same statement when she was questioned by a reporter as she left the foundation. This was reported as fact without any validation, which seemed to be a trend in journalism. Soon this was accepted as the truth, and the community was quick to leave the subject alone for fear of retribution from the mob.

Ty was a private investigator because as far back as he could remember, he loved solving puzzles. Even though Blessing had accepted the mob story, he was not letting it go. It required only a color printer and his daughter. He promised her that this would be the last time he would use her. But she quickly responded that she planned be a private investigator too.

They entered the little bank with a letter on Sampson Foundation stationary, which he had created that morning. The letter stated that his daughter was the recipient of a $1000 Sampson Foundation scholarship. They were to present this letter to the bank, and the funds would be forwarded to the girl's school. The letter was signed by the Sampson Foundation Chair, Rosalie Sampson.

He scanned the bank for the teller who appeared to be the most incompetent or least attentive to details. He spotted her right away, as she focused on her two-inch nails. The girl asked a few questions about the college and proceeded to call up the account information for the foundation.

"There must be some mistake. The foundation does not have enough to cover this scholarship."

One of the managers walked by just as Ty began to question the girl's information.

"What is the problem?"

Ty's daughter proceeded to explain, showing the bank administrator the award letter.

"I am sorry, but this letter should be taken to your school and once we hear from your school, the funds will be sent directly to your school."

Ty in turn began to chastise his daughter. "Didn't I tell you that this letter was just a notification? You might be going to college, but you have a lot to learn." Then he stormed out, dragging the girl with him.

That evening Ty shared the bank exchange with Lena and Klein.

"So, the foundation doesn't even have $1,000 in it?" said Lena. "I understand they have numerous fund raisings, art shows, fashion shows, and they claim that they give out thousands yearly. What if this is what Amanna discovered?"

Snoot had been doing his own investigating. He had contacted everyone connected with the gala.

They all had rock solid alibis: he and 300 other people were their alibis. The only person he could not vouch for personally was Bodine Jones, the custodian. Records indicated that he was working the gala, but no one could remember seeing him. The first time Snoot went by his trailer, he was so wasted, Bodine's girlfriend told him to come back.

Lena knew they were getting close to finding the truth, and she could hardly contain herself. Miss Eliza was doing well in rehab, but Lena didn't know if she would ever be able to manage her home again. She was still surprised that this woman was the age of her brother, Booker. The tragedy really took a toll on her.

People don't realize how a senseless, heartless tragedy affects more than just the victim, Lena thought. *The victim is only one of the victims. All of the family members are victims, except their victimization lasts the rest of their lives.*

Snoot stopped by that morning and provided them with an update, and how he planned to question both Rosalie and Bodine later on that day. When he informed Mrs. Sampson that he had gotten a report of mismanagement of the Sampson Foundation funds, she was appalled but was very cooperative. She presented him with the most recent financial statement indicating all donations, contributions, transactions, scholarships, and the very hefty balance.

When Snoot questioned Rosalie about her background, she unexpectedly broke down and confessed to him that she had been living a lie. Begging him not to betray her confidence, she shared how she kept the fact that she grew up poor from the Sampsons. She told him how her elderly aunt took her in and left everything to her.

Once she left her hometown, she never returned and simply tried to better her life. When he inquired about the foundation's finances, the combination of the bank transactions and the tears convinced Snoot that she was telling the truth. He even admired how she was able to transform her life.

Lena and Klein were anxious to hear the results of Snoot's visit with Bodine, but they were surprised to see him back so soon.

"We finally got a break in Amanna's case. Bodine's woman reported him missing this morning. We just returned from his place. He left this letter.

I can't live with myself anymore. I didn't mean to kill her. Earlier that day I thought she was gone to lunch, but she came back and caught me going through the petty cash. She told me she would be reporting me to Miss Rosalie.

Miss Rosalie never said nothing to me, so I figured she changed her mind. I went to her house and tried to get her to change her mind. I told her I would do anything, if she didn't tell on me. She swore if Miss Rosalie didn't do anything, she would tell Mr. Barnett. I knew he didn't care that much for me and I just snapped.

I told her if she didn't go with me, I would kill her little boy. I told her she was going to give me the rest of the cash in the vault and then I would be on my way, but she was just like a wildcat. I slapped her around a bit, and when we got to the back entrance she took off.

I caught her by her hair as she tried to get away and she tripped and fell down the basement steps. I thought she was dead and I tried to open the safe with my pocketknife, but she came to and started screaming. I just tried to get her quiet and she was swinging like crazy, and I just started fighting her with my knife. Finally, she was quiet.

I cleaned the basement with some of my cleanser and rolled her up in an old blanket. That band was so loud, nobody heard a thing. I drove the truck to the back and carried her up the basement steps wrapped in the rug. Then, I took her back home and placed her in her bed. The little boy was still sleeping soundly. Now you know.

"My deputy and I drove around looking for him, and we saw truck tracks leading to the ramp at Phillips pond. The ramp had collapsed, and we could see the back of the truck sticking out of the water. They are dragging the creek now for his body."

Lena was stunned. "So, I guess the case is finally solved."

"It appears so."

Lena thought she would be excited to finally know what happened to Amanna. But she wasn't. It was as if the murder had just taken place. She couldn't explain the sadness and loss.

The story made the headlines. *Cold Case Solved!* The article provided information regarding the suicide letter and the ongoing search for Bodine's body. They had found his wallet, some clothing, and some other personal items, but they had not recovered the body.

There was a quote from Barnett expressing his gratitude to the police department, and how dear Amanna was to his family. Rosalie even expressed her sorrow, but was grateful that the family could now have closure. Wallace, who still had not returned to work, lay crumbled on his bedroom floor.

Chapter Sixty-One

"It is discouraging how many people are shocked by honesty and how few by deceit."

– Noel Coward

Even though all the evidence supported the suicide, Lena could not explain her unrest.

Ty's detective mind was even more turbulent. "It's just too convenient," he shared with Lena.

"Ten years of no clues, no information, no evidence, and after one day of questioning, the case is solved. And how coincidental was it that the foundation and Rosalie's aunt used the same bank. What about the missing money from the foundation? She could easily switch money from one account to another one if her name is on both accounts. I would bet money that she is involved."

"But Snoot has declared the case solved," Lena added. "He didn't find much on Bodine. He apparently came to town with the county fair. Barnett or someone from the company noticed how efficient he was in maintaining the fair rides, and hired him to maintain the machines at the mill."

"Well, it may look as if the case is solved, but I learned a long time ago, that looks can be deceiving. So, if it's all right with you, I want to check on a few more things."

A trip back down to the east coast only added to Ty's suspicions. The two brothers had gone away on a fishing trip, which they did quite often according to the neighbors. One of the neighbors had a photo of them at a recent pig picking.

They weren't bad looking fellows if you could see their faces behind the beards that hung down their chest. But there was something familiar about them. That evening, he looked at the photo of Bodine that was plastered across the front of the *Blessing Gazette*.

It took a while because he still was not as computer literate as most elementary students. After photo shopping and cropping the brothers' photos, Ty was sure he had what he had been searching for. He was looking directly at the face of Bodine Jones.

Lena could not explain her unrest. She was just as suspicious as Ty, and she shared her apprehensions to Jabo's grandmother. Miss Eliza's words vibrated through her mind each time she thought about it.

"It really doesn't matter. It's not gonna bring her back. I need to spend what time and energy I have left on the living, on my little Jabo."

Lena took the woman's wise words of advice to heart, and began to spend more time with her own children and her parents. Ma Liz was still mute, and the family began discussing getting professional help for her, but Papa Simon wasn't having it. He said she was just grieving in her own way. The trips were still very painful. Their lives had been forever changed.

Chapter Sixty-Two

"The love of the family, the love of one person can heal. It heals the scars left by a larger society. A massive, powerful society."

— Maya Angelou

The ladies were excited but tired. It was time for another farmer's market. It was the last one before the children returned to school. The young men had picked everything that was available from the garden and were loading items into Lena's van.

The ladies had made jellies, homemade breads, cookies, and even pies. Tal Jr.'s grandmother, Miss Polly, had joined the group and became the chief pie maker. When Eddie expressed how Tal Jr. wanted to bring his grandmother to join the ladies, Grace tried to hide her true feelings about having Miss Polly help with the cooking.

When Grace arrived after work the night before the farmer's market, there was Miss Polly with glasses as thick as headlights, rolling pie crust with Lizzie and Summer. The older girls left the making of the pie crust to the young girls, because they didn't want to damage their nails.

Once Lizzie and Summer finished with the crust, the older girls scooped the pie fillings into the crust and the younger girls covered the pies; however, when anyone commented as to how delicious the pies were, the older girls quickly took credit for them.

The older ladies tried not to show it, but they were near exhaustion. They were glad the teenaged girls insisted on cleaning the kitchen, provided there were rubber gloves.

The last of the pies were cooling and Tal Jr. had just taken his grandmother home. The older ladies left the young ones with the dishes and were sitting at Cori's table when Lena arrived.

"Child, you look like you've seen a ghost," said Cori.

"Lord, you're shaking. Here, sit down," Ada added.

"It's Ma Liz," Lena began.

"Lord, have mercy. What is it?" asked Cori.

"She's fine." Lena whispered. "At least I think she is. She finally spoke."

"Thank God," Cori said.

"We were sitting at the dinner table," Lena began. "Nobody was saying much, I guess we were all use to Ma Liz beginning and finishing the conversation. Since she hasn't spoken a word since Booker's death, dinner has been a mixture of attempts at lighthearted talk, to sobs. It's amazing how much a death changes life. After each of us shared a mundane happening of the week, it got eerily silent. Thur's granddaughter, who is a little younger than Lizzie, had joined the older ones around the table and broke the silence."

"I miss us," said Whitney.

"What do you mean, you miss us? We're here."

"We're here, but we are not really here. It seems as if we are all someplace else. In a place when all of us were still here."

Silent heads nodded in unison. Then she was summoned by other little cousins for a Disney movie. After they left, Ma Liz started rocking back and forth moaning, a deep pain-filled moan. All of the girls headed towards her but she waved them away, just rocking and holding herself tightly.

"I couldn't open my mouth...I just couldn't," she began.

"My po' heart done broke in so many pieces. I know it sounds crazy, but I felt that if I opened my mouth, the pieces of my heart would pour out of my mouth and I would just die. I just knowed it." She cried some more, waving away all attempts at assistance.

"My family was all I ever had. I didn't have nobody," Ma Liz said.

"Ma Liz, you had all your uncles, their families, and your grandparents," Béthune cried.

"Naw...Naw, tain't so," Ma Liz continued. Then she squeezed herself even tighter as she rocked back and forth.

"I swore to my Uncle Morris that I would never tell a soul what he told me on his deathbed."

She paused again...as her children held their breath.

"He was dying. We all knowed it. We took turns sitting with him and it was my turn. Granny had my young'uns in the kitchen with her, and he was in the most pain. He just tossed and turned, and I just didn't know what to do. Then he started crying, 'Lord please forgive me.' Tears just rolled down his face."

"'Little gal, I am so sorry,' he cried some more. 'I done killed.'"

"I rubbed his head thanking he was just talking out of his head."

"Uncle Morris, God ain't gonna hold what happened in the war against you. You were following the orders of those in charge. The Bible says that we's supposed to do so."

"Hush little gal and listen to me." He paused for a second, summoning strength.

"We told you a lie. I hates to tell you this, but we did what we had to do. Now, I know I don't have much time. I feel my life leaving this ole body, so you just listen to me. I know we told you that Hiram brought you here after yo' mama died having you, and then went back up North to work. That ain't so. Hiram didn't bring you here, I did."

"You my paw?" asked Ma Liz.

"Naw, now hush and listen," he whispered.

"I had been over to the Phillips seeing my girl. It was bout a two-mile walk through the woods. I was on my way home, when I heard the gunshots. I ran towards the sound, and just as I approached the little cabin that the new family had moved in, it was all in flames. I lay down in the woods, not making a move and barely breathing for fear they would hear me.

"The Ku Kluxers just stood there watching the flames, laughing and talking and chewing tobacco like they were at a baseball game or something. Finally, they rode off. I still didn't move 'cause I thought they might come back. It got real quiet except for the crackling and popping that came from the flames. The stiff, lifeless body barely moved as it hung from the branch.

"After I was sure the Ku Kluxers were gone, I ran toward the house, and then I heard a noise that sounded like a wounded animal. I followed the sound and found Mrs. Clark covered with blood lying face down on the ground. The sound got louder and I couldn't tell where it was coming from. As I got closer, I realized the sound was coming from the Mrs. Clark. I turned her over and there was a tiny baby under her, covered with blood.

"Maw had just delivered that little baby three days earlier. She had stayed with the Clarks and helped look after the older two girls for a day or so, until Mrs. Clark got on her feet. Said that oldest girl won't no more than five or six years old, but could clean just like a grown woman, had been trained real good. Said she was going to make a good cook too. She helped fix all of her mama's meals, and after a few lessons she got really good at baking too."

He paused summoning more strength.

"I didn't have time to think 'cause I was so scared the Ku Kluxers would return. I looked around for the little girls, but I didn't see them, so I grabbed the baby…" he paused. "…I grabbed you and ran through the woods to our house.

"Yo granny grabbed you and started working on you something fierce. Tears ran down her face as she worked on yo little body. Seems the blood was yo' mama's blood but you was hurt. Yo' little leg was twisted something awful, and a bone about the size of a chicken wing bone stuck out of the side.

"Howard and Clay left the room and God knows I thought I was going to faint, but I held you down on the table while yo' granny tried to set yo' little leg. She did the best she could, making a splint out of a wooden spoon handle. Finally, you stopped screaming.

"I thought you had died, but I guess you passed out from the pain. Granny kept rubbing your belly and put a little smelling salts under your nose and you started screaming again. By this time every grown man in the house was crying.

"*I brought this little angel in the world just three days ago, and already she done been touched by evil. Lord, if you let her live, she won't never know no hurt as long as I am on this earth!*'

"All of us men cried like babies. We had already fallen in love with you. Yo' Granny did the best she could making a little splint, but she always felt guilty that she hadn't done enough. It pained her to see you limping and blamed herself for it.

"We were scared something fierce of the Ku Kluxers, and knew that if they had an inkling that we had been near that lynching, we would be next. We didn't tell a soul we had you. About three days later Hiram came home. He worked over in Virginia and had gotten word of the lynching out near his home. So, we came up with the story that we told you. That Hiram's woman had died in childbirth and he brought you home for yo' granny to raise.

"Granny wanted a little girl so bad after having all of us boys and said God had sent you to us. If she hadn't been her age, she would have just claimed you as her very own, but you were her granddaughter instead. We lived so far out, we'd go weeks before we saw anyone and there was no school nearby.

"Us boys walked nearly two miles to the nearest schoolhouse, and when you got old enough, Ma made us teach you everything we learned at school. She said yo' little legs weren't strong enough to make that walk and she didn't want the children teasing you, so she kept you home with her. Now, she made sure you learned. She taught you cooking, sewing, how to pick out roots, make medicines, everything she thought you'd need to know.

"That little cabin had been vacant a long time 'cause it belonged to some relatives of the senator that was murdered at the courthouse. White folks didn't want anything to do with it and the Colored thought it was haunted.

"Yo' Granny made us boys go over and bury the couple. We looked for signs of the little girls, but they musta burned up in the fire.

"But…just listen little gal. I just had to tell you and I don't want you feeling bad about this either. Yo' granny got it right. God sent you to us, and you is ours. We loved you from the time I laid you on the kitchen table."

"Ma Liz said her heart pounded so hard that she thought she was going to have a heart attack. She could hear her babies in the kitchen playing with Granny, and she had so many questions, but she swore to her Uncle Morris and she was going to keep her promise. She never told a soul what he said until today."

"I know they loved me, but after that I felt so alone," Ma Liz continued. "I was in a house with seven uncles and a grandma and grandpa, but I felt like an orphan until I married your pa and had my own family. Now it seems like I'm losing my family again one at a time."

Then she cried, sobbed for the first time since Uncle Booker died.

There was silence, eerie silence. *It was a lot to swallow,* Lena thought.

Cori broke the silence.

"I remember that. I helped my papa in the store some after school. That family, a Colored man, his wife, and two of the prettiest little girls shopped in the store from time to time."

If Cori's mention of the word "Colored" bothered anyone, it didn't show.

"I remember thinking they must have a little Indian in them, with their reddish complexion and long braids. They came in to buy some groceries, and of course I had my questions. They had just moved to the area. The man was a teacher from up North and had come down to open up a Colored school. There was a rich man from up North somewhere who was building Colored schools all over the state.

"Those were some bad days. Two little white girls had been raped, and they strung up the man that did it. They say folks from all over went to see the hanging, just like it was a county fair attraction.

"People were really riled up about the lynching, and then that man comes to town saying he's going to start a Colored school out there near the Kilbey farm, some of Barnett's white trash kin. He musta not a known that the Kilbeys hated Coloreds more than they hated the Germans. They say that the one named Lusky was head of the local Klan. I don't thank a soul cried when he drowned in the Country Line Creek."

Lena hoped the chill that shook her body was not obvious to the group around the table as she thought about the rest of Ma Liz's story.

Uncle Morris continued to Ma Liz.

"I done killed and I ain't talking 'bout no war. I killed a man, little gal, and I am scared I ain't gonna make it in."

"He cried some more and then he beckoned me to come closer. I pulled the chair up close to the bed and he rolled over to the edge getting as close to me as he could."

"I did, little gal. I killed a man. I killed the man who killed yo family."

A few months after I found you, I headed down to the Country Line Creek to do a little fishing, and there was Lusky Kilbey, heading to the same fishing spot. Everybody knowed it was the best place to catch bass and everybody with an ounce of sense knew how much Lusky hated Colored folks. Soon as I saw him I turned to head back, but he saw me.

"Come here boy."

I kept walking.

"You hear me boy. Don't you turn and walk away from me!"

I don't know what got into me but I just kept walking. I guess I was tired. I had fought in World War I only to come back and have them treat us worse than the Germans. I just kept walking.

He picked up a branch off the ground and started towards me swinging that branch shouting, "Never should have ended slavery. Roaming around like this is yo' land. Just like them uppity folks who thought they could just move in here and start stuff. Who they teaching now?

I'll show you who to walk away from!"

He started swinging that branch at me like a madman. I grabbed it and threw him to the ground. He didn't move. I thought he was playing and trying to trick me so I kicked him, but he didn't move. Then I saw the blood. I knelt beside him and looked closer. He had fallen and hit his head on a rock. I was scared to death. Everybody knew Lusky was big in the Klan.

I listened to his chest and couldn't hear a thing. I knew I couldn't leave him here 'cause our family was the only Colored family that lived that close to the creek. So, I did the only thing I knew to do. I took him over near his fishing pole. I took his clothes off and hung them on the tree like he did when he went swimming. Then I pushed him in the water and threw the rock in after him, and I haul tailed home. I never told a soul to this day what happened. But I don't want to carry this with me to the grave.

Cori continued, "Things got real heated around here and they even burned a cross in our yard on account of my papa selling to the Colored. It quieted down some after Lusky's death. The funny thing was that he was missing for about a week before his wife even reported him missing. Seems he would disappear ev'ry so often.

"Had another family over in Chatham County, so his wife just thought he was with his other family. It wasn't 'til some young'uns went fishing and found his clothes hanging near Best Bass place. If you had a taste for bass, then that was the best place to fish. Look like he went for a swim and drowned. They found his body way down near Milton in the Dan River."

Goosebumps covered Lena's arms.

Grace rubbed her arms. "Are you all right, Lena? This is quite a story."

Lena was glad she had not shared the rest of the story. *Ma Liz was right when she said that some of that man's relatives might still be alive. It's best to let that story stay buried with Uncle Morris,* Lena thought to herself.

The story was disturbing to all the ladies, so no one was surprised when Ada excused herself with tears running down her face.

Cori suddenly put her face in her hands and began to shake. Lena rushed to her, moved by how much the story touched the elderly lady. Cori then blew her nose and left the table for the parlor. The other ladies discerned that she needed a moment to herself. She soon returned to her seat wiping her eyes.

"For nights, I cried myself to sleep when I thought about that family and those babies burning in that fire. They were two of the most darling little girls, real mannerly," Cori said. "I could never understand how you could burn a house with two little children in it. Lord, have mercy, Jesus. I never did see a baby though.

"A picture taker was passing through town around then and we sat up a little spot in the back of the store for folks to have their pictures made. That family showed up on the picture day and had theirs taken. When the picture taker returned with the photos, that family was dead. My pa said we'd hold on to the picture in case some of their kin showed up. None never did. Everybody was scared of everybody by that time.

"I kept it in the album with the rest of the family photos and I'd take it out sometimes and just cry. Just couldn't part with it. Here it is."

She passed the photo of a distinguished looking man and woman with two small girls. "As I look closer, I guess she could have been expecting."

Ada returned to the kitchen table, but her steps seemed even more painful than normal. She was carrying a little box, and as she approached the table, her legs nearly gave out. Grace jumped to help her to her seat and she collapsed in Grace's arms, sobbing.

"Miss Ada, what is it?" asked Lena. "Are you all right? Do I need to call Leigh?"

"What is it, Ada?" asked Cori, her voice cracking.

Ada tried to talk, but nothing but sobs came out of her mouth. She simply pushed the little wooden box to Lena who opened it and found some pictures and newspaper clippings. There was one of a beautiful lady with a pearl necklace in a photo similar to her older sisters' graduation photos. She passed the photo around and continued to look through the box. Grace continued to comfort Ada, who was still sobbing uncontrollably.

When the photo made it to Cori, she gasped loudly. "This is her. This is the lady, the mother of the two little girls." Her reaction caused Ada's torrents to abruptly cease.

"Cori," Ada asked weakly. "What on earth are you talking about? What lady? That's my graduation photo."

Cori stated breathlessly, "Merciful Jesus."

Chapter Sixty-Three

"Cruelty and wrong are not the greatest forces in the world. There is nothing eternal in them. Only love is eternal."

– Elisabeth Elliot

———————————◯———————————

Lena, who suddenly knew what it felt like to have an asthma attack, continued sorting through the box with her mind racing. She looked at the photos of the little girls who looked very familiar, but she couldn't remember how she knew them. There was a newspaper article of a lynching…an entire Colored family murdered. The husband lynched…the mother shot…and two little girls burned in their home.

Cori asked, "Where did you get these articles, Ada?"

Ada continued to cry.

Then there was a letter. Lena began reading, trying to control her now trembling voice:

Dear Ada,

If you are reading this letter, I am with the Lord and my dear husband, Ralph. I hate to leave you alone. I know you have been so lonesome since you lost your dear sweet sister, Mary. Please know we are still with you, watching over you, and loving you. So are your parents. You have many guardian angels right now.

I couldn't have loved you any more if I had given birth to you. God revealed himself to me that day in the barn when he sent me you two angels. You were my babies, my daughters. God only knows how you survived on your own for three days. Maybe I was wrong to keep you to myself, and to keep the truth from you, but I was determined that you would not suffer anymore.

Maybe I was wrong to change your names. But folks were so crazy, I didn't know if they would try to take you from me. So yes, I pretended like you belonged to some of my people and you were helping me in the house. Maybe I was wrong to tell you we were playing a game. Maybe I was wrong to pretend you were my house help when certain folks came around or when we went to town. I have prayed for forgiveness for hating Coy. I will always believe he killed my Mary, and God knows if that woman's husband had not killed him, I was going to kill him myself.

You have always been such a gentle soul and I am so proud of you. Miss Steepleton is always telling me how smart you are. I know you are going to make a wonderful teacher.

Since I was your only kin, I have been worrying myself sick over what is going to happen to you if something happens to me. So, I went to Greensboro and talked to a man at the Colored bank there and your schooling is all taken care of. Plus, there is money to take care of you after your schooling. I also had titles to the homes and lots made for each of the families who have helped me so much over the years, and I left my house to the church as a parsonage. The pastor is a good man, and he will make sure nobody bothers those families. I left that sorry nephew of mine enough land to keep him satisfied.

Miss Steepleton has agreed to be your guardian in the event something happens to me, which I guess has happened if you are reading this letter.

My darling daughter, I simply existed, and then you and Mary came into my life. You brought me so much joy. I know you will cry for me, and there is nothing wrong with that. "Weeping may endure for a night but joy comes in the morning." I pray that you find joy and that you find love.

I love you so much, sweet little girl.

Ada cried uncontrollably.

Lena placed the letter on the table. She studied the photos of the little girls who looked like…looked like the photos of her mama when she was a little girl. "Miss Ada… Oh my God…"

***

It all seemed so unreal. Lena cried in her *Aunt* Ada's arms. The ladies went from crying, to laughing, to praising God. The children arrived, and after learning of the new revelation, joined in the celebration.

"I knew it," Tay shouted. "I knew it was something about you. I just knew it. You're my aunt. Oh my God! You're my aunt!"

Lizzie jumped up and down screaming, "She's my aunt, Summer!"

Summer smiled, but Grandmother Victoria instantly saw the sadness in her eyes. While the children doted on their "new" aunt, she hugged her grand-daughters tight.

"Summer, these are my sisters in Christ!" Grandmother Victoria began. "That makes Ada and Cori your 'aunts' also!"

Little Robbie, who was visiting, was awakened by the commotion, ran downstairs, and joined in the celebration, even though he wasn't quite sure what it was about.

"Wait until Ma Liz hears this. Can I call her, Mommy?"

"No, Ma Liz needs to hear this in person. I'm driving out there and I am going to tell her myself."

"Can I go? Please can I go?" begged Lizzie.

"Me too?" Tay added.

"Miss Ada, I mean Aunt Ada, may I borrow this picture?" asked Lena.

Lena was not surprised to find the lights out at home. Her parents both went to bed early, especially on Saturday night. They took their Saturday night baths, Ma Liz prepared the Sunday dinner, and they anxiously anticipated the Sunday service and the family dinner.

Papa Simon answered the door. "Lord, chile, what is you doing here this late?"

"Daddy, it's not that late, it's only 10:00."

"What's wrong?" Ma Liz shouted as she came through the bedroom door.

"Nothing is wrong, I just had some news and I couldn't wait to tell you.

"I was visiting Miss Ada and Miss Cori, and I know you didn't want me to tell Uncle Morris's story, but I just had to tell them."

"Lena, didn't I tell you not to breathe a word of that story to no one?"

"I know Ma Liz, but just listen. After I finished telling the story, Miss Ada was so disturbed that she had to get up and leave the table. When she returned, she had this box of stuff and this letter. Now listen."

Lena read the letter. Then she handed her mother the newspaper clippings, and then the photo of the little girls who were mirror images of her childhood photos. Ma Liz began trembling and little Lizzie ran over and grabbed her. "Ma Liz, it's a miracle, that's what it is. As Reverend Limberson says, 'Look at God!'"

Within minutes, all the brothers and sisters were at the house rejoicing. It was like Christmas and birthdays rolled up into one.

"Ma Liz, I kept telling her over and over how much she reminded me of you!" said Tay.

"He sure did, Ma Liz. Even talked about how her sugar cookies tasted just like yours," said Lena.

"I guess they did. We had the same recipe!" Ma Liz laughed for the first time in months. The whole family laughed.

"Do you think it's too late to call her?" asked Ma Liz.

"I doubt if she is sleep. I doubt if any of us will sleep tonight," Lena said.

Chapter Sixty-Four

"Rising on the Wings of the Dawn!"

– Psalms 139:9

It was decided that the two sisters would meet at the church. There was so much excitement in the air, a passerby would have easily mistaken the church parking lot for a carnival. Cars lined the road just as they had done for Booker's funeral. News traveled fast. Someone had even contacted a television station and they were camped outside the church.

Ada could not believe how spry she felt, considering she didn't sleep one wink. She tossed and turned as she went from exuberance to sadness. She was giddy one moment, and the next moment she sobbed into her pillow; living right next door to her own nieces and nephews and not even knowing them.

She thought about the endless evil repercussions of slavery. How many mothers unknowingly lived next door to their own children? How many sisters and brothers possibly married, bore children with birth defects or worse, died because they were victims of a demonic, totally legal system that purposefully dissected and destroyed family units with no concern or remorse? And after slavery, another a hundred years of oppression, brutality and injustice simply because the color of a person's skin.

Although she was happy, she was also angry that she lived in a country that still refused to admit that it contributed to and legitimized the destruction and dehumanization of an entire race. So yes, she went from joy to sadness. She tossed and turned some more and was only able to sleep after a conversation with God and her Mr. Passmore.

Ada had contacted her children, who for once were on the same accord with love and compassion. They all agreed to meet at Cori's and drive the ladies to the reunion. Cori was touched, but decided to ride with her family, who were going to the service too. Grandma Victoria and her family followed in the

PETA van. Jesús, Maria, and their family joined the caravan also.

Bobby Lee was glad the Taylor family had requested reserved parking spots for the families.

He would have had to park a mile down the road. He could not believe how fast the news had traveled.

The choir was already singing in full force, "O Happy Day." People were standing out in the yard, singing in unison with the choir. Just as Frederick helped his mother out of the car, the congregation in the yard broke out into applause. Ada felt an instant kinship with the folks.

The choir continued to sing as they made their way up the church steps, and when the door opened, this time Martin ushered his mother through the door. Smiling people reached out to shake the family members' hands as they processed down the aisle. Ma Liz's family was in the very front of the church and was not yet aware of Ada's entrance. Ada's entourage was about halfway down the aisle when Lizzie could no longer contain herself. She ran down the aisle and grabbed her great-aunt's hand.

The choir ceased singing, and then there were whispers that turned to shouts. "Praise God! Thank you, God! Praise God!"

Ma Liz looked right in the eyes of her older sister. "Lord Jesus, oh my soul," she said.

Ada didn't speak. Her tears spoke for her.

She limped to Ma Liz as Ma Liz limped to her in unison. Then they grabbed each other, sobbing and praising God.

Sniffling could be heard throughout the church. Young Reverend Limberson signaled to the choir to continue singing softly, as he gave the microphone to Old Reverend Limberson.

O Happy day…

"We are witnessing a miracle!" Old Reverend Limberson began.

"*Yes!*"

"We are witnessing answered prayer!"

"*Amen!*"

"Somebody prayed for these women. Somebody prayed for them when they were nothing but little girls!"

"*Yes!*"

"We are witnessing His love that is everlasting that endureth through all generations! We are witnessing the power of God!"

"*Yes, Lord!*"

"Ain't God good!"

"*Yes!*"

"Stand to your feet and give God some praise! Some of ya'll don't know the story. You've heard bits and pieces, but I want to make sure you get the real story!"

"You see, evil touched these ladies when they weren't nothing but babies! Evil hung their daddy on a tree and shot their mama dead. But goodness triumphed over evil. A God-fearing woman raised one and a God-fearing woman raised the other. A White God-fearing woman raised the other."

"You hear me?"

"A White God-fearing woman took two little children in and raised them like they were her own. A Black God-fearing woman took a newborn baby in and nursed her back to health and raised her as her very own. Both those girls were loved and taught in the way of the Lord. They have walked with the Lord all of their lives, not even knowing that the other one existed."

"Then Miss Ada moved down South from Detroit and answered an ad. Folks thought she was a little crazy to move in with an old White woman." Some in the audience laughed. "But they are like sisters now. That White woman lived next door to our Lena."

"Look at God!" shouted Old Reverend Limberson.

"And God used a child, or little children."

"Little Lizzie and her brother Tay have had a relationship with Miss Ada for months now. She and Miss Cori look after them and several other children in their home. I know you've been seeing them in the news. Oh, they don't play."

"Tay kept telling her, 'you remind me of my grandmother.'"

"Now she had met Deacon Taylor, but every time she tried to meet Ma Liz, something came up."

"I say, the Lord wanted them to meet for the first time on this day, in this place. This is a God thing! You have children of the North and children of the South. You have White, Black, young, old, Mexicans, Muslims, rich, poor, living together, playing together, studying together, praying together, and look how the Lord has blessed them and is blessing us!"

"There is so much division, hatred, racism, anger going on right now. This is a victory over every divisive, hateful, racist act of evil. To God Be the Glory!"

"We gonna do things a little different today. I want to ask all the folks who came here with Miss Ada to stand, and I want Lena to introduce them. Now I know we know Ma Liz's family, but she has kin here who don't know them, so I want them to introduce themselves too."

"Then we gon' have the benediction. Deacon Simon says Ma Liz has cooked a feast, and these folks want to get to know each other. I know you want to meet them, but let's give them this day. I am sure they will be back."

Bobby Lee and Grace and their families decided they would give them some space too, even though Cori was dying to stay behind with Ada. She was already feeling a little left out. The entire experience was overwhelming to her.

All these years she had thought of the little family. Something would draw her to that photo, and she mourned their deaths just as she had done for her own relatives. And now the realization that one of the girls had actually been living under her very own roof, sharing her life with her. She had been taught many things in Sunday school, and heard many stories and clichés in church, but when she looked at the photo of a young Ada, the spitting image of the lady who she had mourned for so many years, she felt the brush of angels' wings. For the first time in her life, she truly knew the almighty power of God.

Ma Liz's house was not big enough for the group so they decided to have Sunday dinner at The Time Out. They had not been there since Booker's passing. There would be tears, but this time most of them would be tears of joy.

Ada could not stop looking at Ma Liz. She looked so much like Vivian that it brought tears to her eyes. For the first time, Ma Liz was a little self-conscious of her dialect, but Ada threw in a few of Mother Damaris' sayings to make her feel comfortable.

Frederick's children had already met their cousins Lizzie and Tay, and stuck pretty close to them. Papa Simon's joy returned as he seemed to find his kindred spirit in Frederick, whose personality reminded him so much of Booker. Martin bounced around from cousin to cousin. Ada bristled when Martin brought up that Frederick was a Republican. She had heard the whispers when his name was called out in church.

If it fazed Papa Simon, he didn't show it.

"We need folks around all the tables. That's how you get things working."

Frederick smiled and added, "That's what I keep telling them. We got to stop limiting ourselves and go through every door that opens for us."

The biggest surprise was Damaris, who seemed to fit right in with all her female cousins, especially Béthune and Harriet. Every few seconds a shrill of laughter came from their table. The gospel music that had welcomed them at the center had transformed into Motown without anyone seeming to notice.

As the evening progressed, some of the cousins took to the dance floor. Ada sat with her baby sister, smiling at all her nieces and nephews, and at her own children, who were truly happy for the first time in a long time. She felt a peace that had evaded her since her Mr. Passmore's death. Then "The Electric Slide" began playing.

Nieces and nephews of all ages joined in. Lizzie ran over and grabbed her grandmother's and her Aunt Ada's hands, and pulled them to the floor too. As they joined in, holding each other's hands for stability, the nieces and nephews formed a circle around them. The music ended and Papa Simon prayed.

"Lord, this family done gone through a lot, and just when we think we can't bear no more, you come in and turn our mourning into joy. Nobody but you could do this here thing. My cup just runneth over. My Booker built this place to bring the community together, to be a blessing for the young. His dream for this place is being fulfilled this moment. His body might not be here, but his spirit is sho' nuff with us this day. Thank you, Lord, that you knew about this day, even when we didn't, and we sho' nuff thank you. I pray that from this day forward that you would continue to bless this family. Guide us and draw us closer to you and to each other. We thank ya, Lord. Amen."

***

For a minivan full of people, it was a quiet ride home. They stopped at Cori's new favorite restaurant for dinner, but Cori was still upset that she wasn't allowed to stay back with the family. Plus, she never liked waiting to be seated in restaurants, and Sunday afternoons were the busiest time for the Home Place.

Of course, little Robbie had a blast playing with all the toys in the little general store. The food was good as usual, and the conversation was upbeat as they reflected on the day's events.

"It was like watching a movie and being in the movie at the same time," Eddie said.

"They probably had enough food to feed all of us," Cori said.

"Now Grandma, the preacher was right. They need a little time to themselves. I imagine Ma Liz will be coming with Papa Simon to town from now on."

"If Ada doesn't stay on out there with them," Cori said.

So, that's what was bothering her, Bobby Lee thought.

The thought of Ada not being a part of their daily lives seemed to deaden the conversation altogether, until Robbie broke the silence.

"Aunt Ada has to come back. She didn't take a suitcase."

And that seemed to clear up the matter…a little.

All the excitement wiped little Robbie out, who fell asleep as soon as he was placed in his car seat. Once again, the minivan was quiet as everyone savored the memories of the day. Cori had not said much since her family insisted that she return with them.

"I bet they're doing 'The Electric Slide'," said Cori.

"Grandma, what do you know about 'The Electric Slide'?" asked Tara.

"I can do it," Cori stated emphatically.

"She can," Eddie broke in. "I wish you could have seen her at the after-prom party at Lena's house."

"After-prom party?" asked Tara. "Grandma?"

"Lizzie says they do it at just about every event," Cori continued.

Eddie laughed because he knew that "The Electric Slide" was a part of nearly every African American event that he had attended.

"Do you think Ada's gonna stay out there with her sister?" asked Cori.

Grace, noticing the nervousness in the question, responded gently.

"It's just as Robbie said. Ada didn't take anything with her, her medicines, clothes or anything. Of course, she'll be back."

The question silenced the van again as each passenger entertained the possibility of Ada leaving.

Chapter Sixty-Five

"How many times do we miss God's blessings because they are not packaged as we expected?"

– Unknown

There was an invitation.

"Our house is empty now, with all of the young'uns gone. We got plenty of room for you. I wish you'd move on out here with us. We yo' family," Ma Liz stated emphatically.

Even Ada's children liked the idea.

"Let's pray about it. You know what they say about houseguests and fish. After three days, they start to smell," Ada responded.

"You ain't no houseguest. You is family," Ma Liz continued.

Ma Liz waited for a response from Ada. She had noticed that Ada was fancy and educated, and she reckoned they weren't high class enough.

Ada sensed the tension.

"I tell you what. How 'bout I come over on Friday and stay 'til Saturday 'til we can get used to each other."

She purposely regressed back to the dialect of the folks in her childhood community. Her Mr. Passmore was often amazed at how she could weave in and out of different socioeconomic circles with ease.

"That'll be just fine. Papa goes to town every Friday. I'll ride with him to pick you up."

***

Grace, Tara, Bliss, Summer, Grandmother Victoria, and Cori rehashed the day's events. Cori was a jackrabbit, hopping up at the slightest sound.

Bliss checked her phone every few seconds. "They are turning down the street and should be here in a few minutes."

At this proclamation, all the ladies joined Cori at the front door as Lena's minivan pulled into the driveway. Leigh had barely put it in park when Lizzie jumped from the vehicle. Tay was carefully assisting Ada, and Cori's breathing relaxed for the first time that day.

Summer started asking questions right away, when Grandmother Victoria spoke up. "Will you at least let them in the house?"

***

Finally, they had all gone. The two ladies sat around the table joking about how tired they were. Cori noticed Ada's limp had gotten noticeably worse.

"Too much electric slide, huh?"

Ada smiled and let Cori help her to her bed. That night, Cori prayed to God that Ada would not leave her. The thought of being alone in her home again caused her to toss and turn the entire night.

Of course, she'll want to move in with her sister and be around all of her nieces and nephews...But she has nieces and nephews right here who love her too...I don't know if I can live by myself again...I've gotten used to having someone in the house with me.

It had been a long time since she had such a restless night. She finally closed her eyes as the sun peeked through the blinds.

Ada, on the other hand, slept better than she had slept in many years. Even after she awoke, she lay in bed savoring the moments of yesterday.

Cori is usually stirring about now. I hope she is all right. Probably too much excitement for her too.

As ritual, she turned her television on to catch the day's weather. It was funny how as the years went by, the weather became such a matter of significance.

The ring of the telephone startled her. "Who is calling this early in the morning?"

"You up and about?" asked Ma Liz.

"I wish. Just can't seem to get moving. How about you?"

"I'm kicking but not too high, but I got a sayin'...if you lay down, you stay down."

***

Upstairs, Cori finally stirred. *Lord, have mercy. I reckon Ada thinks I've gone on to glory. I don't know the last time I've slept this late.*

Cori wrapped her old robe around her and made her way down the stairs, taking one step at a time. It took her a while but she finally saw the wisdom in her Robert's warning about hurrying on the steps.

The last thing I need is a broken hip. Seems like all my friends broke their hips, went to the nursing home for rehab and never returned. Before they knowed it, their homes were sold right up from under them.

She could hear Ada on the phone laughing when she entered the kitchen. It was a joyful sound, but it also stirred the discomfort in her stomach that caused her to toss and turn most of the night.

Just as the aroma of coffee floated through the kitchen, Cori heard Ada end her conversation. Within seconds, she heard her anvil steps toward the kitchen.

"I guess I'm moving a little slow today."

"I didn't get much sleep, just tossed and turned." Cori said. "I 'spect you gon' be moving on out with your sister."

That's one thing that Ada loved about Cori. You didn't have to guess what she was thinking. She got straight to the point.

"Well, she did invite me to move out with her, and we talked about it for a while. We decided that I'd go out to the farm on Thursday evenings and come back on Saturday mornings. So, I *'spect* you're stuck with me for a while longer, if you'll have me."

"Suit yourself."

And the ladies did something they rarely did. They looked at each other and smiled.

The moment didn't last long, and in no time the little kitchen was full. Bobby Lee made his customary stop and the younger girls soon followed, nearly out of breath.

Apparently, they were waiting and watching for signs of life in the kitchen.

"It was just like a movie," said Summer, "except we were the stars."

Soon Lena, the older girls, Tay, and Jabo appeared, and added to the joyful banter with the "Grannies."

Tay's intuitive nature observed Miss Cori each time they referred to Ada as

"Aunt Ada." It was decided that since Cori was such a "Grand" lady that she would be called "Grand." Cori feigned displeasure, but broke out into a smile each time she was addressed by her new title.

"I hate to break up this party, but the open houses are this week, and we haven't done one bit of school shopping," said Lena.

"With all the excitement, I simply forgot about school starting," said Victoria. "Lena, do you mind if I tag along with you and do some shopping for the girls? Their parents left early this morning for a PETA event in Charlotte."

"Sure. I usually let the older ones venture on their own, and once they've decided what they want, I go and decide if it's what I want."

"Sounds like a good plan to me," replied Victoria.

"Is 11:00 too early?" asked Lena.

"No, that's perfect. Ladies, I would love to sit with the two of you, but I've got, what do you call them Cori, 'young'uns'? I've got to take some 'young'uns' school shopping."

"That is probably the happiest woman on earth," said Cori.

"The second happiest woman on earth," Ada added.

Chapter Sixty-Six

"Love overflows and joy never ends in a home that is blessed with family and friends."

– Unknown

Cori's worry about Ada's leaving soon disappeared. Ada enjoyed the time out in the country getting to know her new "kin," but she was just as excited about returning to her rooms at Cori's. She and her sister talked endlessly about their families. They patched together pieces of their family history and nieces, nephews, great nieces, and great nephews who lived around on the family land wore out paths through the kitchen door. It seemed that Ma Liz cooked all day long as the platters continuously emptied.

They dropped off toddlers, ate lunch, grabbed food out of the freezer or canned goods from the cabinet, and Ada initially thought they took advantage of Liz and Simon. But she saw how much the grandparents adored the great-grandchildren, and even though Ma Liz fussed about her canned and frozen vegetables, she also noticed she always gave them more than what they asked. It took her a moment, but she slowly discerned that the visits were how the children and grandchildren touched base with them and kept them from sitting around grieving all day long.

She tried not to complain about the heat. The window air conditioner unit kept the kitchen and the front room cool, but the heat was so unbearable at times, she thought she would suffocate. Yes, she looked forward to spending time with her baby sister, but she also looked forward to returning to Cori's.

Cori on the other hand, had gotten used to having Ada's company, and did not look forward to an empty house. She wondered if the children would continue to visit if their Aunt Ada was not around. She didn't have to worry long.

Tara moved in with her parents while Michael finished his coaching contract in Charlotte. To Cori's delight, she and little Robbie spent Friday nights with their Grandmatoo.

Tara had enrolled Robbie in a pre-school and signed up to volunteer on Fridays. One of the volunteers could no longer help, so she asked Grandmatoo to assist her. Grandmatoo thought about Ada's words, and questioned who actually was the happiest woman on earth.

***

The children kept both Lena and Grandmother Winthrop hopping. The boys were busy with football, and Lena was ecstatic that all of them made the football team.

The cheerleaders had a new coach, who also coached their competitive cheer squad. She personally asked the girls to try out for the squad, but they both declined. The elder ladies listened as the younger ones explained why they didn't want to be a part of the squad. Even though the ladies saw the girls' points, they also thought they should give it a try with the new coach.

That afternoon as the ladies supervised the younger girls' homework, Unique and Bliss strutted through the door wearing their new varsity cheerleader uniforms. Cori, Lena, and Grandmother Winthrop chauffeured the girls to the boy's football games and cheered right along with the girls.

Chapter Sixty-Seven

"This is important: to get to know people, listen, expand the circle of ideas. The world is crisscrossed by roads that come closer together and move apart, but the important thing is that they lead towards the Good."

– Pope Francis

Ada could hear the excitement in the kitchen. She had watched the Republican convention the night before and was shocked right along with the others.

"Now you know I support John McCain, he being a Vietnam Vet and all," Bobby Lee began, "But I don't know about this Sarah Palin. I never even heard of her before yesterday. But she gave a really good speech and the crowd just went crazy when she spoke."

"How in the world is a woman with that many young'uns gon' be able to run for Vice President? It just sounds a little kooky to me," replied Cori.

"I was listening to the talk shows before I came over, and people are real excited. As much as I like McCain, he is pretty boring. Now, he's leading in the polls," added Bobby Lee.

"I don't like it, but if it's gon help beat that Muslim, then I'm for it."

"Mama, I've told you he's not a Muslim. You've got to stop listening to Johnny. I swear he's gone plum crazy."

Ada felt her blood pressure rising, but didn't let that stop her from joining the couple at the table.

"Did you see the convention last night, Ada?" asked Bobby Lee.

"Yes, I was really surprised that he chose a woman. That's a first. She's real pretty."

"Got a bunch of young'uns. They say she named her young'uns after places she had visited. It's a good thing she never went to Timbuktu."

Ada tried to suppress her laughter.

Cori continued nonchalantly, "One of them is just a baby and something is wrong with him."

"He has Down Syndrome. Her story was very moving," said Ada.

"Well, I better run on over to the store and get things going," said Bobby Lee. "I stay right busy now, thanks to you ladies and all of your vegetables and canned goods. I am still surprised at how much these young folks like fresh and homemade goods.

"Eddie thinks we should go through the attic and see if there are any items that we are willing to sell. He says antiques are big business and our attic is full of old things, Mama. He says we need something to keep the store going once we sell all the produce. He's been a real big help at the store. Got a good business mind. What do you think?"

"It's so much stuff up there, I wouldn't even know where to start. Y'all just go on up there and get what you think might sell. If it's gonna keep the store open, then it's all right with me. Let me see it first, and if it's not something I got some kind of attachment to, then go on and sell it."

That evening Bobby Lee, Eddie, Tal Jr., and Tator arrived to sort through the items in Cori's attic. Her mother's sewing machine, the old cast iron that propped her parent's living room door open for so many years, the old flour sifter, and wooden ironing board were the first things to go.

"You ought to see how Dad has changed things around," Eddie stated as he searched Ebay for prices on his laptop.

"It was your idea," said Bobby Lee.

"He has two card tables set up in the back of the store with checkers and cards. Lindsay donated a big flat screen TV and Mr. Raymond and Mr. Pate camp out there most of the day."

"Don't forget Tadpole and Leroy," added Tal Jr.

"Yeah, they thank me a hundred times a day for letting them play cards. Mr. Raymond and Mr. Pate keep them in line too."

"I imagine one day soon when they open the doors of the church, they are going to shock some folks," added Tal Jr.

"Miss Inez gave us some of PM's things, and we hung them on the wall by the tables," said Bobby Lee.

"I can see PM smiling that big smile right now," Cori said. She marveled at the friendly and loving banter between her son and grandson.

That night Cori prayed, "Lord, just when I think things can't get any better, you prove me wrong."

***

Ada's life became a routine of trips to the country with excitement, and equal excitement about the trip back to Cori's.

But she was not imagining things. Each week, Cori was short with her or appeared to be angry with her about something. She even heard Bobby Lee discussing it with his mother.

"Mama, I wish you would go with us to church. Johnny has lost it and the closer we get to the election, the crazier he gets. He's so angry all the time, I wonder if he still believes what he preaches. Plus, I can't tell you how much it means to worship with my whole family."

"I can't stand all that loud music," Cori began. "I talked to Lucy Mae the other day, and she told me she goes with her grand young'uns and she turns her hearing aid off and can still hear just fine."

"I don't like it either, but he preaches some really good sermons. They are right in line with the Bible too. He doesn't get stuck on one issue. He preaches about love…loving the least of these and helping the downtrodden.

"Did you know that there are over 2,000 scriptures on the poor? So, the church has opened a soup kitchen. It provides a place for children whose parents work in the evenings. It also provides adult day care for senior citizens who are not able to stay alone. There is HIV testing, and Alcoholics Anonymous and Narcotics Anonymous meet in the building, and each week we have people standing up in all the overflow rooms.

"I work in the parking lot, so by the time I finish my shift, the praise music is over and it's time for the word. You could help in the nursery. They have speakers in there and we could worship as an entire family."

Cori listened, and Bobby Lee thought he saw her face light up at the mention of all the four generations worshiping together.

"Robert Edward is buried in the cemetery. I've purchased my plot and Johnny and them have a new rule, that only members can be buried there. I can't bear the thought of not being buried beside my Robert."

Bobby Lee decided not to press it any further. It was heartbreaking but heartwarming to see the love and devotion that his mother had for his father, even after burying him over 50 years ago.

312 | Vickie Morrow

Bobby Lee decided to change the subject. "I guess you heard about Sarah Palin's daughter."

"Yeah, Johnny's wife, Laurie June, says it shows that all of us have clay feet and we need to pray for them and their baby. Least she and that boy are getting married."

Bobby Lee was surprised at how understanding and supportive his mother and the church were to Sarah Palin's daughter, when they had kicked several young girls out the church. He was shocked but glad to see something other than hate coming out of the church.

Ada noticed a pattern. Sunday afternoons were the worse. Cori was short with her, sarcastic, and at times, downright rude. Monday's were just a little better. By Tuesday, she was pleasant and by the time the Wednesday morning Bible study rolled around, she was somewhat civil.

The ladies decided that they would not discuss politics and they would pray for all the candidates. Ada couldn't help but notice that Cori was very quiet when Senator Obama and Senator Biden's names were mentioned.

Chapter Sixty-Eight

"Lord, grant me the serenity to accept the things I cannot change, the courage to change the things I can, and the wisdom to know the difference."

– Saint Francis of Assisi

This was going to be a big weekend for Ada. She would stay with the family out in the country until Sunday because Martin was going to reopen Booker's Place. She worried and prayed that Martin would take this seriously. Booker had poured his life into the community center, and it was closed only when his illness worsened.

Martin appeared to be genuinely interested in the center, and was so excited about the possibility of continuing Booker's legacy that Ada decided to support him. She prayed that this would not be another one of his whims. Of course, he had a lot of ideas as to how to make the business more profitable, but Papa Simon insisted that they run it just as Booker had run it.

Ada was surprised at how quickly Martin capitulated and the re-opening was scheduled for this weekend. Most of the family showed up to help, which was a good thing. All the booths and tables were full. Nyra felt that it was too soon for her and decided not to attend, but Aretha showed up to chaperone.

The opening was a huge success. Martin had a portrait of Booker enlarged and placed over a mantle with a shadowbox with his medals. He had an equally sized photo of Emmett placed on the wall over the arcade machines. Ada was touched as she witnessed the warm embrace between Papa Simon and Martin. She hadn't seen Martin this happy in years. This just might be what he needed.

Ada loved the gospel music at the country church, but the service was never ending. She thought the deacons prayed entirely too long. She even started longing for the prayers at Cori's church, which came from a book. She wondered if her legs would move when it was time to depart.

She remembered what Lizzie had said about Miss Jade, and anxiously awaited her scream. Lizzie, who was sitting beside her, elbowed her just as Miss Jade yelled, and young Reverend Limberson started winding down.

The best part of that day was the ride home, listening to Lizzie's antics and imitations. Ada and Cori looked forward to this each Sunday evening, and Ada now laughed at the reruns right along with everyone else.

Lena insisted that Lizzie wait until Ada had rested before joining Summer for their visit with the ladies. Plus, Lena sensed that the ladies needed some time alone. She had to admit she was as shocked as her Aunt Ada when they arrived at Cori's. The McCain-Palin sign was placed right out front for all to see, and there was no doubt who Cori supported.

Cori was sitting at the table cutting coupons when Ada arrived.

"I reckon you are tired," Cori said.

"Yeah, I am. I think I will lie down for a minute before the girls come over."

At 6:00 sharp, the girls and Grandmother Victoria made their way up the back steps. As soon as they arrived, Lizzie filled them all in on the grand opening of the Booker Taylor Community Center, or Booker's Place, as it was called.

As much as Ada enjoyed the joyful banter, she was still somewhat distracted by the sign in Cori's yard.

It is her yard after all, Ada thought. *She has the right to put up any sign that she wants in her own yard.* She didn't know why she felt so agitated about it.

The next morning, the ladies ate in silence. While Cori washed dishes, Ada left to run a few errands. She wasn't gone long, when Cori heard her pull in the driveway. Just as she parked in the garage, Cori glanced out the window and thought she felt her heart stop.

Right on the bumper of Ada's car was a bumper sticker saying "Obama-Biden." Ada had barely made it up the steps when Cori lit into her.

"I will not have anything with that Muslim's name on it in my yard!"

"He is not a Muslim, and I paid for that car. I will put whatever I want on it," Ada responded just as sharply.

"Well, you are going to have to park it somewhere else!"

"So, it's okay for you to put a McCain-Palin sign in your yard, but I can't put an Obama-Biden sticker on my car?" asked Ada.

"Like you said, you can put whatever you want to on your car, but you can't park it on my property!"

"If my car has to go, then perhaps I need to go too."

"Suit yourself."

Bobby Lee and Grace came by that evening and Cori was in a tirade. Nothing they said could calm her down.

Ada heard the commotion through her closed doors.

That next evening Eddie and Tara dropped by to visit their grandmother. They listened to her, but neither of them had the nerve to tell her that they were voting for Senator Obama.

Tara was glad she didn't bring Robbie. She checked on Ada, who was just as defiant. She was determined to keep the sticker on her car, and planned to move as soon as possible.

"Will you move back in with your son?" asked Eddie.

"No, I'll go on out to the country with my sister until I can find a place of my own. I've sort of gotten use to my independence."

"Miss Ada, you and Grandma just have to work this thing out," said Tara. She had told her grandma the same thing she told Ada.

"Grandma, after all the two of you have experienced together, all the battles you have fought and won together, Daddy being accused of PM's death, I can't believe you are going to let something like politics come between you."

"It's not just politics. It's good versus evil," shouted Cori.

Tara didn't respond. She was very familiar with this "Grandma." It was the same one who told her if she married that Colored boy, she would have Satan for a father-in-law.

Tara never could figure that one out, but she knew when her grandmother was in that state of mind, it was best not to cross her.

Fortunately, the girls had afterschool activities that week. Lena kept them away as long as possible. She didn't want them to have to try to choose between the two ladies they had grown to love and adore.

At the Wednesday morning prayer and Bible study, the tension was thick enough to cut with a knife. Miss Inez led the morning prayer with a stern and powerful admonishment about the need to forgive.

Ada informed Cori that when she left this Friday, she would be gone for at least two weeks.

Cori responded as she always did.

"Suit yourself."

Chapter Sixty-Nine

"Love is the only force capable of transforming an enemy into a friend."

– Martin Luther King, Jr.

The packing was not going well. It was hard to plan for her time in the country. The temperature went from extremely hot to extremely cold. She hated to admit it, but she had gotten very comfortable at Cori's home. But that was the problem. It was Cori's home.

She was just a boarder. If Cori wanted to put campaign signs in her yard, it was her choice. If she didn't want a car with an Obama-Biden sticker in her garage, that was her choice also. She made that very clear, and it was also very clear that it was time for her to move on.

It was always supposed to be a temporary arrangement, she told herself.

Frederick, of course, had offered his home to her again. Lena even offered to convert her office back into a bedroom and let her live there with them. But she decided to take her baby sister's offer and move in with her and Papa Simon.

When you are this age, you should be settled down. Not moving from pillar to post, she thought. She felt the same loneliness she experienced after her sister Vivian, her Mother Damaris, Miss Steepleton, and her Mr. Passmore's deaths. But this time no one had died, just a friendship.

Cori, on the other hand, was spitting nails. She was angry, and not just at one person. She was angry at everyone. She ate alone. She refused to ride in Ada's car, so the two ladies no longer ventured to the Home Place for lunch.

She walked to Bobby Lee's as she had done before Ada arrived. Eddie's Wednesday evening visit was shorter than usual because Ada returned to her rooms after cordial greetings, and Cori had difficulty focusing on Scrabble.

The only bright spot in her day was little Robbie's visit. Even that was painful, as he questioned her about Aunt Ada. Ada, hearing the boy's inquiry, joined Cori and Tara in the kitchen and for one brief moment, the ladies were civil.

Tara hoped this was a crack in their armor.

The next morning, Ada listened for Cori to make her way down the stairs. Bobby Lee would be over soon for his cup of coffee. She listened a few more minutes, hearing nothing.

Cori could be quiet as a mouse when she wanted to be, so perhaps she didn't hear her come down. As she entered the kitchen, she noticed the light had not been turned on. Now she really was worried.

"Cori?"

Nothing.

She walked to the bottom of the stairs and yelled again.

"Cori? Are you all right?"

Silence.

"Something is wrong. I know it."

She started climbing the stairs. One step at a time, calling Cori's name every step of the way.

As she neared the top of the steps, she thought she heard a moan.

"Lord, have mercy! Cori?"

She had never been up the stairs, and wasn't sure which direction she should take, when she heard Cori moan again.

As she headed to the bedroom door, she heard Bobby Lee knock on the door. When no one answered, he used his key, calling his mother and Ada's names as he entered.

Ada yelled down the stairs.

"I'm up here. Something's wrong with Cori."

Cori lay on the bed, pale as a ghost. She just moaned, "I'm sick. I'm so sick."

By this time, Bobby Lee stumbled into the room.

"Mama, what's wrong?"

"I'm so sick." Then she sat up, disoriented, as if she was searching for something and began gagging.

Ada grabbed the trashcan from beside the bed and held it in front her just as Cori vomited violently in the trashcan. After the attack, she fell back on the bed.

"My head hurts so bad," she said.

Bobby Lee's fingers attacked his cell phone as he hurriedly called 911 and Grace. Since they lived right in town, they heard the sirens almost instantly.

What a blessing to live so close to everything, Ada thought.

"This is it. It's my time," cried Cori.

Bobby Lee, a giant in statue, crumbled by his mother's bedside.

"I don't have long," she continued.

Grace arrived with Tara and Robbie, who joined Bobby Lee.

"Come here, my precious baby," Cori whispered.

Eddie ran up the steps just as Robbie lay down beside his great grandmother.

"I love you so much little boy. I love all of you."

Cori closed her eyes as her body lay perfectly still. Everyone in the room stopped breathing right along with her.

Tara began to sob uncontrollably.

Dr. Crenshaw arrived just as the paramedics arrived. He made his way through the group and began checking Cori's vitals.

"Cori? Cori?" asked the doctor.

Cori moaned softly.

"What hurts you, Cori?"

"My head hurts so bad," she moaned.

"When did it start hurting?"

Cori muttered something incoherently.

"Did you take anything?" the doctor asked.

"Just some aspirin," she whispered weakly.

The doctor looked at the aspirin.

"Cori, these aspirin are 10 years old! Where is your head hurting?" he asked.

She tossed some more, obviously in pain, her long hair draped over the pillows. The doctor checked her eyes. With a puzzled look on his face, he began examining her head for any unusual lesions or lumps. He paused as he examined the back of her head, and his expression revealed that he had indeed found something.

Everyone held their breath. He laughed as he revealed the source of Cori's pain. It was a hairpin, which was probably as old as the aspirin. Apparently, Cori had neglected to take it out of her hair and it had pierced her scalp. Because he had to force it from her scalp, it indicated that it had been in her scalp for several days and had caused an infection. The ancient aspirin had caused her nausea.

"Ada, I love you," Cori cried. "Please don't leave me. I don't care who you vote for. You can vote for that Bama if you want to."

Chapter Seventy

"When God is involved, anything can happen. Be open. Stay that way. God has a beautiful way of bringing good vibrations out of broken chords."

– Chuck Swindoll

⎯⎯⎯⎯⎯◯⎯⎯⎯⎯⎯

The 2008 election fight was very disturbing to Ada, and even though she decided to remain with Cori a little longer, she realized that she needed a permanent home, and it was time for her to leave Cori's.

She had made up her mind; she would be moving next door to live with her nieces and nephews. Lena had returned to work with Klein, and the popularity of Bobby Lee and Amanna's cases brought them quite a few clients. Ada would assist with the chauffeuring of the children, and Lena had no problem with her preparing dinners for the family.

Even though Cori's sickness was not fatal, the infection had weakened her, and she was bedridden much longer than any of them anticipated. Cori's family had to assist with her care because Ada had difficulty tackling the stairs.

Tara and Michael ceased looking for a home and moved into Grace and Bobby Lee's home. Cori finally realized that she needed to move into the rooms which Ada and her own mother had used when her health began to decline. Bobby Lee and Grace moved upstairs, and converted the attic into a great room for the two of them. Bobby Lee's and little Tara's rooms remained intact for little Robbie's visits, and for Eddie and Lindsay's two foster children.

And the best news was that all four generations were worshiping together. Johnny felt called to work for a conservative think tank in Washington, D.C. and the conference appointed Eddie's pastor as pastor of First Church. Tara actually had to take Little Robbie to the doctor because he became so excited that he hyperventilated.

***

Tara hoped the Thanksgiving festivities weren't too much for little Robbie. Even though he had been completely healthy since the breathing episode, she "hovered," as her mom called it. She watched as he scampered from Grandma-too, to Aunt Ada, and to all his new "cousins," as he called them. He played with his "cousins," ate from random tables, and even joined the crowd on the dance floor.

It was Martin's suggestion that they have a joint Thanksgiving celebration. Ada still could not believe the change in her youngest child. Martin planned every detail of the combined Thanksgiving dinner at Booker's Place, from securing enough tables and chairs, finalizing the menu, and personally ensuring that the individual families knew how important their presence was at the event.

His attention to details and logistics was masterful, and Ada could not hide her delight and pride. As everyone began to pour into Booker's Place with boxes of food, Martin was the maestro of the diverse orchestra of family and friends.

Ada expected all the Taylor family, and of course her own family was invited, but Martin had extended invitations to Tator, Tal Jr., and to all the children who Ada and Cori tutored in their homes, as well as their families. Martin coordinated and delegated with such finesse, even Frederick was impressed.

A special table was set for Papa Simon, Ma Liz, Ada, Miss Cori, Miss Inez, Miss Polly, Jabo's Grandmother, Miss Eliza, and Grandmother Winthrop. Papa Simon stated more than once, that Ada's boys had ways like his Booker. Occasionally, someone wiped a tear, but boisterous laughter overcame sadness.

At the end of the dinner, Martin, Frederick, and Thur took the floor. Thur explained how the cousins went to the property where their grandparents had been murdered. They found the graves, which were covered with white rocks and a small boulder at the head, with "Clarks" painted on it. Ma Liz smiled, knowing that Uncle Morris' was probably behind the tender gesture.

Frederick continued by informing the group that the cousins had joined together and purchased the land. He had obtained a grant that would turn the land into the Clark Family Camp. It would host family reunions, retreats, weddings, and summer educational enrichment camps.

They presented a copy of the framed photo that Cori had kept all those years to the two sisters. They stated that a copy of the portrait would hang at the family camp. They also shared that they were searching for an executive board and hoped Ma Liz, Aunt Ada, Miss Cori, and Miss Victoria, Miss Inez,

Miss Eliza, and Miss Polly would consider becoming the first board.

Ma Liz and Ada's radiant faces were contagious as they held hands and gazed to the heavens.

Cori looked around the gathering of people from every color in the rainbow. She smiled as little Robbie skipped with one of his "cousins." It reminded her of another child who skipped across the stage.

Was it just three weeks ago? she thought to herself. She was led to believe that the election of a Black man would certainly kill her, but Barack Obama had been elected President of the United States, and she was still here.

She laughed quietly as she thought, *the earth didn't explode and I doubt if they're going to paint the White House black.*

Cori had to admit, even she was touched when she saw the beautiful family walk across the stage on election night, with the little one skipping much like little Robbie. Watching the young couple with the two children, she was harkened to another time, with another couple with two beautiful little girls.

She expected to experience many things if he was elected, but she was surprised at what she actually felt. She was proud. She was proud of her family, she was proud of her town, she was proud of her country and how far it had come. Cori had witnessed so much in her 92 years, and she thanked God that He saw fit to let her live to see another day. She was eternally grateful that she lived long enough to witness so many of His *blessings.*

Epilogue

As Bobby Lee and Grace entered the kitchen, they smelled the aroma of coffee. Cori had already cooked breakfast and was watching the morning news.

"Did you hear that? That rich man from New York says that the President wasn't even born in this country! He's saying the President needs to show his birth certificate!"

About the Author

Vickie Blackwell Morrow, freelance writer, poet, and editor, was born the fifth of eight children to a truck driver and homemaker in a small town in North Carolina during the peak of the Civil Rights movement.

She is the author of short stories *A Lick and a Promise, Mud pies...A Sock Monkey...and Brotherly Love, Granny's Braids of Hope,* and the award-winning *He Keeps on Truckin'*, which details her father's struggles as a long-haul truck driver during segregation. She also wrote, produced, and choreographed a musical entitled *The Storm is Passing Over.*

Vickie is the wife of a retired Air Force Chaplain, the mother of two adult children, an adjunct instructor, and continues to be an active member in her church and community.